The Sleeper

The Sleeper

RICA HENE

Copyright © 2024 Rica Hene

The moral right of the author has been asserted.

Apart from any fair dealing for the purposes of research or private study, or criticism or review, as permitted under the Copyright, Designs and Patents Act 1988, this publication may only be reproduced, stored or transmitted, in any form or by any means, with the prior permission in writing of the publishers, or in the case of reprographic reproduction in accordance with the terms of licences issued by the Copyright Licensing Agency. Enquiries concerning reproduction outside those terms should be sent to the publishers.

The manufacturer's authorised representative in the EU for product safety is Authorised Rep Compliance Ltd, 71 Lower Baggot Street, Dublin D02 P593 Ireland (www.arccompliance.com).

This is a work of fiction. Names, characters, businesses, places, events and incidents are either the products of the author's imagination or used in a fictitious manner. Any resemblance to actual persons, living or dead, or actual events is purely coincidental.

Troubador Publishing Ltd
Unit E2 Airfield Business Park,
Harrison Road, Market Harborough,
Leicestershire LE16 7UL
Tel: 0116 279 2299
Email: books@troubador.co.uk
Web: www.troubador.co.uk

ISBN 978 1 83628 079 8

British Library Cataloguing in Publication Data.
A catalogue record for this book is available from the British Library.

Printed and bound in Great Britain by 4edge Limited
Typeset in 11pt Garamond Pro by Troubador Publishing Ltd, Leicester, UK

For

Cara, Nico, Joel, Josephine and Rufus

sleeper *noun*
An artefact or work of art that disappears from view then unexpectedly reappears after a long absence.

PART ONE

Eyeing the future

1685

To be a good silversmith, Abraham Barachin said you need to create with a passion equal to God's, to love and, most of all, you need not be afraid of beauty. Abraham Barachin said too that, as with training a bad dog or flighty steed, you must believe *your* will alone will suffice. There could be no room for doubt; the silver held no power over the silversmith. Equipped with such beliefs, you might spend many a year working as an apprentice. If this did not kill your love for the metal, you might become a successful man of the silver trade, providing, that is, you could incorporate flair and perfection into each of your pieces. It was a hard trade, but reward came in the form of contented customers and the satisfaction of each new job improving upon the last.

Abraham was born in Bourges in France, had served an eight-year apprenticeship, and worked two years as a journeyman under Monsieur Clément, a revered silversmith from the South. However, the wars of Louis XIV and the building of an outlandish palace at Versailles had been an extravagance most people did not welcome, least of all those of the Protestant faith. With taxes high, the clients for fine silver plate grew thinner. Monsieur Clément sat him down with a drink, his fine brow furrowed. 'I can no longer keep you. You must find new pastures to tend. This town is too small for two silversmiths. You must travel further afield, perhaps even leave France. I am sorry. Times are difficult.'

Abraham had no wife, and both his parents had died from consumption when he was a young child. Monsieur Clément's guidance had proven helpful to him in the past, so he took the advice and packed his meagre belongings and a letter of recommendation in a sack, setting off on foot for the North. He had no plan and little money for a safe passage. He had spent plenty of time at his own private altar, meditating on his life, and always when he prayed, he held a question in mind; the answer would be delivered, perhaps not immediately or in the way he expected, but nonetheless, it would be provided. This would transpire to be something of value. In this, Abraham placed faith as well as a belief in himself and his ability.

Sure enough, when he reached the border of Bourges, he was offered a cart ride with a man who had lost his wife and needed a kind ear. After many hours of weary, bumpy travel – during which Abraham had listened to endless tales of two boys with a love of swimming in rivers, and a woman whose preserves were the best in the whole of southern France – both men slept in the cart. The next day and night passed in a similar fashion, but his driver's snoring disturbed Abraham and on the third night, he had an uncomfortable sleep beneath an oak tree. He was woken by the dawn chorus. He sat up, scratching his head, and looked to the horizon. Before his field of vision, a great crane rose into the sky. As the bird flew awkwardly off, Abraham drank in the good omen. Cranes were the birds of legends, harbingers of heaven and signs of longevity and good fortune. Enthused, he stood and woke his driver, ready for the final leg of the journey to Paris, where they would part company.

He entered Paris through the city walls, a place he had not seen before but had heard plenty about. Mouth agape, he took in the monstrous city; he took in the architecture and the vibrancy of the people. The stench struck him hard. Abraham had never experienced a reek quite like it. He stopped a passer-by to enquire.

'Bodies in the cemeteries of Paris are not buried deep enough. Too many dead. Dead animals. Rotten food, stink of tanneries, the cesspits. Welcome, monsieur, to the city of mud!'

The Saint Bartholomew's Day Massacre, in which the Catholic mobs slaughtered the Protestants, had happened a hundred years ago, and it was rumoured that the number of bodies had reached three thousand or more. Layer upon layer of foul rotting matter gave off foetid and hard-to-distinguish odours: animal droppings, the contents of chamber pots tossed from windows, the stench of the swamp Paris was built upon, dead animals and mouldering vegetables all contributing to the overpowering, overwhelming stink. There was no perfume, pomade, or pomander powerful enough to disguise it.

In a state of wonderment, Abraham strolled past furriers working on pelts and washerwomen going about their dirty work on the banks of the Seine. All around him were people speaking in an enlivened fashion, but with dead eyes and sour lips, arms jerking and gesticulating, as if the trauma of the massacre remained locked within their bodies, seeking a way out. After purchasing some bread and a little cheese from a market, he entered the church of Saint-Étienne-du-Mont to eat and pray before continuing his journey.

Sitting on a pew, however, Abraham could not bear to close his eyes; the rood screen was of a kind he had never seen before. So intricate was the stonework that it appeared to be carved from butter. Abraham's gaze met the crucifix placed upon the jube and by now his eyes were stinging. Such craftsmanship could often move Abraham to tears. This crucifix was a remarkable example of what a goldsmith, skilled and knowledgeable in the art of metal, might achieve when cost was no hindrance. It was so beautiful that Abraham reasoned that the beliefs of the goldsmith must be irrelevant. Beauty was free from religion, free altogether from harsh judgement. To Abraham's mind, beauty and truth were close bed partners. If man could keep his eye to the appreciation of such things, there would be no reason to bring about massacres, to forge headfirst into wars. Beauty captivated. Beauty transcended, overriding man's lower nature. To appreciate beauty brought man closer to the Divine. He closed his eyes to offer a silent prayer, one concerning safe travel and protection, even though he was not in a church of his persuasion. Not long afterward, he became aware of the presence of a man with hair the colour of rust, a few feet further along the pew. He performed the sign of the cross and glanced in Abraham's direction.

'Parlez-vous-anglais?' he said.

Abraham glanced at the fellow, taking in his wild hair and ill-fitting garments.

'*Angleterre?*' the gentleman added.

'No, French,' Abraham said, his response in his mother tongue hiding his modest ability in English. Most of his English had come from an English monk in his village; a portly, kindly fellow called Father Lombard. Father Lombard was a carpenter and would make many crucifixes and rosary beads in the workshop adjacent to Monsieur Clément's. Lombard spoke little French, so the agreement had been that they would teach one another, over a modest meal at the end of most working days, their respective languages. Yet, by the end, Abraham had come off well under Father Lombard's kindnesses and had learnt more English than he managed to teach French. In the process, he had been the recipient of numerous gifts of cheese and wine made by the monastery. Most of all, he had made a friend in the monk, a man blessed with patience and humour as well as superior teacherly skills. When it came to their farewell, he had gripped Abraham's hands in both of his, and said, '*Merci de m'avoir appris la française*,' pausing before continuing in English, 'I do not think I will return to England but you... you should go. We have a long history of silver-makers in our country.'

Now Abraham turned to his church companion. 'I speak some English, a little,' he said. 'It should be useful to me, for I am on my way to England.'

The stranger scratched his head. 'I don't think I am long for this world,' he said and then sat in silence. Abraham waited for him to speak again.

For a time, the gentleman continued to stare straight ahead and then slowly, haltingly, he relayed his story. He had returned home after a day's work to find his wife gagged, tied to a chair, their son across her lap, his throat gashed open and the blood staining his wife's apron. Alas, the boy could not be saved and his wife, beside herself, could not be calmed. Despite plenty of St John's-wort given to her by the apothecary, together with some lavender, and lemon balm from the herb woman, she still sobbed and shook for days.

'My heart broke for we had only one son. My wife's two sisters, who had already died from the plague in the pest house, were both unmarried. John was our only child and he was taken from us.'

Abraham did not know what to say. It acutely diminished his own predicament. 'I'm sorry to hear this, monsieur. But why, may I ask, are you in France?'

The fellow seemed to stir from his reverie. 'We could not stay in England. We were reminded daily of the tragedy. Everyone looked at us with such terrible pity.' He held his forehead in his palm. 'So, we took a boat from Kingston upon Hull to Rotterdam. Four days by sea. Elizabeth never spoke a word, not one, throughout the whole voyage. When we got to France her health began to fade. The physick suspected a carcinoma of the lung. He was wrong, for I do know that she died of a broken heart.'

Abraham let the man's words settle in his mind before replying. 'Do you not want to return to this Kingston upon Hull?'

The fellow shook his head. 'I cannot, my wife is buried here, in Paris. I do not want to leave her. That said, I do have some things that belong to her family. Some property that must be returned. There is but one cousin still alive. I know it would have been Elizabeth's wish that he should have them.' With that, he put his hand in a sack kept beneath his shabby coat and produced two silver salts and a beaker with a stone inside.

Abraham looked on in astonishment. 'That appears to be good plate. Why don't you sell them?'

'No, I cannot, they are the only items remaining that belong to my wife's family. My needs are few. When I want money, I work. I can turn my hands to most things that do concern wood.'

Abraham looked at the salts. One was silver gilt, but both were impressive pieces that would not have been out of place gracing a fine table in a merchant's house. They were decorative, yet different from one another. The larger of the salts was silver gilt. It stood tall, with a conical cover engraved with flowers and fruit, topped by a finial in the form of a cage. The lower section had a twin cartouche on either side which depicted the faces of a man and woman, perhaps those of its owners. The other salt, which was silver, was a better piece, to Abraham's mind. It was square, with the four corners removed to make it octagonal. The corner sections had engravings of maidens in flowing gowns and the four sides had cartouches filled with embossed fruit. Perhaps because of its incongruity, Abraham found this salt to be more pleasing. The pieces were so very different from the chalices and crucifixes that Monsieur Clément was commissioned to make in his workshop in Bourges. Abraham felt something bright and new stirring in his mind. The third piece of silver the gentleman proffered was a beaker containing a pebble.

'Your wife's family must have been wealthy.' He wanted to hold the objects, to gauge the quality of the silver, but knew that as a stranger in a strange city, whether in church or not, such an action would not be welcome.

'Her father was a merchant and his father before him was Mayor of Hull. Her father established a merchants' society where they prayed to the God Mercury in a ceremony of his devising and the stone in the beaker is the most precious item. It is the symbol of the Society's success. Without it, their complicated rituals would not have led to prosperity.' He passed the pebble to Abraham. He took the unremarkable stone in his hand and appreciated its coolness against his skin before examining it. He spat on his thumb and rubbed the pebble. 'This is nothing but a stone,' he remarked.

'Ney,' the fellow continued, 'this be a stone borne from magic and magic alone: a philosopher's stone. A stone to harness the *energeia* necessary for successful trade. Monsieur, behold magic in your palm.'

Abraham let slip a brief chuckle. 'I believe you speak of alchemy; alchemy is pure myth,' he said. 'That I do know for certain, for I be a silversmith by trade. If a person should know about alchemy, it is a man that scalds himself on hot metal – metal that cannot be transmuted.'

He thought about the beautiful salts and wondered when he would ever be fortunate enough to produce such pieces. Their beauty and his own wistful musings did not, however, detract from the fact that he knew that silver was silver, just as day was day and night was night. He was no more excited by the man's conversation than if he had been speaking of a moon once made of rock and now of cheese.

'To the ignorant, aye, this is what it is – a stone,' his church companion continued. 'But to the family that did keep it, it was of more import.'

The red-haired man slid closer, so that Abraham could see him in a better light and could make out the scales upon his head and his rheumy eyes. It would not be long before he would join his wife and son, he thought. His suspicions grew concerning what might come next.

'You wish for me to return your silver to England?' he said, too tired for bush-beating, but not tired enough to raise his voice in weariness.

The man sniffed. 'Aye. The salts and that beaker must be returned as duty to my late wife's family and the stone, well, for superstition's sake it must likewise be returned to Hull.'

'You think that I – a stranger – will take silver and… what? Travel hundreds of miles to return it to this 'Ull and not steal it from you?'

'Kingston upon Hull,' said the man, emphasising the mistake.

'I could steal the silver, toss the stone into the sea and have a good meal, just as soon as we part?' Abraham suggested.

The man shook his head. Abraham glanced at him to make sure he had not become lost in a reverie.

'God does not disappoint; he only tests a man's strength and his faith. Besides,' he laughed, 'a man who admires a church as you admire Saint-Étienne's does not appear as a man who would rob himself of opportunity! I am a good judge of character, though not as good as God. At least, if that be your plan, I believe you would not speak of it, am I right?'

Abraham laughed at their joint frankness. 'Unless I was cleverer than you might imagine. But the opportunity is all yours.'

His church friend shook his head. 'That stone was once as important to trade as a ship to its cargo. Without it, the clever merchants of Kingston upon Hull would not have prospered so well as they did. The stone formed a necessary part of their ritual. But it is the silverware I be more concerned about. I had, you understand, made a promise to my late wife.'

Abraham looked down again at the unremarkable stone and wondered if the fellow was of sane mind. Was the man lost in the madness of grief? Or was there further meaning to behold?

'For a God-fearing man you do place much faith in false idols,' he said, flipping the stone from one palm to the next.

The man moved closer towards Abraham's ear. 'It must be returned to Hull.' Abraham struggled to understand the man's words. His tone had dropped to a whisper and he spoke at speed. 'You are familiar with the term philosopher's stone, or material prima?'

Abraham shook his head. 'I am a silversmith,' he said, stating fact.

The fellow nodded. 'Yes, yes indeed. But if you wish to profit as a silversmith, you must place faith in something larger. It is necessary.'

'You mean God?'

The fellow shook his head again. 'Nay God, but trade. You see, all business doth require trade. Trade keeps our bellies full and the roof over our heads. Not wars. Not church.' His arm gestured about his head. 'And the Society was formed of people that did take responsibility for their lives. They did not tug on God's sleeve like a bairn to its nursemaid's skirts, crying each and every time a ship sunk.' The fellow let out an eerie, child-like wail. 'Instead, they placed their faith in the philosopher's stone and the god Mercury, and its power to bond with traders further afield.'

Abraham's hand went to his hip. 'I fail to see its purpose,' he said, trying to keep ridicule from his tone. 'Hard work and luck are of benefit to trade. Not stones.'

The fellow ran a hand across his face. 'Nay, it had to be witnessed to be believed. What they aimed to achieve was to encourage man's possibility. They placed great faith in their abilities alone. They did not offer themselves up as God's humble servants, tossed about on His unpredictable seas; they took control at the helm, creating webs of trade built upon faith and respect. Deuteronomy says that thou shalt remember the Lord your God, for it is He who giveth thee the power to get wealth, that He may confirm His covenant that He swore to your fathers, as it is this day. *Gives you power* is what it says. I have found peace in this.'

Abraham did not understand much that the strange English fellow told him. What was of greater import, however, was that the fellow seemed to believe in what he said. *Truth;* Abraham recognised it keenly, for it always sat with ease in the listener's ear and settled in their breast.

He said, 'I still do not see what you are asking of me. For one, I do not live in Paris but am passing through. Our meeting does coincide with my heading towards England and yet—'

'When two incidents do collide in such unusual fashion that is surely a sign of God's hand at play.'

Abraham shook his head, chuckling. 'I am going to England – you are looking for somebody going to England. There may be ten other people in this church who will soon travel to England. *Non?* He shrugged, wishing for his own language to express himself properly. 'It is not so unlikely.'

The shaking of the fellow's head grew more ruthless. 'I feel it in my bones. You listened to my terrible tale, and you looked at the beauty of the silver. All I ask, sir, is that you return this to Kingston upon Hull, for which I will do you a favour in return.'

'What favour?'

The fellow sat taller. 'The town is a good city and wealthy cities have silversmiths. You will find work. Look for my wife's cousin, Jeremiah Graves. Seek him out. Tell him that Gregory Jenkin sent you. That be me.' He pointed to his heart. 'Say that Gregory said that a reward is needed for your selfless endeavour. He will know what is meant. Tell him you are good at your job. I do believe that is so. You do carry yourself well, sir, and you can tell good plate when you do see it.'

Abraham could not help laughing louder. 'You have known me but five minutes,' he said, causing a lady in the row before him to scowl over her shoulder. He smiled and raised a gentle hand in apology.

'A man who has lost all things that he doth treasure, sees people through eyes that hold no grievances. I have nothing. What else do I have to fear losing?' Gregory was speaking once more, his hands held out to Abraham in supplication. 'I see others more clearly, for there is nothing I do strive to surpass or conquer in them, nor them in me. I flow with my thoughts like the river doth flow. I study people, not weapons. In you, I see a hardworking man, given a chance, but you have been disappointed; perhaps suffered under religious massacres and persecution like many.' He searched Abraham's face for an answer, but found none. He continued. 'So, I ask that you do see me as an angel, Heaven-sent. It will be hard but, in exchange of this small favour, you will find in Kingston upon Hull a place where you might make your fortune. Returning this silver beaker and the salts will please the family, who are an important family in the history of the town. And to return the philosopher's stone for the keepsake of the merchants will mean that you do prosper and prosper well. This, sir, is how the Society did work.'

'And this Society, it is not still going?' Abraham humoured the old fellow.

'Nay,' said Gregory. 'It is no longer in service.'

Abraham fell silent. Although shoddily dressed, the fellow did not appear to be a lunatic. Monsieur Clément would often say that if a thing seemed too good to be true, it most likely was. 'Life does not come coated with the make-believe of dreams,' he had often said to Abraham. 'nature is seldom mild, and man may be at the top of the muck pile, but we are still Nature,' he had said, in his husky, wine-gravelled voice, and Abraham would shrug and reply in a frank but sombre tone, 'I am no animal, sir.'

Now his new friend gripped his shoulder. 'What do you say to this plan?'

Abraham felt no threat in the grip, though wisdom told him he should. 'I say,' he said, measured and slow, 'would you trust me?'

The hand loosened. It patted Abraham's shoulder. 'Trust doth lay upon your shoulders, aye.' Jenkin's taut shoulders dropped a little and his milky eyes softened from their fervour.

'And you will receive news that my quest is complete?'

'I will most likely not live that long. Your conscience will be your guide. An opportunity, that is all I offer. Then, if you are a man that is good and loyal, you will find your way in Hull. The townspeople will not desert you. As sure as night follows day, you will benefit a hundredfold. Of that, I do assure you.'

Abraham tried to look for the fault as he might look for a dent or scratch in a piece of polished silver, his mind turning over the dilemma from many directions. 'I do not know if I shall make it all the way to Hull,' he said. 'I know England not at all.'

The larger of the gilt salts was held aloft. 'That is why,' Jenkin said, unperturbed, 'I am to give you Elizabeth's great gilt salt. The other belonged to her sister, Hannah. You are free to sell Elizabeth's gilt salt as you see fit. It is payment for returning the stone and the beaker to their rightful place. The beaker belonged to her sister, Mary. The other pieces I ask that you do return to her relative, Jeremiah Graves.'

The sun streamed through the window and the rood and jube of the church glowed with sudden brilliance. Abraham looked at Gregory Jenkin and he understood. He was not lonely or mad. He was showing duty towards his late wife's family. And Abraham was certainly no beggar. He was, indeed, a man who wished to serve a cause. It mattered not whether it be full of superstition, so long as he might work with silver. The fellow had, as he said, lost everything and a man who has abandoned himself and wishes only to serve his fellow men was no doubt a man to lavish with respect.

'I will do my best,' Abraham said, feeling as he did so the weight of his words. If the man had given up on all else but not on him, a stranger, it placed him in a strange and exalted position.

'I know that you will,' said Gregory, patting down what was left of his wild, burnished hair. 'Here, take them. Hide them for they are of some worth. The gilt salt is yours. Elizabeth would understand, no, Elizabeth would give praise!'

Abraham took the silver beaker, the flat, unremarkable stone, and the two salts, quickly placing them inside his greatcoat. 'I shall see it as an honour.'

'Guard them with your life.'

'Jeremiah Graves, you say? And your name again, sir?'

'Gregory. Gregory Jenkin. And you must seek Jeremiah out and hand him the silver. He must be your guide during your first months in Hull. He is an arrogant man, but he is clever. Tell me, do you see it as an attractive prospect?'

'I see it for what it is,' said Abraham, unable to withhold his honesty, 'a desperate man appealing to another desperate man. God has brought us together and I, like you, have nothing left to lose, my friend.'

With that, each man spat upon their palm and shook the other's hand. Abraham had the strange sensation he was in a dream, but a pleasant and revelatory one. His departure from Bourges was surely leading him along strange paths. 'I have faith that you will reach Kingston upon Hull,' murmured Gregory Jenkin. 'God has taken all from me, yet left me with clear vision and for this I cannot complain. I knew you were the person I must speak to. That is all I can say.'

Without looking back, the fellow shuffled out of the church and Abraham sat there, dazed, two gilt salts, a beaker and an unremarkable stone hidden in his coat.

***

Abraham felt that God had forged a destiny for him as deftly and solidly as a silversmith presses his mark into metal. He had not expected such grace; better yet, he had found it in Paris, the city he had, but all his life, longed to visit. He shook his head as if to awaken from a dream, cleared his throat and exited the church.

Abraham found lodgings on Rue du Chat-qui-Pêche. His room, where he spent an uncomfortable night, was long and narrow, containing a bed with a thin straw mattress, a small table and chair, and a chamber pot. When he flung the contents of the chamber pot out in the morning, the slosh added to the putrid stains on the walls of the house opposite, so narrow was the street.

Not knowing Paris at all, Abraham set off with one thing in mind; to find someone to buy the silver-gilt salt. He purchased some bread and a small pomander, using the last of his money. The pomander was a necessity and, he thought, served to mark the start of his new and hopeful life. At the pump near Le Pont Neuf, he paused to drink. He grimaced at the gritty, sulphurous warmth of it. If this was drinking water to the Parisians, it was, he thought, remarkable that they drank it and survived. He wiped his mouth on the back of his hand. He had not seen enough to decide whether he liked it or not, but he did not think he had the style, the verve or temperament for dealing with the Paris elite. No, it was not the place for him to settle. In England there was the possibility that he might be viewed as somewhat exotic, or, at the very least, unusual. He looked up. Overhead, a seagull swooped in murky skies and dove as it cackled its cry.

'You are right, my friend. I should not stay long!'

What did he have to lose? What more could befall him if he travelled? A request given in a church, after all, is surely a request not to be sniffed at? He chuckled, relieved that, so far, he had not lost his sense of humour.

His meanderings took him over the Pont au Change. He looked down into the Seine, the aorta that kept the city alive, and crossed, finding himself in Place Royale, a large square bordered by fine houses. There were carriages with liveried coachmen waiting to convey their illustrious passengers abroad. Women, more beautiful than he had ever witnessed in Bourges, paraded in the finest silk gowns of lilac and cerise and cerulean blue, the colours as vivid as a rich man's paintings and as wide as a royal cart. They wore frothy, lace-edged bodices that resembled halos, and the powdered wigs on both men and women alike stretching to the Heavens in elaborate curls. As if imbued with fever, the gentlewomen wagged their fans before their faces, and for good reason. Though the golden waters of the Seine graced the city with prosperity and poise, they scented the surrounding air with a rich vegetable stench, mingled with the flowing tide of the city's unsavoury waste.

Beyond the plumed, waving branches of the trees on the square were plentiful shops selling fine gloves, perfume and more. The view was a far cry from last night's lodgings. Near the Palais du Louvre, Abraham spotted the three suspended spheres, hanging above a shop front. He approached and entered the narrow wooden door of the *monte de piété*. Slipping past several people, milling in ragged garments, he rang a bell. A fellow appeared through a gap in a wooden partition, to the rear of the counter. His eyes were a lifeless grey, and he wore a short grey periwig. He grunted a greeting.

'Monsieur, I would like to sell this, please,' Abraham explained, taking the salt from his bag to lay it upon the counter. It gleamed. He was still marvelling at his good fortune to be given it and by a stranger at that.

The pawnbroker bent to take a closer look. After some time, he looked up. 'The marks tell me it is not French, and it will be difficult to sell in Paris. You are not from these parts, are you, Monsieur?'

'No. I come from Bourges.'

'Then I will hold it for one year. But you won't be back to claim it.'

With that he handed Abraham a bag of coins and turned away to see who was next in line. Abraham pocketed the coins. He suspected that anyone visiting such an establishment would not be in a position to argue. But the bag felt heavy enough. Later, when he counted the contents, he found it was perhaps enough for his passage to England and board and lodgings for a short while thereafter. He felt a stirring in his breast and looked out of his narrow window and over the roofs, towards the distant grey smudge of the horizon.

***

There seemed little point, Abraham thought, in leaving the city without tasting some of its wares. Outside a house on Rue Marie Stuart, a tall and once beautiful woman, Estelle Murais, beckoned him to her room in the shabby building.

'You know why it is called Rue Marie Stuart?' she asked.

Abraham shook his head.

'It used to be called Rue Tire Boudin but when Mary Queen of Scots arrived in Paris and was riding through Paris in a coach, she asked the name of the street. Embarrassed, one of her ladies told her it had no name and that she should request that her husband, François II, name it after her. Some people still call it Tire Boudin.'

Estelle had not come cheap, but since the pawnbroker had paid him a handsome sum, it had seemed important to reward himself. It did not take him long to decide that he liked Parisian women. In fact, he liked them a lot.

'England? Why there?' Estelle asked, stroking his chest.

'To make my fortune,' he replied, matter-of-factly, liking how the words sent a thrill through him.

She stroked his unshaven face. 'A handsome man that is rich is a rare thing.' He laughed.

She said, 'The rich, why they have to have silver? For what? Meat tastes the same if it is served from wood or from plate, no?'

'Silverware to the rich in society has significance: every outward manifestation of a person has special significance. It is anything but superfluous, madame.'

He was arguing the import of his trade, as a mother might defend her child. He had been educated about his customers by Monsieur Clément. What he had learnt most was that everything had relevance; a small silver beaker, like the one he carried in his bag, might have as much significance at, perhaps, a baptism as an overdue meal might to a beggar. 'The rich,' Monsieur Clément, would often recount, 'beneath the surface of their frivolity, are weighted by obligations and standing. Where is the freedom in that?' Abraham had never believed him and suspected Monsieur Clément placated himself with these thoughts. The rich did not bother Abraham; rather, he loved their affinity for the finer things in life, their attention to detail and matters of beauty. Surely, as a silversmith this was to be applauded.

Estelle had laughed just like the whore that she was, or so Abraham decided.

'Such society is constricted. It is not about pleasure but about pain,' she said – of course he had chosen a philosophical whore. 'And that, monsieur, is why the men of such society come to Estelle to find pleasure.'

She laughed again as she stroked his chest, but he'd had enough. He pushed her hand away, flinging back the bedcovers.

'Why do you want England when you have France, when you have Paris?' she said, lying back and watching him. No doubt she wanted regular business from him, particularly given that Abraham had not been a brute – a refreshing change to her usual clientele.

'England is a country that the whole of this world looks up to. I am told it is the seat of glory and one in which many exiles, like myself, do find a home.' Abraham leant his forearms on the windowsill and looked out into the dark.

'Will you come back when you are rich?'

'No. When I am rich, I will find a dainty English wife.' He threw the comment over his shoulder like salt. It was common knowledge that no man could resist putting down a whore, once he was satiated. Yes, Abraham thought, they were always much more attractive before the act.

He stood up, swaying with tiredness as he pulled up his breeches, followed by his stockings and worn-out boots. He left some extra livre tournois beside the washbasin then let himself out. Outside, the streets were quiet aside from a sheep bleating from afar. Then a voice cried, 'Jean-Pierre?' It was Estelle.

A street vendor handed him a pamphlet, free of charge. He glanced at the first page showing an image of a hapless nobleman on bended knee, signing a document, and a green-clad dragoon pointing a musket at his head, a cross coming out of the end of a barrel. It read, '*Whoever can resist this is very strong... irrefutable logic... brute force triumphs over reason.'* Abraham could fill in the gaps.

There were warnings of yet more religious persecutions in France. Once again, Protestants were being hunted. Abraham tightened his jaw. No. He no longer considered it safe to call France his home.

Abraham heard Estelle cat-calling, trying to attract the attention of her next client, as he left. He shook his head with a smile. He had not gone far when he felt his stomach growl with hunger. He entered a better eating establishment than he might have before his visit to the pawnbroker and ordered himself some meat and wine, sitting down at a roughly hewn table outside.

No sooner had he settled, when he heard the menacing boots marching on the cobbles and saw a group of soldiers, bright in their gaudy livery, stop in front of the townhouse set beside the inn. They battered on the door.

The loud hammering as they struck the wood with the thick end of a blunderbuss drew the attention of passers-by who hastily lengthened their strides and ducked their heads. Abraham remained fixed where he was, staring, the soldiers feet from him. The front door opened a crack and the face of a young servant appeared.

'Don't bang so! What do you want?' His face grew pale at the sight of the men.

'Sir to you, boy, sir', a soldier barked as he kicked in the door and sent the young boy flying across the entrance. 'Call your master.'

'Th-there's none in...sir,' said boy gibbered.

'Then we wait.' The soldier beckoned to his comrades,

his face split in a wide grin. 'Come in, lads, and make yourselves at home.' He strode into the house and Abraham heard his voice booming down the hall. 'You, boy, fetch us wine and food.' There was a cacophony of clanging weapons being dropped to the floor and ornaments breaking as they were swept off tabletops for amusement. The dragoons' laughter floated out of the still open front door. Then came a commotion, raised female voices and the snide drawl of the captain, 'Well, what have we got here?'

Straining his neck, Abraham looked through the open door and into the parlour beyond. He heard a young woman's scream and through the tangle of soldier's legs he saw a petticoat. Whistling, crude comments and laughter followed as a sword was used to lift the bottom of her skirt. A woman's voice pleaded on behalf of her daughter, 'Take me instead.'

'An old hag like you? No man would prefer that.' Laughter echoed once more and the door to the parlour was pushed closed.

Abraham's mouth went dry. He was appalled at the thought of what those ruffians might do to such a young girl. Surely someone must do something? Say something to stop them? A window to the parlour stood ajar at the front of the house, the drapes drawn open. Hardly knowing what he was doing, Abraham hurried to the window and crouched below.

'Madame du Cros and her pretty daughter Louise, I presume,' said the captain's voice.

'Let us go or I'll call the gendarmes.' Madame du Cros's voice was rich and strong, though it shook with fear.

'It will not help you, chère madame. There is no one here to help you. We apprehended your maid whilst she was at the market and your manservant when he was outside. We are here to ensure the decree in the Edict of Fontainebleau that all French citizens return to the glory of the Catholic Church is followed. You must surely know, madam, that the religious freedoms granted by Henri de Navarre no longer hold.'

'But, monsieur, we pray every day and go to confession every week–'

'Silence, madame. We know that you and your family worship your Protestant God in a secret chapel. Do you need me to tell you where it is? No, I think not. Ah, you have gone quite pale madame. Pray, be seated. But alas, the chairs are all taken. When your husband comes home, we will tell him who denounced him. We will stay as long as it takes to make him sign. Voluntarily, of course. Sometimes, it is quick, sometimes it takes longer. Not usually more than a few days. But with your pretty daughter here, I think he will not tarry long.'

The hour dragged by and still Abraham hunkered below the window, desperate to offer at least some witness should the soldiers act against the poor women. The evening grew colder as the shadows lengthened. One of the soldiers lit a fire, stoking the flames with any bits of furniture he could break with his bare hands.

Abraham jumped as the surrounding church bells rang out 6pm to call the faithful to recite the Angelus. A figure strode across the cobbles and Abraham ducked into the shadows. Before he could call out to him, Monsieur du Cros had walked through his front door.

'Ah, monsieur, good evening,' the captain's voice was slippery with derision. 'On your feet now, lads, show some respect to Marchand du Cros.' The soldiers rose to their feet, filling the room.

'Papa,' bleated Elizabeth through a sob.

Abraham saw Du Cros's shoulders rise and fall as took in the scene, saw the terror in the faces of his wife and daughter. The smell of stale breath and the stench of sweat reached his nostrils, drifting out from the airless room. It was sour and sharp – the smell of fear.

'Who denounced me?' Monsieur du Cros whispered, staring straight ahead, his hands shaking at his sides.

'You refused to honour a debt to Marchand Aubert. This caused him hardship. When he signed ten days ago, he gave us your name. Here is the paper, a feather and ink. Your signature here, if you please.'

After a long pause, du Cros bent his head and Abraham heard the scratching of the quill. The captain seized the parchment. A cheer went up and the dragoons clattered towards the door. Abraham started and hurried back to his table, where his food had long since grown cold. As swiftly and unceremoniously as they had arrived, the soldiers burst from the house, stopping only to piss against its outside wall, waving the signed declaration triumphantly.

He left Paris the next day. He huddled, squashed into a half-mouldering cart with his meagre possessions and a host of others leaving the stinky city. He was not sorry to go. Without the sale of the silver gilt, Abraham acknowledged he could not have afforded such travel or the comfort of a clean straw mattress and good, hearty food at the inns where they stopped. The women that served him here were friendly, anticipating his every need. He had not found serving women to be so forthcoming in his hometown, where arrogance was often applauded over friendliness. He liked the convivial nature and the banter of the serving houses, found peace in the passing tapestry of the countryside and rolling lanes, and amusement in many conversations that he had struck up with his fellow passengers. The journey was a bright one. To Abraham, to unearth humour was oftentimes all that he required to appreciate life. To laugh was to release fear.

By the time they crossed from Lille into the Netherlands, often travelling no faster than a man might walk, a presiding question circled in his mind: was it a coincidence that he had met Gregory Jenkin? The smoothness of his journey thus far would imply God's grace in action and Abraham took great comfort knowing he was precisely where he was meant to be.

The coach ploughed vigorously along ruts in the tracks left by former wheels, or else entered a sucking quagmire of clay, the three horses heaving them free. Countless other coaches, overloaded with passengers, accompanied them as well as packhorses laden with goods, and flocks of sheep, and cattle and swine herded on their way to market. Abraham struck up a conversation with a man who sat with a canary in a cage, its yellow feathers a spot of brilliant colour against the grey and churning mud splattering below.

'Four days to Rotterdam,' the fellow said, 'same time if you walk, mind.' He tapped the cage. 'Though less if you were to fly a' winged.' He gave Abraham a toothless smile.

Sure enough, when a man set off on foot the next morning, as their cart rolled from its hitch, he arrived at the next inn at the same time as Abraham, so treacherous was that stretch of road. Whenever the cart lurched through a ditch, rattled over rough ground or foundered in the clay, someone would exclaim, 'Royal Roads, why, they are not royal at all!' A chorus of complaints would rise in reply. Even Abraham had to admit, the King's claims to have connected Paris to the world seemed limited in their success.

Abraham endured more than two hundred miles, three coaches, four overnight stops, a change of horse at Amiens and innumerable bruises to his stiff and weary person. All told, it had taken more than six days. Now, standing at the port of Rotterdam, scanning the flat, boggish surroundings and the tall, narrow, red-brick houses, he was uncertain if the base of his backbone would ever recover. Four of the men aboard were so far gone with the numbing effect of wine that they had to be carried off.

Rubbing his back, he found all enthusiasm for silver-making had long since departed. A soft mattress and a crust were all that he now desired in life, with perhaps a bottle of burgundy to accompany them. How foolish a man must be to start a journey without a plan. But to be guided by the loose plan of another, and a stranger at that, must make him a *vrai imbécile*. A fool indeed.

He began to shiver. There were other dangers too. These Northern seas had offered an escape route to his fellow Huguenots and as such there was a posse of Dutch customs officials milling about. Abraham kept his head low, thankful for the meagre dawn light. As he walked towards several large ships moored in the harbour, one caught his eye. Draped in graceful, white sails, its bronze guns gleamed as they peeked from their ports on both sides. It seemed, to Abraham's mind, a work of art; every rope, every piece of waxed and shining wood serving a unique purpose. Snuffle hunters offloaded cargo. People shouted instructions to one another. The air was alive with busyness, and with something else. Hope, perhaps? No, it was more than that, it was the sweet brightness of prosperity. On the journey toward Rotterdam, he had been told of the port's long history, how it dated back to the 900s. The number of ships, both magnificent and obscure, seemed to confirm this. The Rhine River – the great artery of the Continent – and the Meuse rivers flowed into the port's deep waters and the place was bustling and full of alacrity, despite the early hour. 'It is a golden time for the Dutch,' the old gentleman with the canary had said, pinching his chin between thumb and forefinger and fixing Abraham with a steady eye. 'Nor is trade their sole boast, for they are artists and scientists true. It is a land of broad knowing we travel to.'

Abraham had no knowledge of science, nor did he wish for any. What use was science to the common man? Trade, however, interested him greatly and, by virtue of his own profession, art did too. Trade was a comforting notion: one skill, swapped for another; one man supplying the needs of another. It kept the world turning and food on the table. It kept his hands at their work. He would smile at other men complaining of their labour, for when he sat down to tend, hammer in hand, to a good piece of silver, it felt akin to riding a prized and thoroughbred steed. There was a sense of a seamless fit, of being able to accomplish tasks without effort, with the lightest touch or turn of a hand. There was knowledge too, a joyous burst of knowledge that this skill would never leave him, that he would always prevail and had not reached such a position without hard work. Years of it. But day by day, Abraham's will had been shaped until silver became more than his employ but his *raison d'être*. He grew to believe himself armed with this profession, his skill a tried and trusted sword, and though his mission was one of peace and beauty, he liked to think that by the end of his journey, he might indeed conquer something.

This thought livened his stride as he walked closer to the harbour, the majesty of the Dutch ships catching his eye, some with sails arched like winged mythical beasts, others standing stark and bare, skeletons stripped of their grandeur. Their bones turned Abraham's mind to the ugliness of trade. There had been long wars here, he knew; the Dutch East and West India Companies commanded the spice trade, much to the chagrin of the English, and wars had thus ensued as so often they do over wealth. Theirs was not a conflict he fancied himself caught up in, but the North Sea would not seal itself with land for his passage. His crossing was inevitable, with all the risk it carried.

More immediate needs soon drove the thought from his mind, hunger and a means of traversing the seas themselves. Where should he begin? He cast his eye about. The port was as pungent as Paris. The stench of rotten fish was almost overpowering and yet he soon found a seller carrying pies, set in neat rows upon his wooden tray.

'Florins?' the man cried, when offered Abraham's livre.

Abraham shook his head; it had not occurred to him that French money would not be welcome here. The man shook his head in return and waved him away. Abraham's hunger had by now filled his mouth with saliva.

'French?' a voice behind him asked in his native tongue.

Abraham swung round to see a squat, ruddy-faced man leaning on a walking stick. 'You are French?' he asked again.

'Yes,' Abraham replied.

If not for Gregory Jenkin, Abraham would have bidden the man good day, but the interference of strangers had thus far served him well. He inclined his head in greeting. The fellow tapped Abraham's shoulder and pointed towards a medium-sized vessel. It lay at anchor, dwarfed by two larger ships he guessed to be more than one hundred and thirty feet long, the kind of ships necessary, he thought, for crossing the North seas.

'This is your boat?' he asked, eyeing the smaller vessel, maybe forty feet from stern to bow, squashed in between its harbour fellows. Its name was not apparent.

'Yes,' said the fellow, beaming with pride. 'And you are a Huguenot looking for a crossing, am I right?'

Abraham felt a jolt of alarm. 'Why do you ask?' he said. The open walkways of the harbour seemed suddenly exposed and he drew his coat around him.

The fellow chuckled, but not unkindly. 'There have been a great many of your kind recently arriving at Rotterdam seeking passage. Do not fear, I do not judge, monsieur. I am a man of business. It matters not if you are from France or the moon, and besides, I do prefer the livre.'

Abraham's shoulders loosened. 'I need to get to Kingston

upon Hull,' he said, his lips struggling against the foreign words.

'But first you are hungry, am I right?' The man had read his mind and Abraham found himself too famished to refuse.

'Come, I have some bread, some cheese, a little wine on my boat. Follow me!'

With some relief, Abraham followed the fellow into the bowel of a boat named *De Engel*. The man was as good as his word and Abraham realised only after his belly was satisfied that such generosity did not come without recompense.

He wiped his mouth on his sleeve. 'You can take me to Kingston upon Hull?' he said, emphasising the 'H'.

'I can,' said the man, brushing a breadcrumb from the scrubbed wooden table.

'For how much?'

'How much do you have?'

Abraham was no fool. 'Not much.' He showed the man the money he kept in his purse, whilst the remaining coins from the sale of the gilt salt sat strapped to his undergarments.

The fellow rocked with laughter and clapped Abraham's shoulder. 'I know that is not all that you have, but do not fear, it is enough. More importantly, do you have permission to travel?'

'Permission?'

'Yes, you need permission from a notary or from the mayor of your town to sail.'

Abraham had indeed been given a letter of recommendation from Monsieur Clément. It was a good letter, no doubt fuelled by his employer's guilt at banishing him. The gentleman did not ask to see it. He seemed a man with little concern and considerable trust.

'How big is your vessel?' asked Abraham, looking about him.

'Fifty feet.'

'It does not seem big enough to sail rough seas.'

'I have been sailing the North for these past twenty years.'

'But there are no guns on your vessel. How do you remain safe?'

'I know, I know, the Dutch West and East India boats are all equipped with guns, for merchant men are oftentimes men of war. But I am but a sailor to my core. With the choice between money or death, I always choose money.' He laughed with enforced joviality.

'I think I would be safer in a larger boat,' Abraham said, with no qualms about his honesty.

'That you might think,' said the gentleman, his laughter gone but his eye still light, 'but it is of advantage to be smaller, for we are less noticeable on the high seas. These big ships do not bother us, believing perhaps that I am a harmless fisherman. It is good, monsieur, for other people to think you are something other than you are.'

This did not imbue Abraham with confidence, and he shook his head. He was not eager to be dragged below and drowned for the sake of spending less coin. 'I do not wish to risk my life.'

The fellow continued, 'The Dutch have an eye on England. They are ruthless when it comes to the English but, rest assured, *De Engel* is safe. You know what *Engel* means?'

Abraham shook his head.

'The angel,' the fellow stood up and dusted down his lap. 'And that is what I be for your crossing, monsieur. There are ten other passengers below deck.'

He jangled Abraham's gold coins in his palms and Abraham watched as he crossed towards the helm. Hunger had been replaced by a sudden gnawing feeling in his belly. He had not so much as crossed a river before, let alone the sea.

'Wait!' he said.

His skipper turned back, wearing an impassive expression that seemed to imply the negotiations were complete and there was nothing further to add.

'How long will the journey take?'

The old sailor shrugged, 'It depends.'

'On what?'

'The weather. And if I can remember the way.'

'Remember the way?' Abraham's jaw tightened.

'I play with you, monsieur. It may take up to four days.'

'That is longer than I thought.'

'It depends on the direction of the wind and how strong it is. If it comes from behind, it is helpful. If there is no wind, we don't move, or we drift where the current takes us, and if there is a storm, well, we pray.'

Abraham felt something cold sink into his stomach. He paled. The skipper watched him with steady eyes.

'Do you have a seaman's legs and belly, monsieur?'

'Meaning?'

The skipper laughed. 'You will understand soon enough. One more thing: you must bring provisions for four days. If conditions are good, we set sail in the morning. You don't need me to tell you to keep your possessions close to you.' With that he raised a hand in the air before disappearing to the front of the small and insubstantial boat.

Having acquired some bread, cheese and some apples from the landlord's cheerful wife at his port-side lodgings, Abraham boarded *De Engel* as the grey dawn broke over Rotterdam. Their departure did nothing to calm his nerves. Weather conditions were perfect and the sky an open and breezy blue, but the jostling for space exiting the harbour filled Abraham with terror. It seemed miraculous that they escaped at all, and without being crushed by the larger vessels that loomed, creaking alongside, throwing the deck into deepest shadow and oftentimes grinding along their rails with a terrible screeching. It took several torturous hours before they pulled clear from the other vessels, which scattered towards their different destinations. Abraham breathed the free sea air with some relief, happy to see open water to either side. Leaning over the side, he watched the blue-grey waters slipping past, as swift and smooth as his journey thus far. How simple it had been to find a passage, almost as if the skipper had been waiting for him. Was this how divine grace worked? Deftly carrying a man towards his higher purpose. Abraham knew himself to be a simple man who knew little about the wider world. Perhaps, therefore, such coincidences were normal. All he knew for sure was that in his heart, the journey felt good. He felt no darkness or foreboding, no clutching doubts. He would trust in fate. Yes, he would try hard to make something of himself in Hull.

That night, still tired and aching after the rigours of the coach and the port inn's thin straw beds, Abraham dropped into sleep in a hammock strung up on hooks. Alas, his dreams were as turbulent as the seas. In his sleep-swayed mind, he carried a skull in his hand as he entered Hull, crowds gathering to see the spectacle. He awoke, tossing, in a cold sweat, light beaming through cracks from above. He was grateful for the hammock, suspecting he had perhaps paid more for the crossing than the other passengers. Throughout the night, every so often, noises had roused Abraham from his sleep before the ship's creaking and rocking returned him to slumber once again. He swore at one point, he had felt a man staring at him, breathing foul breath into his face, but he could not be certain if it was a dream.

Shaking off the hole-riddled blanket, Abraham stood up. He saw that the other passengers were still at rest, forming a living, breathing rug upon the floor. One man slept with a knife gripped in his hand.

He took the ladder to the upper deck, holding tight to the rough rungs as the ship rose and fell a little. Cupping a hand over his eyes, he saw that the sea was calm, stretching ahead in a great, grey expanse. The wind was strong and blowing from behind and the boat seemed to glide over the wave's surface like a bird upon a current of warm air.

He encountered the skipper behind the wheel, no doubt impervious to any sickness incited by the motion of the ship upon the water. Abraham's belly was not faring too well, and he suspected sea legs might, in that moment, be beyond his grasp, but he was content to revel in the adventure of it all.

'Morning, monsieur,' said his skipper with a broad smile.

'Good morning,' Abraham replied.

'The wind is coming from a favourable direction, and we

are travelling these northern seas at a speed of eight knots,' the skipper said, as if Abraham was about to question him on the finer details.

'Voila!' he announced to Abraham, grabbing hold of the wheel once again.

The wind died down, was now moderate, and the sun was gaining height in a clear and pale-blue sky.

'Tell me, how did you sleep?' the skipper asked.

'Badly.'

'It takes time to get used to the sea. Look – a magnificent waterspout!'

Abraham followed the captain's gaze portside to see a plume of water reaching twenty or thirty feet into the air. 'What is it?' he asked, mouth open in amazement.

'A great whale. They are plentiful in these seas. The oil is used for lighting and all manner of things.'

'Are they dangerous?'

'If you hit one!' The skipper chuckled and Abraham began to wonder if he was soft in the head, like an egg not quite boiled. It was not a comforting thought, given his very life now rested in the fellow's hands. 'Further north there will be many more whaling ships. It is great business in Hull. Hard and dirty work, but much money to be made from the blubber for oil lamps and soap.'

The day passed in quiet contemplation upon the deck. Abraham liked how the sea provoked new and earnest thoughts. Its openness and endlessness inspired exploration of the mind, as so many hermits seek in isolation. Monsieur Clément had often told him that to discover character, a man needed to travel. 'When a man travels, not only the world is renewed, but his mind too.' Abraham was beginning to understand. At first, he conversed with his skipper, learning that he was a fisherman prior to ferrying people to England. When asked why he abandoned his trade, he answered, with a gentle seriousness, 'It did open my mind and heart to the high seas and all their beauty, that much is true. But it did deaden my very soul.' Abraham questioned him further, asking if it was the action of killing that had deadened him so.

'Not exactly,' the skipper replied, 'I was working on the herring busses. You know what these are?'

Abraham shook his head.

'You can always recognise them for they do have three masts, a topsail, a rounded stern, and a protruding bowsprit. This vessel is herself a herring bus. The boards used to smell of herrings to the core of their grain but the wind, the sun and sea have cleansed them, as they have me the same.'

Abraham shook his head again for he had never entertained a conversation about herring, nor bow sprits, nor boats, certainly not in Bourges. More likely talk would be about truffle hunting, which he imagined sailors did not speak about often. The skipper went on. The herring buss, he said, was the work of the Dutch ships with workshops which meant that the herring could be salted at sea. The fleet had grown to five hundred busses but, according to the skipper, competition from the Scots was growing.

'And you did not like the competition?' asked Abraham.

The skipper pinched his pipe stem between his teeth as he squinted ahead, and said, 'No, I, well, I had an accident.'

'And could no longer fish?'

'Not exactly. I... I, well, got into a fight.'

'A fight?' said Abraham smiling. He did not fight personally, but did not mind watching a brawl every now and again. Fighting was good entertainment. 'And you lost, am I right in my thinking?'

'Not exactly, monsieur. You see, I fought a man from the East Indies, small but with brawn. We fought, cleanly, no knives, no biting, but he was vicious, aimed low and... well, eventually, I had had enough of his punches.'

'And you pulled out your knife.' Every man carried a knife, this Abraham knew well for he carried his own, and not solely for eating.

The skipper shook his head. He puffed several times on his pipe. 'No, I did something worse.'

A seagull swooped low over the deck, screeching as if cackling at them.

'No, I reached for an axe that was kept on board for the job of killing the fish quickly. And I hit the boy over the head and, well, alas, I clean killed him.' The skipper paused, and his eyes stared far into the distance at something which Abraham could not discern.

'I see,' said Abraham. 'And this was the crossroads at which you left fishing to become a ferryman?'

'It was not so easily enacted. I spent many months going to sleep with a bottle of rum still in my hands. It was during this time that fate lent its merciful hand, and I won *De Engel* in a game of cards.'

'I see,' said Abraham again, not knowing what else to say. 'Well, you seem content in your new trade.'

'That is so.' The skipper reached beneath the boat's

wheel and brought out a skull – clean, brownish in colour and polished-looking.

Abraham felt a shiver run down his spine as he peered into the smooth and empty eye sockets.

'It has brought me much luck, you understand,' the skipper said, holding the skull aloft, appearing to smile at its inane grin, before turning to Abraham. 'Here! You have it. It has brought me luck, and if you do not mind me saying, you look like a fellow who could do with some luck. Keep it.'

He thrust the skull at Abraham's chest so that Abraham had no choice but to grasp it with both hands, finding it both smooth and cool to the touch. He fought against his every fibre that longed to drop it, to hurl it over the side and away into the water. He was not in a position to offend the skipper.

'Thank you,' he said.

'His name was Aakil, but that may or may not be true. In the end, his name quite suited him, do you not think?' The skipper's laugh carried a sardonic edge. Abraham smiled with difficulty and resolved to wrap the awful gift amongst his belongings and rid himself of it as soon as he landed in Hull.

'I do not know,' he said, 'but it seems that you made a good decision with your boat. I hope that I have done similar in taking this Aakil.' He looked down at the head he held and shuddered as he recalled his dream. He felt a hand on his shoulder and jumped, looking up into the skipper's careful gaze. 'All decisions can be good so long as the mind that made them is resolute. Determination is more important than destiny. Do you understand me, monsieur?'

Abraham felt the weight of the words and turned them over in his mind, as he would for many years, until understanding came and he remembered a penniless young man that had journeyed across the water to an uncertain future.

That night, at two of the bell, Abraham was awoken from his dream of a comely English girl. The foul breath of the man was unmistakable. Under the cover of the storm raging above, his 'visitor' from last night was trying to rob him. *De Engel* was being tossed hither and thither; children were wailing, and the cabin air was filled with the acrid tang of bile. Abraham pulled out the skull and hissed through his teeth, 'This is what happened to last person who tried to cheat me.' With that, he shoved the man hard and he reeled backwards, landing on the vomit-spattered floor with a thud.

Abraham staggered up to the deck where the wind had the captain's coat billowing behind like a great dark sail as he held onto the wheel with all his might. All around them, the sea was unrecognizable, black, treacherous, and roiling. The ship's boys had scampered up the rigging and lowered the sails, as waves towered to either side, capped with white foam that whipped through the air and stung Abraham's cheeks. He squinted against the burning salt spray that seared his face like iron filings borne upon the gale.

'Get down!' bellowed the captain at Abraham. 'You will be swept away. Get down, I say!'

The boat was being tossed like tinder and rocked from rail to rail, as if it might not right itself again. Abraham lost his grip and was thrown back down into the ship's hold. He wiped his face and climbed up again to secure the hatch. His attacker was huddled in a corner weeping like a child. He did not look to be a threat anymore.

'It is a bad storm,' said a pale-faced young man, clutching a bottle of rum. 'You want some?'

Abraham shook his head. It was not the time for drinking. 'I am not sure we will pass through this night. It is fearful rough out there.'

'We will come through,' said the young man, taking another slug. 'I have done this trip four times before. That skipper understands the sea like I understand...' he held up his bottle, 'the power of liquor to bring comfort. We will be fine.'

Abraham doubted that. Another wave came crashing over the boat, water raining through the hatch so that his boots were now submerged. He reached for the hammock and tried to hoist himself into it as the boat rocked and rolled. With a lurch, he was thrown to the floor into the freezing northern waters that washed over the boards.

The hours rolled and thundered by, the water below gathering until it was a foot deep, the men bailing it out as fast as it was coming in. Children and belongings were held overhead. By the fifth hour, the roaring noise and bucking of the ship seemed to be abating, yet still the water continued to enter the sleeping quarters from all directions and Abraham was now so wet that his skin had wrinkled, and his hair sat plastered to his scalp. Like a spider trying to escape a well, he struggled against the waters, trying again and again to get back inside the relative safety his hammock. At some unknown and unremembered time, he must have achieved his goal and fell at once to sleep.

When he woke, the boat was so still it may well have washed up upon the shore. Sunlight streamed once more through the boat's various chinks and knots. Abraham pushed hair from his eyes and looked about for the other passengers. The water still stood a foot or more deep on the hold's floor but people – men, women and two small children – had climbed up onto a high shelf and were sleeping at odd angles, propped up against one another, bare feet hanging over the ledge. Abraham felt his cold and aching limbs, unable to believe he was still alive.

He splashed to the floor and waded across to the ladder past the floating and uncovered cargo. He examined the sodden sacks, wondering if their contents would now be ruined.

'Good morning, monsieur!' said the skipper as if they were about to break their fast in settings of grandeur.

'Is it?' asked Abraham. 'I feel shattered and sunk, even if the ship is not.'

'But the storm has passed! How are the passengers below deck?'

Abraham studied this queer fellow, who had spent the night embattled with a raging sea but appeared, though damp, cheerful, unperturbed, and with a distinct glint in his bright blue eyes that were so keenly set upon on the horizon.

'As bad as me, I suspect, nay, worse. What cargo are you carrying?' he asked.

'Whatever I can find to carry,' replied the skipper. Abraham asked no more.

'Well, it now looks to be wet,' he said.

'And so is this sea.' The skipper's face remained impassive.

Then he smiled. 'My boy, he is down there? Did you see him? He usually is with a bottle of rum. This is his fifth crossing now. He is to take over to allow me some sleep. According to the skies, that was the last of the storm.'

Abraham contained a sigh. Setting a drunken youth to steer the limping ship did not seem clear judgement.

'Can I steer?' he offered. 'It will keep me occupied.'

The skipper's expression flickered from a smile to a frown and back to a smile again. 'Would you let me do your work?' he replied.

Abraham shook his head, for he would not entrust his work to anyone.

'Sit back and appreciate the journey, monsieur. Two more days and we will be landing at Hull.'

And two days later the boat was indeed nearing land. The last night had been spent in slumber despite the cold and endless wet. Abraham could not imagine ever feeling dry again or rubbing the ache and damp out of his bones.

'We are nearly there,' a burly male passenger said and prodded Abraham's side, startling him. He pulled himself out of the hammock for the final time and took the ladder to the upper deck, narrowly missing his hand being trodden upon when the same fellow stumbled backwards.

'And so,' Abraham said to the skipper as they pulled into a large harbour alive with plentiful ships and hardly dissimilar from Rotterdam, 'this is Kingston upon Hull?'

The skipper gesticulated in a grand fashion. 'It is indeed!'

Abraham stared out at the town, a citadel of sorts, much like those surrounding his hometown. The walls were high, with watchtowers evenly spaced around the edges, great

English flags flown from the tops of most. Abraham knew that these fortifications had much to do with the town's prosperity. If one was to trade overseas, one needed to give the impression not only that trade was possible, but that conquering was not. Towering over the ramparts was an enormous church with a magnificent steeple. The size of the fortifications and the great weight of carved stone exuded wealth and stability.

'It is a town that kept out its own country's king. It is like the island of Paris, somehow separate, different from the rest of the country,' said the ship's master.

The thought appealed to Abraham. 'I see,' he said. 'I like the look of it.'

'Looks are not everything in life! I am not permitted to tie up two abreast. I am required to berth stern on and to unload over the stern. To boot, they keep us waiting in the Humber for as long as possible. Plenty of rivalry for berths in this harbour and far too many collisions. And fires too. Just look at the closeness of the wooden buildings to the water's edge. The corporation has banned fires and candles aboard ships but, alas, this is not easy to enforce. Not so long ago, there was a big fire on a boat called *The Dragon*. But I don't have so much worry given that I am captain of the *De Engel*.' The skipper laughed, despite his litany of complaints. He pinched Abraham's arm. 'I see my girl tonight and leave tomorrow, and back to my wife when I return to Rotterdam.' He clapped his hands and pointed. 'Look, berthed three abreast! The place is too busy to control. And too many rules. Half of a ship's ballast is to be offloaded. Also, there is weighing cargo and payment of tolls. But this is not to concern you. Look all you like, monsieur.'

Abraham took in the scene. They sailed past a wreck, its charred and blackened bones scarred by fire, and joined a queue of larger boats lined up ready to enter the main harbour.

As they drew closer, it was possible to make out cranes and large warehouses behind which were – what must be – the merchants' houses backing onto the river. Cart sledges loaded with cargo passed them by and men with their backs bent double were pushing heavy loads. The vessel heaved laboriously past the buoys, sailing from the fast-flowing waters of the Humber to the calmer waters of the port of Hull.

On his right, he could see the decaying garrison, its waterside out of bounds, according to his skipper, to both shipping and trade. 'The ships will be tied there when enough coin is paid. When we tie up, you must get off and move right away. I have a bill of lading for the goods but nothing for you. Sometimes they ask questions.'

To the left he pointed out a thousand-yard wall of merchants' warehouses, behind which were the merchants' houses with private access to the riverfront, and staithes running up into the town. Ahead, lay a dense forest of masts, or spars, as his skipper called them. Abraham had learnt all manner of words since he set sail, as if shipping required another language entirely: stays, shrouds, lifts, sheets, tacks, halyards, jeers, ratlines and blocks; it had been an education of sorts.

'The harbour master has authority to cut adrift any vessel ignoring berthing instruction. I often wish I could do the same with my boy!' The skipper laughed again.

Abraham looked about at the other ships, some in midstream, loading cargo onto lighters or keels, from larger vessels. With every yard they drew closer, he felt the tingle of excitement in his chest. Something told him he would be happy here. He could not explain why.

'You have my skull?' The skipper spoke from beside him.

'I do.' Abraham did indeed have the skull, hidden amid a few items of clothing, wrapped up inside a blanket. He still, however, intended to dispose of the ghastly relic.

The skipper narrowed his eyes. 'What is your trade, monsieur, you never said?'

'I am a silversmith.'

'So, you like to leave your mark on life, am I right?'

'On silver.'

The skipper grinned. 'The desire to imprint a mark on something holds a deeper desire to leave a mark upon this world.'

Abraham shook his head and shrugged. 'I like to make beautiful objects, that is all.'

The boat reached its berth, alongside a great and daunting vessel. It was with a mixture of relief at his arrival, fear he had been mistaken in his journey and hope for his future that Abraham landed on English soil.

'Goodbye, Mr Barachin. Something tells me I will hear your name again.' The skipper bowed his head to Abraham, his eyes twinkling.

'I will not be returning to Rotterdam again.' Abraham said, uncertain as to the intent in the man's words.

'Au revoir, monsieur!' was all the skipper said.

Abraham traversed the worn gangplank and, setting foot upon the cobbles, walked towards his new life. His was fixed on finding lodgings, somewhere to dry his clothes and a good plate of hot food. He would have his shoes mended and then set about finding Gregory Jenkin's wife's cousin. Eager to avoid the officials on the bustling quay, he kept a smart pace and slipped up one of the narrow streets into the town, away from the Dock Office and Weigh House.

'Hot pescods,' a street seller cried. 'Hot sheep's feet – and riches and green.'

Abraham did not stop to purchase any food, preferring to wait until he could be seated. His first meal ought to be an occasion of sorts, he thought. He passed a market where he took in the wares and food – partridges, vegetables and meat brought in by country carts, and oysters, whelks, eels, fish large and small brought in by fishermen. The colours and smells filled the air with a vibrancy Abraham could taste and, coupled with the fresh breeze, he felt his heart uplifted.

It was on Silver Street that Abraham stumbled upon his accommodation, at least for the time being. Ye Olde White Harte was a hidden-away tavern with rooms above. The young serving wench asked him to pay up front for one week's board. Searching for his purse, he emptied out his belongings on the counter, including poor Aakil's shiny skull.

'We do not permit devil worshippers here,' exclaimed the young girl, who had red hair and matching freckles. She shot away from the counter, waving a hand at Abraham. 'You must take your business elsewhere.'

He laughed. 'Devil worship?'

When the girl made out she had horns upon her head, Abraham grasped the meaning of her fears. 'Ah! No, no. It was given to me, on a boat. Here!' He held it out to her, amused by her jumpiness.

'I do not wish for it!'

'It brings luck.'

'Luck? What kind of luck?'

'It is a special kind of luck.'

'Special, how?'

'To keep it is to make certain a young maiden will be soon married.' He said an inward prayer for Father Lombard, for his English was swiftly improving on English soil, no doubt inspired by the beauty of the girl before him.

'Is that so?'

'Oui, so I was told.'

The girl looked at the skull with suspicion. 'Who is it?'

'A young man from the East Indies. Again, so I am told.'

'Where is that?'

'Far away. Do you want it or not?'

The girl shook her head.

'Very well, I will put it back in my bag—'

'I will take it.' The girl's fierce and curious expression defied him and he relinquished his hold on the skull, pushing it towards her.

'You do not have to, mademoiselle…'

With which the girl took the skull and placed it on a shelf behind the counter. 'I won't take it home in case it haunts me. But if there be a handsome man in the inn, then maybe your spell will be proven to be true.' She blushed a little.

'Perhaps,' Abraham said, smiling. 'Now for some wine, please?'

'Wine. We sell ale and beer, whiskey and rum, sir.'

In France, the English were known for their ale, Abraham knew. He ordered a tankard of ale and took a seat beside the fire. He drank a further ale and, though it tasted good, it did not addle his mind as much as he had hoped. He was in a particular mood for addling as he sat before the warmth, drying at last. He saw the wench stroking the skull, doubtless explaining how she came by it to a large man wearing an apron, with a cloth over his shoulder. Listening to the two of them was a fellow of similar age with a mass of black hair. The large man waved the wench back to her work, came over and introduced himself as landlord of the establishment.

'John. John Goodman. Winter is fair on its way,' said the fellow.

Abraham recalled that Father Lombard had explained the Englishman's propensity for discussing the weather.

'Oui,' said Abraham, nodding, the ale making him forget where he was.

'French?'

Abraham nodded this time, keeping his ale-fogged tongue behind his teeth. The fellow with the thick black hair joined them, and sat himself down on the other side of the fireplace. He lit a pipe, looking at Abraham as the glow rose around his dark-brown eyes. 'Good day,' he said, nodding his head and smiling. Though his look was strong, Abraham heard only warmth in his voice. 'From your clothes I would say you are a stranger to these parts?'

'I am,' Abraham replied.

'Are you stopping here in Hull or—'

'I want to make a life for myself in Hull,' said Abraham, his words both eager and frank, for a man could not entertain pride when seeking employment.

'Why Hull? Do tell me your story.'

Abraham paused, uncertain how much to divulge. Yet again, he thought, in conversation with a stranger. He began. At first, he started recounting his tale with caution. He mentioned the religious intolerances in France and the danger for non-Catholics; how he set off for England without any true destination and the chance encounter with an Englishman in a church who had suggested he try Kingston upon Hull. He had been told, he said, it was a thriving town with wealthy merchants and he knew that merchants liked to adorn their homes with silver. He explained, his tongue now loosened by the ale, how the strange Englishman had told him a fanciful tale about worshipping the god Mercury, and then, by way of explanation, he told them he was a silversmith, and hoping to find a master to take him on. 'And this, good monsieurs, is how I set sail for Hull.' Abraham drained the last of his tankard. He had noticed the barely perceptible change to his drinking companion's mien, but he continued his tale of his journey through France and his voyage across the sea. 'All, you see,' he chuckled, 'at the suggestion, nay, the whim of a broken old man who feared his death was close. Perhaps I am no more than a fool, but a hopeful fool at that,' he finished, with a smile. The retelling of the journey seemed to lift the damp out of his limbs as swiftly as the blazing fire in the hearth.

His companion looked at him, long and hard, then stood up and drained his tankard. 'Meet me here at the same time tomorrow,' he said, his face giving little away. 'I may know someone who could help – no promises, mind.' With that, the fellow left the inn and Abraham was left alone, staring into the fire.

2015

Clare Cartwright was not used to being alone in a house with five cats. Before Harry's death last year, there had been a visit almost every weekend from one of Harry's children, or else from his five grandchildren, or from Amber and Joshua, her own children, now grown. Amber had named the cats Jinx, May Day, Jaws, Q and Pussy Galore after Bond characters; Clare had never worked out exactly why this was the case, though could only guess it must come from Rory – the boyfriend's – influence. At night the creatures prowled the house like shadows from the past. Responsibility for them lay firmly upon Clare's shoulders. She fed them whenever they appeared, which was rare. Occasionally, she might stroke them while watching *Antiques Roadshow* on a Sunday (television had never appealed to her in the same way it had Harry), but the trouble was that the cats' free-spirited presence could never be guaranteed. This produced a mirroring effect in Clare, which amounted to little or no emotional connection between her and the cats. It was, in essence, a marriage of resentment.

After Harry decided he'd had enough of playing golf in Berkshire, they'd moved back to London to be nearer the children. Both Amber and Joshua had gravitated to the city as wasps to beer. Amber had subsequently brought Misty home from university. Clare considered this to be a thoroughly unoriginal name for a cat, though still easier to pass off to guests than her current collection's names. Soon after Amber had moved into a tiny flat with her boyfriend in Bayswater, she had asked Clare to mind Misty for a few weeks, omitting to mention that the tabby hadn't been spayed. It was a Sunday morning when the kittens appeared, wriggling like giant earthworms in a patch of light upon the kitchen tiles. It had taken Clare back to the birth of her own children, and she felt a melting in her breast before noticing with a pang that Misty wasn't moving. She had apparently died during birthing, and this, combined with the vulnerability of the tiny, blind, squeaking kits made her refuse Harry's offer to strangle them. Being country-raised, Harry was unsentimental to disposing of animals. Amber screamed when he told her his plan and instead insisted on performing a naming ceremony, complete with a Bond theme tune. She gave no indication when she might want them back. Clare treated them much like her cleaning lady: feeling a sense of duty toward them and every so often remembering to provide treats, especially at Christmas. So used to having cats was she now that when one of them died, she used the same name for the replacement. But after Harry had died, she had begun wrapping Christmas presents for the cats, an action that Amber – who had studied psychology at university – claimed was co-dependent and a result of suffering empty nest syndrome, and that Clare must make a deliberate and concerted effort to find her purpose.

'I'm seventy-one, for heaven's sake!' Clare had snapped.

'So?' said Amber in a way that made Clare wonder whether, in her new role as an estate agent, people bought houses from her out of fear.

Clare tried to set her face into an expression of conviction, wondering if a septuagenarian could pull-off such a look. 'I was caught in a horrible marriage, had the two of you, went through a hideous divorce, kept a roof over our heads and eventually inherited Harry's children to bring up. I would prefer not to be lectured on purpose. Did I ever tell you I had a job share with a neighbour? We looked after each other's children whilst one of us helped as a dresser at Sadler's Wells. I can find purpose when I want to. Let's just say, I am henceforth happily retired.'

Amber crossed her arms, an action Clare had come to associate with defiance. 'Mum, it's something you need to do. Your friend Elizabeth still designs her curtains, doesn't she? And she's a few years older than you.'

Clare kept her eye on Amber's arms, she would know when she was let off the hook. 'For her friends, yes, but it's hardly what you'd call a business, darling.' The arms loosened a little.

'And I'm not asking you to have a business, just something to make you...' Clare waited, face set with a smile; it was a mystery to her why, now she was in her eighth decade, her daughter thought she required parenting. '... Happy, Mummy,' Amber finished. 'It's been a year. The first year is the hardest but Harry would have—'

'Don't you dare say it,' Clare warned, holding up her index finger. Amber had made no attempts to get to know

Harry when he was alive, and she would not have her preaching about him in the wake of his death. Showing care towards her was one thing but overt manipulation was quite another.

Clare was willing to admit, only to herself, that, yes, after Harry had died, she had become quite attached to the cats. In fact, it was like having children without any of the associated guilt. Cats were perfect pets in that way: independent, beautiful, aware of their own needs, all the things Clare had been lacking most of her life. She often regretted not having had a cat herself before marriage. Yes, cats had taught her something about life. Not that she would relay any of this to Amber, of course, who had eventually left in surly defeat.

Suffice it to say, at seventy-one, Clare was finally putting her own needs first and for that she didn't need a purpose. On the contrary, she had been dreaming up means of escape from all that. Elizabeth, whose husband had also died last year, and who had become Clare's rock of late, was thankfully keen to travel too. Elizabeth had always had an independent streak, which perhaps came from having had four husbands – two suddenly dying on her – and amassing a small fortune in the process. She was an eternal optimist and Clare knew she was good for her. Clare could live comfortably off what she had. Harry may have been inconsiderate when it came to taking care of his health, but financially he had taken pride in caring for his family.

Clare checked her reflection in the hall mirror: French, gilded, baroque. Harry always said she looked young for her age, but she neither looked nor felt it anymore. Lack of sleep was to blame. Clare did not like taking the pills that the doctor had prescribed. A couple of glasses of red wine was her preferred means to help her wind down but then, of course, she would be awake in the night, prowling the house like one of her cats. On more than one occasion, they had startled one another, both exuding pain-ridden sounds of surprise.

'Be good!' she called out to the cats, just as she once had to Harry, picking up her handbag and keys, and remembering her umbrella at the last moment. Harry had been goodness itself, hadn't needed reminding, and he certainly hadn't deposited bloodied mice on her pale-beige carpet. Aside from smoking the odd cigar in the house, she'd found him entirely faultless, in fact, no doubt something else Amber would put down to the blind spot in her co-dependency.

The walk to Kings Road took no more than twenty minutes. The weather was warm for May and Clare was glad she'd worn just a raincoat, though the promised rain held off. She exited Onslow Gardens and crossed Fulham Road, past various antique shops, heading south onto Old Church Street; her body moved robotically as if it were urging her forwards and not her mind. Perhaps it was. Perhaps when life loses meaning, the brain gives way to the whims of the body but, even when she tried to feel the excitement she had once felt at discovering an unusual piece of silver or an interesting piece of ceramic, she experienced only a sense of effort. One cannot generate excitement, in much the same way as one cannot generate love, she often thought; it was either there or it was not. Harry's death, it would seem, had robbed her of not only joy but even the anticipation of it. Could one even exist without the other anyway? she wondered. She walked along Old Church Street and passed Chelsea Arts Club, where, unbidden, a quote from Charles Kingsley, an early nineteenth-century Anglican clergyman and writer, came to mind.

We act as though comfort and luxury were the chief requirements of life, when all that we need to be really happy is something to be enthusiastic about.

Enthusiasm. Well, that was a feeling Clare could scarcely remember. Yet here she was heading to an antiques fair, hoping that that enthusiasm might join her. So far, however, she felt numb to it. No doubt Amber would agree with Mr Kingsley's views. No doubt it would slot nicely into her ethos, and occasionally her lectures, on the close association between purpose and happiness.

'Good morning,' said the security guard at the door.

She handed over the entry ticket, pulled the briefest of smiles and kept walking. When you are feeling hellish, keep going. Wasn't that what one was supposed to do? She was in a kind of limbo rather than hell, a limbo in which nothing seemed to matter. Her children no longer needed her, her cats merely used her, and even shopping for antiques no longer brought any joy. There must, at some point, be an exit to this dreary parade, she thought. It would require a great deal to get through the rest of her life feeling so emotionally wrought.

As she wandered around the fair, Clare recognised a few faces and offered greetings and, 'Hello', offering a few perfunctory, unmemorable remarks. If conversations continued for any length of time, she would likely mention the passing of her husband and, today of all days, she was not in the mood for sympathy. After a year, she was unsure where grief ended and self-pity began. This was, in part, why she was determined to buy something today, if for no other reason than to see if it brought a glimmer of happiness. Since Harry's passing, she had put off purchasing anything, not trusting her own judgement, until her lack of trust had morphed into disinterest. Looking about at the rows of gleaming silverware on the pristine tables, she felt a veneer of the same disinterest. But beneath it lay a faint but distinct desire. Desire was perhaps too passionate a word for it; if anything, it resembled a craving, almost like mild hunger. For a moment, she wondered if it was in fact hunger, but like her emotions, her appetite this past year needed to be coaxed continuously. It was just before reaching Malcolm's stand – Malcolm had been her most trusted dealer for many years– that she felt the stirring of an acquisition, the sense that there was something to be discovered. It was followed by a faint fluttering in her gut, a feeling she remembered from first meeting Harry: a sense of want and satisfaction simultaneously presenting themselves. I won't dismiss you, she said to herself as she approached Malcolm's stand, *I won't*.

'Ah, Clare, how lovely to see you!' Malcolm said, walking around the stand and kissing Clare on each cheek. 'It's been a while. How are you?'

Clare appreciated Malcolm's delicacy. She had sent him an email some months back explaining Harry's death and he had expressed his condolences. What she saw was genuine kindness, hovering in his watery blue eyes.

'Some days are easier than others,' she said, waiting for the usual rhythm of their conversations to commence.

'The good days will increase. I lost my twin brother some years ago. Tore my heart apart for a time. You never think you'll have a day when you're not ploughing through the grief, but you will.' Malcolm's lips were pulled in, and he seemed to read Clare's mind. 'But I am sure you're here to distract yourself. Tell me what you think of this eighteenth-century candelabra, it's stunning, eh?'

Clare blurted out, with excessive honesty, 'It's lovely, Malcolm, but you know the grand pieces never appeal to me.' Immediately, she regretted her abruptness. Malcolm smiled kindly and seemed to move back behind his stand with renewed energy. 'How can I forget your love of the unusual, Clare! What do you make of this? It's a lovely piece.' Malcolm held up an ornate beaker. 'A Swedish silver-gilt beaker with a cover, Stockholm circa 1680. The maker was Stahle.'

Clare peered at the outer cage of delicate filigree work and the three ball feet. The piece was six inches high and had the effect of causing the fluttering in Clare's chest to cease. 'How much is it?' she asked. It was not her intention to be abrupt, but it seemed to require excessive effort to pretend something mattered when it did not.

'Fifteen.'

Clare had set her budget at ten thousand, so was somewhat relieved the piece was beyond her limit. 'I… I'm not excited by it,' she said. For some reason, she was thinking of Harry's habit of leaving cigar stubs about the house. She'd find them on shelves in kitchen cupboards, on the cistern of the loo. How she regretted telling him off; what she would do to find a cigar butt now. Tears stung the backs of her eyes. 'I suppose I'm not excited about very much, at the moment,' she confessed, lowering her voice to hide the tremor in her throat.

'You're here, at least,' said Malcolm. 'Give it time. What about this? I know you have a piece of silver from Hull. Well, this piece is a real gem. It's a tumbler cup.'

A loss of passion had, it seemed, been accompanied by a loss of memory; Clare could not recall having previously bought any pieces from Hull. She took the piece in her hand and turned it over. 'I'm not sure,' she said, suddenly unsettled. 'But it's not a tumbler. I'll show you.' She placed the tumbler on its side; it rolled a bit but did not bounce back onto its bottom. This suddenly made it all the more appealing.

'Take it if you like. You and I are old friends. Pay me next week, if it grabs you, that is.' Malcolm picked up the silver piece and handed it to Clare.

She took it, anticipating feeling nothing, except perhaps a slight sickening feeling at the loss of her former joy. Her heart skipped a beat and her stomach fluttered. Clare frowned, bemused. This was nothing new, she decided. In the last months, her emotions seemed to ebb and flow as reckless as waves of confusion upon an expansive shore. They could not always be trusted.

'It's not very eye-catching,' she said. This had ever been her role, the cynic, the one determined to avoid humiliation by astute businessmen.

'Given, but do yourself a favour, Clare, take it home and live with it for a few days.' Malcolm smiled.

Clare felt her old verve returning, and it urged her to turn the bowl upside down to inspect the hallmarks. She lifted her glasses from their chain around her neck. Her eyebrows rose. The image on the side struck her at once. 'That's an odd image of Mercury,' she said in a half-whisper. The figure appeared old, almost disfigured. It brought her a strange kind of comfort, though she could not place her finger on precisely why.

'One of the last silversmiths to have their work assayed in Kingston upon Hull. After this, the silver went to York to be assayed, for their quality.'

It was interesting, but Clare was certain it wasn't responsible for her fluttering chest. 'Who was the maker?' she asked, hiding the stirrings of excitement out of habit. She was sure Malcolm pitied her and would likely give her a good deal on some obscure piece from Hull. But what about it was causing her heart to stir?

'Abraham Barachin,' replied Malcolm. 'As I said, Clare, look at it at home with the rest of your things and let me know what you think.'

Their moment was passing. A pushy man with a pompous accent was enquiring about the grandiose candelabra.

'Very well, I'll take it,' she said, 'what's your best price?'

'Seven,' Malcolm called.

Clare nodded. 'I'll be in touch.'

Malcolm's smile was kindness itself. 'I look forward to it, Clare.'

***

'What do you mean you're going to spend seven thousand pounds on a teeny-weeny pot, darling?'

Clare held the receiver away from her ear. Elizabeth often insisted on speaking from her garden where she was invariably bent over weeding, resulting in a not inconsiderable amount of bellowing. When Elizabeth's business took place, Clare could never fathom. She suspected Elizabeth might install curtains for friends who never questioned her timing. Speaking to Elizabeth at her home in Kew meant having the constant barrage of the sound as aircraft came into land at Heathrow. This also contributed to Elizabeth's tendency to speak at high volume. She would often say that the aeroplanes were the price to pay for a two-acre garden in London. Clare thought that to hold onto an eight-bedroomed house for its garden when Heathrow grew year on year was also a direct measure of Elizabeth's eccentricity. It was this eccentricity, however, that kept them firm friends, with Clare's unconscious pragmatism and sensibility providing balance. It was, therefore, unusual to be the one under examination.

'It's seventeenth-century. It's quirky, but more importantly, it seemed to speak to me.'

'Speak to you? Lord! I have never been able to work out whether women our age with cats start out sane and are driven mad by the creatures, or whether mad women simply adopt cats.'

'Elizabeth!' scolded Clare. 'Speak for yourself. I'm certainly not mad.'

'Oh, look, I'm more than aware I'm throwing stones from my glasshouse, darling. Anyway, I thought you and

I were going away together. Will that still happen if you're buying up Seagrove and Atterbury Auctions at a rate?'

'It wasn't Seagrove and Atterbury,' Clare replied, biting her tongue to stop herself adding, '*And I wouldn't spend what you do on face-tweaking.*' Elizabeth seemed to adjust her appearance as often as she did her client's curtains. 'Thank you for your concern.'

There was a long sigh on the other end. 'Oh, I'm sorry, Clare. You mustn't take me so literally. I'm up to my elbows in compost here. Let me find my coffee and sit down a moment. Now tell me about this silver piece. I do understand how these things excite you, even though I don't get your fascination with the past. But if it makes you happy, it can't be all that bad.'

Clare couldn't help but defend herself. 'It all comes down to legacy. Anybody of any worth always leaves a mark on the world, and that's what interests me most. I like thinking about to whom the pieces might have once belonged, whose hands they may have passed through. Then I ponder precisely what they went through to get it. I suppose there always seems to be a story lurking in the pieces that speak to me, even if it's mostly made up.'

'You always did have a good imagination, but you mustn't take me too seriously, darling. Are we still heading off for a break to foreign parts next month or not?'

'Oh, Elizabeth. I'm not certain I feel like it right now.'

'Left to your own devices, you would never feel like it. I think a break would do you good. It would take your mind off things. Leave it to me, I'll book it and pay for it all.'

'No, you are not paying for me… and where were you thinking we should visit?'

'Look, you have always had this ridiculous pride and heaven knows why, as you know better than most, I'll have a hard job dividing up the money when I'm gone, you know, with no children of my own. So, this is what I choose to do with it, and all I'm asking is that you go along with it. If it's not too much of a bore, that is. You always said you wanted to go to St Petersburg and, I don't know, I haven't thought much beyond that. Grief has made you quite blunt, you know. I like that, but for once, accept something from me graciously, darling. The trip was my idea, after all. It would make me happy to see you not having to think for a few days.'

If Clare gave in too easily, she would likely be under Elizabeth's thumb for the entire trip. Having controlled her husbands (until they'd found a means of escape), Clare always felt Elizabeth was halfway on the lookout for a substitute puppet. So, over the years, Clare had worked out the best means of holding onto autonomy in her friend's company and, though she was never sure if Elizabeth was aware of her approach, the ritual had nevertheless become an important part of their friendship.

'Oh, I don't know,' Clare said, shaking her head, realising that grief might hamper her performance this time around

Elizabeth, replied, 'Come on, Clare, you can't live too much in your head at the moment. It's not good for you. As you more than know, I only do things I want to do, and I want you to have a good holiday.'

Clare wondered if she could substitute Elizabeth's enforced generosity by paying her way with their food. She did not relish trying to wrestle with Elizabeth for the little silver tray at the end of each restaurant visit, but in her grief she did not wish to be treated like an invalid either. Doubt turned over in her stomach.

'Oh Liz, I'm just not sure I'm ready to go away yet.'

'Nonsense. You just have to do it without thinking about it too much.'

Elizabeth never seemed put out by these discussions, which was another reason Clare kept arguing for her autonomy. 'It might cheer you up. It's always the things we don't do in life that we regret, never the things we do. But you know that. Look, little silver pots are great, darling, but it's experiences that are worth so much more in life. Why do you think I've had four husbands?'

Elizabeth's enthusiasm helped to diffuse the remaining tension. Clare sighed. 'You're very naughty, Liz. It's very lovely of you, really it is. You organise it then. Surprise me. But I'm accepting only because you're too insistent.

'Moi? Insistent?'

It was only afterwards that Clare realised her laugh had been, for the first time in a long while, not conscious of itself, nor doubtful of whether it was warranted. She just let it ripple out.

'I'm being ridiculous, aren't I?'

Darn. She had relaxed a little too much and forgotten that to put herself down in Elizabeth's company opened herself up to attack. There was a smacking of lips on the other end of the line as Elizabeth applied lipstick. Chanel, Clare assumed. 'Now you mention it, yes. But as you're so often ridiculous in ways I can't even begin to express, I'm not surprised. In fact, if you weren't ridiculous, I'd perhaps be worried about you, darling.'

Clare smiled. Of course, even if she had to remind herself of this every so often – Elizabeth trumped on her ridiculousness every time. The dye was cast.

Listening to Elizabeth's upbeat tone began to grate, reminding Clare how far out of reach a holiday mood felt. She knew that it would be better for her to go, but that it would also mean colossal effort. Grief had proven people to be useful, and necessary, if only as a brief distraction. The trouble was she felt she had so little to give that she limited time with friends so as not to be a silent, remote and melancholy burden. Elizabeth, of course, understood grief better than most. But before Harry's death, only Clare's family had felt truly necessary to her. Recently, the opposite seemed to be true. Her children pity her. Amber fussed over her or ordered her around, peering into every area of Clare's life like a secretary into an errant file, thinking she knew better. Joshua's input was mild by comparison, but just last night, he had rung her to tell her to buy chamomile tea and spray lavender oil on her pillows, as if she were suddenly senile. She'd told him, 'Thank you, sweetheart, but I'm doing quite well with wine at the moment.' That had shocked him. Joshua, unlike his sister, had a habit of falling into silence when thrown off guard. Clare had hung up.

Now she bid Elizabeth goodbye before she could settle into her topic, and put down the phone. It was dawning on her that she had no-one, at least, no-one truly close. She wondered whether there were buried bits of personality, fragments of self that had never really had time to grow or which had been obscured which would, or even could, emerge. When her parents had died, there had been the distraction of family. Now that Harry was dead and both sets of children were gone, she would have to decide what to do and get on with it. 'At my age, nothing is likely to emerge, so just get on with it.' It would not be true to say she envied Elizabeth with her carefree existence and four husbands, but she could see how such an attitude might be liberating.

Shakespeare was right, the elderly did return to childhood; Clare thankfully hadn't reached the sans teeth part, but instead seemed to be in the throes of edging towards greater independence, just as her children had fought for similar rights during their adolescence. With a trip in the pipeline, Clare would demonstrate an ability to flit off; she would make them worry about what kind of chamomile tea she had been drinking. Children. Why did nobody warn you that the reason good parenting was so essential was because, one day, it would be reversed and applied to you with fervour?

That's all you're really left with, she told herself: cats, a crazy friend, and small, irrelevant thrills from the past.

'Isn't that right, Q?' But Q, the tabby, merely headed towards her bedroom where he would languor in a square of sunlight upon her bedspread for most of the afternoon. God save me from that stage of life, Clare thought.

The study still smelt of Harry's cigars. When he was alive, Clare would tell Harry that the smell would remain forever in the drapes. Now she hoped that it would. All the years she had spent detesting the smell and appealing to Harry to look after his (and her) health, and now stale cigar smoke was the best smell in the world. Love always seemed to be such a battle but, in the end, it amounted to loss. First the heat of the crush fades to the softer depth of love, if one was lucky, and then romance tended to fade too, except on rare occasions. Finally, the person faded. Forever. A heart-wrenching, catastrophic fade. She took a deep breath, determined not to cry, as she sat down in Harry's hefty desk chair and opened a reference book on silver. In it she found the correct word to describe her pot; it was not a tumbler cup, as Malcolm had called it, but a dram cup or a *hottwater taister*. This was something men once carried about their person, as they would a knife, thereby always ready to buy a dram from a street seller. She was determined to hold onto this curiosity. Any emotion other than grief was to be grasped at. She knew now what the Buddhists talked about when they spoke of the impermanent nature of life. It was all so fragile. All so fleeting. All so beyond her control.

'Come on, little pot. Show me that you have a history; that some solidness exists in this damned world.'

***

Malcolm had given her such details as maker, town, and date, which had to be approximate as there was no date letter, but this was not unusual for regional silver of the period. Looking up the details after any purchase usually meant fixing them in her mind. Having done that, she did what she always did next, and that was to see what information there was available on the silversmith. For this, she bypassed leafing through countless books and turned to the computer. She looked first at the Hull Museum website to see what, if anything, they had by Abraham Barachin. It showed a few pieces, but nothing quite like the little cup in front of her. A broader search on Barachin followed. Now there was something to make her sit up and take notice. An article appeared on the screen from the record of acquisitions from the Art Fund. Described was a silver bleeding bowl made by Abraham Barachin. It listed the vendor as Seagrove and Atterbury, and the description of Mercury holding a caduceus on one side and the initials M.A.R. on the other seemed to fit the little bowl on Clare's desk. A pair? she wondered.

'Marvellous,' she murmured and tapped away at Harry's keyboard. Both pots seemed to match until it came to the weight, the description and date. She continued to stare at the screen. The pot they catalogued weighed ten ounces whereas the pot she held in her hand could be no heavier than one ounce. It certainly was not a bleeding bowl. The date was given as 1710–25 which seemed far too late to her. This bowl and her own could not possibly be the same piece. This served only to deepen her intrigue. She would keep it.

This meant Malcolm needed paying and she set off, once again, the next morning, to the fair. It was the last day and the dealers who had fared well that week would be looking forward to packing up. Those who had fared poorly would be left behind, wondering what went wrong. Malcolm was, as usual, in the first group and greeted her warmly.

'Clare, good to see you.'

Malcolm put down the phone he'd been examining.

'Have you had a good week?'

'Yes, I would say it has been a satisfactory week,' was all any canny businessman would admit. 'What have you decided about the tumbler cup?'

Clare reached into her handbag and brought out the silver dram cup. 'Well, I was right,' she said. 'It's a hot water taster or dram cup and not a tumbler cup. I found a picture of one in Philippa Glanville's book.'

'What did it say?'

'It just seemed to ring true; in particular, the weight made sense to me; dram cups are no more than one or two ounces.'

'Of course. Yes, that's right,' said Malcolm in an affable way. 'I certainly could use a hot water taster on my desk right now, together with the whiskey to go in it.'

They both laughed.

'But there's something odd about it, Malcolm.'

'How so?'

Clare stared at the image of the old Mercury. 'Well, it is an unusual depiction of the god. He's usually depicted as a fit young man hurtling through the sky, but I like it and will take it. Seven thousand is what we agreed, isn't it?'

Malcolm smiled. 'It is charming. Yes seven. I'm glad you are taking it. I think it will sit well in your collection.

'Fine. I much preferred it to the filigree piece, which was twice the price, so I somehow feel as if I'm getting a bargain,' she tried to joke but her tone felt flat, foreign as well as effortful. She handed Malcolm her credit card with a brief smile.

As she tucked her receipt into her bag, she added, 'I almost forgot to mention, something else showed up in my search. A pot similar to this one was stolen from the Museum of Hull in 1986 and apparently never recovered.'

'Good Lord!'

Clare reached forward and touched Malcolm's arm. She did it out of instinct and the touch of his tweed jacket jolted her, making her think of Harry and the jacket he had worn far too often in Berkshire. She blinked the sensation away. 'It's all right, or so I think. You see, I searched the name Abraham Barachin and that's what it brought up, but I know that it can't be this little pot. It showed up as an acquisition by the NACF, you know the old name for the Art Fund, and I found a piece that describes this particular image of Mercury precisely, but they called it a bleeding bowl and the weight was completely wrong. Ten ounces. The given date of 1710–25 didn't seem right either. This looks and feels a lot earlier.'

Malcolm stared at her, and his eyes narrowed. 'If there is any suspicion that this is the stolen piece, it needs to go back to the museum.'

Clare smiled. 'No, I'm sure it is not. There were far too many differences. I'm very pleased with it. Look, I'm sorry to have even mentioned it. I feel a little silly now. I'm not quite myself at the moment.' Who did one become in those moments when one was not oneself? A former self? Somebody else entirely?

As she left the fair, she spotted a free black cab and, since a light rain was starting to fall, extended her arm. Her eyes flickered over the advert on the taxi's roof: *The Great Museum Heist*, now showing at Waterloo Vaults. She laughed at the absurdity and climbed inside.

***

Malcolm watched Clare's back until he lost sight of her in the thinning afternoon crowds. He felt for the back of his chair and sank into it, bile rising from his gut. What if the piece *was* stolen and, worse, from a museum? How had he not recognised it as something unusual? Clearly it had spoken to something in Clare. They had known each other for years, not as friends exactly but as buyer and dealer, a type of relationship of which he had many. Not all her visits had resulted in sales and many dealers regarded such people as a nuisance and gave them short shrift when it became obvious they were just looking. But not Malcolm. He always felt there could always be purchases further down the line and, sometimes, introductions to other potential clients. He liked to play the long game and Clare always seemed very interested in understanding what she bought. Now, her assiduous interests might cause him some bother.

'Barbara,' he said over his shoulder to his assistant, 'do you know anything about the little cup that Clare came to pay for?'

'Not really, nothing beyond what it said on the label. Why?' Barbara looked up from the back of the stall, where she was packing boxes with tissue paper, ready to receive the silver headed back to the shop.

'No reason,' said Malcolm, running his thumbnail over his lip. 'Can you remember when it came into the shop? I noticed it when I labelled it and meant to ask you. Must've been distracted.'

'Whilst you were away in Scotland looking at that

private collection. I found it in a box of odds and ends with a few other small pieces and a broken ivory candlestick. Oh yes, and some scrunched-up newspaper as filler. It was the sport's page dated 1986 – nothing significant in that, I don't think. The paper was so filthy I threw it away. The box was damaged and the contents in need of a clean. It was in the stock room.'

The stock room was not exactly a place where only surplus stock was kept but a dark and dusty section of the storage cellar full of odds and ends. It did contain some hard-to-shift old stock that had become unfashionable, but mostly it housed boxes with long forgotten content. Barbara had been working with Malcolm for some fifteen years. She had started in her twenties and almost everything she had learnt about the antiques trade she had learnt from him. In an effervescent moment when they were celebrating a rare find, she had told him that she believed him to be the most honest, decent, hardworking man she had ever met. Malcolm hadn't been keen on being placed on a pedestal, but had accepted her compliment with a small smile, and had blushed a little nonetheless. Barbara had said nothing. Over time, she had come to read Malcolm's moods like a seasoned weather reporter reads a changing map.

'I've got to pop out,' he told her. 'I'll be back in a few hours.'

He strode off without explanation, leaving Barbara to mind the stand, her eyebrows raised in surprise at the sudden desertion of his usual bonhomie. Something had clearly happened, but she knew better than to ask and he, she knew, was under no obligation to tell.

Malcolm left the fair and sank into the back of a cab, having given the driver the address of the shop. He thought about the year of the dirty old newspaper. 1986 was a significant year. It was the year he moved out of the Silver Vaults in Holborn to his new premises on Kensington Church Street. The antique trade had not represented a burning ambition for him, but had been something that he had more or less stumbled into after completing his history degree at Exeter. A friend of the family had offered him a job in his silver business, and it wasn't long before he was gripped.

He started at the bottom, doing any menial job that was asked of him, all the while looking closely at hallmarks and the shape of the various objects. He took the time to read about them and was gradually allowed to deal with customers. He earned his employer's respect and took over the lease and stock when old Mr Goldman retired. Malcolm had never really liked working underground and had moved the business to Holborn, to a neat little shop with a brass door-knocker and a wide, Edwardian twenty-pane front window. He'd been far happier behind the counter looking out at the street, and where his customers could look in. He had moved again to his current premises in Kensington, where he had been for over ten years. He had done well for himself, built up his client base, only borrowing money when he really needed it and never defaulted on his overdraft. A sizeable sum from a family trust also came in handy on numerous occasions.

But the real point was, he thought, interrupting his own musings and watching the traffic crawling by, his reputation meant everything to him. It could all be undone in an instant if he had passed on stolen goods, inadvertently or not. This was not a crime taken lightly in England, not at all. He wiped the palm of one hand across his face. He needed to calm down. He needed a whiskey. More pressingly, he needed to work out how he had got into this awful position in the first place.

The cab pulled up outside the shop. Using the keypad, he let himself in and greeted his staff who had nothing significant to report on their morning. This was not unusual during the week of a major fair, as most collectors and curators would be in attendance there, knowing he would have his best pieces on display. The same was true for all the dealers.

'I'll be in my office if you need me,' he announced to nobody in particular, unable to think of anything other than the possibly stolen silver taster he had sold to Clare Cartwright. He fired up his computer and put the name Abraham Barachin into the search bar. Sure enough, the short article as described by Clare popped up:

Hull Bleeding-Bowl by Abraham Barachin
English, 1720–25
Silver, tapering body, engraved on one side with two seated figures, supporting Hermes holding a caduceus. Later (Victorian) initials 'M.A.R.' on the other side. 'I.G.' within a cross-formation of mullets on the base.
Weight 10oz
Bought in 1969 with a grant of £300 from the NACF
Stolen in 1986

Why hadn't he thought to do an internet search himself? The cup, itself, was not a significant item. It was the type of drinking vessel that would have been made for stock. It had, however, been well crafted, and its distinguishing feature was the oddly shaped engraving of Mercury, which made it stand out from other objects of the same shape and period. But nothing more than this. More ornate and far more interesting pieces had been made at the time. The fact it was regional silver of the period did it some favours, since far less regional silver was made at the time than was made in London. It meant there were fewer regional survivors, even amongst ordinary forms. Next, he split the screen and called up the photograph and description that had been prepared for taking it to the fair. His entry simply said:

> Hull Silver Tumbler Cup
> Maker: Abraham Barachin
> Date: c1690

The discrepancy in date was not of great concern. Many regional pieces of the period had no date letter and it was largely a matter of opinion using style as a guide. He did, however, believe he was rather nearer the mark in guessing the date.

He agreed with Clare's assessment; there were similarities and there were also differences. It was clearly not a bleeding bowl and although he had not weighed it, it did not take an expert to see that it did not weigh ten ounces. Any ten-ounce piece of regional silver would have caught his attention; they were rare enough at that weight. Despite feeling a gnawing discomfort about the whole business, he decided to sleep on it before contacting Clare. The fewer people who knew about it, the better. Yet, he needed to voice his concerns. The churning worry was too much for him to contain altogether. He decided on Barbara, on whose discretion he could count. She was methodical and very reliable, he thought, she would have something sensible to say.

He shut down the computer and headed back to the fair. In his absence, Barbara had sold an early eighteenth-century lace-back trefid spoon made by Lawrence Coles in 1705. She reported a regular visitor to the fair was doing the rounds and would return later, as he preferred to speak to Malcolm, and, no, she couldn't put a name to him.

'If you would like a break for a couple of hours, now would be a good time to take it,' said Malcolm. 'I wouldn't ask because I know it is a long day finishing at eight this evening, but I need to discuss something with you, and it can't really wait. Would you be able to join me for a bite to eat after we close and if you can't do that, would you be able to spare half an hour for a drink?'

By eight-thirty they were seated at a table at the Botanist on Sloane Square. Malcolm ordered a whiskey and Barbara a glass of white wine, prompting him to order a bottle of sauvignon blanc. He didn't feel like eating anything at all but felt he should and ordered two fish specials of the day. He was not often lost for words, but he didn't really know where to start.

'So, you found the taster in the stock room?' he began.

'That's right.'

'I rarely go in there, you know.'

'I know,' said Barbara, sipping her wine.

'I haven't given those boxes much thought since I opened one of them many years ago and found it contained a belt and one cufflink from the 1920s.'

'Is that right?'

He nodded, managing to chuckle. He also knew several of the boxes contained papers belonging to his first boss, but chose not to mention that. The historian in him didn't allow him to throw papers out before reading them.

'This is the problem I want to talk to you about. Mrs Cartwright, Clare – looked up the silver dram cup or taster cup; it seems to go by two names and, well, it appears it may have been stolen from a museum in Hull in 1986. There are some reported discrepancies in weight, but it otherwise looks very much the same to me. Too similar for comfort, in my professional opinion. Effectively, I may have sold a stolen piece. Have you ever found anything else in any of the boxes?'

'I've been through most of them over the years and some did contain silver, which I logged.'

'You are nothing if not meticulous, Barbara.'

'Thank you. I put them in the stock room with similar objects, but I don't recall anything of great interest. Most were substandard to what you stock now.'

'Good to know one thing is going in the right direction,' he said, forcing lightness into his tone. He leant forward and continued, 'I now need you to go through all the boxes and catalogue anything you find.' Barbara did not have to be told she had to keep it to herself. She ran a finger around the rim of her glass.

'I found the dram cup in one of the boxes and I'm sorry for not bringing the piece to your attention. I should have realised all regional silver and any early silver was potentially important.'

'None of this is your fault; I did see it when we were setting up the stand. The buck stops with me.'

'What are you going to do next?' Barbara asked.

'I'll call Clare in the morning and ask her, if she feels uneasy about her purchase, to return it. And, I suppose, I'll then contact the museum in Hull. It will be a difficult conversation to have with them because I will not be able to explain how I came to have it to sell.'

'Your reputation speaks for itself, surely,' said Barbara.

'I hope so,' Malcolm murmured, swirling his whiskey around his glass and draining it. 'I certainly hope so.'

The conversation moved on to more general matters, but he could not stop his mind wandering off in the direction of police investigations and adverse publicity, all over a small piece of silver he had no recollection of acquiring. He paid the bill, and they said goodnight. He did not expect to sleep.

***

Clare had gone out to catch the early post and upon her return, she found the light on her answerphone machine blinking in the hallway. She unwound her scarf and pressed play. It was Malcolm, saying he would like to speak to her and that he would come to the house or meet her elsewhere. She set some tea to brew, fed the cats and called him back and they settled on coffee at Claridge's at eleven. She was tempted to stay as she was, in simple slacks and a comfortable cashmere jumper, but changed her mind and rifled through her wardrobe for something a little more suitable. She was sure Claridge's would be peopled with well-dressed women. She did not pretend to be counted amongst them; the best she could do would be to look neat. As the taxi stopped on Brook Street, the doorman stepped forward and opened the door for her. She marvelled at the Art Deco entrance as she walked through it, the front of the Roman stone façade showing a screen of glass and swirling metalwork and the fluted, cream, glass lanterns set against the wall like upturned shuttlecocks.

Clare saw Malcolm before he saw her. He looked tense, she thought, his shoulders hunched and his hands restless in his lap. He stood up as she neared the table. The pillared foyer was filled with low tables and comfortable, low-slung chairs placed around a towering flower arrangement which, today, was filled with a variety of blue and pink blooms. Some of the tables were covered with white tablecloths and set for lunch. Malcolm had chosen a discreet table in the far corner which had not been set.

'It is very good of you to come, Clare. Would you like anything with your coffee?'

'No, just coffee, black and strong is what I need at this time of day,' said Clare as she sat down. Some stilted small talk was hastily abandoned and Malcolm took a breath.

'I don't know where to begin. I apologise, again, for the awful position you find yourself in. I wish I could tell you that I have spoken to the person I got the little cup from and that there is a perfectly reasonable explanation for how he acquired it. Sadly, I cannot. For me, the situation is about as bad as it can get. The least I can do is tell you the truth.' Clare said nothing and Malcolm paused, watching her with concern.

'As soon as you told me of your suspicions, I looked online. On the minor points, you are correct. The date stated is wrong, it is not a bleeding bowl and, thirdly, it did not weigh ten ounces. It weighs much less. I can safely say that without going anywhere near any scales. But the piece of information that jumped out at me, and probably did not strike you, was 1986, the year it was stolen from the museum. I had taken over the shop in the Silver Vaults together with the stock some years earlier and we moved premises to where we are now in 1986.'

He paused again as the waitress brought the coffee to the table and poured it. They watched her in silence, as Clare wondered where the story was going and how it would end.

'The previous owner of the business, bless him, never seemed to have thrown anything away. There were boxes and boxes of papers, and his stock-keeping was not very sophisticated, is how I can best describe it. I am not seeking to blame him, and over time, we developed a very good system of keeping our stock, noting where each item came from, the date it came in, who bought it and so on. You know Barbara, of course you do, well, she told me she found the cup in one of the old boxes recently, entered as much information onto the stock list as she could, and included it in the items sent to the fair. I did notice it earlier in the day but did not get around to speaking to her about it. Barbara is not to blame either but as the proprietor, I must bear full responsibility.' Malcolm finished and took a sip from his coffee to steady his nerves, his hand shaking.

'Well, how incredible,' Clare said, staring into her own cup. She looked up at Malcolm and smiled. 'First of all, I don't feel myself to be in an awful position, a little awkward maybe but no more than that. Not that I think I should even feel awkward because I made a legitimate purchase from a dealer of standing, at a fair that is visited by international collectors and curators. I don't really know what to say or even think. Do you think the previous owner bought it?'

'No, he couldn't have, he was dead by 1986. It is a puzzle, and I cannot begin to fathom it. It goes without saying, Clare, that I will refund you in full but is there anything else you think I can do to help matters? If you would like to give it back to me, I'll call the museum and tell them what has happened.'

'Let me think for a moment,' Clare said. She found herself in a peculiar situation. 'I have never been involved in any criminal activity, I don't even watch crime drama, neither on television nor in the cinema. I'm just not interested. No, that is not strictly true, I am fascinated by forgery – paintings mainly. Forgers are often such talented people that I wonder why they simply don't paint an original themselves.'

Malcolm's shoulders relaxed a little; he seemed relieved to engage for a moment in a new topic of conversation.

'Money is usually the reason,' he said. 'A successful forger can earn vast sums by forging a masterpiece or producing a work of a subject that a well-known or slightly out of favour artist may have done and passing it off as one of theirs.'

'Envy and *crimes de passion* are other reasons, I suppose.

To go back to your question about phoning the museum, as I am holding the hot potato, so to speak, I would be happy to phone them. For the record, Malcolm, my long-held good opinion of you has not changed. I don't think you are capable of doing anything dishonest, any more than I am. We've known each other for so long, I could not possibly think otherwise. We just have to wait and see what happens.'

'That's very kind of you to say so. If there is a problem, it would be better to deal with it sooner than later. I would be grateful if you keep me in the loop with any developments.'

'There may well be no problem and it may be a fuss about nothing. There are too many discrepancies. Perhaps I shouldn't have said anything. But, of course, I will keep you in the loop if there is anything to report.'

'Maybe you are right,' said Malcolm without conviction. As there did not seem to be anything else to say on the subject, they parted company to go their separate ways. As Clare stepped onto the pavement, she paused and watched Malcolm walk away, his head bowed, no doubt troubled by the situation and concerned about his reputation. Clare was less troubled than she felt Malcolm to be, but decidedly more troubled than she had been when she had woken up in the morning. So far, it had not occurred to her to call the museum, but she would now as soon as she got home. By the time she got home, she still did not have a clear idea of what to say and decided to sleep on it, hoping for inspiration.

***

By morning, the seeds of doubt sown by Malcolm had taken root. Clare had now begun to waiver in her certainty. The more she looked at the dram cup and again at the NACF entry, the less sure she became they were not one and the same piece. Perhaps she should have let Malcolm make the phone call. Beyond her routine of getting up, feeding the cats, and having one cup of tea before showering and dressing, she did not feel she could settle to anything while she waited until an acceptable hour to make the phone call. To fill the time, she went to the newsagent and picked up a paper to read while she had breakfast.

What to say? Nothing she turned over in her mind sounded quite right – most of it sounded downright silly. Pushing self-ridicule aside, she looked up the phone number of the museum. Suddenly and unwillingly she saw herself through her daughter's eyes. *Mummy, the things you'll do not to admit you're lonely. Buying clutter kept you in Harry's shadow, precisely where he wanted you. All successful men want the same: a woman to inhabit the shadows to leave them more space to be grandiose in the limelight.* Of course, Amber had never said such a thing outright, she did not need to, but she frequently alluded to the subject. She discussed other couples, friends of hers, holding Clare's eyes and speaking in that arch manner that Clare put down to the estate agent's superior tone.

Clare leant on her intuition, as other women leant upon beauty. It was always this side, the side of unknown forces at play, that encouraged her. Frankly, both her children could think what they wished. At her age, she no longer cared. As for collecting, it may have been small-scale, but Harry had taken an interest in every single piece, had only asked casually about cost then joked about how the auction houses and dealers would feel the pain when they both croaked. 'We know they're beautiful and yet our children will never appreciate them, sweetheart.' Clare had agreed with Harry's sentiments, but that wasn't her point.

'I want them to have a little piece of me when I'm gone. To leave solely money seems somehow crass, impersonal. A sentimental piece of silver on the dressing table lends itself to memories more than a pile of money. Well, that's my theory at least, and I'm sticking to it.'

Harry would kiss her on the nose and tell her that it was a beautiful theory and that she was a wonderful mother. They both knew, of course, that her ways were often impractical, old-fashioned and rigid but Harry loved her, at least too much to point any of this out. Of course, had Amber known, she would have told Clare that she was being patronised by her husband. But Clare knew her own ways of thinking were viewed as dated, even as viewed by her contemporaries, but a traditional marriage had suited her. She never felt Harry had patronised her. That was what Amber did. The younger generations seemed not to understand the real meaning behind love; they were too eager to move on to the next conquest when difficulties arose. Love, real love, was patient, kind, enduring and forgiving. Whereas the young had turned it into something fleeting, their heads rushing at the pace of churning social media as they took off on their dispensable lives. But platitudes still had a place. Clare's first marriage had taught her this and more, but she would rather not think about it. All she knew now, from bitter experience, was that opportunists turned her stomach, and she had acquired the ability to spot them quickly. It was how she had come to trust Malcolm; he genuinely seemed to want to improve his clients' collections. There was, she mused, nothing ulterior about Malcolm's motives. He was an honest man. Very honest indeed, she thought, as she turned her attention to the phone once more.

Clare dialled the museum, asking to be put through to the silver department. A disembodied voice answered after two rings.

'Yes?'

'Good morning, I have a query about a piece of seventeenth-century silver made in Hull. I read something online about a break-in at your museum in 1986 and there were similarities between a stolen piece and one I have recently acquired.'

'Before my time,' came the abrupt reply.

Clare felt taken aback and half-imagined the man might hang up on her. She reminded herself that he was working for the heritage of the country and that she was perhaps overly sensitive given her state of mind. 'Might it be possible for me to come and look at your archives?' she asked, forcing excessive politeness into her tone. His brusqueness had made her feel oddly small and much younger than her years.

'I don't think we've got any,' came the second, sharp response, laced with a distinct lack of interest. Clare opened her mouth to enquire if he had any further resources, but stopped herself. If they had no archives, they had no archives. Besides, she suspected she would not glean much more from this charming gentleman about her little pot. There would be other means, she was certain of it. Might as well hang up, she thought, so she did. She keyed in Elizabeth's number at once and relayed the conversation.

'Perhaps he was having a bad day, it happens to the best of us, darling.'

Yes, although it was an unsatisfactory conversation, Clare was without doubt having a bad year and had perhaps not been clear enough. Maybe this was why she hadn't felt heard. Harry had often said, 'When it comes to people, delivery is everything, sweetheart.'

'I had such a sense of my own ridiculousness, I suppose.'

'Come now, all human beings are ridiculous in our own unique ways; it's what makes us human, darling. The point is we must navigate one another's ridiculousness as best we can. I take it you were looking into your new acquisition?'

'A bit, I always do. I have a feeling about it that I just can't shake.'

'You and your feelings. I'm always telling you that logic's the best way forwards. Men have got it right, which is precisely why they don't endure much of our agony!'

'Liz, you are so matter of fact. I don't know how you manage it.'

'Years of surviving men with big egos, darling. If you can't beat 'em, join 'em. Always remember, darling, all's well that ends well. Several million pounds later and I'm certainly not complaining!'

'Lizzie!'

'I know. But it's too late to change. Now we need to discuss our holiday...' After saying her goodbyes to

Elizabeth, Clare looked up various articles listed online, marvelling at the very notion of having all this information at her fingertips. It was commonplace now and most people took it for granted, of course. But Harry had kept a full set of the *Encyclopaedia Britannica*, as well as the *Year Books* until they were discontinued, which even she consulted less and less. The information in a book had used to seem more real, but time moves on. She was not sure how the young coped with the relentless influx of information, how they could sort it all out in their minds. Perhaps they didn't anymore and a single online hive mind was the future. Yet, ultimately nothing, not even the internet, could be depended upon forever. Nor could looking forward to decent twilight years with your husband. She blinked away sadness and, as she attempted to turn her thoughts towards a lunchtime sandwich, something occurred to her. She abandoned the computer and took the little pot back downstairs again.

The Victoria and Albert Museum held the National Collection of English silver, and for that reason was usually always Clare's first port of call for enquiries. The free service provided by the museum took place on the first Tuesday of each month and was within walking distance from Onslow Gardens. Clare passed beneath the museum's impressive Chihuly chandelier in the entrance, checked where to go and then waited on a narrow wooden bench for somebody to appear, tapping her heels on the wooden floor. After a short wait, a man appeared, and Clare was reassured to see he had a security badge dangling from a lanyard around his neck.

'Good morning, I'm Andrew. How may I help?' he said. After the bruising encounter of her earlier phone call,

Clare felt this was someone who was going to listen. She stood up to shake his hand.

'Clare Cartwright,' she said. 'I have brought a silver cup, seventeenth century, for an appraisal.'

She opened her handbag and took out the grey anti-tarnish cloth and unwrapped it. As she did so, a knot, which was nothing to do with nerves or even grief, began forming in her stomach. Aside from her recent meetings with Malcolm, she had spent the last few months with a handful of close friends and family, so it was most likely that the knot was caused by having to appear normal and unbothered by the inevitable ravages of life.

Andrew turned the cup deftly in his hands, frowning slightly as he looked at it from every angle. After a moment or two, 'What is it you would like to know about it?'

Instead of feeling foolish at bringing what was probably an insignificant object to one of the most important museums in the world, she replied, 'Mercury, it's an unusual image, don't you think?' From this perspective, grief offered a shield, some protection against the rest of the world: a bubble through which little penetrated. The benefit, Clare supposed, was that right, at that moment, she gave little consideration to what anybody else thought about her.

'Indeed.' Andrew placed a magnifier against his eye. 'I can't say I've seen anything quite like this before. You're right, the image is…' he peered even closer, '…unusual.'

'Look,' said Clare, feeling the knot in her stomach morphing into a nauseous ache, 'I found something on the internet last night. Something worrying.'

'Oh?' said Andrew, raising a single quizzical eyebrow.

'I... I read about a stolen piece from the Museum of Hull. It was on the Art Fund's webpage, and it said it was stolen in 1986, almost thirty years ago. The weight was wrong, however, and I don't think it's as late as 1710, which was the date given online. But the description was very similar to this piece – engraved on one side with M.A.R, and two figures and an elderly Mercury holding up the caduceus on the other side – but it said it was called a bleeding bowl, even though they gave a dimension of only four centimetres.'

'Well, it's far too small for a bleeding bowl, not the right shape,' said Andrew, once more peering at the hallmarks, his nose a millimetre from the silver's surface.

Clare's sense of anxious nausea was growing.

'But it also had Abraham Barachin's marks,' she said. 'It seemed an absurd coincidence.'

Andrew looked up. 'A simple case of misattribution, I suspect.'

Before Clare got the chance to ask Andrew anything further, he took the eyepiece away from his face and nodded.

'What would you like me to do about it?' he asked.

Clare had not allowed her thinking to reach this far. Step by step, moment by moment: this was how one walked the path of grief. To cope, she supposed, she'd applied it indiscriminately to all areas of her life. 'I'm not... I'm not certain,' she said.

'Will you excuse me a moment? I think I'd like to check on something.' Andrew took the dram cup and disappeared back through the doors from which he had appeared. Clare was left standing, gripping the anti-tarnish cloth, wringing it between her hands.

Was it Buddha or Jesus who once advised being in the world, but not of it? Whoever it was, she now appreciated what they meant. She knew she had some sort of part to play in life, but without Harry and with her children patronising her, her role felt muddied and unclear. All the same, here she was at the V&A, and it seemed, in some ways, like an act of defiance against her family's expectations. Though she felt detached from her surroundings, she could not deny a sense that she needed to be here. It was a sense that this was it, the so-called purpose they had been asking her to embrace for years.

Waiting on the bench, she closed her eyes. Let me feel anything other than numb, she instructed a god she did not entirely believe in. Casting her gaze down, she noticed that her knuckles showed through white as she squeezed the anti-tarnish cloth on her lap. *Let me feel anything other than numb.*

A few minutes later, she heard the tap-tap of shoes echoing back along the corridor. She took a deep breath and sat up tall. She had a strong suspicion that he might have looked at the Art Loss Register. Nausea and nerves were now joined by a sense of dread, and though not a vast improvement on numbness, there was no denying that she did feel very much alive.

'Where did you purchase it from?' asked Andrew.

Clare thought of Malcolm and his kindness towards her. 'From a respectable dealer,' she said, 'at a respectable fair.'

'Do you have a receipt?'

'Yes, of course.'

'If you've bought it, it's yours then.'

There was always a place for stating the obvious, but it wasn't proving much help.

'Well, I've certainly paid for it. Look…' She had to bravely tell the whole story, there was no escaping it now, but naturally, it was hers to edit as she saw fit. 'I actually spoke to someone at the Museum of Hull, but the conversation was particularly unsatisfactory. I asked to check their archives to see if a piece was stolen and got nowhere with that either.'

'Ah,' said Andrew.

'I am, to be frank, feeling quite sick about it.'

'I'm sure. As I mentioned earlier, it might be a simple case of misattribution.'

Clare bit her lower lip. What had she to lose by asking for help? 'I wondered if you might… whether you might speak to them? I think curator to curator you might… have a little more weight than just me.'

Andrew took a deep breath and seemed to focus on something further along the corridor, though its long stretch was empty aside from a few benches. After a moment, he said, 'It could do. Why don't you follow me.' Clare, not wishing to break the look of concentration that had settled upon his expression, nodded, and followed the click-click of his heels, her head bent.

It's exciting, see it as that, sweetheart. Life has a funny way of helping us out. At the interception of Harry's voice into her thoughts, Clare stood taller, reasoning that the experience must be having some benefit, as she had not thought about Harry for ten minutes or more.

They entered an office containing four desks, metal filing cabinets, and rows of shelves lined with black files. A young girl paused from tapping at her keyboard to smile.

'Take a seat,' said Andrew, as he sat behind a large desk scattered with the detritus of a hectic workday. Clare eyed the monochromatic room and considered how hard it must be to sit in such functional surroundings when your job was to care for the largest and most beautiful objects in England, no doubt the world. The whole museum's essence, with its sculptures, ceramics, furniture and some much more, was one of beauty but, then again, perhaps this hub of office functionality was necessary to balance the museum's overarching dedication to aesthetics.

'Let me find the number and see what happens next,' Andrew said, and Clare could feel the rest of the office pretending not to listen, glad no doubt for some intrusion into the practical monotony of their days.

'That's very kind,' said Clare, hoping she'd achieved the right volume. Nevertheless, her words seemed to carry across the room . She tried to smile. She needed to trust that it would all be well. Trust that she had done the right thing in coming here. Yet, the feeling of nausea was mounting; was this intuition, or was it nerves alone?

Once the call connected, Clare listened to one end of the conversation. Andrew was nodding. '…Yes, I have the piece in front of me... How about I pass you over and you can ask her yourself? Will do… Here's Clare now… Thank you.' He must have pressed mute, for he then said, 'He wants to talk to you?'

Clare hesitated before she extended her hand. If he spoke to her in the same manner as he had during the previous call, she was determined to hang up on him. She reluctantly accepted the handset and took a deep breath, staring at the brick wall beyond the window.

'Hello,' she said, hating how child-like and timid her voice sounded.

'Gordon Thompson here. I wondered if you could please send through some photos of the dram cup?' It was a different voice. She felt her shoulders relax a little.

'Yes, I can do that.'

'Thank you. I'll then check the archives here and get back to you.'

'That's very kind,' said Clare.

'If you have anything else that you think might be relevant, could you let me see that as well?' All she had 'else' was the receipt but did not volunteer to send that.

Clare handed the phone back to Andrew, who placed the receiver against his ear, shrugging his shoulders. 'He seems to have gone. There's nothing to do now but wait.'

Clare looked down at the anti-tarnish cloth she was clutching. 'I suppose so,' she said as she looked toward the pot. 'That was a helpful conversation. Let's just hope it's not the stolen piece.'

'I'm sure it's a case of misattribution.'

'Yes, let's hope so,' she said.

She rewrapped the taster in the cloth, returned it to her handbag and, as she left the museum, pressed the bag to her side feeling as though it was flashing like a Belisha beacon. She looked up at the speckled bark of the plane trees on the pavement and felt relief wash over her. Andrew had listened to her and had taken action.

PART TWO

Looking back

1969

Dottie was convinced she must be pregnant. Whenever she recounted in her mind the shameful events that led up to the act, she couldn't help but blush. And if Mr Barton-Jones happened to walk into the fiercely lit office, it was humiliating to the point of being painful. But, Dottie thought, looking down at her belly, the changes happening within her body were undeniable. Kathy, her best friend at work, thought of Mr Barton-Jones as handsome. Dottie had not told Kathy what had happened. She couldn't. It was a cliché; even when it was happening, she had felt like an actress in a bad play. What had begun as a pat on the bottom had turned into a pinching… oh, why had she not protested? A touching of her left breast, then the other. Mr Barton-Jones had pushed his tongue between her lips, jabbing, as if his intention was to familiarise himself with the terrain, before making a sharp exit.

Dottie put her face in her hands.

'You all right, love?'

A hand rested on Dottie's shoulder, and she looked up at Kathy, whose orange lipstick had smudged on one side.

'Feeling sick,' she said.

'Take the day off, love.'

'It's not that kind of sick.'

'Oh Dottie! You haven't?'

'I might have.'

'Heck, Dottie! Look, come with me. I need a cigarette. Christ knows what you must need, love.'

In the café – or caff as they called it – across the road from the auction house, they bought tea and smoked Rothmans Blue, as Dottie looked through the steamed-up window at the buses stopping outside.

'Come on then, you're going to tell me who the father is or what?' Kathy asked, chewing the side of her cheek, as she always did when she was upset.

'No.'

'All right. Suit yourself. Do you think he'll rise to his responsibilities?'

Dottie shook her head. 'I doubt it very much.'

'What a bugger. Strikes me that this world is full of men like that, buggers who need teaching a lesson. Men! They only take, take, take and see us women as offerings. It's not fair, it's not fair at all, Dottie.'

Dottie tipped the tea from her saucer into her cup. 'I suppose… I suppose I imagined it being easier, agreeing to be a secretary. Not marrying for five years just didn't seem too bad when I was twenty-five. Now I'm twenty-eight, I seem to have, well, my own needs. I thought it might be time to get married.'

Kathy exhaled smoke like an arrow in the direction of Dottie's right eye, forcing her to blink back tears. 'What for? Besides, you can't do that with another man's bun in your oven, can you, love?'

Dottie looked down at her stomach and into Kathy's heavily kohled eyes. Kathy picked a piece of tobacco from her tongue with startling red fingernails.

'Will you come with me?' Dottie asked, her voice thin and frayed around the edges with worry.

'To get rid of it, you mean?'

Dottie nodded, pulling in her lips to hide her shame as Kathy chewed even harder on her cheeks and seemed to take personal offence to Dottie's stance.

'But you have to tell me who it is. You and I are friends. We've weathered some bloody awful storms together. Who's the dad, Dot? Maybe I can have a word with him? What do you say?'

The bell tinkled over the door and Dottie watched a mother wrestle with a pram. She felt no urge to help. If anything, she wanted to scream, '*I'm going to kill mine. I don't think I'll ever be a good mother or any kind of mother after that. Tell me, should I keep it?*'

'No,' she said at last, 'because it's our boss.'

'What! Where on earth—'

'The stationery cupboard. I know what you're thinking, but it's as I said, Kath. I have needs, that's all.' Was she odd or slow in wanting something like this? Was it okay for women to enjoy sex? There were so many questions she wanted to ask Kathy but something, no doubt shame, prevented her. Kathy, she was sure, was born with a better understanding of how the world worked. If only, Dottie thought, she'd had a good relationship with her own mother. It would be nice to have a shoulder to cry on. Her mother had emigrated to Australia as a Ten Pound Pom when Dottie was still at school. She still lived out there with a man half her age, as unapproachable as a lioness. Anyway, it was too late, the milk was all over the floor. What she had to think about was the best means of cleaning it up. Besides, she had cleared up enough in her mother's absence.

Kathy took a long drag on her cigarette. When she was really deep in thought, the smoke quite often would not appear again. Dottie distracted herself watching the curling trails that carried onwards towards the ceiling. 'Have you told him you're pregnant?' Kathy asked in an accusing voice.

Dottie scowled. Kathy knew very well she would not do a thing like that. Lunchtime, and the place would be filled with colleagues from the auction house, queuing for food. At teatime breaks it was less packed – fifteen minutes not really being long enough. A few lads from the mailroom, a couple of secretaries and occasionally a gentleman or two from the valuations department would turn up. One of the mailroom lads had once asked Dottie out for a drink. He was nice enough. Anyhow, she needed this job. She had no inheritances coming her way and was not the kind of girl to have a million Mr Rights queuing at her front door. Employees were not allowed to date other employees: these were Seagrove and Atterbury rules. It did not prevent misbehaviour, of course, but Dottie had seen too many fired on suspicion alone to be tempted. With Mr Barton-Jones, however, it had seemed a different prospect. If he kept choosing to break the rules, there had to be a reason for it, she told herself. After one of their several liaisons in the stationery cupboard, he had told her that his marriage was unhappy. He had said, 'I'm just a cushion to absorb my wife's complaints.' She had taken that as a sign he desired to leave said wife. She had done all she could to not complain to him, not even about the weather. She had shown him only her kind and good side. She had certainly never pressured him. She was waiting, waiting for him to announce his divorce and propose. But that had been months ago and the unhappy marriage was only mentioned before they had…well… and it hadn't been mentioned since.

'No, I haven't told him,' Dottie said, putting the cup into the saucer with a loud rattle.

Kathy tipped her head to one side, seemingly assessing something in the space above Dottie's head. 'You should.'

Dottie had a memory of how she had felt when her mother had told her women should listen rather than contribute at the dinner table. Men needed to be the ones in charge, her mother had always said. Men must be heard, and women have a duty to listen to them.

'I'm not sure I'm up to it,' she half-whispered.

'How can you not be up to *the truth*, Dottie? You're living a half-life if you can't speak truthfully. If nothing else, women are still allowed to do that!' She laughed her raspy, guttural laugh, which always reinforced Dottie's idea that her friend wasn't fazed by any aspect of life. She never worried and rarely complained. Dottie was not sure how she managed it.

'Tell the truth, shame the devil. Did your mother not grind that one into your head from a young age, Dot?'

She hadn't. Instead, Dottie had been told, 'Always look your best when you leave the house.' In fact, that was the only piece of advice Dottie had ever received from her mother, now that she considered it.

But there were lots of truths, which she had frequently ignored. If she thought too hard and too truthfully about her life, she might never get out of bed in the morning. Women like Kathy had got it together in all areas of life. Kathy had men trailing behind her, a landlady who offered to do her laundry, and parents that were well off and had helped her to purchase a Robin Reliant – an *actual* car. It all came down to luck in the end. Luck and something else, confidence no doubt, both of which Dottie had in short supply.

'I think I'd rather sort it out myself, Kath, you know, not bother to mention anything.'

Kathy's eyes narrowed. 'And have this creep have his way in the stationery cupboard for the rest of your days? I don't think so, sweetheart. I don't think so at all.'

Dottie stared at the tea leaves in the bottom of her cup. Her mother would say there was not a problem that was not solvable with a cup of tea. In the end though, she had found a way of solving the problem of having a daughter by running away. Perhaps that had been in the tea leaves too: *Head to Australia*, in clear tea leaf script.

'I'm not sure I'll work there, you know, afterward.'

Kathy stubbed out her cigarette with vigour. 'Of course you will. Don't be daft, love. We know we're paid better than most secretaries in London. We're in a stuffy institution but there are benefits to that; namely, there's more money floating about. You received a ten-pound bonus last Christmas. That's not to be scoffed at.'

But would she still receive a bonus now that Mr Barton-Jones had got what he'd wanted? 'I don't know, Kathy.'

'Yes, you do.' Kathy gulped down the last of her coffee

and dabbed at her orange lipstick with a serviette. 'Yes, you do. Making money out of the likes of Mr Barton-Jones means that at some future bloody point, we'll be independent. Remember our pact. No more crying over men. We'll be free. Free to do as we please. That's what they do after all. Isn't that right, Dot? We'll be free to live independently – just like men!'

Dottie made to open her mouth to agree, but Kathy's pointed finger silenced her.

'I won't hear you say it, Dot!'

Dottie crossed her arms. 'You have no idea what I was going to say.'

'Yes, I bleeding do. You were going to speak about babies. I can see that pathetic look in your eye.'

Dottie leaned closer so that nobody else in the café would hear. 'I do want them someday, Kath. I do and I'm not afraid to say so.'

'But wait until you're married. Anything else is a ruse so that men can chain you to the house to not let other fellows get to you. The baby is immaterial. It's the chaining that's important. You don't want to be a part of that, mark my words. We're emancipated women, Dot. We won't be the servants of the household like our mothers. That's what we're making a stand against. Eh?'

Was Dottie's mother a servant? She could not remember her cooking a solitary meal, and it was Dottie who had visited the launderette. Her mother was a dancer and would perform most nights at a basement jazz club in Soho, a place her mother called the *Grotto* or the *Grotty Grotto,* depending on what kind of mood she was in. She was otherwise asleep when Dottie was home or else drinking herself toward a deep, oblivious unconsciousness.

'I think it's normal to want a baby,' she said, a sulky tone creeping to her voice.

'That's what men want you to think,' said Kathy, opening her compact and checking her lipstick. 'But it's a trap.' The compact snapped shut. 'That's all.'

Dottie glanced across the room where the mother who had entered earlier was feeding her baby. She had the creature across both knees. Mother and baby's eyes were locked as if the rest of the world had vanished. In that moment, Dottie wanted her own world to disappear. She wanted the job but did not want to put up with Mr Barton-Jones. This baby at least meant she had to do something. She just wasn't sure whether it meant getting rid of it and continuing at Seagrove and Atterbury, or getting rid of it and moving on.

'My mother used to say I could paint,' she said, wistfully. 'I think I might go back to school, study something. Go somewhere proper, like art school.'

The shop bell sounded as they left, and Dottie saw a look of fear cross the baby's eyes. They stood waiting on the kerb for the bus to move past.

'Dot, you're twenty-eight. It's a bit late to consider another career at your age. Besides, you've already got a good job.'

The bus moved and they crossed the road toward the auction house.

'I'm typing auction catalogues; it's not exactly brain surgery.'

'Count yourself lucky you're not in a café, what with being pregnant and all. All those smells!'

'Shh!' said Dottie, feeling her stomach turn over. 'And you have to promise not to mention this to anyone.'

'I might tell Mr Barton-Jones if you won't.'

'Don't you dare, Kath. Promise me you won't. *Please.*'

'Calm down! I'm pulling your leg, love. I might be fighting the corner for women but I'm not a raving idiot. We'll deal with this together. All right? That's what us women must do, stick together. The 1960s will be remembered as the decade that women took a stance and stuck together.'

They re-entered the auction house. Mr Barton-Jones crossed the reception area, whistling *Oh Come All Ye Faithful*, though Christmas was months away.

'Ah, Dottie, I need some more of those brown envelopes. Can you locate them and bring them to my office? I have a meeting with Mrs How.'

Dottie bit her lower lip. She didn't feel capable of taking a stance. 'Yes, sir.' Mrs How was treated like the Queen at Seagrove and Atterbury; it pained Dottie to see the reverence on Mr Barton-Jones' face.

He narrowed his eyes, as if reading Dottie's thoughts. 'Do it quickly and I might just overlook the extra five minutes you took for tea. This auction house prides itself on its prompt service, something not helped by our secretaries lolling about. Understood?'

Kath prodded her side. Dottie thought it ridiculous that Kath would think she might start the baby conversation here in the reception of Seagrove and Atterbury.

'Understood, sir,' she said.

'Good. Hurry along then. You too, Kath. I'm sure Mr Shilton will have something to say about your timekeeping.

Thank the Lord this world isn't run by women, otherwise we'd all be losing our faculties and plenty of business to gossipy tea breaks. You've got that silver catalogue to be getting on with. Chop, chop!'

Mr Barton-Jones marched into the auction room, whistling the same carol.

'Well, you did a mighty fine job of standing up for yourself there, Dot.'

'Oh, shut up, Kath!'

Dottie took a deep breath. She felt terrible.

'You alright, Dot?'

'It's nothing. I just…'

Hand clapped over her mouth, Dottie just made it to the lavatory, where she spewed up her lunch, several times. After pulling the chain, she looked in the mirror as she dabbed at her mouth, a tremor appearing in her hand. Her hollow stomach was burning with growing anger.

'Who says I have to get rid of it? It's my baby and my body, and I shall do with it as I please!'

1685

Abraham looked out of his chamber window towards the sky that beamed bright. Never had he imagined these northern skies would hold such luminosity. He sensed a difference in the air between here and Bourges. From the little he had seen, it felt industrious. He felt more than refreshed, he felt alive.

First things first, he needed to mend his shoes. He examined the hole-ridden sole once more. Hull was not large; it should not take long to find a cobbler. After breaking his fast with bread, dripping and ale, he was told where he should go. The smell of leather and rabbit glue assailed his senses before he even spotted the shop where the cobbler sat by the window working at his last. He looked up from the large shoe before him as the shop's bell sounded. Abraham spotted the statue of St Crispin, the patron saint of shoes, on the counter, acknowledged the cobbler's gesture and sat on the adjacent bench. He looked around the workshop. The tools the cobbler used were quite different from his own and fewer in number. He took in the skins hanging from the wall, some with sole-shaped pieces cut from them, sharp moon knives, needles, cord, hammers, tacks, lasts of various sizes and a cauldron hanging above the fire containing the stinking concoction of rabbit glue necessary to keep the layers of the soles together. Some minutes later, the cobbler abandoned the shoe he had been working on.

'Your boots need to be replaced. My cousin, next door, is a cordwainer.'

'No,' said Abraham, putting his foot down both literally and metaphorically. 'They need to be repaired.' He could not be extravagant when he had yet to find work.

'But look, sir, the leather is worn, they are falling apart.' The cobbler pointed out the numerous holes to Abraham, who was more than aware of the problem. 'You will be back next week complaining and wanting new ones.'

'If they fall apart, that is my cross to bear.'

'Very well. I am not a man to turn away a customer,' and with that he gestured to Abraham to hand over his boots. 'You will be needing stockings too, I see,' he added with a grin.

'Aye,' said Abraham, looking at his protruding toe. But there was so much else of import to do first. 'Stockings can wait but the boots cannot.'

With his boots renewed, Abraham set forth with a spring in his stride. He meandered through the town, drinking it in, passing Trinity House. Looking around, he saw a mix of finely dressed, shabbier poorer people and, crouched in the shadows and running between the buildings the slight frames of street urchins. The houses were not all built of brick, some were made of wood and others lime-washed. The streets were crowded with townsfolk going about their business, rows of market stalls, shops, and street sellers jostling and calling out their wares, 'Oysters and hot codlings, posies and chickens, live birds and onions.' Their voices competed with one another and rose above the hum and bustle of the street and the clatter of feet upon the cobblestones. Abraham turned left onto Whitefriargate and out through Beverley Gate into the countryside beyond. It was flat and verdant. He walked around the outside of the ramparts until he came across the murky south end where the least fortunate had their homes between the bog house – comprising a stinking heap of the town's rubbish – and some broken ships. From here, Abraham could make out the warehouses he had sailed past the previous day. The pace here seemed slower than in Rotterdam, though just as vibrantly busy. The harbour was packed with vessels being loaded and unloaded, forming a forest of masts and ropes, and there was a long queue of vessels waiting to come in. The quay was in chaos and it astonished Abraham that the many careering carts and sleds did not collide. He could see the Dock House with officials pouring in and out; the very people his skipper had been keen for him to avoid. He turned and walked along the parallel High Street. In the distance he saw his drinking companion from the night before deep in conversation with a gentleman of about the same age. They did not see him, and he did not disturb them. Instead, he surveyed the impressive red-brick houses with their leaded window – home to the wealthy merchants, he thought.

He found his way to the church he had seen towering over the town. The sign told him it was the Holy Trinity Church and the door stood open, so he went inside. The quiet interior was disturbed only by an old woman sweeping the floor. He nodded to her before taking in the magnificent stone pulpit and the huge carved coralloid marble font, marvelling as one craftsman admiring the work of another. He scanned the soaring roof space held aloft by pillars, with carved figures on the capitals, and imagined how the voices of the congregants would reverberate. He stared in awe at the stone tracery of the windows. It seemed to him the craftsmanship throughout was marvellous. He looked at the effigies of the de la Pole family. The name meant nothing to him but, doubtless, it did to the inhabitants of the town, perhaps they were merchants. Abraham left with the intention of returning. Such a beautiful building took time to get to know. Across the way, through an open window, he could hear the sound of boys chanting their lesson at the grammar school.

Everything he saw pleased him. He felt he could settle here. Yes, he liked it well indeed. But first he needed to find Gregory Jenkin's cousin-in-law Jeremiah Graves. His mind turned to his drinking companion of the previous day and, glancing at the sun as it swung lower in the sky, thought it was time to return to the tavern where he was to meet him.

Sure enough, as he entered the tavern, he was there, sitting by the fire looking towards the door, cradling a tankard of ale. Next to him sat the fellow Abraham had seen him with earlier in the day.

'Glad to see you again, Abraham. I didn't introduce myself yesterday. My name is Thomas Hebden. May I introduce you to Jeremiah Graves.'

Perhaps Abraham should have been more surprised, but he was not. He had noticed Thomas' expression change the previous evening when he mentioned Mercury. He had known something. Abraham reasoned that Hull was a small place and, if anything like Bourges, people would know another's business as if it were their own. Thomas gestured towards a spare stool, and Abraham sat.

'So,' said Jeremiah, 'what brings you to Hull?' There was an element of caution in his voice. Abraham looked into the man's broad face and steady eyes and found no sign of mal intent.

'I was asked to come by a man; some might say a man who had lost everything dear to him in his life. It did seem impolite not to help such a fellow. I wanted to get to England but did not mind which part.' Abraham aimed for a tone not too serious but not too light-hearted either.

'And this fellow's name?' Jeremiah's eyes were flickering in the firelight.

'Gregory, Gregory Jenkin.' A look passed. The two men turned to one another, and a look passed between Hebden and Graves that Abraham could not interpret. He waited for it to be explained, if they had a mind to do so.

'Could you tell us what passed between you?'

Abraham took in Jeremiah's expression and knew that only the truth would suffice. Following Abraham's retelling of his meeting with Jenkin in the church of Saint-Étienne, Jeremiah took a deep breath and sighed.

'Aye, a great tragedy did befall my cousin Elizabeth and her husband Gregory. Hannah and Mary, her sisters, too. What do you want from me? He gave you the silver, do you still have it?'

Abraham was too cautious to hand it over. 'I have one

salt and a beaker with a plain-looking stone which I cannot see as anything special.'

'Did Gregory say much about the stone?'

Abraham repeated what he could remember about the discussion he had with Gregory. How Gregory had been insistent the stone had special powers and that he found this to be incredible, ridiculous even.

'So, he spoke of the philosopher's stone. It is true,' he said, 'my great-uncle, John Graves, founded a merchants' society where each meeting started with an evocation of Mercury. I believe the stone was part of the ceremony. The meetings were held in his basement, out of sight from prying eyes, in the house where I live now. He tried to include my grandfather, Thomas, his brother, but Thomas, alas, was not of the same mind and caused problems for them. May I see the silverware?'

'I do not want to show you here in a public place. I will show you my Letter of Recommendation from M Clément where I served my apprenticeship.' Thomas Hebden did not add to the conversation but sat, listened, and watched Abraham's face all the while he spoke.

'There is only one original member of the Society who still lives. He is an old man now, but he may be willing to talk about it. Tomorrow at six o'clock, eventide, come to my house, 40 High Street, if you would like to meet him and talk further.' Jeremiah stood and nodded to Abraham, his level brow and thin mouth giving little away. 'Good evening,' he said, and left. Thomas Hebden gave Abraham a small smile and followed shortly thereafter, leaving Abraham to stare into the firelight alone.

The following day, as the light began to fade, wan and grey below the horizon, Abraham stood in front of number 40 High Street at the appointed hour. It was not as grand as some of the other red-brick houses, but it was impressive enough. It reminded him of the houses he had seen in Rotterdam, with their tall faces and rounded window-tops. A young maid in a uniform with dark hair and skin like the moon opened the door.

As he entered, ahead he could see a low, arched door which looked as though a man would have to stoop to get through it. The walls in the entrance were oak-panelled and the floor was made of large slabs of stone. He was shown into the room on the right which had a large ornate fireplace, heavy red drapes hanging by the windows, the same light, oak panelling on the walls and a white plaster ceiling which had motifs of various types of grain. Dotted across the ceiling were greyish, yellowish circular stains from the smoke from the candles, particularly the two on either side of the fireplace. On the wall above the fireplace was a portrait of a very good-looking young woman who Abraham assumed to be Jeremiah's wife. The furniture comprised wainscot chairs and a large table with six chairs around it. The table was covered with an oriental rug. To Abraham it looked to be of good quality, but he could not say where it may have come from. It was surely a house filled with beautiful things and he stood, gazing around appreciatively. A clock ticked somewhere in the house.

A few moments later, in came Jeremiah, Thomas and an old, stooped fellow with very few teeth and a walking cane. Jeremiah introduced him to John Minspeak and invited them all to sit down. A libation was served.

'Mr Barachin,' Jeremiah began, 'you have told me the story, but would you be so good as to repeat it for Mr Minspeak. He is interested to hear what Gregory Jenkin told you in the church about Mercury and the Society.'

'Not much, sir. I did not place too much credence when he said successful trade depended on the god Mercury. I disputed this statement, but Gregory was adamant and insistent that he needed to get this beaker and stone back to Hull. He looked to be in a bad way. I wanted to go to England, which I do not know at all, and I agreed to bring it. He also gave me the salts, saying I could sell the one belonging to his wife but must return the other.'

Abraham reached into his coat and placed the silver salt on the table. Hebden appraised it in the same way he had when he first saw it, turning it in stained fingers like those of a man who worked with his hands; they were calloused, coloured, and burnt just like his own had been when he was working. This was something he hadn't noticed in the gloom of the tavern. Jeremiah set the salt to one side and waited while Abraham produced the beaker and the unremarkable stone. John Minspeak became pale, and his lower lip trembled. Silence descended.

'I never thought I would see this beaker again. The ceremony bound us together in a ritual. We donned black cloaks, our founder banged a brass caduceus on the stone floor, and we called on Mercury to assist us. Seeing the low door opposite going down to the basement, dark and mildew on the walls, brought it all back to me.' The old man stopped speaking. A moment had passed, he slumped back in his seat and said, 'We meant no harm. Where are the cloaks and the caduceus?' His eyes looked vacant and it became apparent that he would say no more. General conversation resumed but he could not be coaxed to speak again. The boy who came with him wrapped a rug around his shoulders and said he would take him home.

Jeremiah broke the silence. 'I am very grateful to you for returning the family silver. You saw how important it was in its time. Thomas, here, is a silversmith and is looking for an extra pair of hands in his workshop. He has agreed to give you a trial. I have asked him to let you make a christening gift for my son.' As if on cue, there was a cry from a baby upstairs. Abraham could hardly believe what he was hearing and said, 'Thank you. I won't let you down.' He turned to Thomas, 'Thank you for giving me the chance to show you what I can do.'

Hebden fixed him with a calm look, something akin to curiosity twinkling at the corner of his keen eyes. He inclined his head. 'I shall collect you from your lodgings in the morning and take you to my premises on Church Lane.'

1969

'He gave you a telling off for what exactly?' Kathy asked Dottie.

'For making an error in the catalogue.'

'You're not joking, are you? Oh, Dot, today of all days.'

The two women stood queuing in the staff canteen. It was Friday and fish was on the menu, which, given her morning sickness, was already making Dottie feel nauseous for the second time that day.

'What do you mean today of all days?' she asked, having taken to standing with one hand on her lower back as she'd seen other pregnant women do, despite not yet showing. She could be no more than three months pregnant, but her suspicions had been confirmed. Her decision still hung very much suspended.

'Mrs How's coming. It's an important auction. The one where you made a mistake in the catalogue. Keep it to yourself. You know how the old dragon likes to creep in unnoticed.'

Dottie spotted Mr Barton-Jones eating fried cod at a nearby table. She grimaced and turned her back. 'That's why B-J went barmy! I was going to tell him the news later today, but I couldn't.'

Kath's eyes widened. 'Well, since it won't be good news to him, I'd wait until Monday, love. You want to have a good weekend yourself and all.'

Dottie shook her head. 'Not sure I can wait any longer. Why won't it be good news? He might be pleased.' But her words felt hollow, like an actress in an unconvincing play.

'Do you see that, Dot?' said Kath.

'What?' Dottie followed Kath's gaze towards the ceiling.

'A pink pig flying across the sky. He's married. He has children already. No man wants any more than that. Don't fool yourself into believing this one's any different. All men are the same, love. All the blinkin' same.'

Dottie wasn't in the mood to be defeated. She picked up her wooden tray in silence. She'd noticed other changes since getting pregnant. She was less likely to say sorry to somebody on the bus. Twice she'd told Mr Barton-Jones that she had too much work in her in-tray to take time out in the stationery cupboard. Remarkably, he'd not been bothered. In fact, she'd caught him talking, closely, to Susan in the kitchen. He was telling her about his sailing hobby, the very subject he had spoken to Dottie about before the stationery cupboard had become her refuge, her place of escape, of passion... oh, Lord, what a fool she had been!

'Those chips have seen better days.'

Dottie's gaze wandered to Kathy's finger. 'I think I might get fired,' she said.

Kathy laughed. 'Man's world, that's what it is. Mushy peas! More like pea soup. You havin' any peas, Dot?'

'No,' Dottie pushed her tray aside. 'No, I'm not feeling well. I think... I don't think I'll eat anything.' Out of the corner of her eye, on the next table, she saw a plate of something fried swimming in grease and before Kathy could say another word, Dottie hurried out of the canteen, along the long corridor and into the entrance hallway, running headlong into an old lady in a headscarf and dark glasses heading towards the auction room. Momentarily, her mind was split between running upstairs for her handbag or simply disappearing out of the front entrance. In the end, she went into the ladies, threw up and cried. *Dottie, you've got yourself in a right pickle this time. A baby, no job, no husband. What in God's name is going to happen to you now?*

***

Mrs How never missed an important silver sale. Thursday, 9th October 1969 was no exception. She entered the auction house wearing a headscarf and dark glasses. She did not, unfortunately, have the right physique to be mistaken for a Hollywood film star, though her bouffant hair fitted the new fashion and was the reason she was wearing a scarf to begin with; incognito was flavour of the day. Most people were already seated, and spectators overflowed down the aisles to the back of the room. Mrs How kept her catalogue clamped under her arm. She knew what she wanted. She sat on the left, close to the back, knowing there would be fewer people overlooking who might recognise her. It was the second day of the auction, and she had timed her appearance to be in perfect position. Bidding was brisk; she stayed a while and left before it ended.

She collected her acquisition the following day. Now,

Mrs How parked her silver-plated Jaguar SS100 outside her Pickering Place home and offices in St James, and picked up the package that had been riding in the passenger seat. It was insignificant-looking, wrapped in plain brown paper, but Mrs How held it with reverence. As she swung the car door shut and headed for the gates, three Old English Mastiffs tumbled out of the doorway and onto the porch, clattering across the gravel towards her. They came to a polite halt and looked up at her with mournful eyes.

'I'm not falling for your nonsense, not today,' she said with practised brusqueness, her mind on the package. 'You may well be a Cruft's Champion, Don Juan, but that includes you.' The largest of the buff-coloured beasts huffed softly through its jowls.

Parcel clutched to her chest, Mrs How entered the Queen Anne house and began to climb the creaking cage staircase, passing several poorly lit oil paintings of questionable origin. If pictures were like silver, they would exude light, not necessarily be so demanding of it – or so she retorts to her clients whenever they enquire, with excessive politeness, as to the paintings' provenance. Her dogs' paws padded up the stair runner behind her. Mrs How checked the time on the Joseph Windmills Longcase before throwing open her office door.

'Morning, Martha.' Mrs How's personal assistant – a red-headed girl whose skirts were always unnecessarily short, and all too easily fell into an all-show and no-go state of mind – half-curtsied as she took her mistress' coat and hung it on a silver coat stand behind the door. 'My boys are thirsty, and so am I, Martha.'

'Shall I fetch you some tea?'

'I really have no idea why you have to ask.'

'Pardon me. I'll fetch the tea.'

'And water for my boys!'

The dogs sniffed the office for scraps of smoked salmon and caviar from last night's cocktail party before settling upon their favourite armchairs. Mrs How placed the package on her desk. She sat down as the sunlight streamed through the window, warming her shoulders. She took in the room: the rosewood breakfast table in its centre with its rainbow-casting chandelier hanging above, the silver-gilt cups displayed along the mahogany sideboard, gleaming against the cherry red walls, and the six royal blue ceramic dog bowls lined up like infantry at the foot of Martha's desk. Dogs and objects of beauty; these were the things to trust in life, for, despite the room's immutable and at times overpowering odour, Mrs How had never once questioned dedicating her life to both dogs and silver.

Glad for the solitude, she pushed a jar of Kent honey to one side and clasped the wrapped acquisition in her hands. Naturally, she would have preferred secrecy at Seagrove and Atterbury Auctioneers. She resented both competitors and fools alike. Yesterday, she'd thought she'd arrived anonymously, thanks to a headscarf and dark glasses, but Mr Barton-Jones, who'd been the one to inform her of the little object she cradled in her hands, gave a peculiar sneer and moments later one or two customers, as well as the auctioneer, were likewise looking her way. Yet she had managed to purchase the bowl for seven hundred and fourteen pounds, with commission; a more than satisfactory price. Upon making her exit, she had heard the drawling words, "Mrs How, do you have a moment?" Ignoring him, she made for her car. The word that best described Barton-Jones was sycophantic.

Mrs How's rouged lips curled upwards. She reached for the string of her desk lamp, giving it a sharp tug. With her hands trembling, a shockwave of expectation travelled from her fingertips and into her chest as Father's words babbled in the background: *Never collect anything, Jane, which isn't valuable or useful.* Well, this item was neither, but as soon as Mr Barton-Jones had telephoned, its apparent humbleness had intrigued her. There was more to it and of that she was sure. It had a history... yes, she was quite certain of an interesting past. She had an instinct for such things. But most intriguing of all was the auction house's apparent inaccuracies.

Removing the tissue paper, Mrs How cradled the silver bowl as if nurturing a newly born chick, relishing its coldness against her flesh. She began to admire it from all angles, noting the patina as she turned it this way and that.

'I know what you are,' she whispered, her breath fogging upon its surface. 'I know exactly what you are, and you are certainly not a bleeding bowl.'

Physicians of the past had used bleeding bowls to collect blood from their patients. But such bowls were far larger than this little thing and a bleeding bowl would have had one lug attached to the top edge. Mrs How took in the details of the engraving: Mercury held aloft by what appeared to be little simian creatures or a twin-headed human perhaps. The caduceus was flagged by wings, bringing peace to the intertwined snakes, with Mercury's right finger pointed emphatically towards the heavens. Though such Mercury engravings on silverware were not unknown, this particular depiction seemed rare, somehow crude, as if to imply he was perhaps old, and ravaged. The sneering Mr Barton-Jones had described the engraving as naïve. But she rarely took notice of his unctuous remarks. Though he had some sense of what she liked, he had no passion for silver and that much was obvious. The more she stared, the more Mrs How felt the image was somehow speaking to her.

'Stop your nonsense!' she said, breaking her reverie. 'Silver bowls, no matter their rarity, do not speak. Whatever message you wish to impart, little object of curiosity, I would like to know.'

Silence descended. Mrs How flipped open the Seagrove and Atterbury catalogue, shaking her head. Bleeding bowl indeed! The bowl was a hot water taster, a dram cup. Of course, it wasn't the first time Mrs How had seen a mistake in an auction catalogue; she never pointed them out, as more often than not they fell in her favour. No doubt a put-upon secretary was at fault. She saw no harm in it and was happy to keep such errors to herself to avoid piquing curiosity or, worse, future vigilance. Having set her budget yesterday, she had not been prepared to exceed it. Besides, once the point of bidding had been reached, she tended to trust her instincts, her inner knowing. It rarely, if ever, let her down. She believed that, as her reputation grew, and many of her clients now ranked on the *Forbes Top 50*, her prowess increased. In fact, lately, and she planned to keep such thoughts private, she saw herself as a warrior of sorts:

a Boadicea type, albeit one considered outspoken as well as eccentric, fighting to save silver and hence, beauty for future generations to appreciate in the real cathedrals of this country: museums. No, the absolute ecstasy of these moments never ceased to delight her.

But something else puzzled her, something Mrs How could not quite put her finger on. She scratched her head, sat back in her desk chair, and examined the taster beneath the desk lamp with some intensity, her flattened palm gently bobbing up and down to her pulse as she mentally weighed the object. She pushed her spectacles closer to her eyes and re-inspected the catalogue. Still shaking her head in bewilderment, she rose from her chair and turned to the set of Dairy Balance Scales by Parnall of Bristol. She placed the piece on the ceramic plate and adjusted the weights. The clock on the landing chimed with muted voice. Mrs How ducked down, eyes level with the instrument to make a further adjustment. She thumped her chest to stop her heart from jumping. 'Blow me,' she whispered, 'I was right. Two mistakes in the catalogue for one entry. That must be a record.'

The clock finished chiming. There followed a lengthy pause. The flap of a white dove's wings passed across the window. Mrs How rested a hand upon each hip. She shook her head, pulled herself back to the task in hand and ran a finger around the rim of the cup.

She checked the catalogue again, just to be sure. She inspected the base of the silver bowl. On the opposite side sat the lavish and rather presumptuous engraving: *M.A.R.* Victorian idiocy, she thought, pursing her lips. How dare they! Pompous Victorian men and their insatiable need to plaster objects of beauty with their initials, thereby desecrating them to some degree. Turning the cup upside down so that she could properly inspect its base, she studied the other set of initials, probably those of the first owner I.C., or, there again, J.C. or even J.G or I.G… it was difficult, rather impossible, to tell. The humble initials sat amid the silversmith's mark alongside three mullets. Without a coat of arms, it was unlikely the identity of the owner of these initials would ever be known. Mrs How placed her spectacles on her nose and leant closer toward the Tiffany desk lamp, thin lips parting. So, who were you to have summoned my attention in such a demanding fashion? Do you have something important to impart, little pot? The thought swirled around her.

Mrs How eyed the engraved monkeys at Mercury's feet, noting that they pointed skyward, mirroring Mercury's hand. Monkey, she knew, represented the physical manifestation of God in the Hindu religion and in the Chinese zodiac. It is believed babies born under this sign will be clever. Was this important to whoever had commissioned the bowl? See no evil, hear no evil, speak no evil, little monkeys…

As the front bell rang, a chorus of barks unsettled the room. Mrs How removed her spectacles to peer out of the window. The sight of her silver Jaguar gleaming in the sunshine brought certain pleasure but did not and could not compete with the thrill of her silver collection against the red flock wallpaper in an otherwise sombre drawing room. She recognised below, fumbling for his keys, the familiar bald patch of her husband, George.

Mrs How exited her office and took the stairs down to the commander; another love in Mrs How's life. Theirs was not a love underpinned by passion or romance, but by duty and shared interests, just as any decent marriage ought to be. But there was one thing to unite them above all else: neither Mrs How nor her husband suffered fools gladly. They were both upon this Earth to serve a purpose and that was that. But with descending each step, Mrs How's thoughts drifted from George altogether. She was thinking about whispering bowls and silversmiths that may or may not have had secrets. But first things first. She had acquired the bowl for a specific purpose as she wished it to place it in its place of origin.

She would offer it to the museum in Hull to enhance their collection. Nobody could accuse her of being unthinking in her acquisitions. Each purchase, each donation, was thoroughly thought out. And occasionally, small mysteries, such as a peculiar engraving or an unknown artisan, would be thrown up, adding further intrigue to a piece.

1986

Ricky sat on his brother's black Chesterfield sofa with his feet up on a Union Jack footstool and looked around. He'd always looked at his brother's office as a child did a playroom, knowing that the toys were just more complicated and expensive. There was a treadmill, an exercise bike, a brand-new television, not to mention a full-sized snooker table, a bar, a mirrored table for meetings, and cocaine. Mia, his brother's wife, had hired an interior designer who had given the room a dark edge with its black flock wallpaper, granite carpet and black varnished furnishings. He took his feet off the footstool, planted them on the floor and looked straight at Danny.

'Have you spoken to Pete today?' asked Ricky, staring at his brother.

'No, he hasn't called. Have you?'

'Why would I hear from him? You made all the arrangements. We shouldn't have left without him.'

'He was trying to do a runner with the best piece of silver in his grubby hand. No, if he wants something, like paying for the job, he can contact me.'

Ricky glanced at the television and said, 'Who the hell's that woman performing in her underwear?'

'It's Madonna, idiot,' said Danny, from the centre of the room where he sat at the mirrored table.

'She looks like one of the kids on the estate near us, high on crack. Christ, look at the muscles on her arms.'

'Feminism. It's called feminism.'

'Bloody frightening! Stop doing whatever it is you are doing. We have to talk about what happened last night.'

Danny looked up from examining his latest acquisition with a magnifying lens.

'Adam and Eve. George Petel, 1627.'

'Never heard of him.'

'Mate of Reubens.' Mate was pronounced *maaytttt*. 'Gifted to me by the Rubens Museum in Antwerp when the room was unguarded.'

'Yeah, right!'

'They talk to me, you know, these dead geniuses. They ask me to take them.' The little ivory sculpture had been a spontaneous find on a trip across the North Sea. Europe had felt so exotic to someone who never set foot outside Hull until he was twenty-five. Over the last ten years, he had been on the ferry to Rotterdam and then taken the train to Amsterdam for a few days as it seem to be everything that Hull was not: colourful, interesting and had wonderful museums. He had suggested that Ricky might join him but it never happened. The time he went to Antwerp had proved to be a fortuitous change and the ivory sculpture had travelled home with him, tucked safely into his suitcase.

The delicacy of the carving on such a small scale had appealed to him. A few, but not many, acquisitions were that spontaneous. Mostly when he saw or read about something aesthetically pleasing that he thought he might want, he mulled it over and if it kept demanding attention, it was all the incentive he needed. He was no snob about it either; he could be as enchanted by an antique teapot as much as a Botticelli, not that he had a Botticelli. He did, however, have a network of lowlifes he could call on if he wanted a job done. Within this carefully selected group were those who had different skill sets. Some were better at breaking and entering, others forgery, or disabling alarms without severing the contact with the alarm company or police station – society's misfits one and all. Danny was never short of cash to pay them. His businesses included a second-hand car dealership, arcades with slot machines and a string of small properties. National Trust properties, country houses, antique fairs and small museums were his usual hunting ground for bigger, shinier game.

As a consequence of his habit, his cellar, once damp and full of mildew, now housed his considered and meticulously maintained acquisitions. He had installed a top-notch climate system too, one that specialised in lighting for fine art, and he'd had a white Statuario marble floor imported from an area above Carrara, just to add that art gallery feel. This was Danny's man cave, and it was the only place he truly felt happy.

'Paintings and sculptures only talk to you if you're insane,' Ricky was saying, still eyeing the television. He shook his head. '*Like a Virgin*: who was that bird trying to kid?'

The sculpture had reminded Danny of his wife Mia, before the menopause: soft Mia, gentle, feminine Mia. Hair scrolling down her back Mia. No deep frown lines Mia. He glanced at the serpent coiled around the tree trunk behind them, the unbitten apple in Adam's hand. Go for it, mate! He couldn't help thinking it. Maybe regret was part of this acquisition. Maybe he was looking back at his past before he had eaten from the tree of knowledge. After all, he'd destroyed his own Eve. Or so she kept reminding him.

'A thing of beauty this is,' he half-whispered as he stared at the carving.

'It's a lump of bloody marble.'

Danny ran his hands over the piece. 'Ivory actually. Forgive them, for they know not what they do,' he whispered, looking skyward with a smirk. 'Exhausting just watching that bird dance, isn't it?' He jerked his thumb at the television.

Ricky turned it off. The room fell silent, and only the Louis XVI clock on the grey marble mantle could be heard, ticking portentously, Ricky thought.

'We should have called an ambulance or waited to see if Pete was alright.'

'Why didn't you if it bothers you so much? Why don't you call the hospital to see if he's there, or better still, call the cops and tell them why we were there? Why are you worried about a lowlife like Pete? Do you even know his surname or whether it was his real name? Leave well alone.'

'He was knocked out and there was blood on his lips.'

'Hazard of the job.'

Silence descended for a few minutes.

'So, you're not going to sell that piece of ivory?'

'Nah,' Danny replied, focusing on cleaning the small

carving in his hand. It bothered him to think it might be carrying years of imperceptible dust. Cleaning of any work of art was always carried out by Danny, always in his own time and preferably alone.

'That don't half get my back up.'

'What does?'

'You deciding to keep stuff.'

'Too much gets your back up.'

Ricky sniffed. 'You can put me at risk of the nick for a profit, but I won't do it for nothing. Does that make sense?'

'I don't put you through anything. It's your choice.'

'For Christ's sake! You might be my older brother, but you're not my bloody career advisor, all right?'

Danny looked up, nodding, weighing up his brother's attitude over his words. 'Could have fooled me. Look, I've got people queuing up to work for me. You know that, I know that. You've got to be pretty special not to be dispensable, especially in this game. Do you know what I'm saying, Ricky?'

'Yeah, well, everything's dispensable to you. Even your wife when you met that art collector woman. You didn't see your kids for four months. Four fucking months. Why would you bother about the likes of Pete?'

'Shut it, Ricky.'

'I just want to know what happened to him.'

Danny took off his glasses and pressed a thumb and forefinger against the corners of his eyes. 'If you're going to start banging on about the museum job again, you can put a sock in it, all right?'

'Hit a nerve, have I?'

Danny shook his head. 'I don't know what happened to Pete. He knew what he was getting himself into. There was no mention of a dead body in the paper or on the news. He must have got up and walked away. Happy now?'

Danny put his glasses back on, picked up the sable paintbrush. He picked up the magnifying lens and looked carefully all over the carving. 'I don't offer compensation packages. You know that.'

'It isn't about compensation; it is about decency. We should have called an ambulance.'

'Look, I'm an art thief. If you're going soft about a bloke you hardly knew, maybe it's time to get out. I don't offer dream jobs; I offer dream opportunities. Big difference.'

'I want payment for the last job.'

'You do, do you?'

'That's right. That break-in was over a year ago.'

'And?'

'You promised.'

'I gave you ten grand at the beginning of the year. What the hell happened to it?'

'I was supposed to be getting more.'

'You're beginning to sound greedy, Ricky, and it's pissing me off.'

Ricky touched a crystal pendant on the chandelier. 'That's rich coming from the bloke with a basement full of masterpieces.'

Danny could feel his blood heating up. He'd always looked after his brother but envy, he knew, was the best saboteur to gratitude.

'You know I don't do this just for the money. I love

beautiful things. Always have. If I sell the odd one and pass on the money to my younger brother,' he peered up over the rim of his glasses, 'to keep him out of prison, then that's an added benefit.'

'I've been inside once.'

Danny resumed dusting the statue. 'And that was because you're a crap thief. You needed your brother's expertise,' he blew on the end of the brush, 'but were too proud to admit it.'

Ricky rocked the chandelier, making a hefty jangling sound.

'Oi! That's a bespoke Murano chandelier. Keep your mitts off it, bloody idiot!'

Ricky picked up a sofa cushion and hurled it at his brother. 'You don't change, do you. People aren't just chess pieces for you to move this way and that, you know. Other people have lives, and I don't know if Pete still has his.'

'Yeah, well,' said Danny, 'you still have yours so go and live it then.' Danny punched the cushion and threw it back onto the sofa. 'I know I will. If you think you can do this without me, then I'm gonna to sit back and watch you do it! See how many blokes will break their necks for you. There'll be a dozen more Petes. I guarantee it.'

'You callous bastard.'

Danny watched Ricky leave. He shook his head, shrugged, and carried on with the task in hand, wanting to finish before turning his full attention on how to dispose of the silver haul.

Ricky trembled as he slammed the door of his brother's study. On the way out, he marched down the corridor and into the bathroom to relieve himself, splashing carelessly into the bowl. As he headed to the back door, he paused to compose himself and spotted the silver haul on a shelf in a small windowless room. Nearest to him was the small cup Pete had been carrying when he tripped and fell during the raid. Danny had prised open the lad's fist: the one with LOVE tattooed on the knuckles, saying, 'Oh no you don't, you thieving swine. You don't get to keep the best piece,' as he put it in his pocket. 'Caught my eye on a visit. Mercury. That's who it is,' had been Danny's words. They had kept running through Ricky's mind. That image of Pete lying halfway down the stairs with a twisted neck would not leave Ricky alone. Without hesitation, he picked up the cup and tucked it into his trouser pocket. And with that, Ricky Cole let himself out and walked towards his car.

1685

'This here is our stock,' said Thomas Hebden, pointing towards two shelves laden with silver beakers, bowls, plates and dram cups. It was, thought Abraham, a plentiful amount of silver. 'It looks to be of good quality,' he said.

'The best,' Thomas replied. 'But the best grade silver deserves the best grade silversmith. I have not disappointed one customer, not in all the years I have been in business. I intend it to remain thus.'

Thomas' wife looked up from polishing his desk. Her eyes met Abraham's and she smiled. Funny, he thought, how a man's success could often be judged on the appearance of his wife. Hebden was clearly a man of good taste too; she had a comely face with flaxen hair that she wore braided, wrapped about her head. Her bosom was ample and when she smiled, dimples appeared in both cheeks, endearing her to Abraham still further. It had been a while since he had been in the presence of a good woman. It was clear by the way she handled the objects on her husband's desk, with care and softness, that goodness resided in her soul. As his eye lifted in her direction, he felt a certain lightness, something far removed from the heavy business of silver plate. He would even go so far as to say he felt the rare appearance of joy.

'I am a good silversmith,' he said, his eyes returning to Hebden. 'But I am of the belief that a man can always do better. So…' he sought the English translation of *regarder*, '…I watch myself. I do not drink. I prefer to think. So, I get better and my, erm, relation to silver, well, I find it doth improve.'

Thomas patted his shoulder. 'A man can always do better indeed. My dear? Are they not my words uttered often since this shop opened?'

She smiled. Abraham felt something stir in his heart. He was in the presence of an angel, he thought.

'Aye, husband.'

'I think you are going to do well here,' said Thomas. 'A man who thinks he knows everything is a man in need of instruction.'

'Aye,' said Abraham, but he could not take his eye from Thomas' wife.

Mrs Hebden cleared her throat. 'But we need to see a sample of Abraham's work. Do we not, husband?'

Hebden nodded towards Abraham's crossed arms. 'I know by this man's hands that he is a dedicated silversmith. I may be the one in charge outside my workshop, but here I have found my wife's wisdom for business combines well with my skill with silver. Without her dedication to the accounts, I do not know if this ship would be afloat.'

Abraham was thinking about the way she had said his name. He snapped himself out of his reverie. 'It appears a well-run ship.' He cast an eye around Hebden's workshop.

'I am not Kingston Upon Hull's most profitable silversmith without good reason.' Hebden's smile dropped. 'It requires dedication. Perseverance. It requires that a man's soul does better than was thought possible. Do you know what I speak about, Barachin?'

Abraham nodded. 'You mean do I do my best? Always. Do I learn new things most of the time? Of course. Yet I do not think God works through me. I believe in my own ability, not God's. I believe in the strength of my own soul, Mr Hebden.'

Hebden's arm briefly rested across Abraham's shoulders. 'I see.' Abraham wondered if he might soon be dismissed. 'Then we will do well together, young man. So, make something, Abraham, make a dram cup!' He reached to the first shelf and plucked a pot from a pile of four others. 'Make one to match these and engrave it with what you think will please Jeremiah.' Abraham knew he was being tested. 'He is seeking a gift,' Mr Hebden continued, 'for his son's christening. He will pay handsomely for it if it pleases. He is a man of good taste is Jeremiah Graves.'

Abraham took the small silver pot and turned it about in his grasp to examine it and feel its weight. Cups such as these were standard items made in most workshops. They were small affairs, able to fit inside a pocket. He had made many such items in France.

'Where shall I work?'

'At that end of the workbench,' said Hebden, pointing towards the corner of his workshop: a large room with a low, beamed ceiling.

Abraham was not sure he could work near Hebden's wife but nodded, nonetheless.

'I have a customer to visit. My wife will provide for you whatever you may need,' said Hebden.

Abraham hardly dared look up as Hebden uttered these words, yet he felt reassured by his steady voice and agreeable manner. 'Thank you,' he muttered.

He spent some time laying his tools out on the bench, trying to ignore Mrs Hebden, cleaning behind him. He placed the silver pot before him. He rested his elbows on the bench and let his chin fall into his upturned palms. He closed his eyes and began breathing deeply. It would take time before the piece of silver in his hand would converse with him, speaking of its likes, its dislikes, and the form it wished to embody. This may be grand, simple, impressive, humble… but a word nonetheless followed by a vision and the two would often coincide in a moment of insight. He let his body become calm as he began to hum quietly to himself for reasons he could not explain – all the while trying to ignore the scent of Mrs Hebden as she polished her husband's desk, breathing heavily with the movements.

Abraham Barachin held his new employer's silver dram cup in one hand and pressed his thumb and forefinger of his other hand to the corners of his eye. Monsieur Clément had warned him that, in time, the work would destroy his vision. It wasn't so much a question of being unable to see close up, but that whenever he looked up from his work, the world seemed too large, too blurred, too… there.

Abraham looked around the workshop. The walls were covered with tools of the trade hanging from hooks and placed on shelves. There was also an animal skin hanging there. It had holes down one side so it could be attached to the workbench, and the rest draped over the silversmith's knees to catch any offcuts of silver, which could be melted down and reused. The fireplace was bricked up from the floor to a height where it was comfortable to hold a piece of silver with tongs to heat it to make it more malleable. The first thing Abraham did was pick up the bellows and fan the glowing embers into life, stacking more wood onto them. Next, he surveyed the tools and decided he preferred to work with his own wooden mallet and planishing hammer, which he laid out on the workbench. He selected a small anvil and stake. For its size, it was heavy, and he carried it in both hands, over to the bench. His workspace was as far away from the chimney as the space allowed.

He looked at the small bowl before him, glanced up at the shelf where the rest of the identical cups were and knew he had to make an exact replica. He considered how it felt in his hand, noting its dimensions; the diameter of the base, across the top; the angle the silver departed from the base to make the sides, and he noted the thickness of the metal. He closed his eyes and ran his right index finger round the rim. When it came to silver objects, he could 'see' as much with his hands as he could with his eyes. All this was important if he were to impress his master. Making a piece like this was not going to present too much of a challenge.

He started blocking the disc of silver by hammering it on a block of wood, and continued until the sides began to lift. When he was satisfied with what he had done, he placed the piece onto an anvil and beat it rhythmically with a wooden mallet until he had created the correct height for the sides. As he felt the silver hardening while he tapped away, he paused and used tongs to hold the piece over the fire to anneal it, making it easy to work. It was hot work, the sweat ran from his brow and down the nape of his neck. He felt Mrs Hebden's eyes upon him as he worked, but did not dare turn from his task. Next, he turned the anvil round and placed the little cup on the stake. He corrected the angle of the sides to the base. In his time, he had made enough similar bowls to judge he had got it right. Before the final stage of going over the object with his planishing hammer, he dropped it into the stack of bowls on the shelf. It fitted snugly as he knew it would. Then he spent a long time planishing the bowl by going over and over it to create a perfect finish. He trimmed the top, smoothed the edge, and rubbed the surface with some rouge to clean it.

The engraving was going to prove more of a challenge. He had been given free rein on the design and told he had to do it. In his last workshop under the watchful eye of Monsieur Clément, an engraver would be employed who would have a full range of instruments to ply his trade. As there was nobody around to ask, Abraham left the close, hot gloom of the workshop and went for a walk to clear his head. The sharp wind lifted his sweaty hair from his forehead and brought the smell of saltwater and the tang of the sea. He turned aside from the chill of the street and found himself in The George Hotel. He nodded in greeting to the porter, whose half-face he could see in the narrow slit of the window to the left of the entrance, ordered a jar of ale and a dish of mutton, then settled himself in a quiet corner. He chewed and drank and thought in silence. An idea came to him, a strange image that swam up before his closed eyes and set his heart thumping and his mouth curling into a smile.

Silver, naturally, was the best currency in both England and France. Moneylenders liked silver well and paid according to its weight, though some used scales of doubtful accuracy and had no shame about it. The Civil War, from what Abraham had gathered with his keen ear in the tavern on nights when the room was buzzing with talk, meant that much silver had been melted down to make hasty coins with which to pay the troops. The merchants had thus issued their own tokens, of copper or brass. Many used the arms of trading guilds: the Grocer's arms, Bricklayers arms and so forth, but the spellings, Abraham had found, differed widely. Even Kingston upon Hull had been spelt in various ways so that he was never sure if there was perhaps a town called Hell in England. Of course, even in times of hardship, the goldsmith profited.

Back in Hebden's workshop, Abraham closed his eyes again and saw, as he had seen these past few minutes, the image he had created. It was of Mercury. Not a young and sprightly figure from the ancient world, but older and with a body ravaged by time. With the distorted image floating before him, he looked again at the cup. To his dismay, the image he had in his head did not match his engraving. He was not an engraver, and he knew it. He looked up and like an angel – for the sun bursting through the lattice windows behind had encased her in a bright light – Hebden's wife stood before him, smiling.

'Some ale,' she said, in a voice so comforting, so reassuring that Abraham felt all his present worries wash away.

'Merci, I mean... thank you.'

'You don't need to thank me, Mr Barachin. My job is to make my husband's business thrive in whichever way seems fit. You are part of our family now.' With which, she smiled, and Abraham found her presence as illuminating as the sunshine of a long French summer.

He smiled back. 'What do you think?'

She peered at the engraving upon the silver. 'I like it. The man—'

'He is a god,' interrupted Abraham.

'The god, he is pointing to the Heavens or to the drink inside the taster?'

He chuckled. 'I had not thought to look at it this way. My thought was to Heaven, but yes, perhaps he is encouraging the owner to drink.'

'The snakes and the rod, what is that?'

His heart swelled at having this beautiful woman examine his work with such curiosity and admiration. 'It is Mercury's caduceus. The staff is intertwined with serpents and there are dove feathers at its end.'

'What does it stand for?' she asked.

'Stand for?' Abraham thought about this for a moment. 'Monsieur Clément had been a great scholar of the Ancient World. He described Mercury as a messenger. In the Bible, serpents are named as being wise and the feathers relate to peace,' he said.

'And what does it stand for, for you, in your mind, that is?'

Once again, he was touched that she'd asked, touched

that her smile showered down upon him with such palpable kindness. 'In my mind? Well, that is an interesting question.' He sighed. 'He reminds me to look to the Heavens, as you did so point out, but he is a messenger too, a messenger from the underworld. He came to my mind today.' He paused to search his vocabulary, which somehow at the tavern he seemed to absorb without much effort.' 'I feel that I am to be…' He felt weak admitting such a thing to a woman, but could not say why. 'I am to be happy here. That was his message.'

Taking him by surprise, she leant forward and tapped his arm, and a powerful sensation passed across his skin. 'Then so you shall, Mr Barachin! Mr Hebden feels delighted that you are working here. He needs someone in the workshop to help him. But more importantly, you did return the family silver to where it belongs.' She poured over the cup again, gazing at its sides. 'It will be a handsome gift for a baby boy. But the monkeys, Mr Barachin, tell me about the monkeys.'

Before he spoke, Abraham revelled in her gaze, revelled in her interest and the respect he beheld in her eyes, then cleared his throat to reply. 'Monkeys make mischief,' he said, wondering if she could see the spark in his eye, and how difficult it was going to be for him to work there.

'I am not familiar with monkeys.'

'But monkeys are also messengers between people and…' he lowered his eyes, '…the divine.'

'I see. Will you be needing anything?'

Abraham's shoulders slumped. He looked down at his work and at the backs of the monkeys and could imagine them laughing at him. 'No, thank you. I need nothing.' He picked up a polishing cloth to buff out any finger marks. He felt she was staring at him but was too afraid to look up for what his eyes might give away.

'I will instruct the maid to tend to the fire. I think Mr Hebden will be pleased with your work, Mr Barachin.'

After she had exited the room, Abraham held up the taster to the candlelight to examine his work. As Mrs Hebden said she liked it, he was pleased, although the inept image should have shamed him. His decrepit Mercury offered appeal, and a certain kind of wisdom, of knowingness, seemed to reside within him. Mercury, the protector of merchants, the divine trickster and, to Abraham, he had certainly played a trick on all those who believe a pagan god made any difference to a successful trader.

1986

Ricky had no idea what to do with the small cup he had removed on leaving Danny's house. Danny had displayed his usual sangfroid. Products of the same difficult childhood, in younger years Ricky had always looked upon his elder brother as a hero who promised to look after and protect him. When Ricky thought about him now, he wondered how he could have been so naïve. Danny was a thug, for all his living in a fancy house surrounded by beautiful things; he could see that clearly now.

The story of the break-in at the museum had been reported in the *Hull Daily Mail,* making it impossible to shift the haul locally since all antique dealers would be on the lookout for silver with Hull hallmarks. The article made no reference to their possibly dead accomplice, Pete. This surprised Ricky. Local papers usually revelled in dramatising any death, the more dubious the better. There was no mention of the theft on the national news either, making it difficult to gauge whether it had made the national papers. Pete was one of Danny's many contacts from the underbelly of society. Danny had used him from time to time because he was 'knowledgeable' about picking locks and bypassing security systems. Ricky could not remember whether he had come across him on other jobs and could hardly claim even to be an acquaintance. It didn't matter. Whatever Danny had promised to pay Pete for the job, he had not deserved to die. He shuddered to think what might have happened to him. It had crossed his mind that Danny may have had his body quietly disposed of.

Ricky looked down at the little cup. He knew he had to rid himself of it, and fast, before more details about the break-in made it into the press. He would have to leave Hull. Without a real plan, he boarded a train for London, with an aim to deciding what to do when he got there. He had learned some useful skills during his career as a thief, housebreaker, pickpocket – call it what you will. He could blend in and move about in a crowd unnoticed, without ever drawing attention to himself. The trick was to act neither like you wanted to be seen, nor like you didn't. The middle ground, that was where you became ordinary and invisible. He boarded the train at Paragon Station and headed for London, leaving Danny, he assumed, blissfully unaware of his missing piece.

On arrival, Ricky made his way to the familiar haunt of the Silver Vaults in Holborn. On more than one occasion he had helped himself to the odd small piece of silver (just for the fun of it) and then sold it on to some unscrupulous dealer of his acquaintance. In 1885, when the Silver Vaults opened, they were known as The Chancery Lane Safe Deposit which, while its name and location had changed in 1953, remained otherwise much the same: a rabbit warren. Ricky moved along the corridor, looking through the windows of several units – the old vaults – until he saw somewhere with open shelves and a large central table crowded with small silver objects. Through an open door at the back, he could see open packing cases, though whether they were being packed or unloaded, he couldn't tell. The assistant was engaged with a client who was probably a regular, and the two ignored Ricky, who made a point of acting like he belonged there. Taking advantage of the opportunity, he surreptitiously slid the cup out of his pocket and placed it gently on the table, losing it carefully amongst the sea of small pieces. Then, he sauntered out. To calm his racing nerves, he walked a roundabout route back to King's Cross, breathing steadily in the smoggy air, before boarding a train back to Hull, his conscience still very uneasy. He couldn't shake the thought of what might have happened to Pete, of what might yet happen to him.

It did not take Danny long to realise that Ricky had helped himself to a piece of the haul. Once he had stopped swearing, it occurred to him that he had better dispose of the rest. Ricky had as much to lose as he did if he grassed him up but still, he did not want to take a chance. Generally, they watched each other's backs since they were both culpable. Not in equal measure, exactly, as he was the mastermind. Pete's untimely death, accidental though it may have been, had changed everything. Holding his nerve, he had made a few calls. Yes, Pete was indeed dead. He made another call and within an hour, Pete's body had been disposed of. Danny never enquired how these things worked; he simply handed over twenty thousand pounds in used notes and told himself he was clever to have such a healthy cash flow. With his lifestyle, there were unforeseen expenses from time to time. He accepted that.

Jaw set, he made his way to the garage, found a clean hessian sack and placed three loose bricks inside it. Back in the house, he took exquisite care in wrapping each piece of silver in chamois leather and placing them in individual, tarnish-proof bags so they would not incur damage should they knock against each other. One after the other they followed the bricks into the sack. Even he could see the irony in what he was doing, but the force of habit made him treat precious objects with respect. He opened the boot of his Ford Cortina. He never drove a fancy car, no need to draw attention to himself. Average was invisible. Should he ever want access to a smarter car, it would not take much to get it.

With the cargo safely on board, he took a careful route along a stretch of the Humber which was too deep to be dredged, cruised around for a while until he was certain he was not being followed, and parked the car on Queen Street near the junction with Nelson Street. It was gloomy, the few streetlights broken and their yellow glow feeble. The weather was not conducive to being out and a sepia fog was curling off the water, drifting at ankle height and swallowing what light remained. The area was derelict. Danny walked the short distance to the disused pier and, in a single movement, dropped the sack into the murky water. He waited long enough for the ripples to dissipate. He imagined the sack sinking gently into the silt and drove back home, putting the matter firmly behind him. He was, after all, well-practised at putting matters firmly behind him.

1685

Thomas Hebden held the cup up to the light and narrowed his eyes. Small though it was, he had to admit that the task had been expertly executed. The proportions were correct, the sides evenly raised and the finish, flawless. The image was crudely drawn but the engraving itself was of good skill considering it was not common practice for a silversmith to engrave his own pieces. The man who could make this would be well able to handle the type of wares that were made in the workshop. Thomas nodded to himself. Aye, he would be happy to have this Abraham work with him. The next step would be for Jeremiah to approve of the present to mark the occasion of his son's christening.

Later that morning, his heart squeezing in his chest, Abraham opened the door to the dusty workshop and ushered in Jeremiah Graves. Jeremiah took the cup from Abraham's outstretched hand and studied it for a time. When the gentleman looked up, his eyes flashed so that Abraham thought he appeared displeased. They scarcely knew each other, to be sure, but Abraham knew that customers never held back on their true thoughts.

'I like it,' Jeremiah said, jarring Abraham's face into an

unrestrained smile. 'I like it a great deal. It is a pleasing shape and useful thing.' The man's face broke into an open and ready smile that tickled Abraham's soul. The French, he was beginning to realise, were far less forthcoming with their praise. 'But tell me, Mr Barachin,' Jeremiah continued, 'why is Mercury shown as an old man with the two monsters at his feet, or is that a two-headed monster? You have etched Mercury in a less than favourable light. Be there good reason for this?'

Abraham tugged at his collar, swallowed the challenge and said, 'Mercury is, by all accounts, an old man, sir, and if we are lucky, we will grow old too. I intend it to serve as a reminder to the boy of his ancestors...' He considered whether it was wise to continue, but saw genuine curiosity in Jeremiah's eyes. '...And the monsters are not monsters, but monkeys. They represent the cunning that is so necessary for trade.'

He was not sure his words made sense. He was not sure he should be speaking so freely in a country that was not his, but when Jeremiah smiled and patted his shoulders, an understanding passed between the two men caught in the glint of the other's eye.

By the time Abraham's explanation had come to an end, associations appeared to have been made in Jeremiah's mind. He fixed Abraham with a genial but level look.

'You are of the belief that the merchants and not the god Mercury made their own way in trade. Am I right, Mr Barachin?'

Abraham looked up at Jeremiah's crooked smile and could not hide the sparkle in eyes; he did so enjoy to debate his beliefs with a willing mind. Jeremiah's lopsided smile told Abraham all he needed to know. 'I would say so.'

'It is a good thing we were not alive when my great-uncle was trading.'

Abraham shrugged. 'I should say that this god has no more profited your business than the sun doth make money grow on trees. Men giving their power to a dead god is, to my thinking, a group of men driven by fear.'

'I do agree with your words, Mr Barachin. You do have insight into the world, which I do believe doth come from travelling far from your place of birth. I have witnessed it often enough to know that it be true. If a man shall choose it, to roam doth profit a man's thinking.'

'Travelling can do that, aye,' said Abraham.

'Fear makes the men huddle together for shelter.'

'Like cows under a big rain cloud,' said Abraham, following this with bold laughter that was too loud, too disrespectful, but he could not help himself.

'Like cows under a cloud, and is this what amused you when working on my son's christening present?'

Abraham heard flatness creeping into Jeremiah's tone, knew that he had gone too far with his freethinking. In the tavern, he was excused as *being French*, but those from foreign lands have to adapt, at length, to the customs of the land they find themselves in. The English, Abraham was finding, said one thing and did another. He was not quite sure whether he could, or should, master that.

'I was not, sir,' he said. Monsieur Clément had been a good teacher in how to treat wealthier customers. 'When I made this cup, I thought of what a young boy would need to arm himself in this world. I know that you are a merchant.'

'Aye.'

'And so, I did realise that in the ancient world, this god did afford merchants protection. He is a messenger for all gods and likewise the god of dreams. The two snakes on the caduceus symbolise giving and receiving, and trade keeps the world alive, no?' Jeremiah looked back at him blankly, and Abraham continued, sweat breaking out lightly on his brow. 'The monkeys, well,' he could not help chuckling, 'the monkeys are mischief-makers.'

Jeremiah's face clouded. He wiped a palm from forehead to beard. 'I do not understand. Why would my son want to have a legacy from his father that did suggest he might take a turn toward mischievousness?'

Still, Abraham was practised at this kind of speech; in France, his customers had been a good deal more critical, not bothering to stretch their face into polite smiles as they spoke. In fact, after so much solitary work, he welcomed the challenge to his thinking. 'All boys will be mischievous,' he replied, 'but if they do turn their head to God or Mercury, god of the ancient world, they will be saved. This is why Mercury doth point to the Heavens.'

Jeremiah looked down at the taster once more, his hard eyes searching. There was a moment's pause, before he looked up, nodding sagely. 'I must apologise, Mr Barachin. I did doubt you for a moment, yet I now see, yes, I see there was no need.'

'Our conversation carried much doubt, did it not?' Abraham laughed.

'It did and...' Jeremiah Graves held up and admired the silver taster in the light. '...I now see that your intentions were measured. I was not alive when my great-uncle and his friends set up their Society. I do not know what they truly believed. I think it bound them together and with other groups they did trade with. He believed in unity over separation. He believed in profit over misfortune. He may have believed in the power of many gods to help them. I do not know. Without my great-uncle's success, I would not have believed I, too, could become a merchant with a profitable business of my own. Many of us here have much to thank the Society for, and this helps to push doubt aside. Does it not, Mr Barachin?'

Given freedom, Abraham would have laughed. He would have said what foolish *absurdité*. He would have pointed out that God provides strength and resolve, but his miracles were reserved for Christ and Christ alone. Unless they were of royal birth, all men had to toil to make a living, to deserve a place in this world. He suspected all the men of the Society worked hard and that their efforts brought them rewards. But instead of saying any of this, he said, 'You must be proud of your great-uncle.'

'Grateful and a little proud.'

It transpired that Jeremiah's forefathers had been lowly gravediggers; to these relations, a man of trade had represented too lofty an ambition. The story came down the family in the manner of a Greek myth that one of his forebears in the sixteenth century, Hugh Graves, aged seventeen, barely a hair on his chin, had strolled into Hull's Merchant House where the merchants met weekly. 'I want to be taught,' he declared to the men in the hall. 'I want to rise above my family's heritage. Teach me what I must do to become rich. I am not a lazy loiter-sack. I am not a bobolyne or a cumberground. I am quick to catch hold. I would rather learn than to be idle. I will work for aught until I can stand on my feet and match thee in trade. Who here will answer my plea?'

Jeremiah told Abraham all this and explained that only the foolish do not admit their ignorance. Abraham agreed.

It seemed that Hugh Graves' ability to remain curious and humble had resulted in him becoming mayor, the townsfolk trusting his honest and generous manner implicitly. And according to the Graves' family myth, he remained as curious as that outspoken youth until the very day he died. Jeremiah continued with the history of his family, explaining that Hugh's son, John, became a Member of Parliament for Kingston upon Hull.

'There were many Johns in our family; my great-uncle, my uncle before him and my great-grandfather and now my son bears the name too, but it were Thomas Graves, my own grandfather, who did turn the tide upon them,' Jeremiah continued. 'His talk did undo the Society in the town. He was nightly *tosticated* and with what he had, he did line the brewer's pocket and that alone. His words against the Society were not kind.' Jeremiah's face grew solemn. 'My father, William, did not take after him. He was a merchant. Though he did not profit greatly, he impressed upon me the importance of trying.' Abraham nodded.

'Though I am hesitant to admit it,' said Jeremiah towards the end of his account, 'it would matter not if I be selling muck to pirates, for the money, the money I make, does ease living.'

He looked at the taster. 'I hope my son will one day will be successful in trade too.'

'I am certain that will happen,' Abraham replied. He kept his resolute dismissal of the Society's god behind his lips, though added, 'From what you tell me, I am not so sure he will understand why Mercury was on the dram cup.'

Jeremiah laughed as he patted Abraham's shoulder once more. 'But that is our secret, is it not, Mr Barachin?'

'Aye,' said Abraham, wearing an impish smile.

'That doth remind me,' said the brewer, 'would you engrave initials upon the base for me? My son was named after my great-uncle who was a decent man.'

'I can engrave it for you,' said Abraham, taking the taster.

Abraham crossed to his workbench. Mrs Hebden had left a cleaning cloth there and as he moved it, his hand squeezed the soft rag tightly before reluctantly letting it go again. 'J.G.?'

'Aye. I am grateful.'

Abraham picked up a burin. 'There is no better way to be remembered than through silver,' he said. 'The image of Mercury continues the family story for your son.'

'I believe you be right, Mr Barachin.'

When Jeremiah took the finished cup, he looked pleased. 'There is no one left now from the older generation. My Great-Uncle John died in unfortunate circumstances. You have heard some of it. It is a long and painful story, and I will not tire you with the rest of it.'

'Most of life's stories contain pain,' said Abraham with

a tilt of his head. Though he did not say so, he was not particularly interested in the misery of other people's lives.

'Thank you, Mr Barachin. I like this Mercury. I like him very much.'

The two men bowed to one another with respect, and Abraham experienced the rush of satisfaction that did often accompany the end of a commission. As Jeremiah left Mr Hebden's workshop and the bell tinkled over the shop door, Abraham stood for a moment shaking his head. *The English and their superstitions.* Yet if he could profit from them, then why not! Who knew perhaps, he would acquire himself a reputation here in Kingston upon Hull. At that moment, Mr Hebden's wife entered with a tankard of beer and Abraham could not hold his mind back from considering her to be yet another ambition but one he should perhaps distract himself from forthwith.

'Was that Mr Graves come to collect his taster?' she asked, smiling as she placed the drink before him, her pretty cheeks dimpling.

'Aye,' Abraham said.

'Was he satisfied?'

'I think so.'

'I am glad. Mr Hebden will be pleased.'

'Aye,' he replied again.

Mrs Hebden smiled at him warmly, too warmly, perhaps. Abraham dipped his head, struck dumb by his own powerlessness to look his employer's wife in her twinkling eyes.

2015

After the visit to the V&A, Clare called Elizabeth to tell her about it. Her answer to most things was to meet up and talk about it over a drink.

'Since there's not much you can do whilst you wait for the fate of your pot, you might as well not think about it until you hear something. Let's concentrate on our holiday. You said to surprise you and this where we are going. Starting off in St Petersburg and finishing in Amsterdam with stops in Moscow and Riga. I know you've always wanted to go there.'

Elizabeth was right, Clare had always wanted to visit Russia. If she and Harry had differed in one area of their life it had been in their ideals concerning travel. Harry had always preferred France and Tuscany, only at certain times of the year, while Clare longed to roam further afield. She dreamed of going to China, Peru, Japan, and New Zealand, but Russia was the country that had always held a special place in her heart. Her maternal great-grandfather had been Russian; a brave man who had harboured ambitions to establish a business. Yuri had remained a legend within Clare's family and an aspiration to succeeding generations concerning the merits of hard work and tenacity.

Likewise, America had been anathema to Harry and Australia had the same effect: 'A nation of convicts can't have much to offer,' had been Harry's usual retort which, though spoken in a tongue-in-cheek fashion, had led to Amber branding her stepfather as *an utter bigot*. And as far as Asia and Africa were concerned, well, Harry preferred learning about them in documentaries. Harry's father first went abroad aged fifty-eight, and despite being a wealthy man, Albert Cartwright had not trusted anybody but his wife. In fact, his first words to Clare had been, 'Trust nobody,' which she hadn't quite known how to take. Was he perhaps warning her not to trust him, not to trust his son, or was he simply declaring that he did not trust her? She'd spoken to Harry about it, and he'd explained that the more success his father had achieved, the more insular he had become. Taking people to court frequently had also meant that Harry's childhood had, rather unfortunately, resembled *Bleak House*. It was also the reason why Harry hadn't once been to court himself. It was yet another place he would never visit. But Russia was the place Clare had wanted to visit most. 'All the interesting Russians are in London, sweetheart,' Harry would insist whenever he saw his summer plans altering. 'I'll happily take you to watch Chelsea play though,' he would add with a wink, referring to the owner of his favourite club. But twenty-five years of hinting had only brought about further retreating to their house in Italy which, though lovely, was not as exotic as the far-flung places Clare hankered after. But Harry was a creature of habit and since most of these habits she loved, she had become willing to overlook one or two of the others. But that had been then.

The journey to Heathrow Airport had a lot of traffic, which had much to do with Elizabeth booking a flight for St Petersburg that left at 8:30am. Clare had ordered a taxi for 5:30am, unsure how the roads would be on a Friday morning. Harry had always said Friday was the worst day to travel to the country but that had been Friday afternoons. Clare had often, of a morning, packed their wash bags and coats to take to Berkshire only for Harry to call at lunchtime to say, 'Leaving soon.'; They had rarely got away until mid-afternoon. She had accepted it and enjoyed the extra time, in the end. It was perhaps Harry's only real fault. To ignore it was perhaps another necessary part of marriage, one she'd never divulge to Amber, who, with her staunch ideas about female independence, would never understand it: acceptance.

The taxi pulled into the drop-off point. She had arrived in plenty of time for the flight. Too much time spent at an airport was not appealing, particularly given her recent dislike of people, *en masse*. She paid the driver and entered the large, open space of the departures hall, trailing her suitcase behind. It would be the first time she had travelled since Harry's death and she felt almost naked without him in the crowds. She had come to realise of late that crowds had the habit of making one feel lonelier. Harry had possessed a knack for sleeping on planes – on business trips it was not unusual for the steward to have to wake him upon arrival. Clare, however, didn't like the helplessness she had to embody when travelling. Used to being the provider of food and drinks, it never felt right to be constantly served, not unless she was dressed up for a dinner party or at a restaurant.

No doubt Amber would put this down to low self-esteem or something else to be ashamed of, but Clare brought it back to her mother having to compete with the officers' mess and the other army wives. Her teas were famous in her circle, and to this day, Clare could not compete with her mother's Victoria Sponge. But, if she were honest, she had often lived for the praise and the gratitude from her children and Harry too. Needless to say, this had grown less as they had entered the wider world, a world that doubtless boasted better cakes, and despite herself, Clare knew she still sought her children's gratitude. That was the other word Amber had pointed out during her marriage to Harry, *needy*. Well, she could not be that needy if she did not require any service on a flight – so there, Amber!

Elizabeth texted as she was going through customs to say she would meet Clare at Caviar House for, 'Some of those teeny-weeny fishes' eggs and smoked salmon, darling.'

At seven in the morning, Clare wasn't sure she was up to caviar. She headed to Boots for some plasters and antiseptic cream. After raising a large family, certain habits die hard. She found the seafood bar, positioned in the centre of the concourse, where a different type of traveller seemed to reside, those determined to prove they were a cut above. No harassed grimaces, desperate reining in of children or enduring limitless delays for them. The sophistication of the caviar-eaters perhaps warded off such things, thought Clare, smiling to herself at the absurdity. These people wore brilliant jewellery, expensive watches, and well-made designer clothing. Sitting on one of the high stools, Clare felt momentarily like a piece of modern art amid a collection of

Rubens or Botticellis; something messy, something needing to be pushed aside for the real sophistication that deserved the stool.

Almost as if Amber had heard Clare's thoughts, her phone rang.

'Are you at the airport, Mummy?'

Clare could not help smiling. It was only at the airport that Clare would be called Mummy. She would say to Harry, 'It's the only clue I have these days that she still loves and needs me.'

'She calls you. That alone is a sign of love from one's child.'

'Even if they call you to tell you off?'

'Come on, sweetheart,' Harry had said, hugging her, 'you must just be happy they're independent, healthy adults. That's the parents' main role, after all. Friendship is just an added – though often unexpected – bonus.'

How she missed Harry's wise words.

'I'm about to meet Elizabeth,' she said to Amber, taking the menu from the waitress.

'Remind me of your itinerary.'

'It is a whistle-stop tour of St Petersburg, Moscow, Riga and Amsterdam.' Do children ever listen to anything they are told?

'Amsterdam is a strange place to go to. People either go there for marijuana or sex. I can't see you going for either of those reasons.'

'Oh, you must think me very dull, darling.'

'Are you and Elizabeth having delayed mid-life crises?'

'I do hope so.'

Amber's tone was accusing but, aside from feeling

discomfort on the stool, Clare was in far too good a mood to be chastised.

'You're becoming ridiculous, Mummy.'

'Does being ridiculous also have a clinical label?'

'Very funny. Well, I suppose you and Elizabeth are both in mourning. Some benefit must come from it. Not sure it's exactly normal.'

Clare smiled; she never had quite believed in the notion of normal and suspected Amber might have a particular blind spot in this area. 'I'm glad to have your approval,' she said. 'You won't forget to feed the cats?'

'Of course not. I'm sorry I never took them back.'

Clare almost lost balance and fell off her stool; an apology out of Amber was as rare as one of the cat's showing gratitude. 'Well, they're keeping me company now, so I'm not grumbling too often.'

'Everything in life happens for a reason.'

Clare shrugged off this display of parenting from her daughter.

'I'm going to the theatre tonight – the Donmar,' Amber continued, 'really looking forward to it. Rory has excellent seats to see *Les Liaisons Dangereuses.*'

That was Clare's excitement quickly swallowed by her daughter's.

'Well, have a lovely time.'

One generation had to give way for the next, she supposed. When Clare had been young, it was all about respecting the ones that had gone before, the dishevelled, worn-out, wise ones who were relegated to the un-hip subsets. Doubtless "hip" wasn't even a word anymore.

'If you forget to bring the key, I've left a spare,' she said.

'Say "hi" to Elizabeth. Enjoy your trip, and don't get up to any mischief, Mummy!'

'Mischief doesn't cross my path these days. I'll pass on your regards to Elizabeth.' With which Clare hung up and Elizabeth was standing before her as if she had been summoned.

'Sorry, darling, my driver took me to the wrong terminal. He's a lovely chap but Russian – it seemed appropriate given where we are going. Only understands a fraction of what I say to him.' Clare had heard this many times before from Elizabeth; it seemed to be a problem she liked. One of her husbands had been a gardener, not her gardener, of course, but the owner of the company from whom she had employed her gardener. It did make Clare wonder whether she had intentions for this Russian chap. Age never seemed to hamper Elizabeth.

'Have you ordered?' Elizabeth hoisted herself up onto a stool. They no longer kissed when they met. As you aged, many formalities slipped away. Though it was not much talked about, Clare suspected that women became more like men in that regard, eventually succumbing to the bare minimum of social appeasement.

'No, Amber just called. She sent her love.' Love was an exaggeration but regards felt too formal for her daughter's godmother. Amber had long ago expressed herself as godless and so had stopped acknowledging any special relationship with Elizabeth on account of not believing *handed-down lies about the origin of humans.* Clare hadn't the heart to mention this to her friend.

'How is she? I do wish she'd come over for tea. She can bring her fella any time.'

'I'll mention it. Amber is very busy with work.' As well as chastising and infantilising me, she wanted to add.

'I do think I'm very blessed to have so many godchildren. I know a lot of it is down to pity, but I've always thought it made up for not having children. I adore them all, you know.'

'I know,' said Clare, 'and you've been marvellous to Amber. She's going through an extra bossy phase at the moment. I'm just hoping that she comes out the other side.'

'I wouldn't count on it, Éclair.' Éclair was the name Elizabeth had quickly adopted for Clare when they had met at a cookery class more than forty years ago. Elizabeth was still with Marcus then – the ex-husband who'd apparently taken her to Amsterdam. She had been instrumental in pushing Clare toward divorce with her first husband, and, for that, Clare would always be grateful.

'Now,' said Elizabeth, slapping her hand down on the black glass countertop, 'are you joining me for some caviar and blinis, Éclair?'

***

'Do you know the history, darling?' Elizabeth asked, pointing out of the taxi window as they drove into St Petersburg.

Perhaps that was Elizabeth's purpose after Harry: to show Clare the world. Lord knew Elizabeth needed opportunities to spend her own late husbands' fortunes. But it didn't rest well on Clare's conscience to be a paid travelling companion, and, in time, she'd have to address this with Elizabeth.

'You mean the history of Saint Petersburg?' Clare asked, stifling a yawn which had been brought on by the pre-flight drink and a further one during the flight. Clare could never keep up with Elizabeth and was annoyed with herself for not refusing. Right now, she had her mind set upon a brief nap. Elizabeth had found it all very amusing, of course, and, for the life of her, Clare didn't quite know how she achieved such a *laissez-faire* attitude.

'Yes, darling. It's rather fascinating. Not so far removed from places like Dubai, at least to my mind. You see, Peter the Great built it as a singular act of sovereign will. He mobilised the fortunes of an empire and enlisted all the best engineers and architects to help him. Tens of thousands of serfs died in the swamps by the River Neva. Poor chaps were struggling to build palaces and dykes and bridges and whatnot. Catherine the Great embellished the city with theatres, opera houses, squares, and parks. In short, it became an almost immediate capital of the world, but it also became known as the city built on bones. You know, darling, essentially dead peasants.' For whatever reason, Elizabeth smiled at this point. 'Kind of romantic, in a peculiar way, don't you think?'

'I don't see that as romantic at all,' said Clare.

'You do take me so literally, darling. Anyhow, the funny part was that terrorists finally blew up Alexander II and now the oppressed were constructing a road to the revolution on the shattered bones of a tsar. Divine retribution, I call that.'

'Oh dear,' said Clare, having a vague recollection of

Harry mentioning this in the past. But for some reason, the words "divine retribution" sent a shiver down her spine.

'It's a country with a terrible history.'

'But it seems beautiful too.' She was looking out of the taxi window at the colourful buildings: palaces with candy-coloured domes. That's what London's missing, she thought: colour. Chelsea had its little streets of pastel houses, as did various other areas, but they were few and far between in London.

'Three hundred and forty-two bridges!' Elizabeth said, smiling rather inanely. 'Built on one hundred islands.'

'Sounds like Venice.'

'Well, they do call it the Venice of the North. There's also a Russian Versailles: Peterhof Palace. Oh, we are going to have such fun here, Clare!'

Clare saw a sign for the Russian Vodka Museum and made a mental note to steer Elizabeth in the opposite direction. She'd known other widowed friends whose relationship to drink in the wake of their loss had been a little too clingy. She let out another cavernous yawn, interrupted as the taxi pulled over.

'Oh, Elizabeth, you haven't!' she said.

'Darling, please don't be a bore!' And in a sentence, Clare filled up with compassion for Elizabeth's former husbands.

'But the Astoria?' she couldn't help saying. The imposing red building with its red-capped alcoves stood proudly beside them. Opposite, shining in the sunshine, the dome of St Isaac's Catherdral glowed like a superb golden eggshell and Clare watched as the traffic purred around the prancing figure of Nicholas I astride his copper warhorse, the monument dwarfing even the ornate lampposts.

Elizabeth's bejewelled and painted hand gripped Clare's arm, pointing at the statue with a wink. 'Gift horses and mouths, darling. Did your mother teach you nothing! And to be frank, the room prices are a fraction of London's. Lenin even stayed here once, you know. Come along.'

The doorman opened the car door with a bow and they spilled onto the streets of Russia. Once they reached their grand twin room, they laughed aloud at the high ceilings and parquet floors. The room was awash with light.

'I don't snore,' said Elizabeth, hefting her suitcase onto a bed.

'It doesn't matter if you do. I grew used to Harry,' said Clare, thinking with a pang that she would never be used to any part of Harry ever again.

An expression of concern momentarily rested on Elizabeth's face. 'Look outside,' she said, her voice softening. 'The cathedral.'

Clare pulled back the net curtain to see the building, smaller than but similar to St Paul's Cathedral in London, even more iridescent from higher up. 'It's incredibly beautiful,' she said.

'My travel agent said that inside is just as impressive. Lots of gold, I imagine.'

Clare sat down on the bed.

'Do you want to have forty winks, and I'll go out and have a look around?' Elizabeth said, peering into a mirror to put on lipstick. 'What do you say? It's so funny becoming a tourist; you have to resign yourself to looking ignorant. Marcus had the best face for that kind of thing.'

'You're wicked, Liz!' But Clare felt the muscles in her shoulders relax a little.

'Must say, it's funny how one so easily dismisses these early warning signs in a man,' said Elizabeth, and she picked up her handbag and exited the hotel room.

Two minutes later, Clare was lying on her back, her coat still on as she fell into a deep, all too brief sleep. She was jarred her into wakefulness by the banging of a nearby door and further rest eluded her.

She got up and crossed to the mini-bar. Harry had resolutely refused to be tempted by a mini-bar and had always pointed out, rhetorically in the end: 'I see it as a test, sweetheart, a test to see how stupid I am. Will I spend a fortune on a whiskey here or get it a few quid cheaper in the bar downstairs?' Though Clare had loved the idea of not thinking of practicalities when travelling (mostly on account of it being a rare occasion, indulged in when they visited relatives or friends for important and essential eventualities), she always accepted Harry's financial advice as sound. He was a banker, after all, whereas her relationship to money had always been a little uncomfortable and precarious. Left with two young children to care for after separating from David, she'd spent many a night awake worrying about it. She took a bottle of sparkling water out of the fridge, resolutely refusing to look at its price and making a note to make some sort of contribution towards the stay later, whatever Elizabeth may say. It was, perhaps, more dignified than fighting her for the restaurant bill.

As if they were actors in a Noel Coward play, Elizabeth burst in wearing a fur hat.

'I've just had a marvellous time browsing at the Gostiny Dvor shopping centre – simply marvellous! Do you like my hat, darling? It's a Russian Cossak.'

Clare thought it looked as if a medium-sized animal had died on her friend's head. 'It looks warm,' was what she said.

'There's something dark and exotic about Russia, don't you think?'

Clare put her phone in her bag. 'I haven't seen that much of it. Do you mean the people?'

Elizabeth flung her fur hat onto the bed. 'Of course the people, darling! The architecture is simply pretty, don't you think?'

'I think the only way I can answer that is if we see the city.'

'Absolutely! Let's head out for some vodka and caviar and then we can play with what we're doing for the rest of the day. Did you manage to sleep?'

To see all that St Petersburg had to offer required a lot longer stay than Clare or Elizabeth had allowed for. In the morning, standing on Palace Square, waiting to go into The Hermitage, they were presented with a show of power. To the right was the magnificent General Staff Building, its central triumphal arch topped with the Chariot of Glory with six rearing horses. Towering over that was the Alexander Column in the centre of the square. On the opposite bank of the Neva stood the Peter and Paul Fortress, the burial ground of the Russian Imperial family. This was easily reached by crossing the Palace Bridge. It was all very imposing indeed, but Clare had to admit it was hauntingly beautiful.

The Hermitage website suggested that 'if one spent a minute within each exhibit, it would take eleven years to see everything'. All too aware of Elizabeth's very short attention span, Clare suggested they allow a couple of hours to walk through it and get an idea of the breadth and scale of its magnificent collections. The pull of the Impressionist Galleries was so strong that they ended up lingering there for a long time, gazing in open-mouthed silence at the mesmerising works. Then, after an inevitable long lunch, they ended at St Isaac's Cathedral, close as it was to the hotel. It was breathtaking. Sweeping arches of gold housed painting after vibrant painting, gilded angels' wings glittered from the sconces and the soaring roof was brilliant with sunlight, the darker corners lit with extravagant chandeliers. Clare stared until her neck grew stiff and she felt dizzy.

Back at the hotel, Elizabeth decided they needed another drink.

'No, no more alcohol,' Clare said, 'a cup of tea for me then I'm going to take a stroll down Nevsky Prospect while you prop up the bar.'

It was a seagull that caused Clare to look up. Seagulls, since Harry's death, had served as some sort of comforting sign. Beyond the reassurance, however, Clare wasn't precisely sure what they signified. One morning, as she was loading the tumble dryer, she remembered how, after retirement, Harry had become quite insistent about hanging laundry in fresh air. 'Somehow seems cleaner,' he'd explained. 'Then that can be your job from now on,' she'd replied, matter-of-factly, surprising herself. And her dear Harry had said, 'It will be my pleasure, sweetheart.' And she'd never had to deal with wet laundry until the week after he'd passed, and tears had been relentlessly falling down both cheeks as she hung up Harry's socks. This was something people never talked about. Nobody openly said it was knowing what to do with his dirty laundry afterwards that added to the heartache, and it seemed only hard-hearted to take it out of the washing basket and throw it in the bin, despite that being where it would eventually end up. But as she hung the last item on the line, she'd whispered to herself, 'Please let this pain lessen.' And she'd looked behind her and at that precise moment, a seagull had swooped so low she could have touched it, had she wished. And Harry had, for a moment, seemed a little closer.

Now, Clare watched as the gull landed on the enormous stained and weathered figure of Mercury high on the wall of a building. There was not enough space, even from the far side of the road, to get a clear view. This did not seem Mercury as the messenger god, but in one of his other guises. He was standing tall with what appeared to be an anchor at his feet, but it was difficult to make out the other attributes. Wandering round looking at various buildings, she stopped in front of DLT Department Store. Above the entrance, in the centre of a large panel, was a caduceus, topped by a winged helmet overlaying the trophies of war. To either side of this confection was a pair of cornucopias supporting a flaming torch. Was this pointing to the spoils of war? It seemed a bit odd to have this image on a shop front. From the little she had seen, to Clare, everything seemed larger than life here. From the great imposing statues of the Bronze Horseman to gleaming gold church spires rising above wide avenues, it all seemed to show off.

It struck Clare as being ridiculous to spend barely two days in a city as rich in history, colour and beauty as this, but she had agreed to the trip and would have to make the best of it. She blamed herself for not taking more of an interest when the trip was mooted. She felt a pang of disappointment realising all the things she was not going to see. They were not going to see the Amber Room in the Catherine Palace at Tsarskoye Selo nor the neoclassical Alexander Palace, nor any of the beautiful grounds. It seemed even more silly not to have factored in a visit to see the grandeur of Peterhof, which was as spectacular on the outside with its cascading fountains as its grand gilded interior. She could quite happily spend a year wandering these golden streets. She resolved to come again and, if she could, it would be with someone with a shared interest. Or perhaps even alone. She smiled at the thought of what Amber would have to say about that. Just thinking such things made Clare begin to feel she was turning a corner and looking to the future. She said none of this to Elizabeth when she joined her in the bar. Her friend was precisely where she had left her.

***

'Moscow, here we come!' Elizabeth announced over breakfast. 'It's a four-hour train journey and, well, why the heck not, Éclair!'

'Do you think—'

'I make a habit of not thinking too deeply for the very reason that you'll always find a reason *not* to do something. It was an epiphany that came to me when I looked back on my life while holidaying in St Tropez with Martin, number one.'

Clare was surprised that introspection even formed part of her friend's thinking. 'You don't mention Martin very often,' she said.

'For good reason. Thing is, darling, I realised that I only regretted the things I *didn't* do in life.'

'I see.'

'So now I do what I can, most of the time. Life's simple, really, you know, darling. It's only people that complicate it. I don't regret Martin, but I do regret the settlement. But much water is under the bridge, and now I'm delighted I married all my husbands. See, no regret, darling!'

With little choice but to be jovially bullied by her friend, they made their way to Moskovsky Station to leave for Moscow. The journey on the *Sapsan* proved unexpectedly enjoyable, as well as fast, and Elizabeth kept Clare entertained for the entire four hours. Moscow was, according to her friend, 'Utterly fabulous!' They headed through Red Square, passing a huge shop called Gum. The store had its entrance on Red Square and Elizabeth said it made Harrods look as dull as M&S. Red Square seemed smaller than Clare expected. Perhaps it appeared so because of the huge crowds filling it, waiting to view Lenin's embalmed body in its mausoleum. Clare shuddered at the idea of the waxy flesh and dull hair. At the far end of the square was St Basil's cathedral, its colourful domes picture-postcard perfect, as bright and glossy as if they were boiled sweets. Beyond lay the Kremlin Palace Complex and The Armoury Chamber with all its tsarist treasures. Clare perked up at this, intent on seeing the ambassadorial silver, which, she knew, included splendid pieces of seventeenth-century English silver-gilt ware.

Once again, Clare couldn't help thinking that this sense of benign distraction had been her friend's mission all along. She didn't know whether to be pleased to have one person caring so effortlessly for her, or aggrieved at being perceived as needing such care and attention. She decided the best thing was to push it from her mind, for now.

After their tour, Elizabeth suggested lunch. 'Dreadfully dull fellow, that guide,' she said. 'I'm not sure he'll ever get over communism, so down at the mouth.'

'Oh, Elizabeth!'

'What? I only speak my mind, darling. We should all be privy to that every now and again. Now, I'm going to Gum to see what I can find. Why don't we meet back at the hotel?'

'If you're sure. I don't mind—'

'I've seen plenty of Russia in the past. Why don't you wander around and we'll meet back in the bar as the sun goes down? Even great friends like us need brief moments apart.'

Sometimes, Clare was uncertain if Elizabeth was enlightened or merely said the first thing that came to mind. She was still musing on this as she turned a corner into a side street, and to her left saw a pair of metal gates. There was no reason to glance at them, but she did, and there, towards the bottom of the metalwork, she saw a gold caduceus.

Clare squinted at the adjacent plaque: *The Russian Federation Chamber of Commerce and Industry.* It surprised her to see quite so many references to the classical world still remaining. She knew they favoured classical styles and the imperialism they implied, but had rather thought they would represent their own myths and legends, if they had them. They probably did, she reasoned, but she was not acquainted with any of them.

By the time she met up with Elizabeth, it had drifted from her mind. Moscow had a history that predated St Petersburg by more than five hundred years, but they were not going to do it justice. The next day they flew to Riga. The speed with which they were ticking off cities put Clare in mind of the film *If It's Tuesday, This Must Be Belgium*, even if they weren't quite visiting nine countries in eighteen days. It was her own fault for letting Elizabeth choose the itinerary. Elizabeth was a friend always best when supervised.

***

Riga was beautiful. Like all old cities that have managed to weather the ravages of time and war, there were more than just traces of the past in its sweeping buildings and banks of carefully maintained blooming flowers. The Old City, home to their hotel as luck would have it, was particularly well preserved. En route, they passed the new Latvian National Library nestled among other modern buildings on the bank of the Daugava River. It was shaped as a free-form pyramid, its base covered with mirrored glass like shining scales and at night, when its brilliant, clear glow rippled across the water to the old, white stone of the city, it was easy to see why it was known as the Castle of Light. The contrast of old and new buildings, on opposite banks, was startling.

They were staying in the Grand Palace Hotel in the heart of the old town. For fear of seeing as little as they had in the two previous stops, Clare had picked up a map and guidebook and insisted on studying both before they set out to look at what Riga had to offer. There was nothing like wandering around a hitherto unvisited place to feel the atmosphere and enhance the experience by looking in depth at a few key sights, she told her friend. Unfortunately, St Peter's Church was closed so it was not possible to go up the much advertised 130-metre tower to take in an aerial view of the city. Elizabeth, already stopping to massage her feet every few minutes, did not seem disappointed.

Their whistle-stop tour took in the House of the Blackheads with its peculiar history of exclusive bachelor societies and intricate membership rules. This story amused Elizabeth no end. 'Sounds like they had their own version of the European Union. Hope they made a better job of it than us,' she said and promptly renamed it a "party palace".

As they left the square, Elizabeth prattling happily, Clare turned and stole a last look at the House of Blackheads. She was glad she did. It was covered in symbols. Of the ones she could read were: a weathervane of St George on horseback slaying a dragon crowning the building, four panels in a row showing crossed keys and the coat of arms of the city (the upside-down key representing St Peter), the Hapsburg coat of arms and a fourth panel that defeated her. Below that stood four sculptures representing the ancient classical world, Peace and Harmony, Poseidon, and, lastly, the distinct figure of Mercury. Mercury, again. She frowned to herself. Somewhere in her mind she felt the soft, silvery nudge of the taster and tried swiftly to quash it.

They passed the day meandering through the narrow, cobbled streets towards Convent Yard, where the medieval widow house stood, home to widows and orphans. The walls of the Porcelain Museum offered still more food for thought, adorned with a set of low-relief panels carved in what looked to be sandstone. The iconography was unambiguous. One panel showed the profile of a merchant with scales to balance good and evil, the next depicted a reaped field with bags bursting with grain beneath a blazing sun and a further panel showed a cornucopia spilling fruit. Two more panels gave thanks for the bounteous harvest. One acknowledged the Christian God, and the final panel was of a caduceus acknowledging Mercury, the pagan god in his guise as god of trade. Clare could now imagine that whoever had owned her little dram cup may well have been a merchant. She had not mentioned her earlier sightings of Mercury to Elizabeth but did so now. Her fatuous response made her wish she had not.

'Well,' she said, 'if you want to research your cup, you now have something to go on and work with.'

'Not really,' Clare said, irritated, 'besides, it's most likely it will have to be returned if it is proved to be the stolen piece. It's just interesting that everywhere we go there are images of Mercury.' Elizabeth's raised eyebrow suggested she did not agree. It was silly, wasn't it, Clare thought, this sense of being not followed, but guided perhaps by the god Mercury. She shook her head to clear it and looked at the map.

They took a circuitous route through the Art Nouveau

area where eight hundred buildings were built at the start of the twentieth century in the Art Nouveau style with curved doorways, floral reliefs, female sculptures and whimsical gargoyles bolted into the fabric of the buildings, alongside some displayed Romantic nationalist imagery.

'All down to a financial boom and the growing bourgeoisie at the time needing homes,' pronounced Elizabeth.

'Thank God for the bourgeoisie then. And whilst we are there, we can look at the KGB museum.'

'How depressing,' was Elizabeth's response. Elizabeth's reply may have been insensitive, but she was right, the KGB museum was depressing. Nevertheless, Clare pointed out, Russia's occupation of Latvia had been an important part of the country's history and it wouldn't be prudent to ignore it. They joined a tour. Their tall, dark-eyed guide had been a member of the KGB and in a measured, polite tone, gave copious details of the awful things that had taken place in the building. He described the interrogations, the privations of food and sleep, and pointed out the bullet marks where prisoners had been lined up against a wall and shot. They could touch them, if they liked, he said. It was chilling. Elizabeth could hardly wait to find a bar and, for once, Clare agreed.

***

The next and final stop was Amsterdam and Clare began to feel she may have been a bit hard on Elizabeth, who had taken her away to cheer her up. The least she could do was to indulge her and listen to her talk. Elizabeth had not chosen the hotel she had stayed in with husband number two, whom Clare had also come to call Marcus, but had booked a small boutique hotel overlooking the Amstel River. It was a good deal more homely than their previous accommodation, tastefully decorated with wooden floors, brass fittings, and a freestanding bath in Clare's room.

Elizabeth came to knock on her door to leave for lunch. 'Ready?' she said.

'We can browse the map and get our bearings. I thought you should choose what we see here, but I admit I have the chosen the Bag Museum for you,' said Clare, picking up her handbag resolutely.

They had smoked eel salad washed down with half a bottle of wine.

'Holidays are wonderful for lifting the guilt of lunchtime drinking, aren't they?' said Elizabeth.

Clare looked at her friend's smooth complexion and wondered if Elizabeth had taken to her surgeon's knife recently. She could easily pass for somebody in her mid-fifties. Clare had never invested in her looks but sometimes wished she had. Doing anything significant now meant being at risk of being rendered unidentifiable by her family. Though, she thought, on certain days, that was an attractive proposition.

'What about you, have you had any spiritual experiences lately, Clare?' Elizabeth topped up their wine glasses. 'I had quite intense visitations after my two husbands died. Michael looked like the Grim Reaper. I called it divine retribution, you know, after that ridiculous affair he'd had with his mother's nurse.'

Clare thought for a moment. 'If you mean, have I seen

Harry's ghost, the answer's no. The cats have been very nice to me though.'

'They apparently see spirits,' said Elizabeth, with some authority.

'I see.'

'They're in touch with other dimensions. I like to think I am too. Talking of other dimensions, you see that statue in the corner?'

'The dancer?' said Clare, looking toward the corner where, upon a pedestal, was a marble sculpture that appeared to be dancing.

Elizabeth took off her glasses and squinted. 'No, it's not a dancer; that's the god Mercury or Hermes, which amounts to the same thing.'

Clare started and turned to look again at the statue, but said nothing. 'I wonder what it was like worshipping pagan gods. I don't believe in organised religion,' Elizabeth was saying, 'but I do believe in spiritual energy.'

Clare nodded vaguely, then asked, 'What do you mean by that?' Midnight mass, christenings and weddings had been the sum total of hers and Harry's spiritual life.

'It's a force, a positive force, that if you follow it – you know, darling, go with the flow, that kind of thing – it looks after you. Least that's my take on Buddhism and I'm sticking to it. Why cry when you can laugh, is always my approach.'

Elizabeth had spent Christmas at Clare's and it had been marvellous having her expert help in the kitchen. Following the cookery school where they had met all those years ago, Elizabeth had opened a restaurant in Kensington and had served, as she had put it, school grub but only the good parts. It had eventually failed, costing husband number three, Stephen, a great deal of money, but it had honed Elizabeth's cookery skills and her sticky toffee pudding and Eton Mess could not be beaten. But after Elizabeth had left, Amber divulged to Clare that her friend had issues around humour and that she was covering up her shallow side, otherwise known as depression.

'And what's wrong with that?' Clare had replied. 'This country won a war by keeping our sense of humour intact.'

'She can be inappropriately happy,' Amber had said.

Clare wondered if this might be true. 'My friend is inappropriate about many things, not just happiness. I can't see anything wrong with being inappropriately happy, though.'

Amber had shaken her head. 'It's inauthentic. She's not in touch with her feelings. She's wearing a social mask.'

This was what Clare loved most about her daughter: the strength of her character and her willingness to warp theories to suit her own beliefs. Since Amber was very young, she had never worried about her being bullied in the school playground. She was far too clever for that, far cleverer than her present career as an estate agent demanded. Whether it was a flaw or a slice of genius, Clare could never quite figure out, but whatever theories Amber had, she would prefer the world to fit her formula, rather than the other way around. Perhaps all people were a little like this and Amber was just less afraid of showing it. Clare knew that as she had got older, silly beliefs from childhood were overlaid with reality. She had always had this vague belief in God, but not a pleasant God. Instead, her God was one that dished out punishment for bad behaviour; if she received a parking ticket it was because she had been a little dismissive towards her cleaner, that kind of thing. But she had carried the weight of these beliefs about, no doubt from school, given her parents were not particularly religious, and so the process of letting them go had been slow, if not deliberate. It had happened after Clare's children had left home and came as a tremendous relief. Harry commented some time afterwards, 'Do you know, I don't see you touching wood anymore, sweetheart. I can't help seeing that as a good thing.' And it had been good for her; years of superstition had resulted in a kind of liberation. And if Clare was really honest, the religious superstitions still pervaded from time to time, but she was better able to jettison these beliefs.

'You were easily conditioned, Mummy. It's not your fault that you're pliable under a bit of brainwashing. But what can be done, can be undone,' Amber would tell her. For, in Amber's eyes, this was all religion amounted to: brainwashing.

Anyhow, for the ultimate elephant in the room, Clare suspected everybody might benefit from a bit of religious brainwashing. In so far as Harry was concerned, she did not have as much belief about him passing through the Gates of Heaven as she did in believing him still to be around. She had not seen him, of course, but she felt his voice strongly in her head, perhaps more strongly at times than when he had been alive. When he had been alive, it had been the rare argument that had repeated on her insistently and which had invariably ended with one of them saying, 'Let's agree to disagree'. She had long found the adage of not expecting people to change for you to be a truism. She could not have un-brainwashed Harry if she had tried and the point was, she had not wanted to. What Amber saw as co-dependency, Clare translated into ultimate respect for another human being. As for Harry, he would say, 'I believe in goddesses, sweetheart. And I have one of my very own.'

Clare did not find it surprising that, having had four husbands, Elizabeth might have shut down her emotions and, if anything, she also felt for the young of today: everything had to be labelled. All areas of life had to be attended to with the meticulousness of a sage growing a Bonsai tree. It was exhausting!

Clare eyed the dancing statue once more. 'The other depictions of Mercury we've seen certainly didn't look as sprightly as that little fellow.'

Elizabeth nodded sagely. 'The Dutch are quite superstitious about him. When I was here with Marcus, we came across many of them. I think it must have been wonderfully reassuring to have a god for every need back in ancient times, don't you think?'

The hairs on Clare's arm prickled. She drew her cardigan together. 'All rather fatuous to my mind.'

Elizabeth buttered a piece of bread, loading the butter as if adding cream to a scone. 'No. It's all power of the mind, isn't it? If you believe this god is taking care of your business, maybe it helps. Glass half-full always produces better results, to my mind. I'm always the glass half-full and I can't change now.'

'A sort of placebo, you mean?' said Clare.

'That's what all religion is really. We simply don't know

if our prayers are having any effect whatsoever. That's why my gods remain love and kindness and, for want of a better expression, positive thinking. I subscribe to it as a kind of insurance policy. Would be horrendous to muddle one's way through death and be declined entry after that. Don't you think?'

'I'm not sure.' Clare looked at her hands. "Death" had recently acquired the same impact on Clare's brain as an unpleasant expletive.

'Sorry, I'm a little effervescent, aren't I?' said Elizabeth, who, despite her fun-loving nature, had a kind heart.

'No, it's… it's me.'

'It's *us*, darling. Now, another half-bottle, or the museum, what do you say?'

Clare, who had never been able to tolerate much wine at lunchtime, not without needing a siesta, suggested they leave for the Bag Museum. Following an espresso and chocolate, they exited the otherwise empty restaurant and Clare paused at the small marble statue of Mercury. She liked the feeling of the marble against her skin as she moved her fingers over its outstretched arm. As she took in the forward motion the sculptor had managed to capture as though it was alive, a shiver ran, once more, along her spine.

The Bag Museum was surprisingly interesting, containing five thousand bags and covering a span of well over four hundred years. Overlooking the Herengraacht Canal, the collection was housed in one of the grand merchant's houses, its wide front boasting high double doors that opened onto the water, the small door for the hook and pulley system still intact. Harry had bought her a bag on her first birthday after their wedding. Clare tried to attain some relief from her own grief as it welled up again inside her. She remembered what Harry would tell her when she had complained if one of the children refused to show empathy for a sick sibling. 'When we're having our tonsils out in hospital, we rarely feel sympathy for those dying in the next ward. It's human nature, Clare.' And although Clare's sadness engulfed her, she clenched her jaw and carried on looking at the beautiful pieces on display without a word.

'Well, that was fun!' declared Elizabeth.

'It was and it hadn't occurred to me that bags are one of man's earliest designs. They've never been improved upon as a means of carrying things, have they?'

'I'm not sure. I'm always keen to improve upon my handbag collection. I have my eye on this season's most fabulous Chanel bag.'

'You would, wouldn't you. It seems to be your job to keep the bag industry going single-handed.'

'I know, a hopeless case is me! What next? Coffee first? I just caught a whiff of marijuana; do you think we could get a spliff?'

'Count me out,' said Clare, looking over her shoulder as she caught a whiff of it too.

They walked a little further along the street then Elizabeth turned to Clare and said, 'Now I think we should head to the Van Gogh Museum and if we've time, the Anne Frank Museum too. And after that, a bar. We might need to be cheered up after seeing the works of a madman and depressed teenager.'

'Oh, Elizabeth, that's shameful! And shameless to boot.'

'I know. Wicked, aren't I!'

But at that moment, Clare looked up and saw, on the facia of the next building the figure of Mercury dancing above the entrance. As she smiled ruefully, her gaze fell on a man passing by whistling as he went. Harry? It was Harry. He had Harry's walk, even Harry's whistle. The moment slowed and, for a second, seemed to stretch into immeasurable time. Clare's head spun in dizzy circles so that she reached for the wall, fell against it, and slid slowly down it, landing in an inelegant heap on the pavement. In the distance, she could hear Elizabeth's panicked voice and feel her hands lifting her up by the shoulders. Shaking, Clare staggered to her feet with as much dignity as she could muster and let Elizabeth help her to a bench. Eventually, the world came back into focus.

'I know it sounds daft, darling,' Elizabeth was saying, 'but I thought you'd fainted at the sight of another Mercury.'

Clare let the memory run through her thoughts. 'I thought,' she murmured, her throat dry, 'I thought I saw Harry. Walking past. I was quite sure it was him.'

'Oh, poor darling! I can't tell you how many times that's happened to me, you know, with the two dead ones. It really made me think that perhaps we all have our doppelgangers.' Elizabeth sat down beside her.

'He is dead, I know he is.' And quite suddenly her own words hit her, hard, and she began to cry in earnest, her shoulders shaking and her nose running. She had never cried in front of anybody except Harry before and, as the sobbing subsided, felt the need to whisper, 'Sorry.'

'Whatever for? Better out than in,' said Elizabeth. 'That's always been my motto.' She took Clare's hand.

'He looked so much…'

'Look, here's another tissue. Amazing, isn't it, what one finds in one's bag in an emergency. Want a bandage?'

Clare laughed as one does after tears. Elizabeth having a bandage in her bag? Tears had the same effect as rain upon a dusty garden; it rid one briefly of greyness and had a mild cleansing effect. 'My pride is wounded more than anything else.'

Elizabeth, who was sitting on the bench next to Clare, pointed to where Clare fell. 'Cobbles are unforgiving. Perhaps we should get you looked at by a doctor.'

Clare didn't like to make a fuss, particularly when it concerned herself. She shook her head. 'No, I'm fine,' she said. 'But I would just like to go back to the hotel and have a cup of tea in my room. I'll join you in the bar later.' Clare looked one last time at the gable stone, but it, thankfully, appeared to be still. 'What work do you think happened here?'

'A merchant, I expect. Yes, look!' She pointed at the stone images below the figure. 'This place used to be a paper mill. See, there are the millworkers and everything they used, and look, there's Mercury again! Even in 1649 they must have used him as a mascot.'

Clare smiled tentatively. 'You could be right.'

***

As there was a knock on the door heralding the arrival of the tea Clare had ordered, her mobile rang.

'Good afternoon. It's Gordon from the museum. Sorry to disturb you.'

'Oh, yes, good afternoon,' Clare said, her heart leaping. 'Have you any news?' She tried to sound guarded.

'Ah, well yes,' said Gordon. 'It seems the silver cup you have, it is – well – it was indeed stolen from the museum.'

'I see. What happens next?' Clare felt her weary head sinking into her shoulders.

'It's complicated. You won't be involved further at this stage. Ownership must be decided and when it is, I will call you back.'

'Was there anything else that was stolen or was it just the taster?' There was a long pause.

'I'm afraid I'm unable to discuss it with you.'

Clare remained silent. She was certain it must be a matter of public record, and made a mental note to investigate further.

'We'll be in contact again when we know more.'

There was nothing else to be said, and the conversation ended and they said goodbye. What a day this has turned into, Clare thought. She sipped her cup of tea and dialled Malcolm. There was no point in delaying the call. He had to be told that he had, indeed, passed on stolen goods.

'I really am ever so sorry. I can't tell you how much the matter is playing on my mind, Clare. What can I do to help? Would it be helpful if you gave it back to me, I'll refund what you paid and send the cup back to the museum?'

'I'm quite unwilling to return the item now, Malcolm, or discuss a refund for that matter, not until ownership is established. We'll just have to wait and see what is decided about ownership.'

'That's understandable. Apologies again that you find

yourself in this position. I do hope you don't think I had any inkling that it was stolen. Not in a million years could I have imagined this happening.'

'Of course I don't think you did. Why would you want to risk putting yourself in this position? It is probably the outcome of some unexplained chain of events.'

Malcolm hung up, sounding distinctly uncomfortable. Clare imagined he was worrying over how his involvement, however inadvertent it may have been, would unravel.

Though she did not feel much like it, Clare went down to join Elizabeth in the bar. She wished she had made more of an effort when she saw Elizabeth dressed up to the nines.

'You know,' Elizabeth said, 'I've been thinking about the images of Mercury you saw in Russia, Riga and now here. Feels almost like an adventure, as if we're following some sort of clue in a Dan Brown novel.'

'You're being silly now.'

'So what if I am Éclair? It's a case of having something pointed out to you and then seeing it often. They were everywhere in Barcelona!'

'I see,' said Clare.

'So, in the end, we asked a bartender what the significance was.'

'Was there one?'

'Yes, and it predates the Dutch interest in him. Actually, it wasn't Marcus but Frederick, now that I think about it. Never suspected for a moment that one was a conman. Anyhow, this barman – Argentinian he was, lovely eyes – he said that according to Greek mythology, there were two brothers called Heracles and Mercury who began a long journey accompanying Jason and the Argonauts in search of the Golden Fleece – whatever that may be.'

'It's a fleece of the golden, winged ram Chrysomallos. It's meant to represent authority and kingship.' Clare had benefited from a husband who studied classics and liked to tell the children stories at bedtime, but the thought caused ringing in her ears and made her eyes blink back tears.

'Oh, yes, clever Harry and his Cambridge degree.'

Elizabeth settled into her seat and continued. 'So, darling, according to this barman, the flotilla consisted of nine boats, one of which was lost on the way and it appeared right by Montjuïc – essentially a hill – and they liked the place so much they decided to found a city and give it the name "Barca Nona", which translates to "Ninth Boat", a reference to the ninth boat lost. Anyhow, after that, Mercury kept popping up everywhere we went. Not quite sure what happened to Heracles. Perhaps he was the less attractive brother. Funnily enough, Fred had a complex like that with his older brother.' She swirled her drink around the glass. 'Did I tell you my thirty-eight-year-old window cleaner proposed?'

'Elizabeth! He didn't!'

'Absolutely he did, and I almost accepted. We must seek joy from whichever place it can be sought at our age, darling. Then I thought, a window cleaner, perhaps not.'

Clare stirred her gin and tonic, shaking her head.

'I think I might turn in,' she said. 'I'm feeling a bit wrung out after the episode this afternoon and the conversation I had with the museum in Hull.'

'Did they have news of your cup?' Elizabeth said. 'Go on then, out with it.'

Clare relayed the gist of it.

'So it *is* stolen. Who is going to make the decision about ownership?'

'I didn't think to ask but I presume the museum has detailed records and a photo to positively identify it. I suppose now they will have discussions with their lawyer, maybe the insurers and I suppose the Art Fund who part-funded it. Then I rang Malcolm to relay the bad news even though I feel sure he didn't know the piece was stolen. I was dreading the conversation with Malcolm, but it went off smoothly.'

Elizabeth sipped her martini and said, 'I wouldn't worry about him. Women worry, men take action; they tend to act in ways that reduce the risk of feeling anything. Remind me, how much did you pay for it?

'You do generalise a lot.' Clare felt a little cornered and slightly irritated by Elizabeth's remark. 'You have lipstick on your teeth.'

Outside of the home, Clare preferred to pretend money did not exist for reasons that were complicated. Firstly, talk of money had been absent from her childhood; secondly, it had always felt unnecessarily personal, akin to discussing one's ablutions; and thirdly, it was really Harry's arena. Theirs had been a marriage in which roles had been traditionally determined, and over recent years she had been aware that, in her daughter's eyes at least, this was not as fashionable as it once was.

'I'm sure there are sensitive men as much as there are macho men. Just like women, they come in all shapes and sizes.'

Elizabeth winked. 'That they do.'

'You really are a hopeless case.' Clare stood up to leave.

'But we haven't eaten yet,' replied Elizabeth, her tone sulky.

'I know, sorry, but I'm going to have something in my room. I would like... I would like to be alone.'

'Say no more. I understand completely, darling. Tell me, though, before you go, do you think that young barman might join me for dinner?'

Elizabeth winked and as much as Clare was glad her life had not known plenty of meaningless relationships, she was also glad to have a friend so vastly different from her. Perhaps this was another reason she was here: to encourage her to live in gratitude rather than regret. As she was always telling Amber, 'I would rather be grateful for my life, darling, rather than be judging of it.'

'Mummy,' Amber would reply, 'self-improvement cannot exist without judgement and discernment. That's just daft!' Which just made Clare sigh.

There was a knock on the door. Clare sat up in her hotel room on the edge of the bed and rubbed at the back of her head. She checked the time. She had overslept. Peering through the peephole at the distorted image of Elizabeth, she suddenly remembered they were heading to a museum before going to the airport.

'Oh no,' she said, drawing back the door, 'I'm so sorry!'

'We need to leave fairly soon. I was going to offer to take your case down. Mine is at reception. Pieter took it for me earlier.'

Clare tightened her robe. 'Pieter?'

Elizabeth leaned forward conspiratorially, 'The barman.'

'Oh no, Elizabeth, tell me you didn't!'

Elizabeth removed her sunglasses, which she was no doubt wearing for hangover-related reasons. 'Of course I didn't! But I did prove a good shoulder to cry on. His fiancé recently dumped him. I didn't object to holding that lithe body against mine, not at all!'

Clare shook her head. 'You're so badly behaved, Elizabeth!'

'*Moi?*' Elizabeth laughed, then winced, her hangover curbing enthusiasm. 'No doubt the fella thought I was being maternal. Men ran away from me in my youth for being maternal. Now they assume I have plenty of these feelings in abundance. Little do they know I'm almost entirely devoid.'

'I'm sure that's not true.'

Elizabeth shielded her eyes behind her glasses. 'Oh, it absolutely is and I'm no longer ashamed of the fact. Any maternal feeling is really a sign I'm taking advantage, but at this age I intend to take thrills from wherever I find them. Speaking of which, I'm going in search of a Bloody Mary. Shall I meet you downstairs?'

'At this time of day?'

'I'll be in the reception. I don't want to ruin the barman's ideas about my maternal side by drinking at ten in the morning. You never know, I might come back to this hotel.'

Clare shook her head and closed the door. There was perhaps something to be said for uttering almost every thought that passed through one's head: nobody could ever take Elizabeth the wrong way. Self-absorption was her main asset, but it was like a huge wave of enthusiasm that swept others up in its wake, and Clare did not possess the desire to resist it. She had slept well and, despite her tender head, was pleased to be going home. Maybe she too could embody Elizabeth's enthusiasm now that there was little to be enthusiastic about in life. Perhaps the excitement came first, and life duly followed. Draining as it was, maybe grief was going to teach her more about this peculiar life of ours than she had initially thought.

Once her belongings were packed into the small suitcase, Clare pulled back the thick, obliterating curtains, and peered between the nets. On the street below, a road sweep was leaning on his broom, smoking a cigarette. The light seemed particularly fitting, soft but clear. Suddenly, it was as if Clare saw the scene through Vermeer's eyes, saw the beauty in the moment, of an ordinary man engaged in ordinary activity. She felt transfixed by the beauty, *his beauty,* as if suddenly she was able to see the world minus her lens. She smiled to herself and whispered, 'Thank you, Elizabeth. Thank you. After the rain, comes the sun.'

They didn't make it to the Van Gogh Museum, the Rijksmuseum, the Anne Frank House, or any other museum. Instead, Clare joined Elizabeth in the bar before leaving for the airport and another boozy lunch where more alcohol was consumed than food before boarding the aircraft. In fact, *not* seeing things seems to sum up the break but, at least, at home Clare would not have to drink at lunchtime!

1692

Jeremiah Graves stared out of his bedchamber window toward the Heavens above Hull. So long had he lain here that he now knew the movements of the clouds and the patterns of the stars better than his body's ailments. He knew he was not long for this world and called for a scrivener to write his will. In it, he intended to leave the little cup to his son together with some money. James Atkins, a good friend, would keep hold of the money until John was twenty-one and, until such time, the taster would belong to Elizabeth. Jeremiah knew that men younger than twenty-one were wont to exchange silver for gold and, thus, he preferred not to place temptation in his son's path. These were, perhaps, the imaginings of a dying man, a man with too little to fix his attention upon. He would also leave his son a silver cup that had been his wedding gift to his wife, and engraved with J.E.G; both his and his wife's initials. He was no longer able to sit at his table to write it himself or even had the strength to hold a pen. His physician, a man more given to medical discoveries than the healing of his patients' bodies, spoke to Jeremiah about carcinoma of the spine, speaking with some authority. He spoke of a Greek physician called Hippocrates, whom he said was the Father of Medicine, and all the while Jeremiah passively listened. He could, after all, do little else. Besides, he was sick, he had weakness in his limbs and, whatever the cause, it could not alter that fact. From Hippocrates, Dr Jessop would head exuberantly towards recent experiments at Oxford University. Apparently, Dr William Harvey was the first to describe how the body's circulatory system worked.

'The blood moves around the body through the expansion of the heart and the contraction of the arteries,' Dr Jessop would say as he prodded and poked Jeremiah's spine. 'But then it is perhaps of no great surprise, for the heart is responsible for so much, is that not so, Mr Graves?'

'What do you mean?' asked Jeremiah, the first time he'd broached the subject, not realising it came from a restrictive staple of anecdotes.

'I ask, where would most men of this town be without their heart? It is, after all, the whims of their soul that lead us towards the love of a good woman. Is that not so, Mr Graves? Is that not right?'

Jeremiah remained silent. He knew this was Dr Jessop's means of buttering a patient in preparation for a sizeable bill. The apothecary had visited four times, and despite a range of herbal tinctures and teas, Jeremiah's health under his care had grown steadily worse. Jeremiah had been purged, cupped, and leeched to no avail, and still he became weaker and weaker. Elizabeth had pleaded with him to put up with Dr Jessop's bedside manner. Having heard the circulatory story enough times to repeat it word for word, he wished only to tell Dr Jessop that the heart was your enemy when you lay dying. That it made a man weep for the living. By all accounts, his short life had not been absent of love, though inevitably it had taken him along many winding paths as love is wont to do; but it had been Elizabeth's belief in his ability as a man of trade and, together with her help, it had brought about his success. From the outset, Elizabeth had kept the company's accounts in order while he went out into the world, inevitably colliding with risk, with setbacks, and though not a swift or easy journey, he had always felt anchored in every storm, with Elizabeth by his side. Yes, Elizabeth had been a good wife. But he was dying a wealthy man, and the Bible taught, and rightly so, that it was hard for a rich man to enter the kingdom of Heaven. Jeremiah was not ashamed of his achievements; on the contrary, he felt buoyed by the strength of them, by the resilience of his soul and by the abilities discovered therein. All the same, it did nothing to lessen the pain of leaving his family or of leaving a young wife.

He was barely thirty years old, and Elizabeth was to be left with a young son to raise alone. He had no brother to take care of his family, and despite telling himself the cruelty was God's and God's alone, it did not bring comfort

What would happen to his business until his son came of age? What if, like his grandfather Thomas, his son John succumbed to the Devil's brew? But when he relayed his worries to Elizabeth she would merely say, 'Place faith in God. He knows better our desires than we know them ourselves. Surrender to His wishes and His wishes alone.'

Now, of course, he had no choice other than to surrender. But why did Elizabeth's words make him angry?

What did she mean? It was not easy for a wife to watch her husband dying. Yet he saw resignation upon her face and, truth be told, it frightened him. He felt he even detected a certain smugness in her actions too, in her bed duty and her competence. Oh, perhaps he was imagining these things. But the wind blowing through his window at night did not whisper messages of comfort and nor did the birds. Every gale, every morning chorus told him of the error of his ways as every dying man must look at his life as it winds down. A palace built on sand did not weather many storms. God may not be fair, but He was always just.

But now, of course, as Jeremiah lay dying, there were no defences. In his chamber, a sign that perhaps he had once made a success of his life, was a small silver pot, a dram cup that sat upon the mantle shelf next to the wedding cup, gleaming in a strip of sunlight coming in through the south-facing window. The taster had been made by Abraham Barachin, the stranger, a fellow Jeremiah had liked as soon as he met him. When he had first met him, his English had been poor, but he was immediately accepted for returning Jeremiah's great-uncle's silverware that had been so important to his family.

Jeremiah had liked Abraham's wry smile. He had sparkling eyes in a face that was a web of deeply etched lines, though he could not be more than thirty. It was a face that had known great hardship, but the eyes revealed that his spirit had not been, perhaps could not be, broken. Jeremiah had found reassurance in the engraving on the cup; he liked that Barachin did not appear a man to favour convention. He fretted over the business, worrying that, as with his grandfather, it was all too easy to take wrong turns and end up at the beginning, back to their ancestral name of grave digging. It was this that woke him in the night in a hot sweat, this that made lying there so unbearable and, in truth, it made him resent Elizabeth's bedside cheer, for she would continue living.

'Mercury, protect my business when I am gone.' He did not know why he had uttered these words or if he had said them out loud. It was not something he believed; belief in the helping power of Mercury was a belief from the past. As if the howls and the dawn chorus of impending doom had not been enough, the room went suddenly dark. Jeremiah turned his head toward the window; though the skies had been clear moments before, they were cast in darkness. Abruptly and with force, the chamber door was thrown open. Elizabeth stood beneath the doorframe, clutching their son, John, pressing him to her chest.

'Have you seen?' she said, her voice hushed and her face pale. 'The sky is as dark as night. The sun hath completely vanished so that even the birds have ceased singing. Mary says it is a potent omen.'

Mary, the maid, thought that a stork flying over a house was a sign of a full womb. No number of storks in the past seven years had brought another child into his family, and, alas, one son served as no protection against any plague.

'It is a cloud. Clouds pass,' he said, neither believing his own words nor feeling the fear that he ought. What was the omen Elizabeth referred to? But, as a man who lay dying, it seemed the only sure thing in life was its uncertainty. Oh, his head was a muddle of unspent thoughts, of wishes, of fears.

'Come to the bed, John,' he said to his son.

Elizabeth set him down, and the boy crossed the room.

'Light a candle, Lizzie,' he instructed his wife.

Elizabeth used ember tongs to light a flame. She stood tall.

He asked, 'John's christening cup on the mantle, bring it to me, please.'

Elizabeth did not smile as she picked up the dram cup with one hand and brought the candlestick over to the chair beside the bed. Theirs had not been a master and servant bond, but both had taken instructions on things that the other knew best. Elizabeth would tell him when he was being charged too much for grain, tell him if his boots were too caked in mud for the house, while he would ask her to find items of clothing or papers he was sure he had placed in a safe place, yet not so secure as she could always find them. Elizabeth knew where things were kept and saw through people who were puffed up on self-importance. They were rowers on the same vessel, heading in one direction, each sure of their roles. Or so he had thought. Elizabeth did not like the significance of Mercury, engraved on their son John's christening gift. She knew the reason for it and sometimes wondered whether he had believed in Mercury's mythical powers as his ancestors had. She had not slept beside him the night he had brought it home. From time to time, she spoke to him as she would to the simple boy who lived further along Church Lane. And yet still there was something in Elizabeth's manner he did not understand, something queer.

So, he now lay within his home, drowning, battling currents his family could not even imagine whilst Elizabeth, without knowing, taunted him with her aliveness and her beauty. Yet beauty was no weapon. Certainly, it had drawn him to her before they were wed. But now, like a nemesis, she seemed only here to enrage him with her health, reminding him that she would continue whilst he would not. He hated his thoughts but felt powerless to prevent them.

'Where is the sun, Father?' asked John, sitting on the edge of the bed, his smooth skin needing much effort to scowl.

'No darkness lasts forever, son. It will appear again. All things must pass.' And as he said these words, he glanced at Elizabeth, who stood beside the bed, gripping the silver taster, fingers obscuring Mercury. He saw her eyes become glassy in the candlelight. With her blessing, he might even conquer this sickness, battle with the fancy Latin words that poured forth from Dr Jessop's mouth.

'Here, husband,' she said. 'John's pot.' She placed the pot on the bed linen, and he made no effort to grasp it, knowing such movement was presently beyond him.

'This,' he told John, 'you must take pains to keep. Each time you look at it, it shall remind you of your wealth and your ancestors. Do not be tempted to pawn it for that will be a sign to your soul that you have given up hope. Instead, make it your quest to pass it on to your children with whatever other silver you do accrue. Work hard and there will be plenty. In that way, the family's fortune will follow suit and the Graves family will not be lost to history. Do you understand?'

John, too young to understand such talk, tentatively nodded and attempted to smile back, before his face crumpled again. 'The sun, Father! When will it be back?'

But as he spoke those words, the world seemed to respond. Sunlight bleached the darkness in bright and hopeful life, as if its purpose had been to precede his exit from this world.

'Just a cloud,' said Elizabeth, tucking in the bed linen.

In a great effort, akin to trying to swim to shore against a fearsome sea, he tried to reach for Elizabeth's hand but had not strength to do so. 'It's more than a cloud. I'm sorry for this sickness. I'm sorry, my dear. I'm a young man and know now that I shall not make old bones.'

Elizabeth shook her head. 'John will be sure to receive the cup when he reaches twenty-one years, of that I do promise. You must be peaceful now, husband.'

What did his wife mean by this? Wasn't to *rest in peace* something reserved for the dying alone? Besides, with his pain, peace was the raft that continuously drifted out of reach.

'I'm sorry if the engraving of Mercury offended you,' he whispered. 'Really I am.'

'There is no need to apologise,' said his wife.

But he resented her calm disposition, the light that still shone in her eyes. He was all but useless now. He had to hand over this ship to her...

'Have you called for the scribe?' he asked.

But Elizabeth had already snuffed out the candle and scooped John up, though he was too old for scooping. She kissed his forehead in a way that made him question if he had, in fact, asked the question. She left the brightly lit bedchamber, and light once more gave way to the dark. At least, for now, thought Jeremiah.

A wife still very much alive was a painful sight to witness, though he wished he did not hold such thoughts. Jeremiah suspected that this, rather than anything in his blood, was the thing presently hurting him most. Through half-closed lids and a door partially open, he heard a knock on the front door. He saw Elizabeth hand John to the maid then turn to go downstairs and to open the front door. He next heard the voice of a clerk who looked over the accounts, Arthur Thatcher.

He heard, or at least thought he did – it was hard when under the influence of Dr Jessop's concoctions – a conversation between Arthur and his wife.

'Good morning, Mrs Graves.'

He swore he heard Elizabeth's soft laugh, in the manner she had laughed prior to his sickness, his all too unhelpful sickness.

'Come in, Master Thatcher.'

'I do not wish to trouble you.'

'Are you here to visit Mr Graves?'

There was a long pause into which Jeremiah heard his heart's beat reflecting off the walls of his bed chamber. He was not expecting him to call.

'No, it was you I wished to see, Lizzie. That is, if you have the time?'

Lizzie, not Mrs Graves, Jeremiah noted. Not even *Elizabeth* but *Lizzie*!

The door dragged over the flagstones, muffling her reply.

And that was how it happened, he supposed. The old made way for the new. He was not old, but he was dying, however much the doctor said he could cure him. That was the order of things. Life was simple really. Only... only, wretched feelings tended to complicate it all.

For three days, Jeremiah drifted in a twilight world between sleep and wakefulness, not being clear-headed for more than a few hours on any day. On the fourth day, he closed his eyes, and though he resisted the grip of sleep, behind closed lids he was in rough seas, swimming with effort to keep his head above water. A ship passed by, but the crew appeared as ghosts, their eyes boring straight through him. 'Save me!' he cried, uselessly. 'I only ever wanted to do my best.'

A man who appeared to be the captain removed his hat, holding it to his chest, head bowed. 'Nobody can save you now,' he shouted over the sea. 'You cannot escape God's wrath or the forces of nature that grip you. We make mistakes and must pay the price. *Ahoy!*'

And the water poured into Jeremiah's mouth so that he soon gave up choking, for it did fill him up and pull him under like a mighty monster. He sank. Down. Down. Down until he finally met the image of God himself, there on the ocean bed: a young man apparently in flight, heels and helmet flanked by wings, gripping a caduceus with two intertwined snakes, nothing like the elderly Mercury on John's cup but young, virile, ready for more of what life had to offer. His son would be all right.

'The boy will be all right,' he whispered, and with this, Jeremiah took his last breath.

2015

On her return from her sojourn with Elizabeth, the unpacking and laundry all taken care of, Clare looked around her home thinking, wouldn't it be nice if homes, like hotels, had an endless supply of staff to clean, polish and dust every day? Undoubtedly some did. In the absence of such help, she selected the pieces of silver which had been somewhat neglected and the usual remedial wash in warm soapy water would not be enough to remove the tarnish. She applied a thin coat of polish, pink when wet but turning whitish as it worked its magic, and only then could the gentle rubbing with a polishing cloth take place.

Next, she carefully removed a plate off the top row of the plate rack, all the while wondering why she was being so careful, as most of them had hairline cracks or small chips. None of this damage bothered her unduly as she imagined them having serviceable lives before becoming mere decorative objects. All were made in an era that predated dishwashers by several centuries, which meant there was nothing for it but to hand-wash them one at a time. She started with a marbled slipware plate that had badly nibbled edges. This kind of damage was not uncommon and occurred when plates were hung on a wall by a wire plate hanger to display them. She looked closely at the yellow-ochre and pistachio-green marbling on the rich chocolate base. Whoever the unknown potter was, he or she would have understood how slip behaved so as not to have turned into a muddy mess. The viscosity must have been just the right consistency for a wide-toothed comb to have been dragged gently through it, leaving its wavy tracks across the surface.

Next to that was an early eighteenth century salt glaze plate. She wondered what possessed someone to throw salt into the firing oven which resulted in a glaze that resembled orange peel. Even though it wasn't true, she thought salt glaze ware looked brittle.

There was one plate that may have had some value and did warrant extra care, and that was a Chelsea Botanical plate made of soft paste porcelain featuring an exquisitely painted aubergine on a stem showing the foliage, flowers, three butterflies and a wedge exposing the inside of the aubergine. The plate had been given to her by Aunt Agatha and as she washed it, she thought fondly of her before putting it back on the shelf. It dated from the second quarter of the eighteenth century and, miraculously, it had never suffered any damage.

Another piece that Clare cherished was a blue and white Chinese pilgrim flask which had a missing ear. She had no idea why they were called ears when the only thing they had in common with these organs was that there were two of them; one on either side of the flask's neck. She suspected the one she had may have been a decorative item rather than a functional object and reminisced when she and Harry had bought it during a weekend away in Wales, many years ago. Harry had made a replacement ear out of plaster, painting it a matching shade of blue. It did not stand up to close inspection but looked fine from a distance. The memory of it made her sigh; there would be no more of these trips.

She turned her attention back to the silver, touched one of the pieces and thought the polish needed a little longer to set. She didn't enjoy cleaning much and wondered if anyone really did. Next, she surveyed the assorted glass drinking vessels she had picked up over the years. She so admired the skill of any craftsman who understood their materials so well they could blow a blob of molten glass into a goblet and then attach a twisted stem filled with spirals of small bubbles, serving no purpose other than to show off his skills and to delight the eventual owner. It was remarkable how many of these delicate objects survived to be passed down the generations.

But the material and craftsmen Clare admired the most had always been silver and silversmiths. She would have been hard-pressed to say why exactly. She liked the look of it, the feel of it, and always thought meals tasted better using silver flatware.

The warmth and depth of the patina of early silver was much more aesthetically pleasing to her than her perceived brashness of the finish on contemporary silver pieces. Using a silver polishing cloth and wearing cotton gloves, she turned her attention to the job in hand and gently started polishing. She was glad she preferred pieces that were not ornate, which meant the job was relatively straightforward. She started with the argyll and worked her way methodically through a pair of Georgian silver salts, a pepper pot, some spoons, an old Sheffield Plate wine coaster. She always wondered about the wisdom of polishing Old Sheffield Plate as she supposed the silver plating would eventually disappear and all that would be left would be the underlying copper, so she rubbed it as gently as she could.

Next, she picked up a small beaker. As the polish came away on the cloth and the silver's natural lustre came alive, Clare stopped and stared. Malcolm had reminded her she had bought a piece of Hull silver from him previously, but she had no recollection of having done so, even with his emphatic reminder. There on the base she recognised the Hull town mark, but even more astonishing were the owner initials: J.G. In fact, as she bent closer, she saw it read *ex dono JG* in the same script as on the dram cup. Even though she was certain she would have done so when she bought the pieces, she went to the bookshelf to consult her trusty copy of *Jackson's Hallmarks* and reconfirmed the beaker dated from c1652 by James Birkby, having been made some fifty years before her newest acquisition. She felt a thrill of excitement. Surely, this meant they must have belonged to the same family in Hull over three hundred years ago. By some extraordinary twist of fate, the two pieces were united once again, in her possession. What was the beaker's history? There must be a story to unearth here. But what and how? No more cleaning took place that day. Clare remained seated for some time, staring at the ceiling, in stunned silence.

She called Elizabeth but was secretly quite pleased when no-one answered the phone. She didn't really think she would be that interested nor would understand. Despite not believing Amber would be any more understanding or sympathetic, Clare asked her to call round that evening. Waiting for her to arrive, Clare found the receipt for the purchase of the beaker. She placed the beaker and dram cup side by side and stared at them.

There wasn't a day before Harry's death that Clare had not felt satisfaction upon entering her dining room, where most of her collection was kept. These moments (there had been many) compared to trying on a new outfit, say, when returning from a shopping trip. The pleasure was at its height, but with a new outfit, this satisfaction soon faded after the first wearing. With a new piece of silver or porcelain, however, the pleasure was longer-lived. This had been true up until Harry fell ill. As she stared hard at the two pieces of silver, she did not really know what she felt. She liked to think of herself as a sort of guardian of bits of the past. More than that, everything that surrounded her represented a happy marriage. Lately though, she wasn't sure how she saw herself anymore. She was no longer a wife and her children no longer needed her. From teenage years onwards, it seemed a parent's job was to take steps backwards, to give gentle opinions and to pretend one never had a life prior to having children. In other words, it took a great deal of restraint. The important moments, "conditioning" as Amber would call it, took place prior to the teenage years, she thought. During the more formative years, your children admired you, needed you, believed in you as chief problem-solver. An unhappy first marriage meant she had not managed it as well as she would have liked. She had been too lenient, tried to placate rather than discipline in an attempt to make up for her then husband's obvious deficits. He had been a heavy drinker. He would either shout at the children or ignore them, and so she found herself compensating by over-giving, so much so that, eventually, she had spent three weeks in bed with pneumonia. As a result she became, in her children's teenage years, the proverbial doormat.

It was Harry who had pointed out that air stewards and stewardesses tell you to place the oxygen mask on your face before your child's, and for good reason. He had been a kind but strict father: principled and fair. His children had adored him, and he ensured in turn that they had all respected her. Parenting his children had, as a result, turned out easier than parenting her two and, if she were honest, they had all turned out more genial than either Joshua or Amber. Yet, she supposed, it had been out of her hands. She had been virtually a single mother for more than five years. Quite why she had stuck it out for so long was perhaps an example of her tenacity working against her, but the point was, she had tried until she could try no more. Having Harry appear had been akin to a white knight or a guardian angel and a whole host of other clichés. By then, her children were teenagers and saw Harry as an intrusion, little more. What she had reasoned since was that no matter how dire a child's early home life becomes, it's still their version of normal, and they grasp onto it as a baby does its mother's thumb.

Just as Clare was taking a cottage pie out of the oven, the doorbell rang. She pulled back the door to see Amber standing there wearing a long camel-hair coat over a black suit. With heels, she was a few inches taller than Clare, slim and with good posture. Her hair was tastefully highlighted, and she had her father's dark, inquisitive eyes. Her nose and forehead were, however, Clare's.

'What's the emergency? If you need some light bulbs changing, you know I am not the person to ask,' Amber said, entering and immediately removing her shoes.

'Hello, darling. No, God forbid. Follow me, I have something to show you.'

'By the way, how was Elizabeth abroad?'

'Elizabeth abroad is much the same as Elizabeth at home; flamboyant, annoying, and generous. I do think her intentions are good, though. Besides, I do feel I have turned some sort of corner.'

Clare took Amber up to Harry's study. It would always be known as Harry's room for as long as the smell of his cigars lingered here. In some ways, it had become a kind of shrine.

'Good God, this place could do with a clear out!'

Clare bristled at Amber's response but bit her tongue, reaching instead for her silver taster and beaker which sat glowing under the green, notary light on Harry's desk.

Amber looked down at the desk with the computer pushed to one side to make room for two pieces of silver and an open book. 'Please don't leave me any of this silver in your will. You know I'd never get around to cleaning it. Rory would love it though!'

'I wanted to show you something. Take a good look at both these pieces,' said Clare, holding the taster and the beaker in Amber's direction.

Amber threw her camel coat onto the back of Harry's

desk chair, pulled down her glasses from the top of her head and brought her eyes close to the beaker. She then did the same with the taster.

'What am I looking for?' she said, wrinkling her nose. Amber shook her head. 'Are you all right, Mother? Did you have another think about those counselling sessions I mentioned?'

'No, and I don't intend to. I haven't reached this age without some ability to solve my own problems. Look at the initials, darling.'

Amber peered closer. 'J.G.?'

'Exactly!'

Amber ducked down again. 'On both!'

'Precisely!'

Amber looked up, taking her glasses off, clearly unimpressed. 'It's a coincidence, they still happen in the twenty-first century.'

'And both are from Hull,' said Clare, feeling now like a stand-up comedian depositing a punchline.

Amber's expression verged on the sarcastically patient. 'And your point being?'

'Isn't it obvious? Both from the same time, the same place and the same initials and *both* now in my collection.'

Amber shook her head. 'Listen, Mummy, I know it's been hard for you, you know, living alone since Harry died. But you will engage with life again, I mean, properly engage. I promise. It just takes—'

'Please!' Clare snatched the two silver pieces from Amber's hands and placed them back on the desk where they gleamed in the desk light as if winking in collusion.

'I am engaging – in the way I wish to engage. And something tells me I am onto something.'

'Oh, Mother. The only thing you are onto is a big, gigantic waste of time.'

'Very funny, darling. Well, I shall just have to prove to you that my intuition is right about this one. Okay? They must have belonged to the same family all those centuries ago.'

Amber sighed and rolled her eyes. If she wasn't so beautiful and together and a daughter to be proud of in so many other ways, Clare would be chastising her right now.

'Or alternatively,' Amber was saying with a smirk, 'you could find an enormous haystack somewhere and start looking for needles.'

'Do you know, I'm glad that you're underestimating me,' said Clare.

'Why?'

'For you will only be surprised when I stumble upon something!'

'But what do you imagine that might be exactly?'

When precisely did this happen with one's children? One minute you are teaching them everything and the next they believe you to be an imbecile. Clare intended to hold onto her marbles for as long as possible, if for no other reason than to prove a point to her daughter.

'I think I might try to trace both the taster and beaker's owners. With two pieces with the same initials, it may be possible to discover who they were.'

'In Hull?'

'I suspect so.'

'And have you ever been to Hull?'

'No, but I imagine I will have to go there.'

'Is this really how you envisaged your retirement: day trips to Hull of all places?'

'Why not? It's as good a place as any to have a day trip.'

'What, when you have South America or China to explore?'

'I would rather engage my brain in something. I've told you that before.'

'You could learn Italian? Or the piano?'

'When I need you to organise my life, Amber, I will let you know.'

Amber ran a hand through her hair and her bracelets jangled. 'Then if you're going to do this, please do me one favour.'

'What?' said Clare, her mind returning to the cottage pie.

'Please don't mention this to Rory. In fact, please don't mention this to *anybody*.'

Clare decided she'd had enough. 'Oh, for goodness sake, Amber! Age does not always equate to idiocy. I have good intuition, and always have had. You of all people should know that.'

Amber laughed. She had a beautiful laugh, thought Clare. Shame she didn't do it more often instead of taking life so intensely seriously. 'Agreed,' she said. 'Do you remember that time you appeared at Charlotte's fifteenth-birthday camping party knowing there would be boys there?'

'You see! Yes, you were caught out good and proper. And I feel all this has been quite synchronistic too and for that very reason I feel... I feel I'm somehow meant to find the answers. Rather, I feel this particular problem has been given to me to personally solve.'

'Romantic, but unlikely to be the case. Just also promise you won't write a book about your findings. Nobody believes coincidences in books.'

'And what about coincidences in real life?' Clare asked, somewhat tentatively.

'I suppose you will just have to see. What's for supper? Did you say you had supper?'

With that, the usual mother-daughter parameters trickled into place again.

'Cottage pie,' said Clare. She gave the silver a last look before turning off the desk lamp. She would return to the polishing in the morning, in the daylight.

'Great, your cottage pie is always truly delicious, Mummy! And I need to tell you all about my promotion. I have been given a junior to mentor. It doesn't mean more money at this stage, but I'm hopeful.'

'Well, done, you' said Clare, and did not add, 'how is that a promotion?' Instead, just said, 'Would you like green beans?'

'I'm only eating organic… wait a minute!'

Clare stopped and turned back. 'What?'

'You're visiting antique fairs again? That's marvellous! Having a hobby is necessary for one's mental well-being. It can give you purpose, and purpose is essential for a healthy old age. The Japanese…'

And Clare had switched off, her mind returning to her taster, to the possibilities it had presented and to the inbuilt magic of life. Thank you, she thought, unsure who praise was to be directed towards. *Thank you.*

1654

In the narrow confines of his cellar, John Graves fastened a black cape over his doublet and pulled the hood low over his forehead. A curl of hair, which might otherwise have been a fashionable lovelock, escaped over one shoulder. As a man of trade, John Graves had little time for the frivolities of fashion. His interest lay in providing the cloth to fuel such frivolities. He flicked the stray lock over his shoulder and picked up the caduceus, finding reassurance in the cold brass against his flesh. He sat down on a hefty oak chair and looked at the men facing him. Where the arched ceiling met with dank walls, long rush-lights burned brightly, casting flickering shadows across the floor, making the men appear on the wrong side of sinister. Time was marked by water dripping from the arched ceiling into a small puddle on the flagstones behind. The air was fetid. It had the overpowering smell of mildew and burning fat from the lights. The room lay several feet beneath his family's home and was the most private space John Graves could think of for the Society's monthly gatherings. That said, it did his lungs no good venturing down here.

His good friends, Timothy Lumn, Robert Winton and John Minspeak also attired themselves in capes. They bowed in turn before taking seats in a rough circle with John Graves' chair at the head, adjusting their hoods to cover their heads as they sat down and arranged their clothing. Last into the cellar, as usual, came John Graves' brother. Thomas' dragging feet did not go unnoticed by the other men, nor did his usual expression of discomfort as he half-heartedly performed his bow to his brother. In his nightly prayers, John Graves asked that Thomas might understand his position as the grandson of Hull's mayor, recognise it and rise to it. A prosperous life was his for the taking. Their forefathers had fought hard to shake off the taint of name and, truthfully put, a man had a duty to uphold a family's ascent with honour and to do so with dignity. But as if they had sprung from various beginnings, he and Thomas floated along different pathways. As with a river whose tributary leads to more extensive banks and eventually the expanse of the open sea, John's business had flourished with the help of his second wife, Margaret. Margaret had known more about keeping accounts than John could ever hope to know, but of more import was that she had always refused to let a customer get by without paying his business. Kindness starts with your family, she would frequently remind him. This was perhaps the only reason that John had continued to help his brother Thomas. He had made a habit of acknowledging his wife's kindly ways since the day he had married Margaret but, if pressed, his patience with his brother was down to the last dregs.

Like himself, Thomas had also benefited from a good education. He had married a wife of the same name as his sister-in-law, but the family called her Meg, and they had been blessed with a son. John and Margaret had three daughters. He worried about his daughters' future, with no brother to look out for them, however. He thus hoped that Thomas's son might rise to the task at hand, which was another reason to wake Thomas up to prosper. Yet Thomas always seemed to veer back to the river's source, to the spring that appeared to travel nowhere, seeping back into the wretched earth as day after day he dug grave after grave behind the mass that was Holy Trinity Church.

On occasion, John had lent his brother money to start up in business. Each plan of Thomas' lacked a practical foundation. They were, to John's mind, too lofty and ill thought out. Following the previous loan, he had seen his brother buy a fishing boat, an enormous vessel with which he planned to hunt whales for their fat. Two months later, with the ship sunk, his brother had been penniless once more. As for Thomas, he would have drowned if not for a passing Norwegian fishing boat, steered by men far more equipped for the icy seas. Yet John persisted in inviting Thomas to their Society monthly meetings hoping, one day, he might realise that living in poverty was lazy, not noble, and that grave digging was merely punishment when a more substantial, steadier income was his for the taking.

The men settled. John banged the brass caduceus against the flagstones three times. The caduceus was an exact replica of that held by Mercury in the statue of the god at the cellar's entry. Mercury was best known as the messenger god but was, amongst other things, the god of shopkeepers and merchants; he served as the Society's protector and no ritual was ever held without his presence.

'Good evening, gentlemen!' said John Graves, nodding to each man in turn. 'I have much to report tonight. Do any of you have a subject you wish to firstly address?'

Robert Winton raised his hand. Winton was older than the other men, appearing weathered but wise. He was a successful furniture maker who had profited greatly since the Society had begun, five years earlier. Business was slowly improving following the harrowing Civil War. 'We did well to lose as few men as we did after the last assault of the plague,' he said, looking about the circle. 'But we need to make sure that there are more men of trade in this town to ensure it remains a grand town, one to be revered. To this end, I have given a sum of ten pounds to the grammar school, for I do see this as the place to kindle ambition in young men.'

All the men, aside from Thomas, nodded in agreement.

'A good and grand gesture,' said John Graves.

Robert Winton smiled. 'I wish to encourage other gentlemen in our Society to do the same. We are all able to keep our families,' Robert Winton went on, as John could not help looking to his brother, whose face remained blank, 'so now we must look to our legacies, not only for our children's children but for the young men of this town, men who will one day meet, just as we are doing now, with a desire to improve Hull's trade and standing.'

A few 'ayes' passed around the room.

'Thank you, Robert,' said John. 'We will endeavour to match your kindness. I have given a sum of five pounds towards the restoration of part of the merchant's meeting house above the school. As you know, the gale last Autumn destroyed much of the roof. It is to be completed by Christ's Mass, and the town is to celebrate such an occasion.'

The men nodded in sombre unison.

'But as you gentlemen do know, not every merchant of this town believes in our methods; this has caused us much past difficulty. Thus, we must continue with the meetings here, in my cellar. I am grown ever more attached to this dripping wall. Aren't you?'

The men laughed alongside John Graves.

'Difficulties there are!' said Timothy Lumn, a grain exporter and learned scholar. 'Of late, I have been accused that I be a Satanist twice and at church. My wife she did nearly faint with the shock. I did not take well to it, not well at all, John.'

John Graves shook his head. 'But rumours we can ignore. If it is proof that is required. Then we are all in agreement that trade with the Continent is kept between us and us alone; they shall be hard put to find any evidence. Who in this room would cut off their nose to be disloyal? I do think that none of you would indulge too much liquor in public. Am I not right? Thus, none would betray our methods. Is this not true?' This time John did not meet the eyes of his brother. Thomas' wife, Meg, said that liquor was to blame for his returning to grave digging after each business gamble failed. 'Early bird catches the worm, John, and this brother of yours cannot shake himself out of bed, up all night as he be in the tavern,' Margaret would tell him. Yet, John was sure Thomas would not bring trouble for himself. He was John's younger brother, and family, after all. No, Thomas would not betray them, John was certain of it.

'We have profited much more than the other merchants of Hull,' said Robert Winton, 'and people are both suspicious and resentful.'

'Envy is a sin,' said John. 'But without proof they can only cast aspersions. We must take solace in our plan working thus far, gentlemen. That is all that we must go on and so it be all that matters. No man can predict what the future holds in store. We have clean consciences, and we did take the time to speak with other merchants of this town, but when they did hear of our plans they did speak in wary tongues. We were careful to veil our intentions and to make suggestions appear as if by chance, all of you showing much prudence, but we were all in agreement that we should include no more men.'

'I am grateful that you took the time to speak to me first,' said John Minspeak, a fellow cloth merchant.

John Graves smiled. 'I have a sense of those friends I would trust with my life,' he replied. 'This is why I confess here first; it has been my intention to make Kingston upon Hull a thriving town of trade, bigger than Norwich or Liverpool, or even Bristol, and a recognised enemy to London's Port. This ambition in my soul I did inherit from my ancestor, John Graves, who was a Member of Parliament. Hugh, his father before him, was once an alderman, a chamberlain, a sheriff, and mayor of this town, as well as a merchant too. I had, you might say, a great deal to live up to. However, my father did speak of uniting England in trade with the Continent but did not progress any further with such an idea. As for us, we see no future divisions in our mind, gentlemen. As far as trade is concerned, we are one nation. Tonight, I would like to take opportunity to speak of an agreement reached with Holland that will benefit us all in different ways. As you are aware, Adelbert always has our town in his prayers.'

Brief mumbles ensued.

'Need I to be here?' asked Thomas.

John's inclination was to bellow, '*Be quiet.*' But he quickly overcame his low feeling with a deep breath. 'Is it not a choice between here and the tavern, Thomas?' he asked with as much patience as he could muster.

'So what if it is?' replied his brother. John Graves took a breath to calm his tongue. 'Learning is a lifetime occupation, dear brother. What you may learn tonight will surely be of benefit to you in the coming years of your life.'

Thomas shrugged. 'Aye, if I felt that I was learning a thing of import. To have friends, to laugh and to have camaraderie with the men of this town: these things I do value more than gold coins that you do so worship, brother. This cannot be a sin. But to sit in a cellar making spells, well, that must be a sin worse than witchery.'

'Nay spells!' said Robert, stomping his boot.

'You know very well what we do here, Thomas,' cut in John Graves, wishing to soothe Robert with his words as much as he did his brother. 'Our methods come from ancient philosophical texts, from the cleverest minds of Ancient Greece. We aim to instil order amid chaos. Thus far, we have met with success, as well you know, dear brother.'

Thomas stood up. 'What you do here is naught but wasting time, time that would be best spent with my friends, folk not gripped by temptation but living in the light. God's light not Satan's darkness!'

Timothy Lumn, although by far the most learned man in the room, was naturally shy, and forever wore a look of concentration etched upon his narrow face with its sad eyes drooping at the corners. He stood up and rested a hand upon Thomas' shoulder. 'I understand your fears, my friend, I do. And yet I do believe that what we have established here, in John's cellar, is an important ritual, one that unites us with similar men that do perform similar rituals in Amsterdam, in Riga, in Madrid, in Stockholm as well as the darker corners of London, and I have likewise heard St Petersburg sits amongst these important trading towns. Our rituals help us speak a common… language.'

'Pah, family!' spat Thomas. 'Latin nor Greek be not what a grave digger doth need!'

John hit the caduceus hard against the floor. 'A grave digger needs money, Thomas. Unless he considers his brother, the draper, his moneylender?' His voice rose in volume, shaking imperceptibly with withheld anger.

'Charity is charity,' said Thomas, kicking the toe of his boot into the flagstone. 'Your gripe is with God, not with me, John. You is you and I is I. Charity is something that be different and it is your choice to give it. That is why God has given you such wealth. Charity begins at home.'

John shook his head, his brow darkening. 'I do not consider it entirely God's doing, as you well know. Besides, it is not God but you that favours liquor and that it be liquor prevents you from arising to catch the worm,' said John, his voice shaking with plain rage. Suspicion was growing that Thomas had spoken freely in the tavern, and this enraged him still further. 'We are all churchmen here, as you well know, but we do not place all our faith in Him alone. God helps those that do help themselves, Thomas. God requires deeds. It is then that he rewards plentifully. What if God has chosen us to improve our town? We have been blessed by the Humber's deep waters. We have by tradition shipped much wool and in turn we have received much flax, pitch and tar in return. In hard times we import corn and in the good, we export it. We now export cloth made by my own looms. Lead export is increasing, and some say it will replace cloth in time, is that not so, Robert?'

'If I have my way!' Robert Winton laughed, a laugh that suited the size of his portly figure but not the sombreness of Thomas' expression. Robert Winton must have sensed this and quickly cleared his throat. 'Give him time, John, give him more time.'

John Graves nodded sagely. 'So, if we enact the ritual, if we commune with the spirits to aid our plight, wherein lies the harm?'

'If it were all above board, you would meet with other merchants in the room above the Grammar School,' stated Thomas.

But all too familiar with his brother's stubbornness, John shook his head. 'Anybody would think you are the Devil's advocate, for all that trade has done is benefit this town. If merchants from the countries that we do trade with visit us, we come together for the ceremony, for the ritual of it. It doth create a sense of trust between us and brings us together for reasons aside from money. Can you not see this, Thomas?'

'Your trust is in the Devil,' snapped Thomas. 'Why not

come together at church? With a proper God? Unless you be afraid that what you do is under Satan's protection and his alone. That be devil's work, to my mind, and that is all it be!'

John Graves knew it was no good to annoy his brother further, for there was no telling what would be spoken at the tavern if he did. He drew a deep breath and momentarily closed his eyes, twirling the brass handle of the caduceus in circles as he tried to get a hold of his thoughts. He would not confess to Thomas that when he entered church, he felt like a beggar going in with a bowl and coming out empty; too many of his prayers had gone unanswered. With the ritual in the cellar, he did not feel so much like God as a trusted captain of God's vessel. He no longer felt himself to be the victim, one without power in the way church so often made him feel, nor did his thoughts feel improper. God, he was beginning to learn, resided as much within as without. And that was all there was to it.

The other men knew not to intervene. They sat in silence, eyes cast toward the floor, as Thomas appeared to grow steadily taller.

'So, you will no longer be attending these meetings?' John Graves asked, his voice softening with some effort.

Thomas shook his head. 'Nay. I neither wish to meet nor be asked to sail to Flanders to do more of the Devil's work there. I am a man of simple tastes and do like a plain life. One man cannot say what makes another happy, nor can he map his path. I answer to God and God alone.'

John took a deep breath of stale cellar air, coughing as he exhaled. 'And what if, as your brother, I can see more in your soul than you believe is there? What if... what if, Thomas, God had placed me in your path for the reason of steering you straight?'

Timothy cleared his throat as the ceiling dripped into silence.

'You speak of souls yet practise the Devil's work,' said Thomas. 'You say you have faith in God then pray to the god Mercury. Now you tell me you are of more import than God! I have had enough of this, brother. If God still plants charity in your heart, then I shall accept with as much grace as I can afford but, henceforth, I shall not be part of your secret Society. I am a free man. I say to you...' He looked at each member in turn. 'Beware, gentlemen.' He gestured to the rest of the circle, appearing to look each merchant in the eyes before looking back at John Graves. 'Beware of God's vengeance for your acts of sin. God's wrath serves a good and necessary purpose.' Thomas looked hard at each man in turn, kicked his stool to the floor and exited the cellar.

With Thomas gone, John Graves at last felt his shoulders relax. He took a deep breath and hammered the caduceus against the floor in four equal thumps.

'We must begin, gentlemen,' he said. 'We have wasted too much time already.'

'Yes, Master,' the men said in unison.

'Robert Winton, do you have the stone? Timothy, the beaker?'

'Aye,' replied both men.

Timothy unwrapped the beer cup from a swath of black velvet cloth and placed it in the centre of the circle of stools upon the flagstone floor.

'John?' John Graves asked his friend, the fellow draper, a man whose face was a latticework of red veins.

'Aye,' said John Minspeak as he unwrapped the red, flattish philosopher's stone from a square of royal blue cloth and placed it beside the beaker.

'*Mercurie, dux umbrarum ad Orcum, deus lucri et commercii, concede notib fidem nostris consiliis et crede illis cum quibus negotiamur,*' spoke John Graves.

'Mercury, guide of souls to the underworld, god of financial gain and commerce, grant us faith in our intentions and trust in those with whom we trade,' said the men, chanting John Graves' words back to him in English.

'As sure as the sun rises in the skies after the moon sets, we four men attest to the stone's power.'

'It is so,' repeated the men.

'It is the belief of our Society that as our wings spread further afield and promises of trade increase, so do our powers. We are not limited by our *geographia*, nor by human doubt. We do not give credence to the physical state of the world being set in stone. It is our belief that God is working through us to show us that great power lies within us, a power that is rightfully ours as the sons of the Son of God.' John Graves held up the caduceus, a wand once awarded to Mercury by Apollo, a wand also comprised of Hull's own brass. He waved it over both the stone and the beaker, repeating in Latin, trade for the good of us all, under his breath several times, closely followed by, '*Noster mundus locus commercii est.*'

'Our world is a net of trade,' repeated the other three men, their voices deep and steady with belief.

'To those absent,' John Graves added, fearing as he always did for his brother's safety in the world. 'May God guide their journeys.' Time and time again, he failed to impress upon Thomas that there were powers, certain *energeia*, at work in the world and that these could be coerced by man, or else man could become victim to their whims. God was a vessel through which belief in such powers, as well as belief in the self, was made possible. The men understood this in the same manner that they understood that all was possible with belief that it began with belief over one's own soul and, ultimately, over God.

Once John Graves had returned the caduceus to his side and the bent heads of the men straightened, Timothy Lumn turned to him. 'You spoke of Holland. What news do you have, Master?'

John coughed softly, as was his habit. 'As you gentlemen know, our Dutch friends are equipped with a large fleet of vessels. Calvinism, it seems, has equipped them with the attributes of thrift and a good education. The Dutch have plentiful stock. This doth mean they can keep prices steady and take advantage of the opportunities of profit. As you know, years passed, following the Dutch visit to our port, they have put much faith in our undertakings and, as such, have volunteered their ships to take back return stocks of our base metals and cloth. For this, we pay a small fee and accept gladly the small risk this affords. It is a situation in which we have both handsomely profited. We are now to begin to send a crew back to Flanders as a precaution against pirates as well and guard against the thieving snuffle hunters at the port. This was at Adelbert's suggestion. Of great import here is that a deep sense of trust has developed between us and, as Mercury has shown, a belief in the transmutation of our minds is as important as that of the power of the philosopher's stone. You do not need me to point out that it has brought much success to us all. We are all now captains, captains of a ship sailing into a new world of trade both in the Continent and, in good time, further afield.' This was as close as John Graves ever came to naming his dominion over his God, his fate; he felt no need to add anything further. 'The news is, gentlemen, that with Adelbert's generosity of spirit, we too shall conquer trading cities such as Riga, St Petersburg, Moscow and Lisbon as well as Amsterdam, which we are now familiar with. The world, gentlemen, is to become our oyster shell. Are you of the mind to begin fashioning pearls?'

There came murmurs of appreciation from the men.

'Gentlemen,' he went on, 'all hail the Dutch Republiek der Verenigde Nederlanden from where great business is promised.'

'Hail!' echoed the men.

John Minspeak picked up the philosopher's stone. He kissed it and passed it to Robert Winton, who did the same as did Timothy then, and he passed it to John Graves, who held the stone aloft; this was the part of the ceremony that always brought doubt, but fear was an initiation into trust and trust, he well knew, was the basis of a good life. He nodded almost imperceptibly to Timothy Lumn, who reached for a torch hung from the wall. He kneeled before John Graves, head bowed, torch extended in both hands above his head. John Graves brought the stone closer to the flames. He nodded this time to Robert Winton, who reached for the silver beaker and stood behind Timothy's back.

'*In deo fidemis!*' he said in a low, deep voice.

'*In deo fidemis!*' the men repeated into the stuffy confines of the cellar as the three objects were brought closer together.

John Minspeak whispered reverentially, '*In alchimia credimus!*'

A moment later and the torches blew out. John Graves knew of the draught that blew through the cellar, but the extinguishing of the flames always seemed timely. As darkness obscured the men's vision, the wind howled along High Street.

'Amen!' the men chorused just as John Graves fell into a coughing stupor. His body shook, his eyes poured, and the other men looked on helpless. From the walls, the steady drip of water onto the dank floor continued. Eventually, John Graves fell back into his seat exhausted. Given he had become used to steering his own ship, he objected to the uncomfortable feeling that the cough had grip of him.

John Minspeak whispered, 'God protect, Master.'

The flesh on John Graves' arms puckered. As he cast his eye to the statue of Mercury, young and lithe, in the corner of the room, he panted as he recovered, and for the first time, the god's appearance offered something sinister rather than reassuring.

As they were all getting ready to leave, it was at last John Minspeak who spoke the words his companions had withheld. 'Are you sure, Master, that it is wise to keep including Thomas? He could undo us.'

2016

Clare seemed to spend every spare hour so called *surfing* the net, seeking some clue or other about her recent acquisition. She tried stolen silver, thefts from museums, odd images of Mercury – each time hoping something, anything, would give her a concrete lead. She had so little to go on. Now her desire to know never seemed to leave her. Her taster was on her mind almost all the time. First thing in the morning and last thing at night she often looked at it on her bureau, glowing alongside her beaker.

'You need some social media accounts,' said Amber, dropping in the next day with some cakes. Amber had done such acts of kindness often since Harry's death. It surprised Clare, but she would accept these offerings graciously and then invariably throw away the rest of the sweet treats. Amber, from a young age, would look at the pudding menu first in restaurants, but Clare, who did not have a sweet tooth, never did. Amber had never seemed to have noticed.

'Social media?' Clare had replied. 'What for?'

'You'll be amazed how easy it is to connect with people – all over the world. Someone, somewhere, might have some information about your silver pot.'

Clare could not imagine how this might work.

'You'll have to show me,' she said. 'Thanks for the cake, I'm sure it will be delicious.'

Amber deposited the box on the kitchen counter.

'I was meant to be meeting Rory for a drink but he's working late – again!' Amber stretched out a perfectly manicured hand. 'Mother, if you pass me your phone, I could set you up now.'

Amber was always complaining about Rory, but Clare didn't comment and handed Amber her phone.

'I'll set you up with Facebook, Instagram and Twitter. I won't make the accounts private. That way, you can then post things about your pot and see whether anything shows up.'

'I can?' said Clare, mystified.

'You can put a photo up on a platform and in between the likes you may receive incisive comments.'

'I know about Facebook, and I don't want a Facebook account.'

Clare sensed a whole new language opening up to her: *posts, platforms, likes...* 'But I can't attract too much attention,' she said. 'I'd rather avoid a visit from the police, if possible. It's just, well, it's just I'd like to unravel it. No, I feel I *can* unravel it.'

Amber put on her glasses. 'It's not your fault you bought it,' she said, picking up on the wrong point entirely. 'I think you need to let it go a little.'

Clare sighed. 'I'm really fine. I'm genuinely interested in the mystery of the meaning of the image on my little pot. But I don't want to prod the hornets' nest.'

'Why, don't you want to upset Malcolm? Do you suspect he knew it was stolen?'

'No, not at all! He was without doubt an innocent party, but his reputation will be at stake if this leaks out. It's a very serious offence.'

'But still not really your problem, Mother.'

'I know,' said Clare, thinking how unhelpful Amber's comments could be sometimes. Why did the younger generations have such difficulty understanding those that went before? Perhaps it had to be this way, she thought, perhaps it was simply evolution in action. Yet, whether it was heading in the direction of improvement, the jury was still out for Clare.

'So, how does it all work?' she said, in as upbeat a tone as she could muster.

Amber showed Clare her phone. 'Okay, how about this: Silversurfer will be your account name?'

Clare laughed. 'Okay, very good.'

'You will need a profile picture.'

'What's that?'

'A photo of you.'

'No, I'd rather not.'

'What about a photo of your little silver pot then?'

'Absolutely not. I am not drawing attention to myself.'

'Then another piece from your collection? You need to put something on it, Mother!'

'How about a picture of one of the cats?'

Amber beamed. 'Great! A cup of coffee would go down well with the cake.'

'Oh, it's too late for coffee,' said Clare, not appreciating her daughter's bossiness either. 'Won't you stay for supper?'

'No, I can't. I have to prepare a document for work. Just coffee. I have a feeling I'm going to pull a late one, possibly an all-nighter, with the amount of work I have on.'

'As you wish,' said Clare, 'don't overdo it,' knowing better than to fret over her daughter's health; it only resulted in being *advised*, as if she were an idiot, about the so-called *modern world*.

Clare was trying to work out whether social media might be a little risky, given she was still uncomfortable that the police might want to talk to her, even though no-one had suggested this. Why did modern lives have to be lived so publicly?

It was all so synthetic somehow but, if the social media accounts helped her with her quest, then at least they were serving a purpose.

By the time Amber left, appearing particularly satisfied at having introduced her mother to the twenty-first century, Clare had Instagram and Twitter accounts all in the name of *silversurferCC*. It seemed *silversurfer* had already been claimed.

'Great minds think alike!' said Amber.

'My experience is that great minds rarely think alike,' said Clare, 'and this is what makes them great.'

'Well, you may have to lower your expectations somewhat for social media.'

'I see,' said Clare, not seeing much at all.

It took half an hour to demonstrate the ropes to Clare, who couldn't shake the notion that surely real life was somehow better than anyone's virtual platform. It already concerned Clare that vulnerable young people were awaiting approval, in the form of *likes*, as they showed themselves off, more often than not, in ostensibly enviable settings. What she did like, however, was the notion that it somehow made the world smaller, that people, no matter where they lived, had similar values and similar needs. She was sure it helped to transform the world into a more curious place too. Whether it would be of much help to her research remained uncertain.

As Amber *scrolled* through people's *posts,* having searched "antique silver", Clare was surprised to see a few familiar people: antique dealers and collectors whom she knew. She relaxed slightly. Some of the accounts were deemed private, whilst others she could freely peruse and though she could not shift the notion she was somehow prying, some of these images were quite wonderful, and the photography often exceptional. Amber showed Clare the *account, hull_museums.* How Clare enjoyed looking at the images of Anglo-Saxon brooches and perfectly polished ammonites, but there were no clues to be found so far about her silver taster, or the 1986 heist. It was pure, frivolous fun.

'You need to think of related words,' Amber explained. 'But be warned, it can eat up hours of one's time.'

'I will have a good think about what to research then,' said Clare, doubt perhaps obvious in her tone.

'Do, Mummy. It will keep you busy if nothing else.'

Clare raised her eyebrows and sighed, resenting the way Amber felt that she had to ensure her time was occupied. Doubtless, Amber had little faith in her ability to uncover anything at all. It also made Clare realise that her daughter was still concerned for her well-being.

'How about *museum heists*?' said Clare.

'That's a good one,' said Amber.

The search brought up some interesting images, including a painting called *The Sea of Galilee (1633)*, stolen during one of the biggest heists in American history. Five hundred million pounds worth of art was stolen from the Isabella Stewart Gardner Museum in 1990 and the robbers had apparently dressed up as police officers. Clare's mind returned to her taster. It had found its way back into the open market. But how was it stolen? Was the thief, or thieves, ever caught?

'Do you get the gist?' asked Amber.

'I'll have a play around with it.'

'Okay, silversurfer!'

'Oh, please!' said Clare, laughing.

'One more thing, you need to set up some hashtags like #antiquesilver #Hullsilver #seventeethcenturysilver #silverengravingsmercury.'

Clare stared blankly at her daughter.

'It just means you will be alerted if anything comes up. In fact, I'll put the same hashtags on my account which I monitor all the time. I must fly, I have so much work to do at home.'

'Thank you for setting up the accounts, I'm not sure how useful they will be but I appreciate that you've done it.'

It wasn't until Amber had left that Clare realised how laughter had been so absent for so long. In truth, the research had come at a most timely point. Not that she would admit this to Amber, of course, but the truth was it was proving a wonderful distraction.

After Amber had left, Clare settled into an armchair in Harry's study. She switched on the standing lamp above and, using the remote control, put Classic FM on the stereo.

Look at me on social media! Who would have thought?!

Several minutes later, Beethoven's *Fifth* playing in the background, Clare became absorbed and transported into the world of Twitter and Instagram. The images of antiques and their settings were stunning, and it wasn't long before she acknowledged Amber's words: many hours could indeed be wasted here. She scanned various silver dealer accounts, from home to France, America, Italy, and Holland, appreciating both the photography and the descriptions, getting lost down various tunnels of pseudo-investigation. Following an hour or so of *swiping,* she put her phone in her cardigan pocket. She didn't really see how it would help and, as Amber had said, she would put the same hashtags on her account; Clare would leave her to monitor it.

1654

Evening fell dark and dank over Hull and its harbour. John Graves got into bed beside Margaret. She saw the worry in his face and set down her candle.

'What is it, Mr Graves? Your look is troubled.'

'I did feel faint with coughing at the meeting earlier tonight,' he said, lying back.

Margaret's lip pinched as she arranged her pillow, making a dent in the middle of the straw as she did nightly. 'Do you feel revived now, Mr Graves?'

'I do. And the girls, how were they today?'

'They are all good girls. They did some needlework and did say how pleased they are of the news that Timothy Lumn is to give them lessons.'

John Graves chuckled as he settled on his back and pulled the cover up to his chin, just as he liked it. 'There are not many girls in Hull that do have the same opportunity for an education.'

John reached for her hand.

'It is quite a miracle that Mary, Elizabeth and Hannah shall be given the knowledge that is given to the young men of this town. I do think this will make our girls excellent wives given time.'

John brought Margaret's hand to his lips and kissed it. 'Just as their mother be too! Rather, to have a wife as a friend and constant companion as well as a compass in business is more than a man might hope for. I am of the opinion, dear wife, that we would not be in the position to educate our girls if not for your wise and thoughtful advice. It is to you that they must direct their praise.'

Margaret laughed, covering her mouth with her free hand in a way that had always endeared her to John. 'I give only my feelings.' Tis a difficult thing to be in trade without feelings and it is good for a woman to put her thoughts to such things over gossip.'

John Graves sighed, knowing he was soon ready for sleep. 'I am a truly fortunate husband and I do thank God nightly in my prayers for such a kindly wife.'

Margaret squeezed John's hand. 'As I do, for thee.'

Margaret turned to her husband, who had begun to cough. Quite suddenly, his hand was snatched from hers. 'Master?' she said, fear lifting her voice. But John's body convulsed with shaking, his eyes rolling back into his head as he emitted a low gurgling sound into the darkness of the room.

'John?' said Margaret. 'John?'

Several minutes later and the coughing ceased. John's body softened and Margaret gently patted his cheek. 'Talk to me, husband,' she could not help but plead.

John's eyes slowly opened then widened at Margaret. 'Why are you leaning over me?' he said, blood beginning to trickle from the corner of his mouth and along his chin.

'You did have a coughing fit, husband. It put the fear of God inside my heart, my love.' She wiped some blood from his chin.

'I have no memory of this.' John scratched his forehead. 'Is it morning?'

The blood spread onto the pillow's covering, dispersing into larger, paler spots.

'Still night, husband, and you must sleep. I will blow out the candle. I do think it might be a good caution to call the physician in the morning. Is this how you did feel at the meeting, my love?'

John continued to stare straight ahead at the fireplace. He had the notion he was somebody different. He had the strangest feeling that he was observing himself from above, as if looking through a roofless house from a cloud. He saw the mound of his body beneath the bed linen. He felt his own insignificance, his own fragility. He looked at his wife and saw her concern etched into the folds of her skin. For the first time, he wondered what she would think if she knew what happened in the Society meetings. Now, as if a recusant caught in the throes of confession, he uttered, 'I do think it might be the damp air in the cellar.'

'I do not understand why you wish to meet there when we have a fitting house for you to meet in, dear husband.'

Once again, John Graves looked down at this insufficient man upon the bed. He saw the loving wife, saw that he was the pivot of her world, thought of his three beautiful daughters and felt their fragility more than his own. He was a guardian of four of the purest souls.

Alongside his wife, he had become a successful trader

of cloth, one that had supplied towns further afield than Kingston upon Hull, such as York, where he kept a second house as merchants often did, Norwich, Bath and London. But it was when his mind and body turned to notions of alchemy, to the god Mercury, that trade with the Continent had really begun. He started to make more money, more than even his father might have dreamed possible. His success buoyed him to trade still further. Yet, as the trades had grown bigger, so had his fear, and, before long, he was consumed by nightly worries. He hid this as much as possible from Margaret, blaming it on eating rich food too late. His diet grew steadily simpler as Margaret did her best to correct his sleeplessness. At one time, John had found himself visiting church daily, praying for protection, but when a ship with a large order en route to Flanders sunk, it took a great deal of resolve to both attend church and ship another order to Amsterdam. Shortly afterwards, he met Adelbert van der Berg, a Dutch businessman seeking lead imports from Kingston upon Hull. Robert Winton had introduced Adelbert to John at his house, a building similar to John's and almost directly opposite it on the High Street. After a meal of ravioles of spiced pork, Robert Winton's bottler had opened a cask of good Spanish sack, and the three men had spoken long into the night as candle after candle burned to its wick. Adelbert's English was impressive, his wit excellent. But this was not the only reason John felt drawn to Adelbert. Adelbert was a man who misunderstood limits, who had no guilt concerning his vast wealth and harnessed ambition with apparently no consideration to piety. It was as they were finishing the first cask of wine that

Adelbert began speaking of the god Mercury. It surprised John that a man clearly steering his own ship would allude to such an outdated and blasphemous mode of worship.

'You seek the buried gods of the Romans?' he asked him, jovially.

'A man looks to those greater than himself for help. Rome sought improvement and conquered much. I am not interested in oppression, gentlemen, and this I have found to be the basis of the faith and is no doubt rife in your little church.' The word little did not go unnoticed. Robert Winton shifted in his seat. A brief smile crossed Adelbert's lips, as if he knew of the delicacy of the ground upon which he trod. 'I am not only interested in but enlivened by the notions of expanding and uniting, gentlemen. It is a large world, and it can be a better one too if we do help one another, do you understand me?'

The two men nodded tentatively.

'God, we must accept, does not have his hand on every puppet string. He is a god that perhaps tests more than He doth help, least not in ways we do pray for. Gentlemen, we must take up the strings ourselves, not to tug and pull in an endless battle with forces we do not comprehend but to unite with one another in profitable business dealings.'

He spoke about the alliance of Mercury to financial gain, commerce, grain, eloquence, messages, communication, travellers, boundaries, luck, trickery and thieves, for Mercury also served as the guide of souls to the Underworld. He said that a statue of the god of trade was to be found in Amsterdam in the homes of most merchants, at least those of any worth. He spoke of the caduceus that Mercury held aloft and its two entwined snakes: Apollo's gift to Mercury. Tipping his chin downwards so that his eyes peered over his eyeglasses, he whispered, 'Snakes are a symbol of opportunity, but they are also a symbol of spiritual guidance. Their ability to shed their skin makes them symbols of rebirth, of transformation and immortality. Keep a close watch over your dreams, gentlemen. The forces of this world do speak to us through our night-time dreams. If the snake appears to you, you accept her invitation. To accept is to agree to your fortune.'

What was this strange language Adelbert spoke? It seemed at once blasphemous and enchanting. As the two merchants leaned in closer, they were told that Ovid had written much about how Mercury carried Morpheus' dreams from the valley of Somnus to a sleeping human. As the tale was recounted, John felt like a child on his grandmother's knee again, listening to the tales of folk from long ago, immersed in times of magic; times when man was cast in God's form, rather: when man himself was God.

'But,' warned Adelbert, 'these two gods – Mercury and Hermes – they are not so different. Mercury can be a trickster too. But, in the Society, we uphold the Romans over the Greeks, mostly for their tenacity.'

It was blasphemy yet did not feel like it, thought John. And as if he were reading John's thoughts, Adelbert said, 'The merchants of Babylon had bottomry contracts. Do you know of the ancient Code of Hammurabi, gentlemen?'

Both men shook their heads.

'The Code of Hammurabi alludes to a form of bottomry. It is a way – how do I put this in English?– of sharing risk: an arrangement whereby the ship is used as security against a loan to finance a voyage. If the ship sinks, the Society loses the money, never you.'

The two men shook their heads, gently, as if shaking words of disbelief from between their ears.

'In our Society, which I will speak of in more detail given time, we feel that some – how should I put this? – some assurance in trade is necessary,' continued Adelbert. 'We are, if you like, armouring ourselves against the mercies of the gods. Actually,' he chuckled, 'we feel that we are, in a small way, defeating them.'

John Graves cleared his throat. 'Here in England, we worship one God and He is worshipped in a church.' On one shoulder sat his father and on the other, his grandfather: both could recite the Old and the New Testaments, word for word.

Robert Winton sat taller in his seat.

'As we do so in the Continent, gentlemen. But whether we refer to one god or one aspect of a god, it matters not. What matters are the attributes of that particular god or, if you like, one overall God we wish to be imbued with. We all believe that, if we pray, God keeps us safe. What we have experienced with shipping loads to far off places, however, is that no amount of praying will keep the ship safe. This is a fact, *ja*?'

John hummed a sound of agreement, feeling Adelbert spoke directly to his soul. Robert Winton scratched his head.

'So, in the Society,' Adelbert went on, 'we like to think of it as a bond against disaster. With these bonds, you will be paid by the Society a conditional loan, and you only pay it back, with additional sums, if tragedy does not occur. It is, if you like, a bond against catastrophe. It has come about, gentlemen, out of the necessity of trade and protection against barbarians. Demosthenes of Ancient Greece called it bottomry, and it is moreover a loan with conditions.'

'And if the vessel sinks?' enquired Robert Winton, a look of disbelief etched into his brow.

'There is nothing to pay. You have lost your cargo, but you are able to ship again on account of the loan. Yet we use the term bottomry for in truth it is not a loan and not a partnership either, neither is it pure assurance to the merchant. It is, if you like, a contract to be upheld in coming times, *ja*?'

For a moment, neither man spoke. John Graves had the strangest feeling he was in the presence of an angel. He looked at the smooth face of Adelbert and reached for his beaker of port. He took a long gulp then wiped his mouth on his sleeve.

'What you speak of,' he said, 'is an answer to a long-held prayer.'

Adelbert laughed, rocking a little in his seat. 'I know, I know all too well,' he said. 'It is the long-held prayer of too many merchants. But I am not a ghost from the dead promising you Heaven, gentlemen. For several years we have conducted our business by such means. Our Society has profited immensely, as have our members. We understand that here, in England, such assurance does not exist. Am I correct in my thinking?'

Robert Winton reached for his beaker. 'You are correct. We are men of trade, but we are naturally gambling men too.'

'Gambling against the whims of your God,' said Adelbert.

John ran a finger around his collar at the gentleman's description of the Supreme Being ruling over England's church. He cast an eye upwards as if to ward off punishment. He was a man of business. He knew that if a thing appeared of greater substance than may be true, more oft than not it was false.

'Well, gentlemen, are you with me? But first of all, does your bottler have any more of this Porto wine? It is from Portugal, is it not? I have tasted your English wine and do understand your need to import many casks from Bordeaux!'

The three men laughed in unison, laughter helping to release the tension held in the air.

'There is plenty more,' said Robert and, as he got up to fetch his bottler, he gave John a look, which said, *we have nothing to lose.*

In time, John had come to see Adelbert's proposition as insurance that kept him on the path of a good father and husband. So, as a provider for his family, he was urged toward creating deeper, more meaningful networks with traders overseas, traders he did not share a language with but with whom he felt bound through ritual, and through trust.

***

John Graves' cough had worsened so that he must to sleep in an upright position, his wife holding his hand as he waited for the sweet sound of sleep's little tiptoes. His physician, Dr Montgomery, had fetched a new drug named laudanum up from London for the specific purpose of easing John's cough. For a few nights, the concoction had helped. Soon after, however, the fear of his dreams began to outweigh the benefit of a throat that no longer tickled. And John's dreams were akin to seeing his day-to-day set upon a stage, the cast his family and friends, except these characters seemed exaggerated, sinister, even grotesque. John would wake from these cloying enactments of his daily life, sweating and panting. Eventually, he was thankful for the foresight that helped him realise laudanum may very well be helping his body but was, at the same time, destroying his mind, which John treasured dearly. He cherished his peculiar prowess to discern opportunity. He loved the way he imagined his mind divided into drawers, as with the apothecary's case, and into each he poured an area of life that would at some point require attention: his business drawer, his wife, his daughters, his friends, the broader community of Kingston upon Hull, drawers… and into each he would siphon equal and undivided attention. These compartments of his consciousness he turned to understanding and fixing problems, tending to the philanthropy required of him and, if there was a drawer spare from time to time for his own indulgence, it would be given to good food and plentiful wine, without which his life, he thought, would be half-lived. Most of all, John felt tethered to the Society's enactment of ritual and the power held here. Without this particular drawer, he sincerely doubted whether any other would exist. It had brought more joy than attending church. And despite being careful to keep such understanding from his wife, he feared the loss of the stone's power and Mercury's overarching protection, dreading it almost daily.

Yet following the Society's monthly meetings, John's cough would become unbearable, his breathing effortful to the point of terror.

'You must seek an elixir to cure,' Robert had told him. 'Perhaps we should consider meeting elsewhere? Out of town, perhaps?'

The mould that sprung from the cellar's leaking brickwork had spread along the west end, so that much of the floor and walls were consumed by a thick green and black slime, like a poisonous river that threatened to engulf the house. To even look at it caused John to cough. Of equal concern, however, was the worry his brother Thomas may yet show himself to be a loose cannon.

***

Saturday night was Thomas Graves' most favoured night of the week. His wife, Meg, visited her elderly mother on the other side of town with some food she had prepared, leaving him free to head to Ye Olde White Harte Inn. He liked this place, not a formal inn as such, more a house run like a tavern and with board and lodging above.

John, the landlord of the establishment like his father before him, liked to tell people the plotting against King Charles took place there. Thomas thought he spread such elaborations in order to charge extra for his ale. The landlord was a good-humoured man and his was a comfortable place, with roaring fires and good, honest congenial company. These were men who worked hard for a crust, who bore honest sweat, being far removed from the men who relied on stones and magic. These were men who prayed ardently in church and trusted God with their pleas; the kind of people that Thomas preferred. If the truth be told, they were thankfully not liquor-fearing men, for liquor Thomas did welcome after a hard week set to work in the Trinity burial yard.

'Cold or warm, it all hath the same effect on my head,' said Thomas, sitting down and removing his hat. 'Greetings, men.'

'Greetings!' replied the six other men gathered around at a table too small for the number of tankards and elbows that it held.

'What's wrong with our landlord tonight, he looks down in the mouth?' asked Thomas.

'He just found out his lady love got tired of waiting to become Mrs John Goodman and wed a rich widower from York. I was just speaking about your brother John Graves,' said Michael Mead. 'He has bought a new cart, a handsome one at that. He is doing well, is he not?'

With his mind on the ale he was drinking, Thomas was barely aware he had uttered the words, 'Too well, to my mind,' as he wiped his mouth on the back of his cuff.

'What do you mean?' asked Alfred Brown.

Thomas looked Alfred in the eye. Alfred was a simple fellow, a baker, and a good friend. Each year he brought one of his geese over for Thomas for his birthday. He had not missed one in fifteen years.

'I mean, his ways in business are not God-fearing. I have spoken of this before, have I not?' asked Thomas.

'Aye, but I do not understand what is meant by it,' said Alfred.

Thomas shook his head. He picked up his tankard again and downed the remaining liquor with a loud gasp before the pewter hit the table. 'He and some other men of this town, they think... they think they can act as God.'

'They are more ambitious than we thought!'

The other men laughed too but Thomas banged his fist onto the board; his brother's ambition was a thorn in his side, one embedded deeply. It pained him to see these men taking this news with such ease. John's success was not so much the problem as much as his means of acquiring it.

But how his brother did rile him with his ambitions. He ate, slept, and breathed trade. *Trade, trade, trade* until Thomas would be forever known in Kingston upon Hull as John Graves' poorer brother.

'Tell me, Thomas, how does a man act as God?' asked the landlord.

Thomas felt his angst grow. He stared into the fire as the flames danced and lashed out into the inn as if with anger. When his whaling boat had sunk in icy seas, not far off the coast of Norway, he had seen this as a sign of God's displeasure. Once recovered, he had turned to Meg saying, 'Grave digging doth not require killing but is the means by which death can be shrouded with reverence. God's displeasure has resulted in my humble servitude, and I would rather surrender to his wishes than to serve human greed. Do you understand me, Meg? Please say that you do.'

'I understand very well,' Meg had replied, 'and as a good wife I will honour your decisions, husband.'

'Thank you, wife. Thank you.'

He thought about how his brother had lent him money for the boat so he could trade in whale oil and that had failed. And he was sure his brother enjoyed watching his failure, knowing that it would pull him into the Society, into the throng of Devil worshippers he had amassed. Eventually, Thomas had allowed himself to be reeled in only to get the measure of the group of men. It did not take long before he could see that they believed themselves more powerful than the congregation at Holy Trinity. They carried out their business as if they did not need God's permission to act. They felt empowered by their own force. To Thomas's mind, they acted like angels of Satan.

'He makes a secret society,' said Thomas.

'He does? What kind?' said Alfred, eyes dancing as he sipped his ale.

'One that gathers in his basement on High Street once a month.'

'Are we talking in particulars here?' asked Michael.

'Particulars? What fancy speak! They meet in a basement,' said Thomas, now warming to his audience who now sat and stared, wide-eyed. 'And in the basement, this man who believes he is as powerful as God takes a stone, a common stone, and pretends that it hath special powers.' He did not go as far as to mention his brother's name.

'Of what nature are these powers?' asked Mark Taylor.

'Powers that do prosper a man when he doth use a certain silver beaker and a stone.'

'How doth such command come from a stone? You jest with us,' laughed Mark Taylor.

'He believes in powers that doth transmute a stone and in so doing brings him all the trade and riches he needs. It is a magic of sorts. Full of terrible witchy sorcery.'

'Do you think we can bury bodies with that stone?' asked Alfred, smirking.

'I be serious, deathly serious,' said Thomas, colour rising into his cheeks. 'After the ceremony, ships will arrive from Rotterdam and from Norway, heaving their cargos into our harbour and likewise cargos leave on the boats do travel north to Norway or to the Baltic States or Netherlands or Portugal, and in turn the men of the Society do prosper greatly.'

'And what be wrong with that?' said Alfred.

Michael shot him a look. 'It is the means by which this comes about, Alfred. Thomas, have you been to one such meeting?'

'Aye.' Thomas took a sip of his drink. He did not need to prove anything to Alfred for he had seen what he had seen, and he knew what he knew.

'And was it a common meeting of men of trade?'

'No, it was not common at all. Men of trade do not worship false idols. They do not bow to Satan. They do not make incantations. No, not common at all!'

'Is not the means to be overlooked in favour of making a handsome profit?' persisted Alfred, his eyes now shining.

Thomas nodded. 'Aye, if a man is not in servitude to God but to himself.'

Alfred beamed. 'And that be wrong?'

'Aye! Naturally it is wrong!' Thomas clipped Alfred over the head with the back of his palm.

Alfred sipped his pint. 'I do not see belonging to such a society as being all bad and no good,' he said.

'Be quiet,' said the landlord, 'another jar for anyone? Does Thomas look like a man in need of your foolish remarks? We do not wish to anger God.'

It was Mark, the baker, who sat taller and nodded sombrely. 'But remember, only God takes revenge and that a good man turns the other cheek.'

Thomas stood up. He was going to need more than one tankard tonight. 'Well, I have turned and turned until I am spinning round in circles, and I be no more interested in spinning than in Devil worshipping. I carry my brother's secret no longer. As he soweth, so shall he reap.' Thomas stood for a moment watching the fires dance before him, a mirage of anger and heat. 'And if God shall wish me to be his humble servant in seeking revenge on his lost sheep then I shall surely rise to the challenge. Aye, more ale for me.'

And with an order for more ales, Thomas went in search of a serving wench, a wry smile upon his lips. It would take some time for his friends to clear their heads on the Sabbath, but come Monday they would recall what had been spoken about the secret society. He had not mentioned John Graves, for there was no need. Knowing that people knew of his secret society would be enough to frighten his brother. And Thomas would be glad when John was shaking in his boots. This was a God-fearing town and men that flaunted their blasphemy had no place within it.

***

'I heard from the baker's wife that Thomas talked in the tavern that you are involved in the Devil's work at your Society meetings,' Meg had reported, imposing a visit unannounced upon her brother-in-law. 'I cannot abide that, John. I cannot abide it at all that you do involve your brother, my husband.'

Meg's eyes were wide with fear. John had reassured her amid much choking and sweating but knew that Thomas spilling tales was a potent omen. In this one action, he had shown his lack of respect for the Society and his brother too. The secrecy of the Society had been imperative to its survival these past five years; wives were kept from unnecessary worry by its establishment. Women talked. All the Society's members knew this too well. Likewise, they knew that if the churchgoing residents of Kingston upon Hull were to discover that Society meetings were held under Mercury's watchful gaze, they would fall into disarray.

'If you play with the Devil, you must expect pain. As my grandmother always said, you cannot beat the Devil at his own games, John. Never!' At which point, Meg had burst into uncontrollable tears, leaving John in awkward silence, traversing a moment he was incapable of handling. He'd always been grateful for a wife not much given to tears.

He resisted all temptation to wrongly reassure; he could not bring himself to lie to a person in such a deep state of fear. So with calm and, he hoped, logic, he said, 'We are bound by certain customs. We still worship in church, as you do know, Meg. We still say our nightly prayers. We believe that we are watched over by our Lord.' He hoped it had lent itself to reassurance over deceit, and he waited to see the result of his trying.

'Of that I am glad, dear brother,' said Meg. 'I am thankful too.' She bowed her head.

'Tell Thomas to visit me at my workshop. I will ask him to join us again. There is much profit to be made when we unite. I am sure you could do with some extra money at home?'

'You would not believe how much, brother. But I do fear that the green-eyed monster hath taken hold of Thomas' soul for he doth see you in the guise of a devil not an angel.'

John tried to assess how he felt. Aside from the ubiquitous coughing and spluttering, he felt the familiar cloying presence of guilt, restricting his breathing still further. 'Tell Thomas I will be here at noon tomorrow,' he said, adding, with a hand to his sister-in-law's shoulder, 'and fear not, Meg. Thomas needs only open his heart to the notion of profit, and he will see that each member of our small Society is willing to help carry him toward better times.'

'Thank you, dear brother. I will reassure him. He has been spending too much time at the tavern of late. That be partly the difficulty.'

'I will speak to him tomorrow. Fear not, Meg. All will be well.'

Following Meg's departure, John coughed for a good ten minutes. All was clearly not well, neither in his body nor concerning Thomas' confession. Yet John had not become wealthy in trade by letting fear get the better of him. He would placate his brother. He would use money as bribery, if necessary, for if the town learned of his associations with false idols, it would surely mean difficulties and threaten his family's peace. The North Berwick witch trials had left fear in their wake and, so, if James VI of Scotland could accuse the 5th Earl of Bothwell of witchery, then there was little to prevent John from suffering a similar fate with only the late mayor of Kingston upon Hull as his grandfather to protect his reputation. When facing fear, people rarely spared you their sympathy; it ruled deftly and love, it might be said, struggled to conquer it. Love needed time and plenty of patience, whereas fear conquered swiftly. Even Mercury would perhaps be powerless in surviving such vigour. The Society relied upon the strengthening of bonds between traders. Fear, on the other hand, relied on witnesses being swept up in its wake, hoping to devour the discriminatory powers of those it encountered. Fear, John had often thought, turned men into animals for, without reason, man was always one step away from becoming some kind of barbarian. Thus, his own fears revolved around discovery, failure of his business and perhaps the wrath of his wife and friends. And every time he tried to quash his fears, forcing them into a smaller box within his brain, his cough grew steadily worse as if one were perhaps pointing attention toward the other. He would speak with Thomas tomorrow.

He sat at his desk, overlooking the courtyard. The sun emerged from behind a cloud and lit a scant puddle, making it gleam like a precious gemstone. It provided a moment of encouragement, as God invariably did during trials, if man took time to notice. Yes, John was sick to his back teeth of fear. Fear had no place in life when a man had power over his own sails. His being taken aback by the wind was only momentary, of that he was sure, for he had become both the ship and the wind of late. In the next moment, a splattering of raindrops pounded the window. John Graves looked down, keenly burying his head in his accounts.

At around three, his clerk, David Smithson, entered John's office and announced his brother was here to see him.

John started and almost fell from his chair, for there stood his brother, Thomas, wringing his cap between his hands, swaying so that his unsteadiness meant John did not at first notice the gash in his brother's thigh. Thomas' breeches were slashed, blood had darkened the cloth around the exposed skin and the wound itself appeared deep, wide, and still heavily bleeding.

'What hath you done to your leg?' John asked him.

'Devil's work,' said Thomas.

John tried to discern his approach. He looked outside at the falling rain. It looked dismal in the courtyard; the puddle had been startled out of stillness and the skies were an ominous grey. 'God and his angels cannot be blamed for every sin, brother. We must show accountability for our actions. How else does God test our worth on Earth?'

'Meaning?' Thomas was sneering and surveying John's office so that John had the sense he was looking for something to strike him with.

'Meaning, I cannot be blamed for all of your failings, Thomas.'

'Philip Carter did stab me in the leg, in the tavern. See!' he lifted his knee and pointed to the cut. 'Who do I blame for that? Myself? Nay! I blame your Society. While you reap profit, I reap pain.'

John stood up. Thomas flinched. John made his way to a cabinet where he kept cloth for cuts in case of accidents from the spinning wheels in his workshop. This protection he had learnt from the Worshipful Society of Drapers when he visited them in London in the mansion in which Thomas Cromwell himself once dwelled, at Austin Friars. John had since moved to the distribution of cloth as it was more profitable. Naturally, he was always thinking of ways to increase business and of late had begun importing Dutch or Flemish cloth, which was proving even more profitable. It seemed, oftentimes, forming a trading net across the Continent was simpler than handling the character of a brother always in the throes of arguing for his limitations.

'Here!' John offered him the cloth for the cut.

Thomas took a step back. 'I now know there is a price to pay if I do take from my brother. I chose to thus save myself and take naught.'

John shook his head. 'You turn down help and sacrifice too much,' he said. 'I do not understand your thinking, Thomas. I do not understand it at all.'

As John turned his back, he heard his brother spit. 'I can no longer drink in the tavern.'

John placed the cloth back in the cabinet. 'And that is my fault?'

'Aye.'

Before turning to face his brother, John saw a white dove pass before the window. The starkness of the wings against the threatening skies helped silence his thoughts. A distant church bell tolled. John looked towards Mercury's sprightly statue in the corner of his office. It had been given to him by

Adelbert on one of his many visits and its beauty and grace brought much-needed comfort. Of course, real protection was afforded by trading with fellow merchants overseas. It seemed the more money he made, the more respect he earned and the more money he continued to make. Why could his brother not share in his good fortune, knowing too that it was his for the taking if he so chose?

'Snowdrops flower in the spring,' said Thomas in a cool and foreign voice.

'I do not understand your meaning, brother?' said John, unable to shake the image of the dove from his thoughts.

Thomas closed his eyes and seemed about to fall asleep, but his lids sprung open again. 'For this is when the snowdrop is meant to flower. Just as wheat must be harvested in the autumn. People are talking about your business, John, calling it unnatural. They said that you have formed an alliance with the Devil to profit year upon year without failure.'

'They were offered the same opportunity yet turned it down.'

'For their souls are godly. That be why.'

'There is nothing that we enact that goes against the doctrines of the Bible, Thomas, as well you know.'

'False idols go against the Bible. This I do know.'

'It is no more harmful than father's statue of Saint Paul. Tell me, wherein lies the difference?'

Thomas spat again. 'You are so sick with Devil's work that you can no longer see Truth. Do you not see?'

John remembered to inhale deeply before pressing on. 'We are not animals, Thomas. God helps those that help themselves. God does not wish his flock to suffer. You must understand this much, at least? Is farming Devil's work for controlling Nature? In a similar vein, we find assurances against Nature in forming an allegiance with overseas merchants. That is all. And in so doing, we respect the god that they do.'

John stood motionless for some time after Thomas had left, watching the rain dart against the window. He felt himself to be staring into a chasm, his feet hanging over its edge. What hurt John most of all was that his intentions toward Thomas were pure: he had only ever wanted to help. When a father died unexpectedly, sons grew up quickly or were at least meant to. After Thomas had married, he had thought he might rise to his responsibilities alongside his wife, Meg. When, following the birth of his son, Thomas continued to drift like a feather caught on a current, John had pulled him into the Society, or tried to, and done so naturally with the intent of helping Thomas to profit. Whereas John's drive had been duty, Thomas' thoughts were consumed with ungodly darkness. Resentment towards his brother had built until it had imprisoned him. It was for this reason that John felt no guilt, yet he did feel numb. He had been taken advantage of. He had been mistaken for an idiot. And this did not rest well in his soul.

John ran a finger around his collar. The truth of the situation struck him like a blow: Thomas saw John as a threat to his freedom. Why had he not realised this sooner? True, he had been caught up with his business, with his family, too caught up to consider Thomas might intentionally be thwarting him. But now he saw the situation in this harsher light. Whereas his wife had attuned his thoughts to take pity on Thomas with each new venture his brother sabotaged, John saw that Thomas most likely sought pleasure from his actions. All that Thomas had cared about was turning down John's help in an ungrateful manner. If any person was caught up in Devil's work, it was Thomas, for his thoughts were as dark as a starless night. His mind was not familiar with practising good.

Moreover, it was attuned to hatred and jealousy and taking charity from whence he could find it. Yet holding this knowledge in his fist did not give way to power. There was really nothing John could do, except watch as Thomas continued to thwart him. He suspected that with the ale muddying his thinking further, Thomas would spout even more earnestly in the tavern about his brother's unseemly business dealings.

John listened to the loud ticking of the clock. His hand went instinctively to his wooden money chest. He turned the key and put it in his pocket. John watched the rain falling so heavily it obliterated the view of the yard and the earlier iridescent puddles were pierced as if by arrows. John shook his head and closed his eyes.

'*Mercurie adiuva me*,' he asked, calling on the god of trade's help, and as he waited for an answer, his lungs grew irritated as his body lurched forwards into a coughing fit, he felt powerless to control. 'Mercury, help me!' he cried as he slowly fell to his knees to pray, the rain lashing against the window. '*Help me.*'

***

'I fear I do not understand, husband. I heard it from Meg and the servant girl told me what she heard in the market.'

John Graves felt himself to be standing at the base of a great hill. He knew he had to climb it but knew that the reward for doing so would be nothing more than a long walk down to his humiliation; he did not much relish the prospect.

'We are taught by Adelbert that sometimes more is needed than the Lord's Prayer.'

Margaret's hands were upon her hips. Colour had risen in both cheeks.

'And you believed a man from foreign seas? You did not see fit to question him? Did not see fit to wonder what sin he was committing in the eyes of the Lord? We may no longer have a monarch as our leader, husband, but even so, even under Cromwell's watch, I did think better of you.'

Margaret's gripes were rare and thus, when they came, were extraordinarily painful, attacking not only John's values but also his soul. This was why men and women, for the most part, lived in different worlds. The worlds of work and home were best kept apart for a good reason, for when they came together in combat, it did more damage than two men coming together for the pleasure and pain of bare-knuckle boxing. Margaret was his light upon the shore, his guide; he would even go as far to say that she *was* the shore. So when he had injured her, unwittingly, her words felt as hefty as his shame; they fired against his chest as if musket-fire imbued with poisonous vengeance.

'And if you disgrace this family, your daughters…'

Margaret turned to face the window, fists clenched against her skirts.

'I would never want to cause injury to you, nor my girls.'

Margaret was silent and this frightened John more than her harsh words.

'Would you not agree we have profited these past few years?' he asked, his voice softly quivering, his wife's approval more relevant than any cargo safely shipped abroad.

Without turning to face him, Margaret replied, her voice deep, almost unearthly, 'You think that to profit against God is good. Do you know nothing of the Lord?'

John Graves considered that in that moment he knew very little about anything. If pressed by Adelbert as to whether his wife approved, which had happened once or twice, he would declare with genuine belief, 'My wife trusts that I have her and our daughters' best interest at heart. She is an understanding woman.' It was indeed the case, until Margaret was, well, not so understanding. In other words, John had been of the belief he'd been doing the right thing by all of them, including the merchants of Hull. Admittedly, at first, he had been wary of this god of trade, perhaps apparent in the omission of the Society's use of him to his wife. But over time, as with any sin committed continually enough, he'd grown accustomed to it. The novel had become commonplace. Mercury was no more a sin to the Society than the Philosopher's Stone or the tallow candles; he was just a necessary part of the procedure.

'The Lord has only blessed us with profit. Is this the sign of his disapproval I am meant to look for, dear wife?'

'Do not *dear wife* me. We have profited at the hand of

the Devil, husband. And mark my words, the Devil profits a sinner with the same hand he takes from him too.'

John sank into a chair. His body slumped forward as he rested his head in his hands. 'But we have profited for more than five years. Surely—'

'Surely he sees that your sins are great and wishes to punish with equal measure. Your time will come, Mr Graves. You must turn your prayers to God now if you do wish to prevent your retribution.'

'Is this on account of you fearing what Thomas will tell people, my good wife?'

Margaret's face seemed to swell with ill-suppressed anger. 'I said, do not *my good wife* me, Mr Graves! Your brother has a tongue as loose as the water pump handle. I cannot see how you thought it wise to let him privy to your secrets. Can you not see how foolish this was?'

At last John considered he had an understanding of the real problem here. 'So, it is my including Thomas that be the problem, not the Society or—'

'Don't you get all clever with your words, Mr Graves. You know that one worry is dependent on the other. A sin committed in secret does not any less a sin become. It's what a person does when imagining God is not watching that counts. Not only have you wronged God, but you have also wronged your brother and your wife. I now see that I was not wrong to pity your brother; he has had the misfortune to be caught up in your sins and for that I do truly pity him.'

Margaret left the room. John felt a shiver pass down his spine. Something in the way she'd moved, purposefully, driven by something greater than herself, told him this was not the end of it. Sure enough, a few moments later, Margaret's feet marched down the stairs and across the hall as the front door slammed with finality. John watched a blue tit land on the windowsill. It didn't appear to see him, but rather tapped its beak upon the glass with insistence. John felt the creature speak to him 'Hasten!' it seemed to say. 'Before it's too late.'

John buttoned his waistcoat and put on his coat and boots, angered when his fingers fumbled with the fastenings. He knew where his wife would firstly go and he ran straight up the incline to St Mary's, dispersing a children's game of Blind Man's Buff as he tore through Kingston upon Hull's cobbled lanes.

'You need not have followed me, John,' said Margaret, appearing to catch sight of him out of the corner of her eye. 'I do not wish to speak with you.'

John did not like the sound of her voice, did not like the strength present there; his wife's confident force directed towards his business thriving was one thing, having it directed against himself, quite another. He cleared his throat. 'When you have finished praying, come home and talk to me, Mrs Graves.'

'I disapprove of your behaviour, husband, as well you know by now. God doth not approve either. Leave me be.'

To John Graves' mind, his wife and God's approval amounted to much the same thing. Willingly, he had turned to a different deity for the growth and support of his business perhaps. He no longer felt any guilt concerning this. But, as for his wife's judgment, well, it was as if he were awaiting entry at Heaven's gates. Mercury did not seem to be a vengeful God, at least not thus far, but John could not say the same about his wife.

'Let me reason with you, Margaret. What has set this in motion?'

'What has set it in motion? Your brother hath set it so.'

'I can control Thomas, my love. You have nothing to fear, Margaret, come home and talk to me when you are finished with the Reverend.'

Margaret's head swung so fast it resembled a fox caught wide-mouthed amid the chickens. 'I will be going to church. To pray for your salvation.'

Margaret stared at him with an intensity to make a flower wither in its vase. No words were forthcoming. Though he may trade with some of the richest men on the Continent, as far afield as Flanders and Riga, when it came to it, his wife had always been the one in charge, the one steering the sails; without her, his success meant nothing.

'When will you be coming home?' he asked, plainly.

'I may not come home again. This is why I wish to speak to the Reverend, to understand whose sins are greatest in the eyes of the Lord; yours for worshipping false idols or mine for wanting to end my marriage.'

'End our marriage? My love, I have not set out to hurt you? You presume wrong of me. I love you and our daughters. We have a profitable business and the wolves have been kept at bay for years.'

Margaret looked down at her fumbling hands. 'I presume only to take guidance from the scriptures. To blame another is no excuse for wrongdoing. Now leave me be!'

John could do no more than to remain stationary. He

inhaled a lungful of air to feed his thoughts. If this was divine retribution for worship of a false idol, then at least he knew that God existed.

He turned back to his home. Behind him there rose the high, unearthly scream of a horse and a terrible clattering. Spinning, he saw a cart laden with straw, its horse rearing, as its narrow metal wheels ploughed into his wife. 'Out the way, old hag!' The driver cursed and swerved aside.

John watched, struck motionless as his wife crumpled to the ground where she lay unmoving, appearing to be cut in two. Blood began trickling in rivulets through the cobbles and down the incline.

'Margaret!' John heard his own voice scream as though from afar. He felt his legs buckle as he staggered towards her. But his wife did not move and would not again.

***

Coughing more than ever, John Graves entered his cellar, his knuckles white around a tallow candle. He hadn't been down here since before Margaret's death. He cast an eye about. A servant had deposited a sack of coal by the door. Otherwise, the chairs were still in the same position, arranged in a rough circle with his carver – his chair of authority as he had often jested – placed with its back towards the wall. Behind, a great river of black mildew continued to form as water dripped onto the flagstones, more so in the wake of so much rain. To think such a humble, stinking room had led to their success now seemed so improbable. Peculiar to think that here, in this room, enacting rituals and sharing troubles with old and trusted friends, he had come closer to God than he had in any church. In Latin they had chanted their incantations and either because of the somewhat exotic nature of men like Adelbert that visited or because this was a religion of sorts, but one under their control, they had fostered great faith in their actions. Amongst the chosen men, there were no doubting Thomases at their meetings. All believed in the work that they did. All had faith that it would, in time, bring success. And so it had. This was faith in its rawest, most pervasive form.

But then a doubting Thomas had arrived in perhaps its plainest form. Never had John expected his brother would be the instrument to destroy not just the Society, but potentially his business, and now his family too. Aye, it was always the least expected events that struck a man down, not the ones he considered often or regularly maintained defences against. The things he had been fighting to keep safe – his family, his trade – were of little import now; he had neglected his wife's wishes, his dead wife's wishes, and the remainder was rendered trivial. Of no import at all.

Women and their power of intuition was something men of trade should heed more often. How many times had Margaret warned, and how often had he ignored her? In time, it had been much the same with Thomas's wife. With Margaret he had been bent on saving his reputation over his family, for he had never imagined they might be in danger. On the contrary, they were profiting. Yet the pitiful truth was that though his wife had been killed in an accident, without the anger rushing through her veins, it would not have happened. This was a secret John knew he must carry to his own grave, for he could not bear his daughters to know of it. He had known, to the depths of his soul, his wife to be a clever yet cautious woman. Hence her concern over the way he invoked a pagan god to help him trade. But that morning it was evident she had gone all to pieces and when a woman did reach that state, as his father once relayed to him, there was no reasoning with her, only listening. But he had not listened.

That was the truth of it. He had thought business was not woman's work, other than to oftentimes keep an eye on his expenses. But as to how he managed his affairs, that was solely his decision. Did he not keep a roof over their heads and keep them safe and warm? Why oh why did he not heed his wife's warnings? Why had he remained rooted in stubbornness? For the sake of greed, that's why! Greed and his standing in the town, amid other men of trade.

He wiped a hand across his face, crossed the room and lit two rushlights on shelves towards the rear of the cellar. These were in stark contrast to the sconces and candelabrum above, which did light up the rooms in such a magnificent manner. Though more used to such brilliance, the men had not once complained about the dimness. They knew perhaps that light must come from darkness and that even a child in the womb was cast in darkness for the first few months of its life. And so it was as they grew their networks in secrecy abroad, forming mutually beneficial agreements. The monies earned had spoken for themselves. Their trade existed without judgement, and oftentimes without common language, but through ceremony and mutual understanding they had been united and, as such, leant heavily upon trust for trade's bed partner had to be trust. And in the background – John looked to the statue in the corner of the cellar – there was always Mercury, watching over them.

There was a knock on the door.

'Come,' said John, turning around.

Timonthy Lumn entered. John was glad to see his face first. His kind and intelligent eyes met his through the gloom.

'I am deeply sorry, my friend,' Timothy said.

John bowed his head, though tears were spent for today. 'I am glad to see you tonight,' he said.

'It is the very least that a friend can do at such times. Is it not? And am I right in thinking that our Society had something to do with Margaret's death?'

But it was too soon for him to be able to discuss his wife's death as if debating why a ship had sunk in the northern seas.

'I do not know,' he began before his voice cracked and he lapsed into grief-ridden sadness.

Timothy approached, placing a hand on John's shoulder. 'You did not seek to do evil, my friend. You must remember that.'

'Thank you,' said John, fearing his eyes might give insight into the stone, into what he now felt about their Society.

Timothy picked up the philosopher's stone, which they had used in their ceremonies as a vicar might use a Bible. He rubbed a thumb across its polished surface. 'We have no further use for this. Am I right?'

John sighed, closed his eyes and nodded.

'It is understandable, my friend,' said Timonthy Lumn. 'It has lately been used out of superstition only. We shall all understand.'

John did not agree but was in no mood for argument. If religion worked without tools, there would be no reason for churches nor Bibles.

'I would like to discuss my girls' future with you,' he said when John Minspeak and Robert Winton entered the cellar, boots scraping over the damp stone, and John's conversation was replaced by further condolences for his loss to which he had no reasonable answer other than to express what felt like misplaced gratitude.

'I am given the impression,' said Timonthy Lumn to the other two who had gathered either side of his scholarly friend, 'that John doth not wish to further meet here.'

John once more bowed his head.

'Then we are in agreement,' said Robert Winton, looking around.

'Aye,' said John Minspeak, his face grave and his brows furrowed with concern. 'We will do what we can to ensure the success of your family.'

John looked up. It was no replacement for his wife, but he sought some comfort in the presence of these true and faithful friends. 'Thank you, gentlemen,' he managed. 'I do fear that we must halt all future meetings, for now we know word has spread about our meetings and our rituals.'

'I assume you speak about your brother?' said Robert Winton.

'Aye, you all know what he did and I wish—'

'Save your reasoning!' said John Minspeak. 'We do not

require explanation. We know that your brother's tongue becomes loose with ale. We know that you have done your best to include him in trades in the past and that he did rile against your efforts. Dear friend, we do respect your wishes as your humble devoted friends. I have only of late spoken to Robert about how our nets are not as they originally were – of fine spider's web, prone to breaking if not properly tended to – but through our relationships with societies across the seas, societies much like our own, these nets have been strengthened to resemble that of iron and we do believe they will be in place now for our lives and our children's lives to come. It is to you we are indebted, and it is to you that we now bow at your wishes. From this day, our Society will be disbanded. If anyone should speak of it, we will claim no knowledge. Is that right, gentlemen?'

'Aye,' echoed the other two men.

'We thank you for all that you did encourage in our business,' John Minspeak continued, 'but we understand that your brother has become a danger and we shall do what we can not to rile him further. We shall take whatever means necessary to ensure this doth not happen.'

John bowed his head, grateful for such loyalty. 'I do believe you are right in your thoughts concerning trade. As to my brother, I feel there is perhaps more harm to come and cannot manage to shift such thoughts. But this is something more of import that I wish to discuss further with you tonight.'

'Pray, continue,' said Robert Winton.

John looked to the stone floor. He noticed that the men's boots were wet, but he didn't comment. He could hardly believe that many a meeting would begin with discussions about the weather, about the seas. Now, such speak seemed hollow. Empty. All he wished for now was for his daughters' lives to be happy and safe.

John cleared his throat. 'I fear that this cough I have lived with for many years may get the better of me one day.'

'You are speaking from a low place,' said Timothy Lumn. 'When your grief passes, however long that may take, you will see the world with renewed eyes. Of that I do promise.'

John pulled a flat-lipped smile, acknowledging his friend's widowerhood these three years past. 'Thank you, Tim. But it does still concern that my daughters, who are clever girls, might not be cared for in the way my wife would have wished. Aside from worldly goods, I would like to leave them something more in my will.'

'These are heavy thoughts, dear friend,' said Robert Winton, patting his back, 'save them for another day when, for you, the world is cast a different shade.'

John shook his head with vigour. 'Nay, Robert, I cannot. I must be sure of one thing in this life and if that be the knowledge that I may name you as testamentary tutors in my absence, if God wills it, I swear it would be enough for my head to meet with my pillow at night and for sleep to come. I know that is what Margaret would have wished. I failed her in this life. But I would, God willing, like to meet her needs in rest. What do you say?'

The three men did not speak for a moment and John sensed they were getting a measure of his meaning.

'You would like us to tutor your girls in subjects that

would be of benefit to them?' asked Timothy Lumn, the cleverest of his friends.

'Aye, so that they might live good and proper lives.'

'And continue your family's good name?' added John Minspeak.

In truth, John was not concerned with his name as he was not sure he had one anymore. The safety of his daughters' future was of utmost import now. 'I would like it if you, Timothy, you, John and Robert too could enact this task for my daughters.'

Timothy's gaze sought the other two men and then he spoke. 'It would be our honour dear friend.'

John bowed his head at each man in turn. He took the stone from the beaker. 'Thank you. Please take this.' He held out the stone. 'I have no further need for it.'

It was Robert that took it. 'What shall we do with it?'

John stood up. He had not slept in days but now that he had heard his friends' affirmations, he thought it might now be possible. 'I do not care what happens to it,' he said, waving a hand. 'Give it to my brother. God knows he could do with the help.' No-one said a word, nor thought he meant it.

With that, he took the caduceus and the statue of Mercury, unlocked the wooden chest, and placed them on top of the cloaks they had worn during the ceremony, then locked it again and pocketed the key. 'The chest must be disposed of.'

He took the beaker and didn't argue when Robert said, 'Keep the stone with it, it must not go to Thomas, he does not deserve it. The stone and the beaker must stay together.'

John opened the cellar door, managing to make eye contact with each of his old friends as they now stood shoulder to shoulder watching him, before following him out. 'I have been humbled by your friendship tonight, gentlemen. I do give praise and gratitude for that. Take comfort in the knowledge that what we have done for this town can never be undone, despite how much it has undone me. I bid you all goodnight.'

***

A numbness had settled in John Graves' bones, drawn, he knew, from the cold grey earth in which he had buried his wife. He felt it still some weeks later as he sat at his desk in his office, adjacent to his warehouse, set back from High Street. It had been pouring solidly for two days; great sheets of unrelenting rain. If John were to cast his eyes up at the great mass of grey cloud above, it was akin to peering into the recesses of his battered and bruised heart. The gloom suffocated, muted his grief and obscured any hope of light entering again. This hazy, shrouded greyness was met in John's disbelief at Margaret's passing, but on this subject, his thoughts could presently travel no further. Oh, what cruel fate had God bestowed upon him? What harsh hand had left him a widower, with three daughters and at a time when they were much in need of a mother? It was indeed the worst kind of death imaginable for a husband. Hadn't Margaret told him too often, 'To make up with a loved one is a necessary duty before sleep.' But such things seemed only important to those earnestly living. Emphasis on trade, on profit, had seemed far more necessary and of greater import. Now that Margaret was gone, he could see all that was meaningless in her absence. His profit was the mere froth to the ocean that had been his wife.

On the desk before him sat a copy of his will. There were amendments to make in the shadow of Margaret's absence. It was he who must now secure his daughters' futures, and this would take more than silver, more than money. In her absence, he would continue his daughters' education for it had been a priority for his wife and thus a thing he wished to honour in her absence. He was grateful for his closest friends, sound minds all. Timothy Lumn had been a fine scholar and both John Minspeak and Robert Winton were learned, wise men, and all successful men of trade to act as testamentary tutors. This should enable his daughters, in turn, to marry well and to do their part in keeping Kingston upon Hull a profitable town. He would to each, in turn, leave silver plate that they could do with as they saw fit. The two salts, especially the silver gilt piece, were more remarkable than the *beere bowle*. He would leave a salt each to Elizabeth and Hannah, and to Mary he would leave his *beere bowle* and some extra cash besides as the *beere bowle* was much smaller and less valuable.

He scratched his head. What, he wondered, ought he to do about his brother, Thomas? He had it confirmed now that Thomas had ranted black words about him and his practices in the tavern. John had tried on too many occasions to draw Thomas into the Society so that he may profit, as he and his friends had handsomely over time and, in truth, it had been an attempt to silence him too. Yet his brother preferred to drink rather than think and this had been his overriding problem. He preferred to throw up his hands at the slightest inconvenience, demand that God's will was at play and as a good Christian he was guaranteed salvation. But John had enough experience of life to know well that God helped those who helped themselves. It was following this that a person could see God's compassionate hand in action. If anything, John thought that God rewarded men for bravery, not for turning from their fears, but for remaining defiant in action. Once he had begun trading cloth overseas, he felt grace begin to carry him so that his profit did not increase only marginally but doubled and trebled. He had bought number forty High Street with warehouses. Business, he had mastered, marriage – alas – he had not. The Society he had formed in his cellar, with their ritual, may have shifted his attention from worshipping God, to respecting and forming deep alliances with overseas merchants. He had little faith that Thomas would do the same. As far as his brother was concerned, they were mere Devil worshippers. John, however, knew that whatever men did not understand they more oft than not feared. He settled upon a figure of ten pounds. It was, perhaps, more than Thomas deserved.

With this done, John Graves sat back in his seat. He took out a smoking pipe and filled it with tobacco from the West Indies. He had a good supplier and had found that smoking momentarily eased his cloud-ridden head. The task of writing his will had temporarily distracted him from the chilling sadness that spread outwards from his chest like a black candle's flame, creating undue heaviness in his limbs. But there was still work to do. He must somehow find the resolve to carry on for, if he did not, there was no telling what might happen to the families of men like Lumn, Minspeak and Winton or his own. His brother, Thomas, was now a millstone. There was nothing like a tragedy to spur men into action, but if only his body would comply with his wishes.

John sat for several more minutes, staring out at the water now gathering over the cobbles. Being only twelve yards above sea level, Hull was too vulnerable to flooding. As John stared, after a time, as if in equal measure to the puddles gathering beyond the window, he felt the clouds in his heart burst. As he sat at his desk, he closed his eyes, rested his head in his hands and wept.

Sometime later, John picked up his favourite goose feather quill and penned letters to his friends Timothy, John and Robert inviting them to meet on Sunday 19th December to witness his signature. Afterwards, he pulled himself out of his chair, his limbs heavy, his head sore, summoned his maid and handed her the letters for the post boy. As he spoke with authority, he thought, *life somehow must continue.* But it did not, for not long after he was dead.

PART THREE

Accepting the present

2015

Months had passed and Clare felt she was spending too much time staring at the enigmatic initials. Both sets, on beaker and dram, appeared identical, as though they had been made by the same hand. It took her breath away and even the beaker itself seemed to whisper, '*There's more to this, there's more…*'

Later that day, Clare was watching the autumn gales sweeping leaves from the tree boughs in her garden when her mobile rang. She answered and wished she had drunk her coffee first. The voice was civil, though it was not one she was overly pleased to hear.

'This is Gordon calling from the museum.'

'Oh, hello,' Clare said, her tone bridled with caution. Gordon had written to declare that the issue of ownership had been thoroughly investigated and the dram cup did, indeed, belong to the museum. There was no mention of how the investigation had arrived at this conclusion nor who had been involved in the discussion, though she had her suspicions. She hadn't yet replied to the email so it was inevitable there would be a phone call. She had known, of course, the day would eventually come when it had to be returned. Somehow, in her mind, it was as if she had got the loss of Harry confused with the pot, and to let it go would mean another bereavement. At least, she mused, she had kept it for six months longer than she had thought she might.

'The museum would like the piece back. Would you courier it to us?' was the gist of the conversation. This was it; the discussions were over, and it was now between the museum and Clare to sort it out. She felt somewhat bereft already, but it had awoken in her an even stronger desire to find answers. Who had commissioned the taster and why? She hadn't the foggiest idea where to begin.

'I really don't think it should be couriered,' she said, at length. 'I think you ought to come to London and collect it.'

'If you think that is best, we'll find a date that suits both of us.'

Clare felt palpable relief. 'Considering its history, I think that might be wise.'

She hung up feeling oddly victorious. The taster was theirs and they could have it, but not its story. And there was a story. And it would be *hers*.

Almost immediately, she telephoned Malcolm.

'They want it back,' she said, her voice flat. 'The museum, that is.'

'Clare. I understand. I will issue a refund immediately. Frankly, I'm relieved it's going back to the rightful owner.'

'I think I am too. The whole business was an odd thing to have happened, Malcolm.'

'If you can see it that way, I'll look at it that way too and I appreciate what you've done, Clare. You didn't have to, and I'm incredibly grateful.'

'I have been grateful to you many times in the past, Malcolm. A favour begets a favour.'

'Thank you, Clare.' The buoyancy in his voice did not reflect how Malcolm felt. He was pleased the piece was being returned, but did not feel he was off the hook. He wondered how many questions had been asked of Clare as to where she had got it from and from whom. There was, he knew, absolutely nothing he could do about it but wait and see what, if anything, developed.

***

Before returning the piece of silver, Clare desperately wanted to unravel the mystery of the strange portrayal of Mercury. To better understand the image, Clare needed to break it down into component parts and examine them separately to make sense of it all. The figure was clearly Mercury or, alternatively, Hermes in Greek mythology – the two were, essentially, interchangeable. A herald's wand in his left hand was his attribute, a caduceus. In Clare's understanding, in both Greek and Roman mythology, Mercury was the messenger god, the trickster and the thief. In Roman mythology he was, in addition, the god of commerce and protector of merchants, especially those dealing in grain. The caduceus should not be confused with the Rod of Asclepius, so named after Asclepius, son of Apollo: the god of healing, truth and prophecy, a title Clare found mildly reassuring. The Rod of Asclepius had only one snake wrapped around its staff (seen, for example, in the symbol for the World Health Organization), whereas the caduceus of Mercury or Hermes had two intertwined snakes around a wand topped by wings. To Clare's mind, however, the most puzzling aspect of the image was a pair of two-headed, seated creatures, facing right, beneath Mercury, their outstretched hands almost touching and appearing to hold a feather each, upon which the god balanced on one foot, his other foot tucked behind his calf. What could the image have meant to Barachin or to his customer? Clare turned the taster in her hands to study the initials on the opposite side: M.A.R. Unlike the image of Mercury, Clare considered these initials to be clearly Victorian and of no real interest. There were no systemised records of owners and, anyhow, this addition was not contemporaneous to the cup.

After looking through her collection of reference books and coming up with little of use, Clare decided she must visit a local library. Of course, she needed a better way of phrasing it than to ask for references to two-headed creatures. Further *surfing* suggested *polycephaly* was the correct term for the two-headed state, one that existed in animals, humans and mythology. Yes, animals and mythology sounded promising.

Of the two libraries within walking distance, Clare set off for the one she knew had a larger reference section, glad for the bright sunshine. She felt a small thrill of anticipation hanging in the crispness of the morning. As she walked, she pondered how to narrow the field of research to one more specific. If she was going to engage in research, she needed to be methodical about it.

The library was quiet as libraries were wont to be and, seeking guidance from a librarian, Clare was directed towards the *Dictionary of Mythological Imagery* and, before long, came across the two-headed Orthus, brother of Cerberus. Cerberus, with his three heads, guarded the Gates of Hell to ensure no soul escaped, whereas his brother Orthus, represented as a twin-headed dog, guarded Geryon's cattle. Clare studied the image for a moment before dismissing it. Her figures were far more simian than canine, or possibly humanoid. Further reading taught her that these monkeys may represent cunning; the early meaning of cunning meant possessing erudition or skill. One certainly needed a degree of skill to be a successful trader. Much later, however, the monkeys would represent deceit. But how much of this was relevant in the context of her little cup? She worried she may get forever lost down a rabbit hole.

She set about looking up Hermes, learning that he was the founder of alchemy. She let the concept swirl around her brain. Alchemy seemed such a romantic, though improbable concept, signifying the impossible. A bit like the task she had set herself, Clare thought. She moved on from Hermes to *polycephalus* and came across a number of drawings of twin-headed humans. She also came across a long section on Hermetic *tresmegistus*; too long a word for Scrabble but could be useful for the morning crossword. She found herself none the wiser about its meaning as she read on: Hermes Trismegistus, the father of alchemy, the thrice-great god. Thrice great as king, philosopher and priest and held three parts of the wisdom of the whole world. Further information followed regarding the philosopher's stone and *prima materia*. Clare continued reading and, though *au fait* with these two words, she really did not have much of a handle on what they meant in practice. Alchemy seemed such an esoteric subject. No doubt it would take years of study to understand it and the theories surrounding it. Clare didn't have years. She wasn't sure when Gordon was going to turn up and whisk away her taster, but she doubted he'd wait long. One thing was certain, however; none of the images in front of her showed anything remotely resembling Mercury, nor was there a caduceus in sight. Was it likely then that the strangely rendered god on her cup was anything to do with alchemy? At that moment, she felt the loss of Harry keenly with his knowledge of the classics. He may have been able to shed some light on the matter, or even explain it in terms she would have been able to understand.

She took the photograph of her taster from her handbag and studied it, as if the mere act of doing so would yield further answers. She willed it to reveal its meaning to her. She pressed on for the next hour and a half, trying to make sense of concepts she had, hitherto, not come across, and tried to absorb the information. Her head began to throb. Reluctantly, she called it a day, satisfying herself that she had plenty to digest, though how much was relevant, she couldn't yet be sure.

It turned out to be an equally pleasant afternoon. With the image of Mercury still in her thoughts, Clare set off for home; unanswered questions milling about her mind. *Why did the figure look old? Why was the god so roughly drawn? Where else could she look for answers?* Perhaps it meant nothing at all. Halfway back home, a memory drifted through her head of a guided tour around the City a few years ago. Standing in front of the huge metal door at the entrance to the Bank of England, she remembered the guide had said something about Mercury. In the absence of anything better to do in the sunshine, it seemed a good idea to take another look.

Nowhere in London was difficult to get to by public transport and Clare headed east on the underground. She emerged at Bank Station on Threadneedle Street where the colossal majesty of the bank loomed above. With some difficulty, she pushed her way through the throngs of pedestrians to get a clearer view of the doors. Though she politely asked, the two security guards flanking the door were not amenable to standing to one side to allow a clearer view, let alone permitting her to take a photograph. Despite this, she was able to note that the giant caduceus on the left-hand door was topped with a galleon, while the one on the right-hand side was adorned with a symbol of electricity. Presumably, the galleon spoke of explorers and commerce, the movers and shakers of an earlier age, while the modern symbol spoke of the new age of electricity and gave insight into its importance in powering the world; both activities that needed the backing of the bank.

Opposite the Old Lady of Threadneedle Street (the colloquial nickname for the bank that Clare had always rather liked) lay the Royal Exchange, whose foundation stone was laid in 1842 by Prince Albert. The central figure on the pediment of the Exchange was the personification of Commerce. In her left hand she held the charter of commerce and in her right a rudder, and at her feet a cornucopia. Of even more interest to Clare were the caducei on either side of her. If that wasn't enough of a sign to imply its association with trade, the rest of the pediment was filled with figures celebrating commercial activity across the known world.

So, Mercury and his caduceus were linked with trade and money – that much Clare could confirm. But the image of Mercury on her cup was so bizarre; it remained unexplained. If it had any meaning at all, she supposed its owner must have had involvement in commerce. But that was as much as could be assumed. Taking the stairs down to Bank, Clare thought her Mercury looked, in all honesty, as if he might be more at home enjoying an orgy with Bacchus.

***

The room was the polar opposite of Andrew's office space in the V&A where Clare had listened to that first phone call to Hull. The long boardroom was impressive, with ceiling-high windows, heavy drapes and an ornately mounted chandelier hanging low over the mahogany table. Across the table, Clare faced Gordon, who was accompanied by an associate. Clare greeted both of them. Gordon was as, she had imagined him to be, several decades younger than she was, and serious about his work. Also present was Andrew, who gave Clare a tentative smile and introduced her to the head of regional museums who sat beside him.

After pleasantries were exchanged and refreshments served, Clare was tempted to ask what steps had been taken to establish ownership, but decided against it. She felt certain she would not be told anything significant, and it didn't really matter anyway. The decision had been taken. Still, she thought she should say something. Her taster was safely stowed in an anti-tarnish bag in her handbag. Before producing it, she said, 'I had wanted to unravel the meaning of the image and, if possible, the name of the owner who probably commissioned it. Given there is only a set of initials but no family crest or coat of arms, it seems unlikely that the identity will ever be discovered.' How she wished she had something concrete to say to them.

Clare took out the taster and set it before her, resting it on its protective cloth. *Her beautiful taster.* Clare felt absurdly sad, as if she was giving up one of her children. The thought that kept her going was that, more than ever, she wished to solve the enigma.

Clare said, 'It was stolen, it has to go back.' She pushed the taster toward Gordon. Then she reached into her handbag again and brought out the beaker. 'And there's also this piece in my collection. It seems a strange coincidence that it has the same initials and was also made in Hull.' There was a short discussion on date and the maker but nobody seemed that interested in the beaker.

All eyes were focussed on the dram cup. Gordon got up, walked around the table and extended his hand. Clare smiled and took it. She felt an incredible sense of satisfaction, which she hadn't expected; *the piece was going home to where it belonged.* 'Thank you,' he said, and Clare could hear genuine appreciation. He placed it before her again, one last time. Clare picked it up. *Goodbye, old man.* She ran her finger over the engraving of Mercury. *Lead me to your owner.* She rewrapped the taster and handed it to Gordon saying, 'I would really like to find out who originally owned it. It may have been the same person who owned my beaker. It might be possible, because people of substance always leave a footprint.'

The head of regional museums smiled. 'And usually, only the archivists know where they are.'

Clare left the museum feeling less lost than she might have done. She had a clue: *archivist*. Already her mind was on what she felt she had to do next. The quest to find the owner should start in earnest in Hull. Despite being without the taster, she felt lighter and it lifted her spirits. Yes, lighter, almost unburdened. But within her burned an insatiable desire, a hunger almost, to understand why two pieces of Hull silver with identical initials had made their way into her collection, however briefly. Now that she considered it, it was something of a miracle. It had to mean something. As if to cement the moment, a streak of blue flashed before her eyes as a man wearing a pair of hyacinth macaws, one on each shoulder, walked swiftly passed. She smiled, catching a glimpse of a brighter future in the birds' shining eyes.

***

Clare looked down at her list. She felt a little like an imposter, unfamiliar as she was with research. At the top of the page, she had written: *British Library and the Hull History Centre*. Not much of a list but it was still a start. Further internet searches suggested the library at Goldsmiths' Hall and, following a brief phone call to confirm it was open to the public, she set off. Every journey starts with one small step and Clare's first step was, inevitably, towards the underground.

The Worshipful Company of Goldsmiths was situated on the corner of Foster Lane and Gresham Street and possessed the charm of an urban palazzo. The library on the first floor was of interest to Clare. It housed over 15,000 images on subjects relating to precious metalwork, jewellery, hallmarking and the Goldsmiths' Company itself. She entered the building with a bounce in her stride which, she suspected, had more to do with being close to a wealth of information on silverware rather than the anticipation she might find something.

The reading room was a comfortable, high-ceilinged room lined with books, with a large, dark, wood table in the centre. The librarian brought out a selection of books and documents which, to a greater or lesser degree, had information on silver in Hull during the seventeenth century. By the end of the afternoon, she had found a useful title that provided images of dram cups and, most thrillingly, a book on Trinity House which mentioned the mysterious initials, J.G, as having held office during the era concerned. What was more, she now had a name: John Graves,1686. She hastily scribbled *Trinity House* and *John Graves* on her list for further investigation.

Another volume, *Old Country Silver* by Margaret Holland, shed still further light. It showed a picture of Clare's purchase, describing it as "very rare, and not really a tumbler, by Abraham Barachim, Hull c1685". It mentioned too, "a most unusual bleeding bowl, sold in London in 1969… and described as 'naïvely' engraved. The word is apt, but the ambitious picture serves only to add interest to a most unusual piece". Clare pursed her lips. She was vindicated at last. The National Art Collection Fund entry had listed the date as 1710–1725. She found herself battling a peculiar mixture of smugness and bemusement. She had bought a small, unimportant piece of silver at a fair, where countless pairs of feet had walked past it, and it had been paraded in front of an equal number of eyes belonging to dealers, the vetting committee, and knowledgeable collectors, yet she was the only one who thought it worth having. It *was* an important piece. It was mentioned in literature.

That evening at home, Clare decided her afternoon had been very satisfactory. She knew more than she had that morning and had unveiled more avenues to explore. It seemed the mystery would reveal itself to her piecemeal.

***

Kingston upon Hull was a place Clare had neither the curiosity nor reason to visit until now.

But all I have are the shared initials of the owner and the idea they have been made forty years apart, she berated herself as she watered her plants. *Is Amber right, do I have so little to occupy my mind these days?*

She tweaked away dead leaves of the ruffled fan palm and dusted off the larger, greener ones, making a mental note to buy compost. Yes, her spirits were at least lifting at the prospect of doing something different. And what did it really matter if the mission was a foolish one? There was, after all, nobody here, in her home, to laugh at her exploits. Nobody at all. At the very least she would get to see her little dram cup again. She felt the tingling of excitement in her chest, something she had not experienced for a long while.

Clare wandered to the kitchen. Staring out of the window, she made a cup of coffee in Harry's old mug, wandered into the study and sat down at Harry's desk to research Hull. *Who would have thought an adventure would present itself at this juncture in my life?* She tapped enthusiastically at the keyboard. *And what if I do find the answers I'm looking for? What if!* Enlivened by the prospect, her research felt somehow ordained, as if the past was persistently whispering in her ear, '*Keep going, Clare, there is something to learn here…keep going…*'

The first internet search, however, was somewhat dispiriting: Hull, it transpired, was the one of the most heavily bombed cities in the UK during the war. The Hull Blitz had resulted in over one thousand deaths and German bombs had destroyed, to the point of ruin, some twenty-seven churches, fourteen schools and hospitals, forty-two pubs and damaged almost one hundred thousand houses. In 2003, Hull earned the unfortunate title of Britain's Crappiest Town. Clare closed her eyes and sighed but kept tapping away. She eventually broke through the fog when she read that Hull was being readied to become the UK's City of Culture for 2017 and this conjured up images of an enormous building site; developers indiscriminately, perhaps even callously, paving over the past.

She looked up at the window. *Oh, was this foolish thinking?* She could almost hear Amber assuring her that it was. She spotted a large bird, a bird of prey, a kite or buzzard, circling high above her garden against a backdrop of clear blue skies. She paused to admire its poise and its grace, her thoughts seemingly hovering with the bird's flight.

'Right, I'm going to do this,' she said aloud, 'I really have nothing to lose.'

Following her decision, it was easy to find accommodation at the Royal Station Hotel, adjacent to Hull's mainline station, and to book a train ticket, reasoning that one night would be long enough. There, it was done; in two days' time, she would be on her way to Hull.

Early on Tuesday morning, but late enough to avoid the commuters, Clare took her seat on the train at King's Cross. The weather was set to be good for the next two days, though Clare had long since learned to travel equipped for many seasons: umbrella, sensible shoes, sunglasses. Green and brown, the countryside spooled past, scattered with the grey and red of intermittent towns. When the train pulled into the Paragon Transport Interchange, Clare felt a thrill of anticipation. Who knew what she might find?

After passing through the ticket gates, she was surprised to see a larger-than-life statue of Philip Larkin. On closer inspection she noted it had been unveiled in 2010 and then remembered that Larkin had spent the last thirty years of his life in Hull. What had he called the place? Yes, that's it: *his lonely Northern daughter.*

Once inside the hotel, Clare mentioned the statue to the receptionist.

'He's not really seven feet tall,' the girl informed her.

'No, I didn't imagine he was,' said Clare, smiling.

'There's a Toad Trail around the town to honour him too.'

That's it, thought Clare, toads represented work and financial pressures and other internal conflicts to Larkin; creatures that forced poison into life.

'What sort of toads?' asked Clare, benignly, imagining with some amusement large, live creatures sat patiently at arranged locations.

'Giant, individually painted ones,' replied the girl.

It transpired that the hotel had a legitimate reason for its name: Queen Victoria had once stayed here, when visiting the town in 1854. Apparently, the hotel had installed a throne room, complete with a French-style gilt and cerise velvet throne, or so the friendly lady at the tourist information stall told her, the pride in her town apparent. Clare's hotel room, however, was simply decorated and sans throne, the key feature being its location.

'Where do you advise I start as a first-time visitor?' she asked.

'Why not start with Beverley Gate, or what remains of it? It was once the entrance to the city when it was still surrounded by its medieval walls. Would you be interested in a tour?'

'I suppose I could do,' said Clare.

'There's a lot of information to be gleaned about Hull that might not be immediately apparent. Sarah, my colleague, will be leading a guided tour in half an hour.' As luck would have it, no-one else turned up and it became a private guided tour.

It transpired that the old town was not large. All that remains of the medieval city walls are the foundations of Beverley Gate. A stripe of red paving stones on the roads indicated the path of the ancient wall. The entrance at Beverley Gate was, apparently, the site of the nine-hour standoff between a mounted Charles I, supported by three hundred of his troops on the outside of the locked gate, and Sir John Hotham, parliamentarian, on the inside of the gate.

'As you are on your own, would you like a further history lesson, or would you like to move on?'

'Not that I can remember what I must have been taught decades ago, but if you could just remind me why Hull was so important to the king.'

'Well, it was a very complicated period of history, but Hull was strategically important because it had an arsenal and a port that was its primary value. If you want to see anything else, we need to move on.'

'I would like to see as much as possible with an emphasis on the seventeenth century. I am trying to picture how it would have looked then,' said Clare, without explaining why.

'The bombing during the Second World War means there are very few buildings of that period, but I'll show you what there is.'

Though the ramparts along three sides of the city had all but gone by the end of the eighteenth century to accommodate the expanding town, there were four further gates to be found in the fortified walls: Mytton Gate, Hessle Gate, Posterngate and North Gate. A map of the period showed the surrounding fields, beyond the walls, dotted with windmills.

Clare quickly came to realise the depths of her own ignorance as she listened to Sarah talking. Hull had clearly, from the thirteenth century onwards, been a proud, independent city as well as an important trading port, evident in its solidity and flashes of austere grandeur, much of it being Victorian. Most of its wealth had been generated by the sea.

Sarah pointed out plenty of reminders of Queen Victoria's connection to the city; her statue stood before the Ferens Art Gallery and there was also a Queen Victoria Square and Queen's Gardens, built on what used to be Queen's Dock. To Clare's eyes, the most impressive of the many Victorian buildings, however, was the Maritime Museum, built on the edge of Prince's Dock as the New Dock House in 1881. However, it was Victorian and therefore built too late in history to bear relevance to her little taster.

'Unfortunately, though, the Cod War decimated the fishing industry in Hull,' said Sarah. 'It left many of Hull's families in a perilous state.'

'How did the town survive the damage to the fishing industry?' asked Clare.

'There were always other industries, such as engineering works, and in 1971 a massive roll-on roll-off container depot was built.'

The docks and marina had and were still undergoing major renovations, and The Deep had not long been built: an eye-catching and world-class aquarium, designed, she learnt from Sarah, by the architect Sir Terry Farrell and completed in 2001. It had taken only seventeen months to build and jutted, shark-like and thoroughly modern, across the wide expanse of the river. To the left of The Deep, some distance away, lay the Humber Bridge, the world's longest suspension bridge, built in 1981 to replace the old Victoria paddle steamers that would leave from the now disused Victoria Dock. Once, they had been a regular sight going back and forth across the river, ferrying passengers from Yorkshire to Lincolnshire, but now there were only cars, toy-like as they crossed between the two land masses.

'Yes, Hull's been through much,' conceded Sarah, though her expression brightened, 'but millions of pounds are going to be injected into restoring some of Hull's museums and buildings. In fact, we have been nominated as the UK's City of Culture for 2017. We're really delighted!'

Her excitement was palpable.

'I'm sure you are,' Clare replied.

'You must come again during the celebrations,' said Sarah.

'I shall,' said Clare with a smile

'I can take you to the Plotting Parlour on Silver Street if you're interested.'

'The Plotting Parlour?'

'It's a room at Ye Olde White Harte Inn where it used to be thought Sir John Hotham and his cronies plotted to keep the king out of Hull. It is now known it couldn't have happened there.'

'The style is Artisan Mannerist,' her guide continued as they walked, 'similar to the Wilberforce Museum where we'll head now. There's been a building on the site since 1550.'

'An extremely old inn,' said Clare.

'It has been an inn and private dwelling at different times.'

And must have been a lovely house, thought Clare, given that it would have been tucked away from the busy hustle and bustle.

Sarah gestured Clare inside and they passed by a group of regular punters seated around a table outside, through a heavy and low wooden door with beautiful brickwork and a round, latticed window above, and into a room with low ceilings and distorted beams, two bars gracing either end. Each section was separated by a hefty wooden staircase, and each equipped with substantial brick inglenook fireplaces, with seats either side and panelled walls. It almost seemed possible to hear the echo of thousands, perhaps millions, of conversations that had taken place in here over the centuries. It was utterly British and yet somehow stuck in both the unfamiliar and the familiar past, both iconic and yet oddly homely and comfortable.

Clare approached one of the fireplaces to read the inscription above the mantle: *Gather ye around the ancient hearth, and by its gladdening blaze, unto thankful bliss we will change our mirth with the thought of the olden days*, written in beautiful gold script. She suspected it was perhaps Victorian and her suspicions were quickly confirmed.

'Those tiles are late-nineteenth century blue-and-white Dutch delftware tiles showing landscapes, warriors on horseback and biblical scenes,' said her guide. 'They were made by the Dutch firm Ravestein in Utrecht. The fireplaces, sadly, are not original but Victorian.'

'Very interesting,' said Clare, her mind returning to Hull's former glory and to her little pot.

'But take a look at this,' said Sarah. Clare followed Sarah's finger to a row of tiles to the right-hand side of the fireplace.

'See how this tile is the wrong way up.'

'So it is,' said Clare, wondering its relevance.

'Some believe that it was a sign to the masons of the town.'

'Of what?' asked Clare.

'Again, it's only really a rumour, but it's believed that at one point they met here.' Clare felt a tingling along her spine, though wasn't sure precisely why.

Sarah smiled at her. 'Would you like to see the Plotting Parlour?'

'Very much so,' said Clare, welcoming what might become a strand to her research. Then, just as she set her foot on the first stair of what was quite a magnificent staircase, something behind the bar in the far room caught her eye.

'Of what significance is that skull?' she asked.

'It depends,' said Sarah in a spritely voice as she climbed the stairs.

'On what?'

'On whom you believe. Some say the landlord murdered his servant girl. I've also heard it said the skull was not Caucasian but Asian. The crack is thought to have been made by a heavy object which would have ended her life, if it was a girl. It's unlikely the truth of it will ever be known.'

'But surely they must know the sex,' she said; how horrible to be dead and not even have your sex remembered.

'You would have thought so, but local legend and fact seem to fuse in this place,' said Sarah. 'It's a popular debate these days!'

The Plotting Parlour, likewise, seemed to possess a static air of mystery, as if even the dust mites suspended in the sunlight streaming through the lattice windows, knew something that the visitors didn't. On its panelled walls, which contained secret cupboards, were paintings of men, made out to resemble seventeenth-century plotters.

'Don't take them too seriously,' said Sarah. 'They're modern-day paintings of some of the staff and regulars.'

Clare laughed. 'Yes, their wigs do look a little peculiar.'

'Whilst the plotting to keep out Charles I didn't happen in here, the plotting for Town Taking Day did.'

Clare's eyes widened.

'Another complicated story,' Sarah said, catching her look, 'but in a nutshell, there was a 1688 plot to overthrow the Catholic governor put in by James II following the arrival of William of Orange. The plot did not succeed, and the governor was removed. I'll tell you a story about it when we get to Holy Trinity Church.'

Clare took a deep breath; what heavy conversations must have taken place here. Some of man's lowest thoughts must have been absorbed by these very walls.

'Others say that it was also used during masonic meetings and that the skull was found on a boat and used as some sort of ritual talisman. I guess that's why it's his-story; it's only ever one man or woman's interpretation.'

'Absolutely right,' Clare agreed, wondering whether her little pot had a story to tell.

'And this is the Old Town still?

'That's right. And this here is the George Hotel which boasts the world's smallest window. Before it was called the George Hotel it was known as Ye White Frere Hostel, which referred to Whitefriargate. I like that name rather better.'

It wasn't really a window, more a slit ten inches by one

inch, like those used by knights of old to fire bows and arrows through castle walls. It was apparently used by a porter to look out for stagecoaches without exposing himself too much to the elements. Though impressive, the George Hotel sat solidly on the cobbled street as if it might still be here a thousand years from now, but it did not ignite the same curiosity for Clare as Ye Olde White Harte Inn had. Clare had felt the White Harte might bear relevance to her little taster, though quite why and how she could prove it she wasn't sure. It felt absurd to even try.

From the George Hotel they passed Trinity House and from there it was a short walk to Holy Trinity Church, solid and secure in its seven-hundred year old position. Clare made a mental note of its location – she would visit to follow up on its connection to her elusive "JG".

'On a clear day, you can stand at the top of the tower and see North Lincolnshire on the south bank of the River Humber. If you turn north-eastward, you can see Spurn Point on the East Yorkshire coast and looking north you can see Beverley Minster.'

'A lighthouse of sorts,' said Clare.

'I'm sure it must have been a welcome sight for many a sailor.'

Clare didn't climb the church's tower, but did admire the medieval brickwork. From the Charter of 1299, given by Edward I to form the city, to the start of the English revolution, to slave abolitionist William Wilberforce's baptism – it was all here.

'As the church is being restored, part of it is blocked off. Remember I mentioned Town Taking Day? Imagine this –

the year was 1688 and the governor of Hull under James II tried to force Catholicism on the townsfolk on Sundays but what resulted were two services taking place simultaneously, one at either end of the church with ministers of different denominations attempting to preach louder than the other and occasionally hurling insults at one another. Hardly a reverential Sunday service!'

It did seem like a frivolous story for such a magnificent church with a seven-hundred year history, but a good one and easier to remember than dry facts. Clare thought how much she would love to find a story connected to her pot.

They passed the old Grammar School, now the Hands-On History Museum, but originally built by the Society of Merchant Venturers to educate young boys. In front of it was a statue of Andrew Marvell, metaphysical poet and politician, standing on a plinth engraved with his poem, 'Ode to a Coy Mistress.'

'Two of Hull's better-known sons, Andrew Marvell and William Wilberforce, were educated here,' said Sarah.

From there it was a short walk to the High Street and Wilberforce House where, in 1759, William Wilberforce was born.

'The house, complete with garden walls, was built by William Catlyn in 1656,' said Sarah. 'It was built for the Lister family, who were wealthy lead merchants. Catlyn was responsible for much of the building at the time and his buildings are recognisable for the use of his trademark red bricks. Can you see the similarity in style and in bricks with Ye Olde Harte Inn? It's the only merchant house still standing in an area where many merchants lived in the seventeenth century. They were strategically very well positioned.'

'How did Wilberforce's family acquire their money?' asked Clare.

'From Baltic trade,' Sarah replied. 'Timber and iron ore.'

Where else! thought Clare. 'What other goods were traded at that time?'

'Lead, bricks, tiles, pitch, hemp, timber, coal, whalebone, cloth, grain, wine, wool, dry food such as rice and spices – if it could be put in a barrel or a sack, it could be traded. Hull's importance as a trading city goes back a long way and should not be underestimated.'

The houses on High Street, with land going down to the river, were in prime position for goods to be offloaded from the ships onto the quays. The goods were loaded onto sleds to be pulled by manpower or carried to the warehouses along the river edge or to be taken up the staithes into town and further afield. On the cobbles on Chapel Lane Staithe, the ruts from the sleds were still visible and Clare found herself mesmerised by them.

'Can we go inside the Wilberforce House Museum?' said Clare, looking up at last.

'It's closed today, but open tomorrow. Will you be here?'

Confession rested on Clare's tongue, but how on earth could she begin with her stolen dram cup story? No, she would visit the next day, and visit anonymously.

'I'm not sure,' she replied.

The outside of the house would not have looked out of place on a Dutch street. Clare was looking forward to discovering her cup within the confines of such an important building.

'I think this concludes your whistle-stop tour and I hope you have found it helpful.'

'Thank you, Sarah. It was fascinating – I had no idea about most of it. You've given me plenty of food for thought and brought the place alive. I now think I have a small idea of life here in the seventeenth century. While we are walking back to the hotel, could you tell me about the cream telephone kiosks?'

'Funny, aren't they?' said her guide.

'I think they are rather attractive,' replied Clare.

'I think so too.' Sarah explained how Hull had not formed part of the nationwide coverage of BT but had been run independently by KCOM, short for Kingston Communications, and the kiosks are identical to kiosks up and down the land, all apart from the colour.

As they walked, Clare felt compelled to tell Sarah the reason for her visit. She began with the museum heist.

'I was quite young at the time so cannot remember that,' Sarah said. 'It was sad that the thieves were not caught.'

'I don't know how much was taken but a seventeenth-century silver taster ended up in my collection. It's now been returned to the museum. I'm hoping to see it in situ tomorrow.'

'I see! Now I understand your interest in Hull. You have no longer got the pot, but in knowing where it came from, you can keep something of it for yourself.'

Clare was glad she didn't have to sum this up herself. In some ways, she supposed Sarah was right.

'It's helpful to put it all into context,' she told Sarah.

She asked whether there were any other examples of seventeenth-century architecture still standing outside the limits of the old city walls. Sarah mentioned the Charterhouse, built in the late fourteenth century by Michael de la Pole, who came from a wealthy family of wool merchants. Originally set up as an alms house, only the boundary wall still stood and she showed Clare an image on her tablet of how the gables along the top of the wall would once have looked. Clare was now convinced of the strong Dutch influence in Hull, which was not surprising considering the amount of sea traffic between the two places. Sarah said building materials such as pantiles were often used as ballast, as were red bricks. It meant early travellers would have found Hull familiar to what they had left behind.

'What exactly are you hoping to find here?' said Sarah.

'It is a bit of a problem because I don't really know, but I thought it might be interesting to understand the times and place from whence it came,' replied Clare.

'I know how objects of the past can get a grip on the mind. I think sometimes they even speak to you, willing you to uncover their secrets.' She smiled and Clare smiled too. 'Well, I wish you all the best with it.'

'Thank you,' said Clare and once again felt her inner resolve strengthen.

She went straight to her room to take the weight off her feet for a while and lay on the bed quite satisfied with what she'd so far discovered. She judged Sarah to be the same age as Amber, and presumed Amber presented herself just as professionally when she was work.

Later, having supper in the subterranean dining room, she mentally sifted through everything she had seen and heard that afternoon. Focusing just on the seventeenth-century aspects alone, she tried to imagine the life and times of the elusive JGs. She suspected they had been merchants, perhaps father and son or grandson. They certainly had excess cash to burn if they owned silver objects. They may have lived on High Street and may have worshipped in Holy Trinity. As this was all speculation, there was not too much point in thinking further about it. One thing she was sure of was that during their lifetimes, Kingston upon Hull had been a busy, thriving place with assertive individuals who knew what they wanted and went out and got it. Since the advent of mobile phones, dining alone was not such an ordeal. She searched the internet for the poems of Philip Larkin and read 'Friday Night in the Royal Station Hotel'. The line, "And all the salesmen have gone back to Leeds" seemed apt on that particular Wednesday evening as she looked round. Besides herself, there was only one lone diner at a distant table.

***

It was a bright, crisp day and Clare set off for the Hull History Centre. The building was modern and impressive and she thought it evoked a ship, the entrance wide as though it was the stern and the walls tapering into the bow at the other end. There she found one of the brightly painted, outsized toads titled "Toad in the Hull".

Clare entered the building and explained to the archivists

at the front desk what she was seeking. In a few sentences she gave the background to her quest. When asked how far she had got with her research, she had to admit nowhere. She had come to Hull, she explained, because that was where the story, if there was one, had unfolded over three hundred years ago. She answered no to the questions of whether she had consulted church records or tried the East Ridings Archives in Beverley or The Borthwick Institute in York. She had to confess she was unfamiliar with both places. She mumbled that she was unused to doing research but, by then, the faces behind the desk told her that this much was painfully evident.

And so, it began. Sat at a vast table, she was brought a variety of books to peruse, but they were all too general and without any real idea of what she was looking for, she found it difficult. Next, she leafed through the booklets listing the known graves in the immediate and surrounding areas. They yielded nothing. She was told there was a lot of material she could go through and, perhaps, she should start by looking at the Bench Books, which were essentially the council records of the day. She was unfamiliar with the term. None of it made easy reading. After several hours of intense concentration, she gave up, believing she had enough for one day and could not absorb anymore.

As she trooped wearily out, her mind buzzing, one of the archivists stopped her.

'Excuse me, but you might like to look at this.' Clare was presented with a sheet of paper, which appeared to be photocopied coins. They were, in fact, images of trade tokens of the sort issued by the trade folk in the middle of the seventeenth century. They bore the names of the issuers. On the back of the sheet was a printed list of names and one caught Clare's eye at once: J.G., John Goodwin. Well, well. Perhaps it was Goodwin, not Graves, who would be the needle in her haystack.

Clare set off for her next destination, St Mary's Lowgate, which was a pretty, fifteenth-century building. She had phoned ahead and been told that while Holy Trinity's records were closed during renovations, St Mary's would be happy to help. The Rt. Reverend Paul Burkitt greeted her warmly, taking her hand in both of his and shaking it with a firm, reassuring grip. In the background, Clare could hear the murmur and hum of a social event. She didn't like to interrupt. The vicar, however, was a genial chap and took her to a cupboard in an annex where their archives were kept. She could, he said, look at anything she wanted to. She was beginning to feel like a *real* researcher and imagined this was a researcher's dream. She asked whether there was a Book of Gifts recording anything that may have been left to the church over the centuries.

'It's a good place to start and I know there is one somewhere. A person of some worth often left something to the church in their will,' he said.

Clare had not been asked what she was looking for or why and did not divulge anything. Unfortunately, the Book of Gifts could not be found, but Clare was given an email address and the name of the archivist and left the church feeling somewhat satisfied.

'Trinity House also has archives and might also shed light,' were the vicar's parting words. Clare thanked him and set off once more. It was beginning to feel like an adventure. Even though she had not found anything concrete, it had been a highly successful couple of days.

Although it incited a degree of remorse, she hadn't really thought about Harry at all whilst she'd been away. She had felt slight guilt about not inviting her friend on a return trip, but she knew traipsing around Hull would only be *dreadfully dull* to Elizabeth. Besides, Clare needed concentration rather than to spend the time propping up bars or indulging in afternoon naps. She called Elizabeth when she was on the train, travelling into London.

'What do you mean you have to go back again? Why didn't you just stay in Hull and do what you had to do, darling?'

Clare took a deep breath. She had to do this more and more lately, particularly in so far as her family were concerned, and definitely with Elizabeth. 'Because I'm not sure what I have to do, or what I can or might find, that's why.'

'Needles in haystacks don't get found hanging out by the beach all day if you get my drift, darling. If you're going to find anything, I guess you've got to be there.'

'I've worked on the premise that if the two pieces of silver sought me out, then the answers may be seeking me too.'

'Not necessarily, Éclair. And you're far too passive about it. Maybe you're being called to adventure. See it as that; a Miss Marple call to adventure. How wonderful!'

That afternoon, Clare sat down at Harry's desk and wrote an email to the archivist at St Mary's church.

Dear Judith,

I believe there is a Book of Gifts listing donations to the church. I am seeking to find somebody with the initials J.G, I.C, I.G, J.C., which may sound obscure, but I am researching the initials on a piece of silverware that was stolen from the museum of Hull. The piece would have had to have been made towards the end of the 17th century. It would really be of benefit if...

Amber's voice was ringing between her ears about finding a purpose.

... if you could send me anything of relevance.

She now had to wait and see what would come back. After that, her mind turned to the image on her taster. She meditated on it for some time, but nothing came to mind. Nothing whatsoever.

The sun broke free from clouds and striated through the French doors. Sitting at her computer, a thought suddenly occurred to her: perhaps the original Seagrove and Atterbury catalogue might have something more to reveal about her little taster. She looked again at the entry in the Art Fund Register online, which she had discussed with Malcolm, and it listed Seagrove and Atterbury as the vendors. Therefore, all she had to do was search on this giant encyclopaedia in the sky for the actual catalogue.

Searching on the internet, Clare realised, required perseverance and technique – something she was getting better at. She had come to her own conclusions about things and was, if she was honest, enjoying the process. Perhaps that was the reason that she was able to find what she was searching for much quicker. Within half an hour, she saw there was a single copy of a sale for Seagrove and Atterbury for 1969 in *Star Catalogue*. She didn't have a date for the sale but thought it would be interesting to see what a catalogue from the sixties would have looked like anyway, so it did not matter whether it was the right one or not. So, without another thought, she purchased it and hoped that it would arrive soon. She was, she thought, being proactive if nothing else and now she would just have to wait.

***

It did not take long for Judith to reply saying she had been through the *Book of Gifts* for St Mary's and there was nobody with the initials J.G. listed as having made a donation. She suggested Clare try East Ridings Archives in Beverley or Borthwick Institute for Archives in York. It was same suggestion she had been given in the History Centre.

Clare sighed and sat back in her chair. The silence of the study with its floating dust and the faint smell of Harry's cigars began, for the first time, to feel stagnant and claustrophobic. She drummed her fingers on the arm of the chair, trying to beat back her own frustration. Her impatience got the better of her. Instead of waiting for the catalogue to arrive, she rang the auction house to ask whether she could look through their catalogues from 1969 and was told they were in the British Library.

The British Library was a modern red-brick hunk of a building that sat complacently on Knowledge Quarter, smug in its certainty that it was one of the largest libraries in the world. Clare looked up at its familiar face and smiled. She entered the building and headed to the cloakroom before being directed to the Rare Books Room where she requested the catalogues. It took a full seventy minutes for them to be brought up from the stacks. Clare was presented with six bound volumes to go through, each volume containing two months' worth of catalogues. The tower of paper dwarfed her and cut off her view of the rest of the room. She settled into a seat. It took a long while for her to examine them page by page to find the right sale which, she discovered, took place on the 9th of October.

Clare rubbed her eyes and carefully read the entry. There it was, entry number 137:

A RARE LATE 17TH CENTURY HULL CIRCULAR BLEEDING BOWL, the tapering body naively engraved on one side with a contemporary crest comprising two seated figures supporting the figure of Hermes holding a caduceus and on the other with later initials, MAR, the base also engraved with contemporary initials, 1½ in. high, by Abraham Barachin, circa 1685, 10oz. 18dwt.

Clare's eyes travelled to the image: yes, it was her taster all right. The date was correct, unlike the entry in the NACF's register. This copy of the catalogue was annotated. The "10" had been struck and next to it was written "1", giving the correct weight as 1oz. In the right-hand margin, it noted the hammer price of £680 and the name How of Edinburgh as the purchaser. How was a name familiar to Clare. Mrs How was, in her time, a well-respected expert on early silver. Clare had never met her, but dealers were always happy to share stories about her. She had sounded like quite a character, someone who, by all accounts, was not always easy to deal with and did not suffer fools gladly. If Mrs How thought it worth buying, it gave the piece an excellent provenance. To add to her records, Clare asked for a photocopy of the annotated copy.

Ten days after Clare's visit to the British Library to look for the catalogue, the copy she had ordered landed on her doormat, pristine, unannotated and devoid of the valuable information Clare had almost missed for good.

***

For every small scrap of information that Clare unearthed, she wanted more. After the success with the catalogue, she headed back to the British Library to learn about script, as she assumed she may need to read seventeenth-century documents. If she was lucky, she may, in time, find a name and if even luckier, she may find a will. Better to be forearmed. After another lengthy wait she sat at a table, pouring over a book on secretary hand. Secretary hand was used from the beginning of the sixteenth century before italic writing came into fashion. However, since Henry VIII's time, Italian, or Italic, script had become increasingly fashionable; yet, for the purpose of will reading, it was secretary hand Clare needed to study. There were apparently three different types, just to confuse matters more: mixed, court, and archaic hands. She took photocopies of various sheets. Her mind whirled – it seemed a lot to learn!

Clare enjoyed the sensation of feeling like a student again, albeit one that hadn't the pressure of deciding a future career. She wished she could take the book home with her, wished that she could lose herself amid tomes of knowledge and wisdom. Was it escapism? Perhaps. Did it matter if it was? How she dealt with grief was her business, and so long as she wasn't falling apart, well, that had to be a good thing.

Whilst she was there, Clare headed to the newspaper archives. After trawling back to 1986, she discovered the newspaper article describing the theft and her eyes widened. She asked for a printout. Since she was there, she looked at other articles on silver in the Hull Museum. In 1939, there were several articles about the collection. Her eye lit on a piece about a Lady Waechter de Grimston who was a society lady at the time and had made a significant donation. Clare realised how easy it was to become distracted and to spin off down a rabbit hole and had to stop herself.

'It's becoming an obsession,' Amber had said to her. 'An utter obsession. It needs to stop. Grief is a complicated process, but it is exactly that, *a process*. If you repress it, which, by the way, is precisely what I believe you are doing, you will have problems further down the line. I guarantee that.'

What sort of problems,? Clare wondered. Would she be fined, imprisoned, or would she turn to stone perhaps?

'I'm fine, sweetheart,' she said flatly.

'I'm not so sure. Repression is the root of most psychological issues, you know. It's almost dangerous.'

When Clare was Amber's age, Clare had worried about world wars or nuclear attacks, things outside her head. These days, it seemed the young were more concerned about the contents of their own minds. Clare often thought it didn't leave too much time for the actual process of *living*.

'I'm fine, really.' And, she supposed, in some strange way she was.

'I think you're rushing it all if I'm honest.'

Clare had never known her daughter to be anything else.

'What if you don't find the answers you need? You'll fall into despair again, that's what I'm afraid of.'

The funny part was that this didn't bother Clare at all, and it wasn't just to do with knowing her daughter well. It was because an inner knowing told her she *would* find the answers. She simply knew she would.

'I'll just have to take that risk,' she told Amber.

'I do hope you're okay,' said Amber, soberly.

Clare hung up and looked out of the window as a rock dove swooped before her face.

I feel more okay than I've felt in a long time. I have a purpose, and it's all mine. Clare smiled to herself.

***

It had been a few months since she first visited Hull and Clare now felt the need to return. For whatever reason, she felt sure that being in the town would direct her toward further clues. This time, however, she would keep her travel plans secret, from Amber in particular.

As soon as Clare arrived in Hull, it was clear that the the City of Culture celebrations were well underway. Now, alongside the statue of Philip Larkin in Paragon Station, a full-scale replica of the famous aviator Amy Johnson's *Gypsy Moth* was suspended from the rafters above. The statue, a replica of one designed by Geoffrey de Havilland in 1920, had apparently been made in a prison's engineering workshop. All over town, there was a large infestation of gigantic, individually painted moths over various walls, forming a full riot of colour as if the moths, like herself, had been attracted to an invisible light that Hull was secretly emitting.

Blue-clad volunteers were on hand to assist visitors. The walls all around them were brightly decorated. Towards the high ceiling was a flock of sculpted birds, individually painted by members of the public. Below them was a series of what looked like stained-glass windows which, on closer inspection, were made of coloured film, telling the story of the two million people who had arrived in Hull by boat between 1848 and 1914, mostly from Europe, who then spread out to the four corners of the world. Clare's mind naturally jumped to Abraham Barachin. Where had he come from? Had he planned to live here? Was he successful? All these unanswered questions tumbled through her mind.

Checking into the same hotel adjacent to the station, Clare dropped off her bags and set off for the History Centre almost immediately. As she walked, she tried to imagine the past, picturing the horses trotting over cobbled streets pulling carts behind them. She imagined the markets, the women in big dresses, the men in stockings and breeches and the street sellers. How she wished she could see it, to reach out and somehow touch it all.

She shook her head at the fantasy and, as she passed it, she noticed the Truck Theatre which had now reopened and was showing Richard Bean's *The Hypocrite,* which had opened to rave reviews. Perhaps she could get a ticket for that evening. The Ferens Gallery had also reopened its doors, showing off its magnificent collections and latest exhibitions. A cascade of ceramic poppies, the Weeping Window, tumbling down from an upper floor in the Maritime Museum, marking the centenary of the start of WWI. In futuristic contrast, a huge seventy-five-metre Siemens wind turbine blade lay right across Queen Victoria Square and an audio installation on the Humber Bridge incorporated the great structure's sounds into music whilst one crossed. Clare marvelled at it all, at the town full of life and colour. Cultural events were planned every day for a year. Yes, Hull's celebrations were certainly in full swing!

Clare dragged herself away from the lively streets, entered the History Centre's doors and sat down in the cool quiet to trawl through more seventeenth-century documents and concentrate on immersing herself in them.

She read through Hull Merchant Records, Enrolment of Apprentices lists, working her way through further Bench Book Rolls. Then, with the librarian's help, she came across an entry of a John Graves, witnessing the signing of an apprentice in 1675. Her heart took off at a pace, but unfortunately it didn't make any reference to him being a merchant or hiring an apprentice. And yet it must have been a world he was at least familiar with, which offered a modicum of encouragement. She continued trawling through pages on monumental inscriptions, looked at Freemen Registers and Registers of Persons Bound Apprentices to Burgesses, and decided much of the terminology meant next to nothing to her; it really was a different language. She laughed at the way her parents, growing up, had often seemed like creatures from a different era and so she suspected that people she was reading about, if she could be introduced, would be quite alien too in their outlook. She did learn that once apprentices became free, they were known as burgesses and that becoming a burgess meant you could sit on the council, or bench, as it was known, which explained the term Bench Book. These facts Clare found fascinating, but they weren't useful to her. There were documents pertaining to Bonds for the Maintenance of Bastards, Hull Settlement Bonds, Hull Apprentice Indentures, Hull Bonds to support children; what a quagmire she had to wade through. She was amazed, as she always was, at the sheer volume of information that had survived, amassed, indexed and cross-referenced for the sole purpose of making the past accessible to anyone in the present who was interested.

Yet, despite it all being very interesting, it covered civic life. Since the initials she was concerned with were on pieces of domestic silver, a name was needed for her to pursue the private life of the still unidentified owner – or perhaps owners.

Clare looked through the index box and asked to see everything relating to the initials J.G. Having exhausted that avenue, she tried A.B. for Abraham Barachin to see what, if anything, there was for him. All that there was was a handwritten receipt. It was in beautiful copperplate lettering and pertained to a repair on a piece of silver. It instantly ignited some hope. Of course, she had no way of knowing whether it was Barachin's writing, but there was the chance it might have been. It was, perhaps, the same hand that had engraved her taster. How fascinating such a receipt had survived for a seemingly insignificant job! After further searching, she found nothing more on John Goodwin. *Am I drawing any closer?* she wondered.

Despite finding nothing substantial, Clare left the History Centre feeling buoyed. She rang Trinity House to ask whether she might call in later.

'Four o'clock is the latest time,' she was told.

Following the long session at the History Centre, she walked round the city once again, to clear her head, enjoying the vague sense of familiarity. She walked to the Museums Quarter on the High Street, her feet once more treading cobbles. Once in the Wilberforce House Museum she read the story of the slave trade and its abolition and looked carefully at the artefacts. She thought how poignant it was to see the campaigner's coat in the right setting, not displaced in a museum elsewhere, and how the accompanying writing carried a justified sense of pride. She thought how courageous Wilberforce must have been going against the ethos of his time. Next, she went upstairs to look again at the silver collection, the pottery, and various antiques, feeling content as she often did amid silver pieces. Not only that, but it was a satisfying building to be in, though she couldn't precisely say why. Perhaps it was something to do with it having once been a private house, around the time of her little taster, so it seemed to fit. Yes, no doubt that was it.

From there, Clare passed through the elegant entrance to the eighteenth century building of Trinity House and found the young man on reception happy to assist with her query regarding a Book of Gifts. She knew that wonderful collections were often formed at institutions where outgoing officers donate something to mark their term of office. When she had called earlier, she had stated she was only interested in gifts to the guild during the second half of the seventeenth century. After a few moments, the archivist appeared and handed her a photocopied page: listed was a silver tumbler given by Joshua Greene in 1689 who had once been one of HM Customs House Officers. The date was too late for the J.G. on her beaker but the era was right for her little dram cup. She added another name to the list, three in total now, John Graves, John Goodwin and now Joshua Greene.

How many more J.G.s will there be? Maybe I'm getting closer. Or maybe further away...

Buoyed by the thought of progress, she said, 'Do you know why tumblers are called tumblers?' to the archivist, surprising herself.

'No idea, as a matter of fact,' the woman replied.

'Because they roll from side to side to right themselves.'

'How fascinating!'

'Silver always is,' Clare declared.

Following this find, she was determined to continue her search, telling herself that she was slowly but deftly gathering information. Yet the recurring thought occurred that it wasn't so much that she was *seeking* something but that something was *calling* to her, and this time she was refusing to dismiss the niggle.

She headed back onto the streets of Hull and walked around, trying to reorder her thoughts. She felt as though she ought to have a notebook like some sort of detective, or silver sleuth. The name John Graves had come up several times now, for different reasons. A John Graves was listed as an MP in Hull in 1601, his father Hugh Graves was listed as a merchant. There seemed to be a good number of men who had lived here during the seventeenth century who bore the same name. Were they members of the same family, different branches of a family or from different families altogether? It was clearly not an unusual name, but the beauty of it was that if Hugh was a merchant, there was a good chance his son might have been one too. If she had understood it correctly, John Graves MP of 1601 was later Mayor of Hull, which meant it was therefore not improbable that his son could have been alive and buying silverware some fifty years later, by which time there might also have been a grandson. Perhaps she would check the town's churches for gravestones.

Whilst she was now convinced that the owner of the dram cup was a merchant due to the engraving of Mercury, Clare had no good reason to think the owner of the beaker was one too, though it would be foolish to rule it out. The truth was, there were far fewer occupations in the seventeenth century compared to now and with Hull being a prosperous town, there would have been plenty of merchants. But it was no more than a hunch. There was no real evidence to go by. She was letting assumption get the better of her. Yet she couldn't help envisaging a scenario whereby the beaker had been passed down from father to son, eventually ending up in the same home as the owner of the dram cup. Hadn't her assumptions served her well up until now? Was it so unlikely?

Given that some months had passed since her first visit to Hull, she went back to look at Holy Trinity Church, now Hull Minster. What she hadn't been able to see on the first visit was this time visible and truly magnificent. Inside, she admired the majestic lines of Perpendicular Gothic, the clerestory which had been restored and the beautifully carved collaroid marble font where Wilberforce was once baptised. She admired the stained-glass windows made by Walter Crane, and the Brooks Window and the Earle Window, both named after the families who had paid for them. She took a closer look at the tombstones marked with effigies and after that, the gravestones, but no matter how hard she looked and hoped, she couldn't find any with the initials J.G. In some cases, there were several gravestones for different members of the same families. It felt as if the history of the building was seeping out of its very stones. The floor space was the largest of any parish church in England and Clare found it easy to imagine how it might have once looked when filled; she could even picture the scene, with pews arranged so that half faced in opposite directions, of the shouting clerics on Town Taking Day. Back at the hotel, she looked back at what she had learned and wished she had someone other than Elizabeth with whom to discuss her findings.

It was almost as if, lately, she went about her days with one foot firmly rooted in the past. She lay on her bed and stared at the ceiling, wondering where to look next and what direction might throw up clues. Presuming the two original owners had been men, what would their lives have been like? Did they have wives? What were the women's lives like, and what were their roles? She had read about trade and shipping of that period and could imagine the activity at the port. She could even imagine how a merchant might have lived. What she couldn't imagine was how the little dram cup had found its way back onto the open market, years after it had been stolen. It took such a jump for her thoughts to get here. She found a transcript in Hansard on the *marché overt* in Bermondsey, a market where stolen goods could be sold before daylight with no questions asked; an odious practice going back to the Middle Ages. Eventually, it petered out and became illegal. It was possible the dram cup was offloaded there. Her foggy, swirling thoughts and great tiredness took over and quickly dismissed her earlier idea of a night at the theatre.

The next day, somewhat satisfied, Clare took the train back to London. Yet the gnawing curiosity began to pick up again as distance grew between her and Hull.

More and more she wished the matter resolved. There was still the possibility she could put a name to the owner, and it seemed the next resource to explore would be the archives in Beverley she was so often being chased towards. She acknowledged that this research was a lonely business, with much of it seeming to go nowhere. She stared out of the train window at the grey raindrops beating against the pane and lost herself in thought.

***

The time had come to approach the East Ridings Archives and the Borthwick Institute. Clare wondered whether she had put it off for fear of disappointment. Where else could she look if she failed to unearth what she was after?

When contacting East Ridings Archives, she thought she would start with two of the three names and if they yielded nothing, she would still have a name in reserve to pursue. Graves had come up a lot, Goodwin with his trade token seemed a possibility, as did Joshua Greene. Wills, she thought, might be a good a way as any to start. She made the phone call. Not all wills survived, they said, and not everyone made a will. For the latter group who died intestate, a list of possessions was drawn up. She had to wait for the information to be sent, if there was any.

The news, when it came, was mixed. It seemed John Goodwin was born in 1629, a landlord, but there was no trace of a marriage, children, or a will. Her line of enquiry here was at an end. She struck his name from the list. The news on John Graves was more promising. They could find no reference to a John Graves in the parish records for Holy Trinity, St Mary's Lowgate, Drypool St Andrews and Sculcoates from 1600–1650. There was a list of various names, which meant nothing, but it transpired there were several men called John Graves. One born in 1587, another in 1596 and a third in 1622. But, most importantly, there was a will for a John Graves in the National Archives in Kew: probate had been granted in 1657. The dates fitted. As long as the will was unread, there was still a flicker of hope. Yorkshire wills were housed in Borthwick but during the Commonwealth they were proved in London. Without getting her hopes up too much, it could possibly provide some information about the owner of the beaker. Joshua Greene, then, could still be held in reserve. Clare called Elizabeth that morning to see if she wanted to meet for lunch after her visit.

'I couldn't think of anything better, darling! I tell you what, Éclair, when your story hits the big screen, I would like to be played by Joanna Lumley. Who would you like to play you?' Clare did not dignify the question with an answer.

Clare registered as a reader for the National Archives in Kew. The building sat on a large site in south-west London. The concrete brutalist exterior hid a light, airy interior. She went upstairs, trying to suppress her rising excitement in case this turned out to be a wild goose chase, and it was the wrong John Graves. Eventually, she was handed a print-out of two A3 sheets covered in almost indecipherable writing. She found a table with good lighting and sat down. At first, she was delighted to read "…bequeath to my grandson James Halhead a house of bees …And half my business…" No mention of silverware. Then she realised what she read at the top of the page pertained to the will of someone else, and the relevant will came next. Clare read on, making sense of very little until something caught her eye and caused a sharp intake of breath. She made out the word 'silver'. The writing was too difficult to speed-read, and she certainly could not read it all, but there they were, the names of his heirs, his three daughters. She would have to take it home and struggle with it there. She was glad of the printed sheets and little booklet on secretary hand that she had picked up at the British Library. They were going to come into their own. It seemed she had found the right John Graves, and the right will.

Clare was sorry she had agreed to have lunch with Elizabeth when all she really wanted to do was go home to transcribe the rest of John Graves' will.

'A coffee, darling?' said Elizabeth, pleading creeping into her tone.

'I think I've found the correct will, Liz.'

'Darling, that's marvellous! I do completely understand. Go home at once and promise to tell me your news.'

Many, many hours later, Clare had come up with:

...Also I do give and bequeath unto my daughter Mary Graves thirtie pounds for life money as a legacie to be payd unto her out of my personall estate and above what the rest of my children are to have by reason that are better provided for in some way as to land given them. Also I do give and bequeath unto my daughter Elizabeth one great double silver gilt Salte, unto my daughter Hanna my silver gilt Salt. And to my daughter Marye my best silver beere bowl...

She had no idea what "beere bowle" meant, but it had to be her beaker. The sentence above read, *I do give and bequeath unto my brother Thomas Graves tenn pounds of good and lawfull English money*. At that point she reopened the email she had received from East Ridings Archives some time before and looked again at the list of the names. John Graves, born in 1587, indeed had a brother called Thomas born in 1595. A second pair of brothers called John and Thomas were baptised in 1622 and 1624 respectively. 'Her' John Graves must be the one baptised in 1622 as he was most likely to have had a young family thirty years later. A family tree was emerging, setting its roots and unfurling its branches before her eyes.

She teased what she could from the document. From the tone of the will, she had the intense impression that John was kindly and trying to do the best for his family in his absence. It gave positive confirmation that he was a merchant: a Hull Draper. He had also asked his friends Timothy Lumn, John Minspeak and Robert Winton to be testamentary tutors for his daughters, which suggested they were still young and that he cared for them a great deal. As there were young children, this must be the will of John born in 1622. It also implied there was no mother, nor a brother of any responsibility, for whatever reason. All in all, Clare felt a real connection to this fellow. Such things had, in the past, kept her awake at night, particularly concerning what she would leave behind for her children. And if her own children dismissed her silver collection at some future point, then perhaps grandchildren would come along to claim it as well as its potential stories.

With no mention of a wife and the fact the children were each treated differently, Clare wondered if Mary had been born after her sisters had been gifted an inheritance. The other possibility, she supposed, was that Elizabeth and Hannah may have had a different mother. None of this mattered; the silver is what interested Clare.

Clare knew this was her man just as she had begun

to feel close to unravelling the story during her travels to Amsterdam, Riga and Russia with Elizabeth, as if it was all *asking* to be discovered. This mystery had come to her with a specific purpose. But this was only one part of her story proven right; now all she needed to do was to prove the origins of her little silver hot water taster...

Clare was now curious to know what a *beere bowle* was and wrote out an email to Benjamin Miller, a silver dealer and acquaintance of hers, relying on him to give a full description. Benjamin was not a London dealer. Clare could not explain, even to herself, why she did not want to ask a London dealer. She wondered whether she would ever stop feeling odd about having been in possession of the stolen piece. Benjamin's reply was swift and did not disappoint. It confirmed her belief that the *beere bowle* must be her beaker. He explained how they were often used by the Puritans as communion cups. He listed a few examples of beer bowls being bequeathed in wills of that period. Clare needed no further enticement. He mentioned in the final paragraph that *vessels were often put to purposes entirely different from those implied by their names.* These words fascinated her. Benjamin had also added that such descriptions were often used imprecisely at the time.

There might still be a chance that the dram cup from forty years later, engraved with J.G., might have belonged to the same family. Clare needed proof of that. Until this line of enquiry had been fully explored, there was still no need to investigate Joshua Greene.

Already, Clare was feeling the urge to return north again to the epicentre of the mystery. Walking to the shops the next day, she couldn't help beaming widely; she could feel the momentum gathering. Further reading online yielded more information on Hull merchants, who formed a small yet, apparently, powerful group. Several families were prominent, including the Graves family. She read that they often had more than one home, and though they weren't all wealthy, some had part shares in ships. They tended to live on Hull's High Street and held their meetings at an impressive red brick hall, purposefully built by the Hull Merchants. The upstairs room was used for meetings, while the downstairs was used as a grammar school to teach their sons reading, writing, arithmetic and Latin. It fired Clare's imagination going as she imagined the owner of her little taster attending, growing, learning. But who was he?

***

Next came the archives in Beverley. She longed for another J.G. to fit the time period, but the dates had matched so far. John Graves had borne no son and, unless one of his daughters had married a gentleman with a surname beginning with G, it blew her theory out of the water about the beaker being passed from father to son. She needed to look down another branch of the family. From the will, she had the name of John's brother Thomas. This line had to be explored. Although clues were being presented slowly, perhaps too slowly at times, it did not deter her. What was it Amber had said on the phone last night?

'It's like a bad relationship in some respects. You know

what you're doing is wrong and that it will have to end at some point, but you're willing to go along for the ride.'

Clare had laughed, telling her daughter she really didn't know her mother at all. She so wanted to prove Amber wrong. If she did not, at least she had tried.

Like Hull, Beverley was not somewhere Clare had ever had occasion to visit and was glad she had allowed time to for a quick look at Beverley Minster, with its three phases of build styles from Early Gothic to Decorated and Perpendicular Gothic. She looked at the stained-glass windows, carved musicians, and misericords. As much as she would have lingered longer, she also wanted to see the inside of St Mary's Church, daughter church of the Minster, built to serve the trading community. If the merchants worshipped in St Mary's, did this mean the Minster was for the exclusive use of the nobility and the landed gentry? Perhaps for the gentry only, as aristocratic houses tended to have their own chapels. Where did the lesser orders worship? Where history was concerned, there always seemed to be more questions than answers, thought Clare. The interior of St Mary's, smaller than the Minster, was equally startling with its gilded stars shining down on worshippers from a celestial blue ceiling, a fine example of Decorated Gothic. The archives were beckoning Clare and as that was her reason for being in Yorkshire, she left the church.

The East Ridings Archives were housed in The Treasure House, the treasure now amounting to a library, a museum and an art gallery as well the information services. Once Clare had explained what she was after, the waters muddied again. She was told that to request a will to match the initials J.G. or possibly I.G. for the late seventeenth or early eighteenth century was a mammoth task. Just in the probate index volume were dozens of entries with the initials for J.G. alone in Yorkshire. Another spanner was later thrown into the works as the archivist assisting her told her there was a will for a Jeremiah Graves dated 1692.

'Jeremiah Graves, are you sure?' she asked.

'It looks that way. Would you like to see his will?'

'Of course.'

'Well, you'll find it at Borthwick in York. If you cannot get it there, they'll email it to you. Have you found John Graves' will?'

'Yes, I have in Kew. It's spurring me on to find the wills of other family members. John left his brother, Thomas, some money and I wonder whether you have any information on him.'

There was a colossal rustling and a weighty thump as a great pile of papers was placed before her by the archivist, who had known just where to look. Over the months, Clare had become more and more convinced that archivists really did hold most of the nation's secrets and that they were practiced at navigating their way around the dead.

It seemed Thomas had married and had a son called William, which would make William a nephew to John. William, in turn, had a son called Jeremiah who would have been an adult in the 1690s. Nevertheless, she did not feel that optimistic, as the name Jeremiah had not appeared in the one hundred and forty years of the family tree. Families back then tended to recycle names rather than introduce new ones. Clare had a feeling she might have hit another dead end.

'Thank you, I'll go to York and look for the will,' she told the archivist, her thoughts already leaving the building.

All this information felt like a window into the past, but one smeared with dirt and grime. But, if there was one thing Clare knew, it was that she was not afraid of polishing.

***

From Beverly to York was about forty-five minutes in a taxi. En route, Clare reflected that if Jeremiah's will did not provide anything useful, Joshua Greene would be the last throw of the dice. And if he, too, proved to be fruitless, she would have to accept she was not going to succeed in her mission. That was a possibility she did not feel quite ready to face. The thought of it made her feel oddly lightheaded and breathless. She put it from her mind. Cross every bridge as she came to them.

The Borthwick Institute for Archives was the specialist archive service of the University of York, and it was housed in a modern building. Clare crossed the bridge to the entrance with a feeling of intense expectation and not a little fear that it might all end here unresolved. Where had this sensation come from, this utter belief she could discover the first owners of both a silver taster and beaker from Hull that had both ended up in her collection? It was illogical and presumptive. But so far, she supposed, her intuition had served her well.

The Chinese perhaps had it right in their beliefs about life: yin and yang. Clare had been as low as she possibly could swoop, and in that place of despair, hope, in the form of a mystery (important only to her), had presented itself. She was past believing it was mere distraction now; the secret was calling to her, of that she was convinced, and with that thought she marched inside. Jeremiah's will was here and she was determined to read it, even if it brought her to a dead end.

Looking at the microfilm had given Clare a stiff neck and a tension headache once more. After what felt like hours of streaming through wills, her attention was caught by a messy and challenging document – here it was at last, the will of Jeremiah Graves. Worse was to come when she scrolled down and saw that instead of a signature was the impression of a seal.

This man must have been illiterate, was her first and resounding thought and one of absolute dread. Her disappointment was palpable. She put her head in her hands. *Pull yourself together, Clare.* She shook herself and requested a copy of it.

Is this all that people amounted to, Clare thought on her way back to the hotel, names on a piece of paper in Yorkshire? She had stood too close to death to imagine this might be a good thing that Harry, and she also, for that matter, may one day rest in an archive such as this, laying in a silent yet dignified state for somebody to pore over, or not, as the case may be. She was given a printout and resolved not to try and read it until she got home. Clare was more practised and familiar with secretary hand by now, but it still took some time to decipher the will. Her disappointment lifted at once. It was there. Right in front of her, indelibly inscribed into the will:

In the name of God Amen I Jeremiah Graves of the Towne of Kingston-upon-Hull Beerbrewer being week of bodie but of p[er]fect minde and memory .... I devise and bequeath to my sonn John Graves the summe of Tenn poundes of Lawfull English money ... I give and bequeath unto my s[ai]d son John Graves two silver Cupps one marked JEG and the other marked JG.

There it was, Beerbrewer, the connection to Mercury, the god of grain and trade. The rest of his *goodes and Chattel[e]s* went to his *loving wife Elizabeth* with a few conditions should she remarry. What happened to Jeremiah's widow? Clare wondered.

And though she laughed, the hair on her arms prickled. Something told her there was perhaps more to her story. But she was going to stop looking. She had found the names of the first owners of both pieces of silver and their heirs; it was more than she had ever hoped for. She did not even feel the immediate need to tell anyone; in a day or two would be soon enough. Neither Amber nor Elizabeth thought her quest was anything more than a displacement activity. She simply enjoyed the moment, knowing she had achieved what she had set out to achieve against all odds.

***

Clare put a vase of roses on the table with petals so dark they resembled rich, crimson velvet. She stood back, a hand on hip, deeply satisfied. She thought about Amber's response to her invitation for dinner and how it had momentarily irritated her.

'Has something terrible happened, Mummy?' had been her response on the phone.

'No, why do you say that, darling?'

'You haven't had more than one for dinner at yours for almost two years now.'

Clare cleared her throat. 'How delightful to have you judging my domestic habits.'

'I'm not. I'm judging your mental health improvement.'

Clare half-laughed. 'Well, isn't the fact I'm inviting you to dinner enough of an improvement?'

After a reflective pause which wasn't the standard with Amber, she said, 'Yes, I suppose you are right.' (How lovely to be right about one's own situation, Clare had thought.) 'Maybe soon you can branch out from Elizabeth's company.'

'Oh please!' One thing Clare could not take was any further nannying. 'I think at my age I can organise my social life to suit my needs.'

'We all need help at different stages of life. I'll be there, Mummy. But please do not expect me to join in with Elizabeth and her patriarchy worship. It's completely nauseating!'

Was that what it was! At this juncture, Clare couldn't help smiling at the juxtaposition of her invitation to Elizabeth against the one pitched to her daughter.

'Love to come, darling! Where and when?' Elizabeth's tone had then dropped to an intimate whisper. 'Now tell me, have you decided at last to tie the proverbial with Malcolm? You sly thing.'

It was really a predictable response from both invitees, but Clare remained buoyant about the evening: *she had news to impart.*

For the food, Clare had decided to go all in and had headed to Harrods' food hall; a space dedicated to the most flamboyant of ingredients seemed appropriate given the occasion. She did not purchase much but what she did choose had an edge of perfection in its appearance: scallops, salmon, prawns, a piece of white fish, avocados, peppers, lemons, and baby tomatoes with a handful of fresh coriander, chives and salad leaves. She looked at the patisserie counter and mentally calculated the calories, then walked on. How funny, she thought, leaving the store's busy ground floor, but I would never have noticed such things a year ago and certainly would not have looked forward to the prospect of entertaining!

She now took the ingredients from the fridge and spread them over the counter. *Rigoletto* played on the digital radio, and she hummed along. Her mind was set upon her own version of ceviche which involved marinating the prawns and scallops, cooking cubes of shallow-fried breaded white fish together, with the grilled salmon, then strewn with strips of roasted red and orange pepper, wedges of lemon, coriander, decorated with a few sprinklings of snipped chives and served with a crust of warm baguette and a salad.

She settled into a meditative trance as she prepared the food, helped by the music. The idea of a starter was soon eschewed in favour of parmesan thins which would go well with a glass of champagne. Though she doubted whether either Elizabeth or Amber would want pudding, she was enjoying being in the kitchen, humming as she worked, and decided she would make three individual apple tarts with a biscuit base, covered with an apricot jam glaze, scattered with slivers of almonds. Pity the idea had come to her so late as there was no time to make vanilla ice cream

With Harry, there had been many business dinners held in the dining room, jovial late-night affairs. He preferred to entertain at home rather than in a restaurant. The bottle count, in the morning, never failed to astound Clare. She had taken her role seriously but had not enjoyed the occasions as much as Harry seemed to and the next day the smell of stale smoke and alcohol hanging in the air would be overpowering. Tonight, however, would be very different.

Once the food was prepared, she laid the dining table carefully, surprised at how much enjoyment it brought. She put a pair of twentieth-century copies of de Lamerie candlesticks in position, knowing that anyone with a practised eye would know they were not the real thing; Elizabeth would think they were a decorator's item, no doubt, and Amber would most likely not even notice them. The champagne flutes needed washing, dusty as they were from neglect. Clare took the crystal glasses into the kitchen and set about washing and soaping them, wiping them dry with a fresh cloth. Coasters, plates, fish eaters, salad servers, flatware for the apple pies, glasses for both wine and water, salts, napkins – all the things Clare liked to look at and use were set out. The table was ready, the meal prepared and the drinks in the fridge.

Clare went to shower and change, putting on tailored, navy, wool trousers, a white silk blouse, and some pendant pearl earrings. She smiled at her reflection in the mirror and thought, yes, I do have something to be proud about tonight. All the same, the trousers looked a bit tired and didn't fit as well as they used to, so perhaps it was time to throw a few things out of her wardrobe, donate them to the charity shop. Perhaps she could create a new image for this latter part of her life. She felt pleased that such thoughts were stirring again. They seemed akin to how the sound of returning spring birds could brighten a day following months of dark wintery nights. Yes, she was waking up to life again.

Shortly before seven, the doorbell rang as Elizabeth and Amber arrived together. They were in mid-conversation, chatting amiably as Clare let them in.

'I swear it's true!' said Elizabeth.

'I'm not sure I believe you!'

'That's the way I'd prefer it, dear. Éclair, how are you, darling?'

A pleasant feeling swelled in Clare's chest as she realised how much she loved them both, naturally and in very different ways. Elizabeth was as impeccably dressed as usual, slightly overdressed really, in an elegant chiffon black dress dotted here and there with a generous sprinkling of diamonds. She completed her outfit with a Chanel handbag and shoes with heels too high for someone who'd had four husbands. Amber's outfit of culottes and cashmere sweater, teamed with low boots, looked stylish and flattered her thin frame. Clare was never sure where Amber's style came from but knew resolutely that it was not from her. She considered asking Amber whether she would accompany her on a shopping trip.

'Mwah, mwah!' said Elizabeth, in an exaggerated fashion

as she kissed Clare's cheeks. 'So good to see my god-daughter again at long last. Oh, something smells good, Eclair!'

'Gosh, you look really well, Mummy!' said Amber, also kissing both of Clare's cheeks. 'Hope you don't mind us being early.'

'How nice of you to say so, darling, thank you. Come in!' Clare took their coats, coughing a little as she was momentarily overpowered by Elizabeth's perfume, then led them both into the drawing room. She couldn't help noticing her own anticipation; so shiningly different from how she had been feeling for such a long time.

'Champagne glasses, we must be celebrating something special! If you are not marrying Malcolm, you must have met another man. Don't you think, Amber darling? She hasn't mentioned anyone, has she?'

'God, no. Clare is done with that side of life, right Mummy?'

Not for the first time, Clare asked herself what she had in common with her friend, who often seemed devoid of any verbal filters. At least Amber never needed reminding why a little of Elizabeth went a long way.

'Couldn't be more right actually,' said Clare.

'Let her draw breath and tell us in her own time what is bothering her.'

'I am here, you know!' said Clare, opening the bubbly. 'And to satisfy your curiosity, nothing is bothering me; in fact, quite the reverse. Something rather wonderful has happened. I wasn't going to tell you straight away but as you will keep on badgering me, I shall. But I'll pour us all a drink first.'

'It had better be good after that kind of build up!' said Elizabeth, kicking off her stilettos and draping herself rather awkwardly and in a contrived fashion on a sofa as though she was preparing for a photo shoot.

Amber did not say anything, but watched her mother carefully, causing Clare to hope she could see the shift in her psyche, see that something had irrevocably altered in terms of the shroud of grief she'd once supported like a heavy, obliterating disguise.

She declared, 'You may raise your glasses to me because the last piece of the jigsaw has slotted into place and the story – *my story* – is now complete. There really is no more I can do with it.'

'Now you are the one talking in riddles. These parmesan bites are really very good, darling. But, Éclair, do top up my glass for a toast. I feel one coming on.'

Amber shook her head. 'I think you are going to have to spell it out, what exactly was the last piece?'

Clare had rehearsed this moment. She stood before the fireplace, champagne flute in hand, one arm resting on the mantel. 'I found the will of Jeremiah Graves and in it he bequeathed a silver cup with the initials J.G. to his son John. Everything fits together and makes sense now. It was an extraordinary coincidence that the two pieces of seventeenth-century silver, made forty years apart, both ended up in my hands, having been owned by two branches of the same family all those centuries ago. I think it is even more extraordinary that both pieces were recorded in separate wills. Thank goodness for the terrific record-keeping in the various libraries and archives that are open to all comers. It was serendipitous that I decided not to wait for the catalogue I ordered online to arrive as I found an annotated copy in the British Library. And it was pure chance I saw all those images of Mercury during our whistle-stop tour abroad, Elizabeth, as it helped cement the idea that the original owners must have been merchants. That to me was far better than spending a few days lying on a beach doing nothing. I know neither of you really knew why I was doing it but, for me, it was all rather fascinating.'

'I presume I shall be fully credited for the part I played?' demanded Elizabeth.

'For what? Happenstance?' said Amber. 'You happened to be in the right place at the right time alongside Mummy. That's all, no more, no less. I'm disappointed that social media didn't yield anything further, I must say. Imagine how exciting it would be if the thief had felt bad about it for years and got in contact to confess.'

'Too much for your mother's nerves, I suspect,' said Elizabeth, noticeably not defending herself, yet Clare was pleased that Amber had, instead, defended her for a change. It was only at certain moments that life revealed that one had done well as a parent, and in that moment, Clare could feel the palpable loyalty of her daughter and smiled at this fact; life was still dishing out these silver linings after all. But Clare, no doubt, knew Elizabeth better than anyone else. She knew that beneath her *big personality* there lay a lost little girl. It was that part of her friend that Clare remained loyal to. She couldn't say why. Life just worked that way sometimes. One had a sense about something, just as she had had about the little silver *taister*.

Elizabeth downed the contents of her glass and held it out to be refilled. 'I need a good glass for a proper toast, Éclair!' she said, bringing the attention back to her, of course. 'Fill it up for me, darling!'

Clare took a large gulp of her own glass before heading to the champagne bucket. 'Well, it didn't matter that it didn't yield anything. I was very touched that you tried to help me – both of you. I spent a lot of time looking at documents that yielded nothing and even more time just staring at the ceiling wondering what to do next. At certain points I wanted to give up but am so glad I didn't. Now I have found what I wanted; I have mentally drawn a large full stop.'

'Not a line in the sand, darling?'

'No, Elizabeth. A full stop. It's done and dusted. Mystery solved!'

'Until the next time, darling!' said Elizabeth, holding up a glass.

Clare and Amber exchanged a knowing look and a smile. Clare smiled too, then said, 'Come on, let's eat!'

PART FOUR

Moving on

2016

Every morning, without fail, Dottie read the BBC website and caught up on the country's headlines. It gave her a certain sense of accomplishment. Following this, she would catch up on the world news. It seemed every day she learned about events in far flung countries she hadn't previously known existed, where the people were being persecuted, or dictated to, or starved, or were at war with another nation or themselves. It was bewildering to her that the planet could endure such tension, such suffering. At times the stories would read better than a novel and it amazed Dottie to think that some people's lives were so richly complicated, today's headline being no exception.

A seventeenth-century cup made by a celebrated silversmith which was stolen thirty years ago has been returned to the museum it was taken from.

> *The silver dram cup was stolen from Hull's Wilberforce House Museum in 1986 and was lost until last year when it resurfaced in London. It was identified when an antiques collector took it to an opinions day at the Victoria and Albert Museum.*

> *The cup was then offered back to the original museum.*
>
> *A spokesman for Hull Museums said the cup was bought in 1969 with a grant from the Art Fund.*
>
> *He said: 'It's really important to Hull because it's a work by Abraham Barachin, the last Hull silversmith to use the Hull town mark.*

A museum heist had an air of romance to it. What made people do it? Desperation? The thrill? Or the love of the loot? But what interested Dottie the most was the name Abraham Barachin – why on earth did it sound so familiar?

Barachin, Barchin…

Yes, that was it! She had heard it when working at the Seagrove and Atterbury auction house and, to be that familiar with it, she must have at some point typed it up in a catalogue. How many hundreds, maybe even thousands, of entries had she typed up during the 1960s, Mr Barton-Jones breathing down her neck, often quite literally, as she worked? How many silver cups? So why this particular name?

Yes, there was something absurdly compelling and romantic about a museum heist, though Dot couldn't say precisely why. Just as she finished reading the short piece and set down her glasses, Dottie's mobile rang. It was her old colleague Kath, from Seagrove and Atterbury.

'It's me,' she said, as she always did.

Kath and Dottie had remained friends ever since Dottie had left the auction house in 1969. Their relationship at first had been somewhat lopsided as Dottie leaned on Kathy during her pregnancy, but these strains had evened out as

Dot got back on her feet again and their friendship had subsequently blossomed. These phone calls were now a daily occurrence and, at times, a lifeline to Dot.

'You'll never guess what I have just seen on Twitter!' said Kath, excitedly, launching in without so much as a *hello, how are you?* – which was nothing new for Kath. Without drawing a breath or allowing Dot to reply, she continued, 'Remember that sale of seventeeth-century silver, just before you left? Remember the day that old Barton-Jones was furious with you for making a typo?'

'I remember, the formidable Mrs How was coming in on that day.'

'Yes, for a viewing. See, you do remember!'

'Oh don't, Kath, even now the memory fills me with dread.' Dot couldn't help covering her eyes with her hand.

'Oh, you can't hold onto the past. Anyhow, you'll be pleased to hear that the piece has been found and sent back to the museum in Hull. Apparently it had been stolen years ago.'

Dottie could have saved Kath the effort. 'Well, if you'd let me get a word in edgeways, I could have told you that myself. I read it on the BBC website just now.'

Dottie heard a long exhale which she couldn't distinguish from Kath blowing out cigarette smoke. 'Yes,' she went on, 'but I bet you'd forgotten your association with the name Barachin. See, that's what friends are for! Now, tell me, has your son signed you up on any social media accounts?'

'Signed me up to what?'

'Facebook, Instagram, Twitter, Snapchat—'

'Snap what?'

'Oh, stop being a dinosaur, Dot. You must at least have

heard of Facebook?'

'No, because I like real life. I'm not a virtually-there kind of person. I'm all here.'

'You are funny! Well, social media makes the world a smaller place. We're a global community now, Dot.'

'We are, are we?'

'Yes, we are. I am going to do a bit more digging and see if I can find out anything more about that silver piece. I think I'll also post something on my Twitter account saying I remember it well because I was working there at the time.'

It was news to Dottie that Kath had a *Twitter* account. She had the sense Kath was just showing off now. 'Why would you do that? I'd rather just forget all about it.' She supposed this is what old ladies had to do, amuse themselves with trivia concerning the past.

'It's called *joining the conversation.*'

'Don't tell me, the conversation of the *global community*.'

'Now you're getting it, Dot! Then if someone else sees it, they might join in or contact me through my account. You don't know where it will go after that. It could get quite interesting, you know.'

Dot couldn't see the point of raking up the past. If she looked back now, she saw her life as a tapestry, one that necessarily needed these darker threads for her to become the reliable person she had always been to her son, Kevin, and thereafter all the brighter threads had transpired *because* of her beloved son. She had no regrets. If anything, it had been a comfort knowing she depended on nobody but herself and it had more than made up for a precarious childhood. She still lived in Shepherd's Bush, in her tiny flat in a converted Edwardian semi, and though her pension didn't stretch far, her needs and expenses were minimal and her health surprisingly good. Yes, she was content, but more importantly, she was at peace.

Her peace only lasted until the next day, however, when Kathy phoned again, this time in the afternoon, once more wrapped up in excitement.

'Guess what, Dot?'

'What?'

'Something came up on Twitter.'

'And?'

'We're meeting two women, Amber and her mother Clare.'

'We are?' There was no suggesting or asking Dot whether she would like to go to meet them, but Dottie was more than used to this behaviour from her friend. 'How come?' she added in a disempowered fashion, slumping into the wicker bath chair beside the telephone.

'Amber got in touch. She read my post about once working in the auction house.'

'Who are Amber and Clare?'

'Don't quote me, but I think she was the one who discovered the pot after it was stolen.'

'Amber?'

'Or it might have been Clare – you'll have to come to the meeting and find out.'

'Stop it, Kath! What did you tell her?'

'Only that my friend typed the catalogue.'

'Oh, you didn't!'

'You're missing the point, love; if I hadn't, she wouldn't have been so keen to meet.'

Dottie looked out of the window, over a chaotic patchwork of rooftops. It was beginning to rain, stray dashes spreading across the windowpane. 'Look, I don't know, Kath. They might be a pair of cranks. I'm a great believer in not dredging up the past, leaving it to rest in peace.' It was the only way she'd been able to raise her son, and put the circumstances of the pregnancy behind her. 'I'm sorry, I don't think it's for me.'

'Dot, I ask you, what have we got to lose? It will do us good to have something important to think about. We're meeting in Battersea Park in a café next Thursday and we can always leave if we don't like the look of them!'

Dottie hung up wondering what in Heaven's name she had agreed to.

***

Clare heard the phone but did not manage to get to it before it went to answerphone. She heard Amber saying, 'Pick up, pick up. Something astonishing has happened!' Clare immediately rang her daughter back.

'What is it?' she asked. 'Are you alright?' It was unusual for Amber to call so early.

'All is well here. You will have to remove the full stop.' Now who was speaking in riddles?

'What is astonishing then? What full stop?'

'Your story is not quite over yet. You have one more thing to do. Social media has come up trumps. The story about the return of the piece of silver to Hull has appeared on Twitter and Instagram. Someone who was working in the auction house at the time the stolen piece was auctioned—'

'You mean before it went to the museum?'

'Exactly. ...has posted something on Twitter saying she was working there at the time, made contact through your silversurfer account and the upshot of it was that she would like to meet you and talk about it. It seems one of her colleagues was working on the catalogue at the time. She said she'd see if she can bring her along. I know you weren't monitoring your account, but I kept an eye on it for you. I bet you're pleased I did!'

The catalogue. She had seen the catalogue, what more could there be to say?

'You pretended to be me using my account? Oh, Amber! But what if it's a hoax?'

'I think we have nothing to lose if we arrange to meet on neutral ground: a coffee shop or in the open space of a park. As you would for a first internet date. I'll find somewhere we could meet for coffee and if we are all getting on, it could morph into lunch. They both live in London so it should be easy enough. Look at it as an adventure!'

Clare felt herself beginning to feel powerless in the face of Amber's excitement. She knew nothing about internet dating, but she also knew that she hadn't come this far not to see if there was something to be learned. 'I suppose such a meeting would round things off,' she said. 'Okay, if you think it is a good idea, find out when they are available, and I will make sure not to invite Elizabeth.'

'I should hope not!'

Clare could already imagine the extent of blunders streaming forth from her friend's mouth and was not surprised Amber agreed with her. 'So, let me know when you have arranged something, and I'll check my diary. Lord, I can't believe what I'm agreeing to here.'

'I'll call you, but I have a lot of viewings booked at work over the next couple of days so it may not be immediately.'

It was three days later, with some misgivings, that Clare met Amber at Sloane Square Station. It was a blustery day and as she walked along the King's Road, Clare felt the wind pushing her gently forwards, encouraging, guiding almost. From Sloane Square they took the 137 bus to Chelsea Gate and walked through Battersea Park towards Putt in the Park. The cafeteria was located in the corner furthest from the entrance and they walked arm in arm, chatting, observing and wondering what the day would bring. Clare had a sense that if anyone passing – amid the joggers, the tired-looking mothers with prams and the lost and lonely whom invariably inhabit parks – were to observe them, no doubt they would see a mother and daughter getting along well, almost enviably well. It was funny, she thought, how this was not the usual mode of interaction for either of them. But things had gotten better lately. If Clare were honest with herself, she was touched Amber had become involved and was helping her.

They reached Putt in the Park; a place that got its name from the mini golf laid out before it. Above hung the apparatus of an obstacle course, strung through the trees. There was a look of concentration on the faces of the children and adults as they swayed on the bridges and ropes. It was the nearest anyone was likely to get to doing what our closest simian ancestors did, thought Clare. Next to this was a well-equipped children's playground filled with squealing children, and nearby a football pitch with disparate players kicking balls in various directions. It was in essence, a place of high energy.

The cafeteria was similarly busy: mothers wiping the noses of preschool children or holding bundled babies to their breasts. As soon as they entered the café, Clare spotted the two women at once. One was neatly turned out in a lilac pullover and a mauve scarf, secured around her neck with a butterfly brooch, whilst the other was more casually dressed in a sweater, jeans and an anorak. They were perhaps Clare's age, or a little younger, which added up in terms of their working in the auction house in the 1960s. Life would make a sleuth out of her yet! Both were now looking toward the entrance. Knowing her daughter, Amber probably thought they were controlling the agenda, but this notion was soon dispelled as they arrived at the table, the waitress bringing over two bowls of pasta. 'I'm Kath and this is Dot,' said the woman in an anorak, gesturing to her neatly dressed companion. 'Sorry we didn't wait for you to get here, but as you're late we weren't sure if you'd come at all!' There was no nonsense about Kath, which Clare couldn't help but like.

They removed their coats as the waitress set the food down and took their seats.

'Well, thank you for agreeing to meet us,' said Dot. 'It's amazing that technology brought us all together.'

Clare smiled at both of them in turn. 'Yes,' she said, not wanting to admit she'd had very little to do with it.

'I thought you might have considered us both a couple of nutters and might not turn up,' said Kath.

'Well, sorry we're late,' said Amber, 'it was a longer walk than anticipated. But thank you so much for getting in touch and we are really delighted to meet you. I'm Amber and this is my mother, Clare.' Clare was impressed by Amber's professionalism, having never seen her in work mode before. 'Since you have already ordered, we'll order something to eat too.'

'Dot thinks it is really exciting to meet you,' said Kath.

Clare did not think Dot looked excited at all. Instead, rather solemnly, she ducked down and produced a catalogue from her handbag.

'I don't really know why I kept it, because I made a mistake and got into so much trouble for it.'

Clare found her heart was thwacking against her rib cage. Had she really travelled to a point in this long, and revelatory journey, to find all answers lay in the book, about to be given to her by a woman who once worked at the auction house? The simplicity struck her suddenly as quite profound.

Dot continued thumbing through pages. 'Here's the entry,' she eventually said. 'The Bleeding Bowl. I typed 10oz instead of 1oz. Even now it makes me feel awful looking at it.'

'I should say it was a bleeding bowl, in more ways than one!' laughed Kath.

Clare could see Dot's fingers trembling. She decided there and then that she would not add to her remorse. 'I wouldn't feel bad about a small typo concerning the weight,' she said. 'Your boss should have proofread it thoroughly before it went to the printers and he or she made a much worse mistake.'

'What do you mean?' said Kath.

'Well, as you pointed out, it is described here as a bleeding bowl, but it was no such thing. Its correct description is a *dram cup* or a *hott water taister*. There are many, many dealers out there who crawl through auction houses on viewing days, pour over catalogues and, now that it has been invented, trawl the internet looking for objects that have been misattributed, often picking them up cheaply. I'm not saying that this is what happened in this case, but a case of misattribution is a far greater error than a minor typo in my view. I was given the first clue the little cup might have been stolen in an article I found the internet. The catalogue gave the correct date of 1685, but article I saw said 1710–25. So you see, there were lots of mistakes about such a little object.'

Dot let out a sigh and held a palm to her chest whilst Kath once again roared with laughter, a big and boisterous guffaw. 'Well, who would have thought it, Dot? Mr High and Mighty Barton-Jones made a mistake. That was not the only mistake he made, was it, Dot?' Kath nudged Dot's side and turned back to Clare. 'Is that what you do, Clare? Go around looking for mistakes in catalogues?'

'Oh no, I'm not a dealer and nor do I have specialist knowledge about anything. I know a little bit about a few things, but it doesn't amount to much. The people who do that sort of thing have in-depth knowledge and a lot of patience. But really, lots of people make mistakes. I really wouldn't blame yourself. It was a long time ago.'

Dot didn't speak but lowered her head, staring into her teacup as if reading her fortune there.

'The whole thing is a bit complicated for my friend,' said Kath, also taking in Dot's posture. 'An incident meant she had to leave Seagrove and Atterbury soon afterwards.'

To her surprise, Dot then looked up and blurted, 'The idiot got me pregnant.'

Both Amber and Clare stared at her, wide-eyed.

'Needless to say, Dot's boss – Mr Barton-Jones – showed no accountability.'

'So, the man who didn't spot the typo also got you pregnant?' said Amber, which Clare considered too forthright to utter herself.

'He did and although abortion was legal by then, I decided to keep it. Having my boy was the best thing I ever did with my life. Kevin has done so well for himself, you know. He's the accountant for a small firm in Putney and I'm so proud of him. So please don't think I have regrets. I simply don't.'

Once their food arrived, Dot's former life working as a typist at Seagrove and Atterbury's became clear. Together, the two women explained how Dot's career at the auction house had come to an end before the birth of her son. Her boss had had her replaced, saying she was careless and unreliable as a typist. She had very little by way of savings but with her child allowance was able to remain at home for a couple of months, after which time her friend Kathy, who was pregnant with her own son and no longer working, had offered to care for Kevin alongside him. She was deeply indebted to Kathy, her oldest and truest friend. Kathy had married Reg, not long after Dottie had left the auction house. Unlike Dottie, Kathy had made Reg take responsibility for his attractions and they were wed in a civil ceremony at Marylebone Registry Office, just four weeks before their son Mark was born. Though there had been no such fairy-tale ending for Dottie, with Kathy's babysitting help, she had at least been able to take on part-time temping work, which she continued for more than thirty-five years. She had liked the variety as well as the anonymity of it all. There was little prying into her status as a single parent and the pay had been sufficient to ensure she and Kevin had short holidays, clothes from C&A, and she'd even managed to buy him a second-hand car when he reached the age of seventeen. She had made it her responsibility to be her son's rock; to be everything that her mother hadn't been for her. Admittedly, to begin with, she had missed the glamour of the auction house where she had come across famous artists, collectors and the dealers that kept them in business but with maturity, she had begun to realise the extent of her naïvety; how much working here had eventually turned her into an excessive people-pleaser. It hadn't helped that Kevin's father had refused to acknowledge responsibility for his son. For a long time, even the name Barton-Jones had riled her, 'Bringing angry splashes of colour to both your cheeks!' interjected Kathy. But as far as Kevin was later concerned, 'Your father was a knowledgeable and wise man who made a silly decision,' Dot told him, which naturally placed her in the silly section, but the truth, she confessed, had been too prickly to confront. She knew that from her own childhood, life was challenging enough without the knowledge that your father was a selfish idiot to boot. When confronted with the pregnancy, Mr Barton-Jones had uttered the words Dottie would never forget, 'What are *you* going to do about it?' With firm enough emphasis placed upon the '*you*' for Dottie to realise that anything more would only come about by pleading. She finally realised she was merely being treated as irrelevant and, God knows, she had experienced enough of that throughout childhood!

'He was just trying it on,' enlarged Kath as she sipped her coffee. 'That's what blokes do. You've got to give them an ultimatum.' Her eyes met Amber's and Clare could almost sense Amber biting her tongue at this juncture. 'What Dot should have said, is: I'm sure your boss would be very interested to know what you get up to in the stationary cupboard, Mr Barton-Jones.'

'He would have laughed, Kath,' said Dot, forlornly, so that Clare wished they would change the topic.

'Surely there was a union of some sort to complain to?' asked Amber.

Both Dot and Kath laughed collaboratively. 'You have no idea, do you?' said Clare. She couldn't help enjoying the moment of seeing Amber's ideals being trumped by reality. The truth was nobody in the present could truly comment on a past so different in every regard to their own.

'No, dear,' Kath told Amber, 'what Dot should have done was confront B-J directly. It was her opportunity to show him he couldn't get away with it. She had to play him at his own game but at that time it was not so easy.'

'I didn't really fancy upsetting my baby,' said Dot.

'Well,' Kathy said, shaking her head, 'I really don't know how you took all the pomp and lecherousness lying down.

I think revenge would have been oozing out of the pores of my skin having to endure it.'

'There wasn't really any choice,' said Dottie, patiently, as if she'd had the conversation many times before with her friend. 'I'd worked for B-J for many years by that point. I already knew his motto was: never complain, never explain. He would have just denied it was his and I would have looked like an even bigger donkey.'

'All the same, it was your green card for marriage, love. No man likes to be cornered but that's how it was back then.' Kath appealed to Amber again. 'It was a man's world and any babies that came along were a bit of a nuisance but needed accounting for. But getting him to marry would have been the only way he would ever have respected Dot.'

'He was married already, Kath. He was hardly respecting his wife!' Dot replied.

Dottie then explained that, unlike Kathy, she felt downright uncomfortable wielding her feminine charms to get what she wanted. She'd plainly and simply fell for her boss and, in her darker and more delusional moments, had actually believed it to be reciprocated. A naïve young woman's brain was liable to pull such tricks, she had realised soon enough. But something else she had also come to see over the years was that it was impossible to properly judge the past whilst rooted in the present. Things were changing for women then, but she hadn't known how to contribute to the changes herself. As well as accountability being low, men didn't necessarily know they were doing anything wrong. She loved her job. Most of her friends from school were briefly nurses or teachers before giving it all up for marriage. Though being a secretary was also considered woman's work, the auction house had paid comparatively well and the work was interesting. The environment itself had always felt excessively male and Dot said she was not ashamed to say that, at first, she had rather liked that element. It felt important, somehow dignified. As to how she had been treated by Mr Barton-Jones, well, she merely accepted it as her lot and used it to understand how she perhaps slotted into the world. Even after her son was born, she hadn't raged at the system, had instead seen her fate as in some way inevitable. Anyhow, it wasn't the cards you were dealt that mattered, she surmised, but how you played them that counted; she hadn't been able to play the damsel in distress when required but had done her utmost to rise to the challenge of keeping both herself and her son going. Resilience was one thing she had acquired in spades. which no doubt resulted from her particularly strained childhood.

'And what about you, Kath? Do you have a family?' Clare asked. She was not inclined to pry into Dot's childhood but was grateful she had been so open concerning the catalogue's typo. It would have been easy to blame Dot for the error, but after listening to her circumstances, it seemed blame perhaps lay beyond a secretary's fingers, lying moreover in the hands of the swinging sixties society in which she had lived. Whilst Dot had spoken, Clare had listened, almost spellbound, as did Amber, and Clare couldn't help thinking how it did Amber good to hear how hard it had been for women in her day, how it wasn't just as simple as speaking up and being confrontational. It seemed that in uncovering the truth of her taster, Clare felt as if she had unearthed so much more. How many times had Amber not understood Clare's motives for leaving her father? Perhaps after this meeting, Amber might extend more compassion towards her mother's circumstances in the sixties which, although not as harsh as Dot's, did not come without difficulties.

'I've got my Reg,' said Kath. 'But he was never very ambitious. In fact, he's at his happiest lounging in a chair with an open copy of the *Daily Mail*. We have five sons. Right now, none of them work but I have four grandchildren who keep me busy.' Clare didn't say anything but wondered how she could be so cheerful about this. She noticed Amber's judging eyes widen that much more. 'I read the other week that only children are often more successful and it's down to all the attention they get. Maybe you had the right idea, Dot. Ole B-J, as we called him, was a male chauvinist pig but your Kevin turned out very well, eh?'

'I was working in an office at about the same time, and I absolutely loathed it,' said Clare. 'I remember one girl was fed up with it all and pinched the backside of a young man who was bending over someone else's desk. He was furious and rounded on her. All she said was, "Now you know what it feels like so keep your hands to yourself." We were all surprised, but he did, and life improved a bit after that.'

Kath guffawed even louder, causing heads to turn.

'Truth is, I haven't thought about that period for a long time,' said Kath, when she had finally ceased laughing, 'but the one person B-J was scared of was Mrs How. Did you know her?'

Clare shook her head.

'Well, she was formidable,' said Dot, 'and we all admired her because she drove a flash car and was very clever. There weren't many women around like that then! She was coming in for the viewing and I was feeling doubly sick because of the typo combined with the morning sickness. B-J always said how nobody knew silver spoons like Mrs How did.'

'Probably because she was born with one in her mouth!' said Kathy, laughing loudly again, causing one or two people to turn around wide-eyed. Her friend, however, didn't seem to notice. 'I tell you what, Dot,' Kath continued, 'if B-J is still alive and has read about the return of the cup, it's probably the closest your thoughts have come to one another since we stopped working there.'

'Did B-J ever acknowledge his son?' asked Amber, concern crumpling her face into a frown.

'When he was a month old, I sent him a photograph, but I never heard back. It was not like it is now, with fathers being forced to pay by the courts. It was hard but I just got on with it. That's what we did back then. Got on with it!' Clare could see that Dot didn't want to divulge anything further and was proved right by her turning to Clare and asking, 'Why did you buy the piece?'

'Why? Oh, well, I found the image on it to be intriguing. When I saw it at the fair, he – Mercury – seemed to stare straight at me and lock his eyes onto mine. It seems silly to say it out loud but that's really the reason why.'

'You know what, Dot, the next time we feel like a day out, we should go to Hull and have a look at the little cup in the museum,' said Kath.

Clare piped up with, 'I've been to Hull and I think you'll enjoy it.'

After a genial hour and a quarter, Clare and Amber said goodbye and then left. They walked about a hundred yards without speaking to each other, then Amber asked, 'Why didn't you say you had seen the catalogue already? Or mention the second piece of Hull silver in your collection? They were being open with us, why couldn't you be open with them?'

Back to Amber being Amber, thought Clare.

'Well, the catalogue was Dot's story to tell and I didn't want to diminish its importance. Secondly, I think the other piece of silver was irrelevant, at least to her story. I liked them both.'

'I see. Yes, I liked them too.'

'And Dot had had a really hard time but has done well for herself in spite of it all. Now it is very commonplace to be an unmarried mother, it was not so easy then, that's the thing you have to understand, Amber. Both mother and child could have been stigmatised. It was very brave of her to do what she did and I'm pleased her son is now successful.' Was she speaking up for her own past too? Perhaps, none of that seemed to matter now. What mattered was her taster's history and this was a refreshing, freeing feeling. 'She is obviously so proud of him,' she went on. 'It was quite fun to reminisce about the bad old days of sexism in the workplace. Things are so much better now. It wasn't called sexism then; it was just how it was. Thank you for setting up the meeting, darling. It was a good thing to do.'

Amber stopped and turned to Clare, placing a hand on each of her shoulders. 'Look, there's something I want to say too. I wanted to say it the other night but with Elizabeth there, I decided against it. When you were lost after Harry died and I kept pushing you to find a purpose, I shouldn't have. You were right. You took things slowly and did everything your own way. I'm proud of you, Mother! And, most importantly of all, you seem so much happier and settled now.'

You were right! Now, those were three words Clare had never thought she would hear Amber utter. She linked arms with her daughter and together they retraced their steps through the park.

***

Ricky reread the article in the *Hull Daily Mail Online* for the third time. Stolen Abraham Barachin cup returned to Hull after thirty years. It was the word "Barachin" that caused Ricky's initial pause. He reread the post. *Barachin. Barachin.* He never thought he would hear that name again. He never wanted to hear that name again. He studied the image of the silver dram cup. He clicked on a link, which took him to the BBC website, and read another article. It hit him like a blow to the jaw. How could he forget that rough, almost unappealing image? Months after the robbery, after Pete's disappearance, he had spent hour upon hour staring out of the kitchen window, the image playing on his mind like a dripping tap, so much so he started seeing it in the clouds. Eventually, he'd had the balls to speak to Danny about it,

'It's a bleedin' god, what do you think it bloody is!' he'd been told as if he was asking the colour of the sky, his brother sounding more and more like Michael Caine, demonstrating the usual contradictions in his character, a character Ricky had long since given up trying to comprehend.

Following this, Ricky had carried out his own research in the library, drawing the conclusion it must be the god Mercury, for it held a caduceus in its hands, though in truth it wasn't Mercury's usual image, according to the books he looked at. It was unsophisticated and no doubt his brother had related to that. He did, after all, regard himself to be god like and above the law. Yet, like the image on the little cup, he was also roughly drawn, distinctly shady. But Ricky hadn't thought about his brother's quirks for a long time now. Besides, being quirks he no longer cared for, he had moved on with his life. He now had a purpose, and a gratifying one, as a counsellor. A few years ago, Mia – Danny's wife – had sent a birthday card to Carol, writing, *your man did the right thing in getting out. Only wish Dan would one day. Take good care of yourselves, love, M x.* He had felt no emotion when he heard, some months later, that Danny had suffered a fatal heart attack.

Ricky, in time, had forgotten about the cup, only thinking about it fleetingly as a small enactment of revenge against his brother, one he most likely never noticed. Who would have thought it would turn up again? Ricky shook his head. No, he'd been right to exit Danny's fiascos when he did, right to go straight. At least he could look at the cup feeling removed from it all. With Danny dead, it was never going to rebound on him.

Still staring at the image of the cup, he slumped into his armchair. Below the image were a few sentences about the piece: that it was eighteenth-century, that it was stolen in 1986 from the Wilberforce House Museum, how it was discovered at an opinions day at the V&A and then it confirmed that it was in fact Mercury engraved on it. Ricky laughed. Only his brother could have swiped a cup with the god of trade emblazoned upon it.

But the twisting of Ricky's gut towards resentment was all it took for the whole night to come flooding back in painfully accurate detail; he heard Pete fall, saw him lying motionless at the bottom of the stairs at the museum, legs splayed, left arm twitching, blood trickling from the corner of his lips. He saw Danny, with palpable callousness, remove the cup from Pete's still twitching hand, shouting over his shoulder at Ricky to, 'Go! Get out, you idiot!' Speaking as he often had to Ricky, as if he was an irritating piece of dirt stuck on the sole of his shoe. These images came back in glorious technicolour and the grip of trauma experienced after the theft stirred up inside him again like a tornado of unexpressed pain, placing him momentarily, yet firmly, in the past.

Strangely, after the incident, the fact he'd never known whether Pete lived or died had disturbed him more than anything else, more than the fact they could have been caught. He knew Danny was cold-blooded, soulless and flush enough to have paid someone to go in, remove and dispose of the body, if necessary. This ignorance of Pete's fate had continued to haunt him for decades. Why hadn't the papers reported the death? Or had his brother done with Pete what he did to most people and covered up his contribution, papering over Pete's life as if it were no more than a strip of dodgy wallpaper?

In truth, Ricky had always blamed himself for obeying Danny that night, for running away and not calling an ambulance. They hadn't any mobile phones back then, which had made the successful robberies seem almost miraculous now. But in 1986, times may have been very different and yet Hull had plenty of phone boxes (obvious beige ones to boot) and yet Ricky had mutely followed Danny's lead, letting the loot become more important than human life. *Carpe quod potes.* Danny had this carved into his mantlepiece: *seize what you can.* And he always had.

The disappointment Ricky had in himself, in his character, had crippled him for years. No amount of whiskey seemed to touch it. He knew now, of course, he should have ignored Danny and saved Pete, but for a time, he tried to believe what Danny had said the next day, 'He wasn't there in the morning when the burglary was discovered, so he must have got up and walked away. He was a good thief, keeping quiet like he did.' Danny had squeezed the end of his nose between thumb and forefinger as he spoke, as he always did when he was lying. No, the only reason Pete had kept quiet was because he was dead and the only reason the body had vanished was because Danny had made it disappear. Yet Ricky still knew better than to verbalise what he thought. He had no proof.

Ricky knew his brother would have chosen Pete especially for his anonymity. These were his brother's usual targets for accomplices; men with difficult lives who lived below the radar, no families, no jobs, often no fixed addresses either. It also took one to know one. He had simply vanished, with nobody looking out for him wondering why he had not come home. In time, this fact was to Ricky just as sad as Pete's death.

The toll this episode took on Ricky's life for years had been heavy and ongoing. As the days stretched into weeks and then months, he'd slipped into a deep and seemingly unbreakable depression. Danny refused to discuss the night further, and it was clear he felt neither responsible nor guilty. In side-stepping responsibility for Pete, Danny had somehow landed the responsibility in Ricky's lap. Which is perhaps how their relationship had always played out. Ricky had only one choice and that was to sever all communication. And he did.

To begin with, he started drinking more to forget the night. If not for Carol, he might have drunk himself to death. He drank to forget and to spare himself from all thoughts. If he had been prone to violence, perhaps Pete's death might not have hit him so hard. Of course, Carol had stood by him, and he was grateful for her love, but he never told her what had happened. He didn't want to worry her. She'd always considered him his brother's dogsbody. 'He thinks up the plans, I enact them,' he had always told her, and Carol had known better than to ask more. But in hindsight he could see there was more truth to his words than he'd realised. 'He's a bad penny, that brother of yours,' Carol would say from time to time, and doubtless her womanly intuition had suspected something all along. 'Abused kids go one of two ways in my book, not that you were abused: either they transform and become decent folk, or they become like the abuser. But Danny thinks he's owed something and doesn't care who he tramples on to get it.'

Ricky had gone along with his brother's plans because Danny was the master of persuasion, though perhaps manipulation was a better word for it. He had truly wanted to give his kids a better start than he'd had, and Carol felt the same, having shared a childhood of grinding poverty. Initially, he'd liked that he could provide for his family, give them holidays and nice Christmas presents. It had balanced out the guilt.

But thank God for Carol because after he'd stopped working with his brother, she'd trained to become a nurse. The first few years had been hard; he'd had to look after the kids – often with a pounding headache and unable to work. But Carol went off to college and in the evenings took up part-time cleaning work. How she did it, he couldn't comprehend. Making ends meet hadn't been easy, especially as every problem they encountered – the gas being turned off, bailiff's visits – all fed into his drinking habit which he could ill afford. It was then Carol had qualified that she confided in a doctor about Ricky spending nights sleeping on the sofa, too drunk to make it upstairs. She had apparently broken down, saying, 'He's going to drink himself to an early grave,' and it was Dr Morley who handed her the AA leaflet that changed his life.

It had been a hard battle to fight but, along with his mentor Brian, he'd faced his demons one by one. It took the best part of three years, during which time, slowly but surely, he rebuilt his life. Under Brian's advice he took a job as a shelf-stacker for the Co-op, eventually becoming the manager. Working wasn't as bad as he'd imagined. He made the job personable, greeting customers as they walked around the store, making sure his staff took breaks. Then, after a year of working at the Co-op, he took up a role at the weekends for Victims of Crime: a helpline that dealt with the very people he'd at one time offended. It was the most rewarding thing he'd ever done and gradually that pocket of pain inside him started to shrink, diminishing into a kernel of anxiety. He thought instead about how he would resolve, for the remainder of his days, to be his best self and to make the world a better place in the process. He looked once more at the image on the cup and laughed. *Yes, Mercury, you certainly blessed my trade!*

He got up from his chair and checked his watch. It was almost time for him to leave for the clinic. He went to the kitchen and wrote a note to his wife, as he was wont to do these days.

Without you, I am nothing. Back at 9pm. Love you, Rxxx

Two years of training and at last a counsellor. No more stacking shelves. Now he could help people, in the way he wanted to. In truth, he couldn't quite believe the fact he had a profession and one he could speak about with pride. As always, his wife was his inspiration; he had meant what he said in the note.

***

Malcolm was concluding a phone call when Barbara walked into his office with the post. With much of the correspondence happening via email, there were rarely actual letters to look at. Today was no different. There were some trade magazines with the *Art Quarterly* on the top of the pile. 'You might be interested to look at page seventy-six.' He was momentarily surprised when he saw the image of Clare's dram cup. He hadn't thought about it recently. He skimmed the short article next to it and reread it more slowly, then let out a huge sigh of relief. Beyond saying the item had now been returned to the museum, and had been bought at an antique fair, there was no mention of his name. The likelihood of his having to answer questions on how he came by it seemed to have disappeared. He called Barbara and said, 'As we haven't seen Clare at any of the most recent fairs, keep sending her invitations until the end of the year and if she hasn't appeared by then, I think her name should be removed from the database.'

***

Clare looked around the drawing room and thought back over last few years. She thought of the overwhelming sadness that overcame her when Harry died and how she had slowly moved on by focusing on a pair of inanimate objects. She was surrounded by all the things she had carefully selected to fill her home. Once, they meant something to her by triggering a memory of a place or a person, but now, she could see them for what they were: just objects, inanimate objects that need someone to appreciate them to give them meaning. She had also come to realise she no longer needed a large house filled with possessions in which the next generation showed no interest whatsoever. It was time to downsize. One consequence of the whole dram cup affair was that she had become uneasy as to how much stolen silver there may be out there. She had lost her appetite for it and had not acquired any more. It was too late to ask Amber to take the cats off her hands, but she decided as they died, she would not be replacing them. Clare was ready to shake off the past and start afresh. Wherever Malcolm was, she hoped he knew she believed he was innocent. And, of course, she wished him well.

EPILOGUE

1695

Abraham sat up in bed and rubbed the sleep from his eyes. He remembered what lay ahead and an image of Dorothy drifted into his thoughts, swelling his chest with a deep sense of joy. His beautiful, intelligent Dorothy! She was a pure ray of light in what had been an otherwise challenging and, for the most part, unknown journey toward success as a silversmith. Yet though he was happy to be joining with Dorothy under God's watchful gaze – for today the banns would be called in church – a certain sadness lay beneath the occasion, tarnishing it, like a blemish or a slight scratch.

Abraham's sadness was borne from the loss of his good friends Jeremiah Graves and Thomas Hebden, friends he made in Hull more than ten years ago. Alas, they were no longer alive to share his joy, Jeremiah having died three years past, wasted away, and Thomas not six months past from a disease of the blood. He recalled the conversation that took place with Dorothy, on a night when the skies had glowed puce, which he had taken as an omen of sorts.

'I need to talk to you, Abraham. We know each other well, for you have been living under our roof on Church Lane in the little room off the workshop since you arrived in Hull.' Dorothy had stood hands on hips beside his workbench, her cheeks flushed. 'I need someone to run the workshop now my husband, Thomas, is dead,' she said, softly, 'I need, you might say, a competent replacement.'

Her eyes had held his a little longer than necessary. The way her fingers toyed with a stray lock of hair, told Abraham all that he needed to know.

'Perhaps you should give it time, Dorothy,' he said, not wishing to take advantage of a woman in her weaker moments.

'I have made up my mind. We know each other. We trust one another, more importantly. You are established now as an accomplished silversmith. Your work is good and in demand. Most of all, I know what it is I wish for: it is for you to decide if you are in agreement with my wishes. I think we should wed.'

He could hardly believe what he was hearing. Much later, he would realise this is what he had fallen in love with, a woman who did not mince words, who spoke with forthright confidence, her moral compass always pointed towards good. The opportunity naturally did not escape him. Whatever guardian angel had watched over his journey from France had done so deftly, providing rewards for many an effort made. Quickly he realised that if they wed, it would mean he would not only be his own master in his own workshop in a thriving town, but would, according to the country's laws, become head of the household too.

Then whatever monies Dorothy had would become his. He felt a tinge of guilt, stepping into his master's shoes in the workshop and into his bed. It did not take long for him to see the sense in her argument.

'I am honoured,' he had said, bowing his head. Overcome by the moment that contained both his love for Dorothy and an appreciation for his fate, he dipped onto one knee and took her hand in his, planting it with a kiss.

'But you know,' he said earnestly, 'I bring less wealth to the arrangement.'

'But plenty more talent!' Dorothy swiftly corrected, laughing and releasing the tension from Abraham's expression. 'Do remember, I know thee well, Abraham. I know we will do very well together.'

There was no reason for lengthy negotiations concerning dowries or bride price. Neither had parents alive from whom to seek permission or approval; besides, Dorothy was a widow. Not being a gambling man, or a risk-taker, Abraham had accrued money over the years; not enough to secure him a house or a workshop but enough for him to hold his head high.

He once more had bent to kiss Dorothy's palm. 'As you wish, my love.'

When the banns were read later that Sunday in Holy Trinity Church, the congregation uttered a prayer, one of well-wishing, as was the custom in Yorkshire, and nobody objected to their union. For this Abraham was glad.

Later that day, in what was soon to be *his* workshop, he made gimmel rings, decorated with a pair of clasped hands which locked together when worn by one person. He engraved the word "Always" on the inside of one and the word "Together" inside the other. One he would give his bride on their wedding day, in three weeks' time, and the other he would wear to mark their commitment. He felt satisfied with the work and thought they looked handsome in silver. Pleased with the rings, he felt inspired to give her something else. Over the years, he had made many marriage spoons engraved with the initials of the bride and groom. He searched through the spoons in the workshop drawers, where they lay like dead soldiers in a common grave, and after careful consideration, he settled on a dog nose spoon with a long reeded rattail running down the oval bowl. It was a good size and of a good gauge. A practical, yet elegant, spoon for his practical and beautiful bride. On the back of the terminal, he engraved the initials *A D* over *B*. On the shank, he punched his mark. Gradually, as the day drew to a close, he felt his guilt begin to lift.

On the day of the wedding and dressed in his Sunday best, Abraham walked to the church whistling like a schoolboy, sunshine appearing from behind heavy clouds. He reflected on all that passed since leaving Bourges. He thought how the unusual request of a stranger had led to his long voyage north, to Kingston upon Hull; he thought how sparse his English had been and how he had striven hard to bridge the more obvious gaps in his knowledge, so that these days, his customers were more likely to comment upon how he oftentimes sounded as if he were borne in Hull, not France. But then, late at night, alone with Dorothy, as she tenderly stroked his hair, she would tell him, 'Your foreign voice is charming. I think it is what I love more than your craftsmanship with silver.' And he would silently vow to keep the accent, for as long as his wife did require it.

He arrived at church before Dorothy and waited beneath the porch with his two groomsmen. He watched her now as she walked towards him accompanied by her two friends who attended her when she had married Thomas. She was, to Abraham, a vision of loveliness, dressed in her best blue dress with a simple wreath of flowers threaded through her flaxen hair. Dorothy and Thomas had been young and from poor families when they were married and had made *bride-ale* to be sold at their wedding to cover the cost of food and the musicians. Dorothy had recounted how she and Thomas had laughed at the wedding rituals, such as the one where the bride was undressed by the bride's women and laid on the bed in readiness for her husband, who had been undressed by his groomsmen who then led him to the bed in a night smock. With the sound of music and merry-making running through the house, Dorothy had wondered if she and Thomas would ever manage to be alone. Abraham listened, without envy, as she recalled her memories. Thomas, his friend and master, was Dorothy's past, but Abraham was her future.

As Dorothy drew closer, her eyes locked with Abraham's and her face broke into a smile. Yes, this wedding was to be different, he thought. Besides, Dorothy had not long buried her husband. After the blessing in the church, there would be a wedding feast, with their close friends and Dorothy's cousins, who were all she had by way of family. Following their health being drunk, they would be left alone, just as Abraham wished for it to be. Much later, as slivers of moonlight shone through their chamber window, Abraham took Dorothy in his arms.

'My fair wife, I am a blessed man indeed tonight.'

'For what, dear husband?' replied his wife, somewhat playfully.

'For marrying thee,' he said plainly, honestly. 'Here, I made this for you. It is yours or, perhaps I should say, *ours*.' Even his tongue seemed delighted uttering such a word.

Frowning, Dorothy took the spoon from his hands. She faced it towards the light at the window and smiled. 'It looks to be a handsome spoon, dear husband,' she said. 'I am pleased. Thank you.'

'Engraved with our initials, *A D over B*,' he added, pointing to them. 'For when a thing is set in silver, it has more meaning. Life with its impermanent nature cannot argue with facts pressed into silver, my dearest.'

He was not sure if he had made sense, but he was nonetheless happy to have expressed his love for his wife in silver.

'I do agree, husband,' his wife replied.

'You are too kind, Dorothy. Or, should I say, Mrs Barachin!' And it was his turn to tease and Dorothy laughed, and he took the opportunity to pick her up and lay his wife upon the bed, whereupon he looked her deeply in the eyes and said, 'You have made my journey worthwhile. If I had known that God awards bravery in such a meaningful way, I would have set off from Bourges long before.'

'Mr Barachin, God's timing is always perfect. Besides, we are here now, are we not?'

'That we are, Mrs Barachin, that we are. And I pray this is how we shall always stay.'

Without having to wait too long, God blessed Abraham's union with Dorothy by giving them a daughter, Isabel, a child who proved a constant source of great pride and joy to Abraham. To commemorate the occasion, he made a small cup not unlike the first piece he made in Hull for Jeremiah's son, but this time, he engraved a simple floral motif with her initials in the centre of a rose.

***

It was a strange quirk of fate that wrote Abraham Barachin's name into the annals of English provincial silver, for after 1700, all silver made in the town of Kingston upon Hull was sent to York to be touched. Abraham Barachin, who arrived as a stranger, made good and became, in that moment, the last silversmith in Hull to use the town mark of three ducal coronets. And so it is today.

Acknowledgements

The saying goes 'it takes a village to raise a child'. I believe it could equally apply to writing a book. It would be impossible to take the germ of an idea for a story and get it on the printed page without a supporting cast.

I could not have breathed life into the characters without the unfailing patience and help of archivists who I think of as keepers of the nation's secrets. We are so lucky to have them. As I set out on the quest, I was patently aware that I had very little to go on and even less idea of how to go about it when I had the idea to unravel the history of the dram cup. My naivety and ignorance must have seeped out of every pore. The archivists and librarians, without whom I could not have succeeded, were working in Hull History Centre, Goldsmiths' Library, The British Library, The Maritime Museum, The National Archives, East Ridings Archives, The Borthwick Institute, Trinity House, Holy Trinity Church (now Hull Minster) and St Mary's Lowgate. I shall be eternally grateful to them. As I will be to the editors at The Literary Studio who saw potential in my initial draft and guided me through the process of turning it into a readable manuscript. Thank you to the team at Troubador for being so easy to work with.

There are individuals I must thank too. Angus Patterson of the Victoria and Albert Museum for enabling the conversation with his counterpart in Hull culminating in the return of the silver piece. This would not have happened without them and I am very grateful to both of them for making it so painless to return the piece to its rightful home.

I would like to thank Sarah Milne-Day whose brief it was to bring seventeenth-century Hull alive for me during a guided tour; it was no mean feat. Many thanks go to Philippa Glanville who gave me the correct description of a dram cup or *hott water taister* and for being so encouraging, and Pieter Jongbloed who told me seventeenth century Dutch merchants kept statues of Mercury in their homes and Benjamin Miller of Shrubsole NYC for helping me when I confessed that I had never heard of a *beere bowle*. Barbara Gray and Didier Jonas are to be thanked for their valuable input.

To the people of Hull who were without exception, friendly and helpful, I hope I have portrayed a fair view of what I saw and found in your city. I enjoyed my time in your company.

Last but not least, a huge thank you to my family and friends who stuck with me and read various drafts, and offered their encouragement and criticism in equal measure; it all helped.

This book is printed on paper from sustainable sources managed under the Forest Stewardship Council (FSC) scheme.

It has been printed in the UK to reduce transportation miles and their impact upon the environment.

For every new title that Troubador publishes, we plant a tree to offset CO_2, partnering with the More Trees scheme.

For more about how Troubador offsets its environmental impact, see www.troubador.co.uk/sustainability-and-community